Yesterday's

By

Carol McClain

Bill,

Carol McClain

Copyright © 2019 by Carol McClain

ISBN 13: 9780578411866

Published in the United States of America

Publication Date: January 2019

Cover Artist: Carol Fiorillo

Carol's Cover Designs

Names, characters and incidents depicted in this book are products of the author's imagination, or are used in a fictitious situation. Any resemblances to actual events, locations, organizations, incidents or persons – living or dead – are coincidental and beyond the intent of the author.

Dedication

To my mother, Vera DeFord: Everything good about me, I learned from her.

Acknowledgment

As I serve the King who is the Alpha, my acknowledgment must first go to Jesus who has given me a talent for writing and a unique gift with words. I'm so glad He spoke the world into existence because it parallels my life as I type my worlds into reality.

He also deserves praise for sending me Randy Cook at exactly the right time. Adam Benedict, my antagonist, is a paramedic. I read books, and followed paramedic sites online. However, my scenes would not contain the depth, and the accuracy they have without Randy who, for many years, worked as a paramedic. He taught me their points of view, how they handled severe situations, along with all the paraphernalia used by EMS workers.

Randy carefully critiqued my work. I do accept blame for any errors in procedures as the information had to pass from his suggestion through my mind which leans to the literary more than the medical.

In addition to Randy, I thank Linda Rondeau, who has been my mentor, my burden-bearer, and my doppelganger. No words can express the gratitude I have for her love and support and critiques.

As far as critiques, this work would not be as good as it is without the help of the Scribes 215: June Foster, Laura Hilton, and Deborah Piccorelli. Their acute sense showing/telling and point of view, along with stylistic issues, has polished this work to perfection.

My "baby" sister, Janine Weisse, has been a faithful beta-reader and cheerleader. She inspires me with her devotion to her family and love of literature and encouragement for my writing.

Next, Ellen Mainville, the sweetest woman ever created, helped me with the details about Parkinson's. For years, Ellen cared for her father who suffered from this illness.

Of course, my husband Neil believes in me. In weeks where I wished to quit, he urged me on. He promotes my talent to anyone who will listen -- or not listen. He loves me even knowing my shortcomings. He's a faithful, godly man, and I love him.

My mother, the woman to whom I've dedicated this novel, is an inspiration. Under hard circumstances she raised six wonderful children. Vera became a physical therapist during our youth and has spent her life serving us and her friends. No one believes in me more.

Finally, God is the Alpha, true, but He also is the Omega. It's into His hands I commit this book. I pray its theme of forgiveness reaches you, the reader. Yesterday's poison is potent today.

Chapter One

Her world burned, dissolved into ashes, and Torie Sullivan needed to keep her tears at bay.

Stupid girl. Should've figured.

Torie chugged the last of her drink and waved her hand toward the barkeeper of The Stadium Bar and Grill. "Another, Collin. No ice this time." She struggled to make her voice crisp, in command.

"Easy, Torie. No one's worth what you're doing to yourself." Collin slid a scotch and chaser across the bar.

She grabbed for it, but his fingers lingered.

Collin leveled his eyes at her. The look fired her anger.

How dare he believe I drink too much?

Torie forced a smile. Men. All alike. She lifted the whiskey, winked at Collin, and cocked her head. "A faithful find who can man?" She squinted and mused. "A find is a faithful. A faithful find man?" Giggles hiccupped, and she covered her mouth. "However that saying goes. Cheers." She put the glass to her lips, paused, and placed it back on the bar. "Cheers is all wrong." Torie gnawed her forefinger. "I got a better toast." She lifted the glass. "Glooms." The Jim Beam singed her throat. The sting didn't lessen over the evening, didn't numb her emotions.

Sorrow settled in her chest, a heaviness like her childhood asthma. She hadn't cried and wouldn't. After all, what could one expect from a man who thought with his hormones? Men all acted alike, and Trey Currey proved her expertise. Selene was her friend. Her one *real* friend. Until she stole Trey.

Collin took her empty glasses. "Want a Coke?"

Torie propped her head on her hand and glared at him. "Another boilermaker would fit the bill, sweetheart." To play to Collin's ego, she murmured the words. He was too moral for a bartender.

"Torie." His voice purred with a concern. It pierced her fog.

She brushed it away.

"You've drunk enough. How about a ginger ale?"

Bolting upright, Torie lost her balance and gripped the edge of the bar. Falling over like a common drunk would never do. She wasn't no

1

drunk -- no how. "Come on, Collin. I only had..." Fumbling for the number, she waved three fingers in his face.

"Try five. At least by my count. Who knows who you conned out there?" He nodded at the crowded dining area behind her.

Where she and Trey should've been enjoying a candlelit meal.

"Too many for little old you."

"'S your job to give me drinks." She stood on the chair stretcher and gave a sultry pout, her Rihanna look. It always worked. "'Specially as I'm payin' good money for 'em. You know how many perms I have to give for those dollars?" She tilted her head, gave him the smile that always melted men.

Collin leaned over the bar, his eyes warm in the dim room. His hand caressed her head.

Collin was sculpting gel in her hands.

"Torie, you're cute and fun, but not like this. Have you ever thought your problem might be you?" Someone flagged him down for another drink. He turned away, attentive to his other patrons.

"Me?" She sputtered and tumbled off the stool.

An older guy three chairs down grinned in her direction.

Batting her lashes, Torie tilted her head. "The last step's a doozy." With a wink, she turned back to the barkeep and snapped her fingers -- or tried to. They didn't quite make any noise. "Collin. My keys?"

"No keys, Torie. I'm calling a cab for you."

Collin headed for the phone at the far end of the bar.

With her arms crossed, she leaned forward. "Then at least gimme one for the road. The cab'll take a year or two to get here from Shocari." She shook her head and giggled at her mistake. Instead of correcting it, Torie played it up. "Scho-oochy." A snigger bubbled up. "Why do our towns have to have unpronounceable Dutch names? Skokary whatever? Why can't we name 'em somethin' like Albany or Delmar 'stead of Schoharie?"

"Because those other names have already been taken," Collin called over his shoulder.

With Collin yakking to the cab service, Torie grabbed her purse and stumbled to the other end of the bar. "Schoharie'd be a good place for my new hair salon. The Hairy in Schoharie." She peeked at Collin.

Like vapors of alcohol, her momentary giddiness evaporated. Hurt descended in a heavy-handed fist. She leaned against the bar and heard Collin's mellow voice, his back to her. Pegs at the far end of the bar held the patron's keys. Letting Collin take care of her would feel so good, but she'd tried letting Trey tend to her needs, and what did he do?

She needed to get out of this bar.

Men. Useless. Unreliable. Like adding another log to the woodstove in winter, she stoked her anger by recalling all the wrongs of men -- sex and photographs, demanding dinner cooked the moment they got home, endless sports on TV followed by sex. Then the photographs. She tilted her chin and huffed. Men. Controlling freaks of nature.

Torie grabbed her keys from the peg Collin insisted his patrons use. The stupid booze-Nazi. Stomping past the diners enjoying their Saturday night dates, she teetered out of The Stadium.

Cool night air slapped her face. The stupid town would freeze again tonight. The rest of the stupid world warmed up in May, but not stupid Westfield.

Stupid, stupid, stupid town.

Torie wobbled to her beat-up, ancient Rabbit parked right in front of The Stadium and climbed in. *I can drive. By the time the cab gets here, I'd be sober and not need it.* She shook the thought away. *If I was drunk.*

Her keys slipped from her fingers and fell onto the asphalt. The black of the road blended with the night. Torie leaned out of the car door, flung wide open, and stretched out to get them. Missed her first swipe. A truck, too big for the narrow streets, whizzed by, just missing her.

She snatched the keys from the blacktop as Collin exited The Stadium. He loped down the steps and banged at her passenger window.

"If you drive away, I'm calling the cops."

The glow from the streetlight haloed Collin, like an angel. If angels existed.

"Torie, no man is worth it. Consider AA. You don't have to be like your mother."

She bit her lip. Mumbled. "I'm not like Jean."

Tears threatened, but she wouldn't be a cry baby. Hadn't cried since middle school when... She clenched her teeth and inhaled, let the air fill her lungs. Her mother thrived on self-pity and man-lust. Not her.

With an exhale, Torie pulled away from the curb. Behind her, brakes squealed, and a horn blared. She stepped on the gas, peered into the rearview mirror, and let the black SUV eat her dust.

"I don't need no cab," she told Collin as though he sat beside her. "I'm cool and in control."

The road curved sharply left as it skirted Hookskill Preserve. Torie turned too late. Her car careened into the parking lot of the town's pride and joy, nothing more than a couple hundred acres of trees and water owned by the Nature Conservancy.

After skidding to a stop, Torie patted her hair, squared her shoulders and lifted her mouth in a sultry grin. *Meant to do that. In control.*

She threw her Rabbit into reverse, scooted back onto the main road, rounded the curve, past the Ready Mart, and zoomed out of town.

Speed, and anger at Collin, lost their magic. Collin had been a friend -- sometimes stern, but always fair. Her eyes watered.

The real culprits resurrected -- Selene and Trey. The imprint of Trey's hand on her wrist, inviting her into his bed burned like a brand. Lying next to him, Selene smirked. Her friend *knew* Torie loved Trey -- the first man she dared to not simply date, but to love.

It did no good. He preferred her fat friend. Her stunning, voluptuous, charismatic, sarcastic best friend. Torie's fingers dug into the steering wheel.

Her stomach tossed. She had scruples. Unlike Jean. Unlike everyone else. Yet, the treachery of the two people she trusted most rushed back and blinded her. Collin's rot-gut booze failed her. Her memories remained raw.

Collin was right. She ruined every one of her friendships. Maybe she was--

Her eyes blurred, and her nose ran. Her thought would stay unspoken. Torie fished through her Kate Spade purse for tissues then tossed it to the back seat. Her iPhone fell to the floor. Contorting her arm behind the console, Torie tried to retrieve the phone.

The car hurled itself to the right. The crunch of the shoulder gave way to the bumpy grass. It caught the tires and yanked her down a steep slope. The headlights illuminated tree branches as they grabbed the car, rasped their fingers along its sides as though shoving her down the slope until spider webs of pain showered over her. The Rabbit slammed into a stone wall.

*****

Adam Benedict knew the course of one's life needed a minute to change. Since he was thirteen, this fact burned into his being. Literally for his sister and his parents, along with the drunk who started the fire that killed them. His last call confirmed it -- a three-year-old who fell into a bonfire.

The dispatcher interrupted his brooding. "Single-vehicle MVA. Livingstone Pond Road, EMTs on scene. Need paramedic assistance."

"Let's go, Garfinkle." Levi Stephenson, his EMT, driver, and closest friend, slapped Adam's shoulder and rounded the ambulance. "This call will turn out better." He climbed into the rig and glanced at the clock.

"Should be the last one for the evening. You can get home at a decent hour and make it to church with us in the morning."

Adam glanced at his buddy. "Had you been at the same fire as I? How can you be so chipper?"

"God. It's all in His hands." Stephenson pulled out of the bay. With the flip of two switches, red, white, and blue lights bounced off the other vehicles. He turned left, and sped out into the blackness, the siren piercing the night. "Not death nor life nor angels nor fire can separate us from the love of--"

"Don't start on the God thing." Adam held up his hand and turned his head toward the window. He hoped Stephenson hadn't noticed his smile.

"Don't grin if you don't like my preaching." Stephenson chattered about the love of God, about his church, and the picnic to follow while Adam studied the murky shapes of the trees whirling by. Even after an hour of counseling with his captain after his last call, images of skin sloughing from the toddler stayed glued in his mind. The smell of charcoal and sulfur from burned hair and flesh. Bone-melting screams.

He took off his cap -- ran his hand over his close-cropped curls and reviewed the burn protocols. He had done everything possible to save the three-year-old Cody Lasky. Intubation. Air. Fluids. Even Mid-State Hospital couldn't do anything but get him ready for the bird. Before Adam began his PCRs, the kid had been airlifted to Albany Medical. Probably landed before the paperwork got filed. Died before Adam returned to the station.

Even if he were a doctor, he couldn't change the kid's fate.

"Hey, Garfinkle?"

Adam turned and caught Stephenson looking at him.

"Yes or no?"

"Yes or no what?" Adam scrunched his cap down, as much to hide his buzzed curls as to buy time.

"You listen as well as Justine." Stephenson laughed. "At least come to the picnic at Hookskill. Justine's been cooking up a storm. Teaching Maya how to bake. She'll be there, you know."

Adam twirled his finger, thought of Jennifer, finally now his ex-girlfriend. He'd had enough of women.

"Maya's sweet, Adam. Maple syrup and cinnamon rolls."

"Yummy."

The lights from the accident scene came into view. Relief flooded Adam. Maybe he could redeem *this* life.

Chapter Two

"Nothing is easier than self-deceit. For what each man wishes, that he also believes to be true." Demosthenes

A fireman waved the ambulance ahead of the parked fire truck. Adam and Stephenson backed to the edge of the road. Before the men hopped out of the rig, Trooper Chad Morgan pointed. "Down there."

Deep into woods, where nothing but stars illuminated the expanse, the twin taillights of the wreck glowed red.

"How the heck did anybody find this vehicle?" Adam grabbed the O2 and his trauma kit and skidded down the hill behind Morgan.

"A guy pulled over to take a leak. His wife told him to step out of sight. Good thing for the drunk down there."

Adam skidded down the embankment and arrived at the scene. Emergency lights lit the night like a scene from a sci-fi movie. *How'd anyone survive the mangled wreck?*

"Don't get too close. She might intoxicate you. I'd guess this is the drunk The Stadium owner called about."

Of course, a drunk would survive. A kid would die. Adam winced. He couldn't judge. Shouldn't. Brushing aside the grief of losing Cody, he angled his flashlight into the vehicle -- by the looks of it, an old Rabbit. Through the drivers-side window, shattered and hanging together like a mosaic, the driver's head lay against the headrest. A gash in her forehead bled.

The steering column crowded her chest but hadn't pierced it. Probably broke some ribs -- with luck, not her back or her spleen. The dashboard buckled upward, not into her.

Adam climbed onto the hood. A volunteer EMT from Westfield's VFD had already pushed out the old windshield.

"You guys were fast," the EMT said. "We thought we'd have her packaged for you."

"Slow night." Adam donned blue neoprene gloves. "Glad you got the rescue started, though. Don't want to lose another vic." He reached into the vehicle. "Facial lacs. Unconscious and pulse is tachy." He squinted and peered at the EMT. "Has she gotten worse?"

"Nah. Been stable."

"Let me start a drip." He lay on his stomach. The EMT angled lights on the unconscious driver as Adam cleaned the crook of her elbow and inserted a line. Once finished, Adam hopped off the hood and held the IV bag high.

"Ready to cut her out?" Adam asked a firefighter wielding the metal spreaders.

"Let me at her."

The EMS workers stood back as the firefighter used the spreaders to pop the door.

With the car accessible, Stephenson climbed into the back seat. Together, Adam and Stephenson worked the cervical collar around the driver's neck and slipped the Kendrick's Extrication Device behind her back. They'd end up bundling her like a mummy, but the KED secured her back as they lifted her out of the car. Stephenson held alignment while Adam secured the straps around the KED. All the while, the vic remained unconscious.

Before they immobilized her head, Adam slapped a four-by-four bandage over the bleeding gash. The doctors would clean it out at the hospital and stitch it like an Amish quilt. Her nose, if not broken, would be swollen and bruised. He ran a finger around her eye, careful not to press too hard. She'd have to lay a thick steak on her shiner, but it didn't look like she'd broken her cheek or orbital bone. Maybe she'd escape with a concussion. For now, he wanted her packaged and off to Mid-State.

With her face framed by the collar and immobilized in the KED, something about her looked familiar. The vic was around his age. Small. Dark hair. Given the size of the hamlets in this area of Albany and Schoharie counties, he'd probably run into her around town. With the play of lights in the darkness and her cheek and hair clotted with blood, she couldn't look much like herself.

Adam secured the victim onto the backboard. He wedged in the orange head blocks, then slipped her hands through the straps.

"Ready, Garfinkle?" Stephenson stood near the vic's head.

"On my count. One, two, three." They hoisted the woman. The stretcher was lighter than helium. The smell of her coppery blood overpowered the scent of the pines. Unpleasant, but it beat the stench of charred hair and skin. He stepped, the angle awkward as Stephenson took the lead. With the head of the board higher, Adam bent to get a better grip. His foot hit a rock. He stumbled and wrenched his knee. The pain knifed him, and he wanted to crumble to the ground but refused to drop the vic.

"You okay, Benedict?"

He gritted his teeth. "A walk in the park."

Stephenson's laughter jiggled the board. "You got that -- a walk in

Livingstone Park."

*****

Torie rocked. Each movement sent shards of glass into her head. Her stomach churned as she strained to sit up.

"Easy, there." A face came near. The man's voice too loud.

"Sick." The word stuck in her chest. "Sick." Her eyes wouldn't open. Her scream whispered. No one came to her aid. "Sick. Sick. Sick." Why wouldn't anyone help? At last, she shrieked, "Gonna puke!"

"Did you say something?" A man turned his ear to her lips.

She groaned.

"Sorry, but you're hard to hear." He grinned as he removed the mask. "I worried you wouldn't come to. Hang on, and I'll turn the board."

Her world tilted sideways and a kidney-shaped basin came into view below her cheek. Spasms shook her stomach, and it emptied into a basin. For the most part. The nausea settled, and the guy turned her onto her back.

Torie strained to see what was happening. She was alive. Tied down. In an ambulance, maybe?

The man's face neared. He grinned a Kewpie-doll smile beneath kind eyes. "I'm Adam Benedict, a paramedic from Schoharie Rescue. You gave us a scare. What's your name?"

Her voice felt lost somewhere deep inside. Terror gripped her gut. "Torie."

"What happened to you, Glory?"

"No. Torie." She struggled to speak, but her tongue felt too big for her mouth. The man's face hovered above hers.

"You're right. No glory in your accident." He chuckled. "Can you tell me what happened?"

Sour vomit rocked her stomach once more. The ambulance turned, and the motion sent her world spiraling out of control. Panic roosted on her chest sending searing pain with every breath, and she spun in nauseating tumbles. She wanted to grab onto this man and let his steady calm transfuse into her, but she was wrapped up tighter than a perm.

*****

"She's out again, but stable," Adam called to the triage nurse. "Breathing steady. Pulse one hundred -- slowed since we stabilized her. Name's Glory, I think. Trooper Morgan can tell you for sure." The nurse

8

indicated an exam room, jotted notes on a clipboard as she jogged next to the stretcher. With their patient stowed, Stephenson and Adam joined Morgan, who was filling out forms in the EMS room.

"Twenty-two minutes from call to delivery, boys. Not bad." Morgan stretched his legs as he slapped his pen on top of the paper. "I've bagged plenty of overtime tonight." A yawn underscored his comment. "You, too. Didn't I see you guys at the Lasky fire?"

Adam nodded and stiffened. He opened his laptop to begin his reports.

"Busy day?" Morgan asked.

"Nah. The Lasky kid, one frequent flier, and a lot of downtime until this one," Stephenson said. "Slow night. But a sad one."

"The innocents get destroyed while the drunks only get scraped up." Morgan hitched his head toward the treatment room.

The charge nurse stepped into the room. "Patient's alert. Waiting on the PA. You can see her now, Chad."

"Don't let the ladies keep you here all night. Although they're tempting." Morgan winked at the nurse who rolled her eyes.

Adam caught her slight smile. Morgan always wowed the ladies.

The trooper stood and left the men alone.

*****

Torie yanked her arm. "I'm fine. Quit poking me with needles." She held her right arm up to swat the nurse and tangled it in the IV lines.

The nurse tightened her grip and filled another vial with blood. She capped it off, placed it in a holder, and turned her attention back to Torie. "I've completed the mandated blood work. Can't get rid of the troopers without it." As though to stress her point, a tall cop who had to be double Torie's size appeared in the doorway. The nurse hoisted the bed's guardrails and left.

The cop wore a dun-colored Stetson, pulled low over his forehead. It added to his height, almost as though his head would brush the ceiling.

Torie pushed herself up. With pain searing her ribs, she gritted her teeth to keep from screaming. She fell against the raised head of the gurney and gawked at the approaching cop. His gray uniform was unwrinkled, neat. His gun -- big and black -- advanced toward her. She shrunk back and wished the bed would swallow her.

"Trooper Morgan." He grabbed the brim of his Stetson as though to tip it. "Can you tell me what happened?"

She shrugged.

9

"Know what caused the accident?"

She cowered. The gun, like a magnet, drew her attention. Torie couldn't tell him she'd been searching for her phone and fleeing from her life.

He scrawled something and handed her papers. "Appearance ticket, unless you plead guilty. If not, I'd advise you to find a lawyer."

With the last words, Torie raised her gaze to the steel-gray eyes of the trooper.

His eyes sparkled with kindness despite his authority. She smiled apologetically. The papers, held in his fingers, hovered over her. With hesitant moves, she reached out and took them.

"I wasn't..." She lowered her lashes and figured flirting could help her cause, but her attempted excuse sounded hollow. Her appeal to sex made her feel dirty.

Once more, the trooper reached for the brim of his hat, nodded and strolled out of the room. His black shoes squeaked against the beige tiles.

Torie shifted up on the bed and clamped her mouth tight to stifle a groan. Her ribs had to be as splintered as pick-up-sticks. She eyed her ticket like a spider crawling up her fingers.

The nurse who had taken her blood approached the gurney. "The PA will be here in a moment to stitch up your gash. Judging from its size, you'll be a grandmother before he finishes. Then we'll get you a CT scan and x-ray those ribs." She turned on quiet shoes and left.

Torie let the papers drop and chewed a cuticle. *I want to go home.* Shifting on the bed, she grabbed her ribs and blinked back tears. Did anyone know where she was?

Her head pounded, and her heart tightened. It would kill her when it broke into pieces.

Her fingers grazed her forehead making her wince. *I'm going to look like a freak.*

And this stint in the ER? How was she going to pay for this? The ER, the overnight stay they said she needed? CT scans? X-rays? Drugs?

She'd bought only enough insurance to not be fined by Obamacare. Her copay was a gazillion dollars.

But her gash? *I'll look like Frankenstein's bride.*

She brushed her fingertips against the edges of the bandage. So much blood crusted in her hair, now frizzing like ol' Frank's bride, and more oozed from the gauze.

On the bright side -- things couldn't get any worse.

Chapter Three

"You will burn and you will burn out; you will be healed and come back again." Fyodor Dostoyevsky

Adam glanced at his bedside clock again. Not even six. He closed his eyes, wished for oblivion, but all he saw was charred skin and oozing lymphatic fluids. He turned, but in the creaking bedsprings, he heard Cody Lasky's moans. When his sister, Maizie, burned all those years ago, she must have screamed like Cody when he fell in the bonfire. He squeezed his eyes tight. He'd been camping with his Boy Scout troop that weekend, had begged Mom and Dad to let him go. If he were home, he could've saved them.

Or been dead, too.

He sat up, swung his legs over the side of the bed, and cupped his head in his hands.

Shaking his head to clear the memories did nothing. In their place, he heard Stephenson's cheerful voice. *You think wallowing cleans up the hogs, Garfinkle? Get over it. Come on to church.* It sounded good this morning. His heart yearned to return, to hear the comfort of God's love. He'd surprise Stephenson.

Adam stretched and drew apart the bedroom curtains. His movement scared a deer grazing near the crab apple tree. The blossoms drifted to the ground like snow, pink in the rosy sunrise.

With the coffee started, Adam hit the shower, grabbed a nearly empty bottle of shampoo and lathered. The scent of sour-apple slid over his shoulders, and down his hips. Foam from Jennifer's shampoo bathed him with more bitter memories.

Jennifer. Model beautiful, a mane of blonde hair that glinted gold in the sunlight. Eyes sea green like one of the Crayola's from Maizie's colors. Beautiful, fragrant Jennifer. The men at the station teased him and envied him. No one understood how dull beauty could be. If one's values were built on looks, when age took them away, you had nothing. He'd never date a woman as vain as Jennifer again. Adam needed companionship and depth.

If the past proved the future, he didn't have much of a chance.

Finally, clean and dressed, he leaned against the jamb of his open door. With coffee in hand, he focused on the world before him rather than the one behind.

11

His cabin perched high above a small stream which pooled and fell in gentle spills down the hills. Beyond the stream, the land lay in a patchwork of greening fields like one of Neema's quilts made out of old clothing. Squares of trees, interspersed among fields, offered lots of cover for the whitetail and the bears, not to mention raccoons and skunks and coydogs and every critter in God's good earth. Or every critter capable of surviving the freezing winters in the hills of upstate New York.

He studied the squares, recalled the patch of woods where he snagged his first eight-point buck. In the brown section, he learned to ride dirt bikes in grade school. Another square grew the world's best sweet corn. Quilted memories overlapped. Then his phone jarred him.

"Adam." Neema's worried voice greeted him. "Pop fell in the yard going for the Sunday paper. I can't get him up."

Adam's fingers clenched the phone. "Is he hurt? Do you want me to call rescue?"

"No. You know your grandpa. No flashing lights and drama."

"It'd be faster. They'd come without lights. What if he needs transport?"

"No. Just hurry. Okay?"

"Be right there." He spoke into the dead phone. If Neema hung up on him, panic overwhelmed her.

Adam grabbed the emergency kit he stored behind the couch, loped around his cabin to his truck, and snagged the keys he'd stashed in the console. Within minutes, he pulled into his grandparents' gravel driveway. Not bothering to shut off the F-150, Adam hopped out.

"Pop." He knelt next to his grandfather who lay in the front yard. Neema knelt between him and the road as though to shield Pop from traffic. "Do you hurt anywhere?" Adam palpated his grandfather's neck.

Pop brushed his hand away. "I'm okay. Just give me your arm. I told Grace to bring the car around. I coulda used it for leverage."

"I might've run you over, Harold." Neema ran her hand over her husband's head.

Pop's jaw tightened.

"She did the right thing by calling me. Any neck pain?"

"Jeepers, Adam, get me off the ground before the neighbors start selling tickets to the freak show." With surprising strength, Pop grabbed onto Adam's arm to hoist himself.

"Hold on." Adam took hold of his grandfather under the arms and lifted. Together they wobbled up the porch steps.

The door of the screened-in porch bounced shut behind him, and Adam helped Pop into his favorite, worn rocking chair in the corner of the porch.

Neema tucked a quilt around her husband.

"Stop yer fussin', Grace." He brushed her hands away and rubbed his shoulder. "Jist bruised my shoulder. One injury don't make me a total invalid. Why doncha bring Adam them pull-aparts."

Neema's eyes caught Adam's, questioning. He caressed her arm. "He's fine. The pull-aparts sound good."

His grandma tottered into the house. She'd lost height, and the dowager's hump hobbled her more than usual, melded her breasts to her belly. His heart twisted into a tiny knot. When did his grandparents become so frail? Adam turned back to his grandfather who dropped the hand that massaged his bruised shoulder. "You okay now? I can--"

"Stop fussing. Jist a bump. Next time I take a tumble, it'll have to be near furniture, so I can hoist myself up. Your grandma ain't no spring chicken anymore." He chuckled at his joke. "God is good."

"Good? You were just complaining."

"Not complaining. Jist stating the facts." He rocked a little and a small smile played around his lips. "Yep. God gave me a beautiful morning. Lilacs blooming, and a grandson who knows medicine. What more kin I ask for?"

"How can you find goodness with...?" If he named the Parkinson's, it became too real. "You're my hero, Pop."

"Don't take courage to live with what you ain't had a choice in. Courage comes when you choose your battles. Why don't ya go help yer grandma?"

Adam opened the screen to the house. The aroma of cinnamon and yeast made him salivate. In the kitchen, Neema bustled about fixing a tray of warm pull-aparts and a china teapot filled with Earl Grey. Adam never drank tea, except for hers. Earl Grey with its tangy scent always made him think it should taste better than re-heated dishwater. With every sip, he knew smells deceived like the whiffs of the sour apple shampoo. However, with Neema's home-baking and love, he downed the tea with joy.

"Let me help--" He swallowed his thoughts when he caught sight of Pop's Winchester 30-30 propped against the counter near the door. "What's Pop's rifle doing out?" He picked it up. Checked it.

"You know your grandpa."

"It's loaded!" He racked out the shells.

"Here. Give me it." Neema stuck her hand out. "Pop wants it ready."

"It's not safe."

Her eyes bored into him. Her chin raised.

He couldn't look at her. Instead, he took the empty rifle upstairs. He stopped short at the threshold to his childhood room where Pop stashed the gun safe. The freshness of the Lasky fire resurrected the one that killed his family. Neema used all the money left from the insurance to outfit the spare room for him with a loft bed and colorful rug and quilt. Under the bed, stood the desk he had filled with science paraphernalia. This room made him feel like he was twelve.

Stashing the gun, Adam turned the tumblers to the safe and scurried back to his grandparents.

On the porch, life continued as though no argument had taken place. Glad for the peace, Adam pointed to his grandmother's latest quilting project. "You're almost done."

Her smile bloomed. "Good thing. Shoulder's been cramping. Fingers atingle." She shook a finger at her husband. "Now don't you start in on me, Harold."

"Tell your grandma to get a EK-heart-o-gram."

"Tell your grandfather it's the fine motor work pinching nerves."

"As in love as ever." Adam bit into a pull-apart. The cinnamon melted with the butter and sugar on his tongue. "Neema," he said with his mouth full, "you've done a lot of fine motor work." The quilt lay like pieces of an intricate puzzle. Each section created an optical illusion. The background would pop to the foreground. The overlapping pieces would morph so you couldn't tell where one began and the other ended. "Perhaps you should get an EKG."

"I'm fine. Quit talking with your mouth full."

Adam swallowed. "I can check you out."

"No!" Her head jerked up, and she raised a crooked finger toward Adam. "I ain't going to have my grandson fishin' 'round my naked parts." She nodded toward the plate of food on his lap. "Eat up."

Adam had no choice. When Neema used that tone, everyone listened. He leaned back in his own rocker and savored the morning. Their house oozed peace, despite laying so close to a main road with the constant drone of cars and trucks zooming west to Schoharie and east to Albany. Ten acres were all they had left of their farm that flowed across county lines. The apple trees were overgrown, the fields unkempt, and rhubarb sprung up in patches like hair gone wild on Rogaine. Mornings like these tasted like dark chocolate -- a bitter sumptuousness.

*****

A nurse led Torie to a small room where a guy in a uniform was filling out papers.

"You should *not* leave."

Torie waved her off.

14

"You can contact Social Services."

"No!" Torie caught herself. Half the staff yelled at her already for wanting to leave. "Sorry. I won't be a welfare case."

"You do have someone who will be with you?"

Torie looked her in the eye, made her gaze warm and earnest. "I'll be careful." She held up a prescription. "The Percocet you gave me took away most of the pain."

Sometimes lies were the easiest route. This stint in the ER would cost her a month's pay. Or more. *If* Selene let her continue to work at Curly Girls.

She had to go home.

To do that, she needed a ride, but those ambulance drivers lost her brand new iPhone with all her contacts.

Drumming her fingers, Torie tried to remember someone's number. Trey? He'd be with Selene.

Curly Girls?

Same thing -- Trey and Selene.

She'd have to call Trey. A twenty-mile walk home with a million stitches and a cracked rib didn't seem possible. Not to mention her concussion.

Trey's number rang forever. Voicemail picked up.

She inhaled, but air wouldn't fill her lungs. Wrapping an arm around her torso, Torie strained to take a deep breath. With no other choice, she dialed Selene.

It rang twice. Went to voicemail.

Selene had disconnected the call. Torie dropped her head onto her hand, closed her eyes. Behind her lids, she pictured Trey and Selene together. She'd have to put up with sharing a home with Selene until she found a new place. Saved enough to pay the rent, the hospital, the tow, and her fine. A huge penalty. Points on her license. Fortunate for her, the cop said she'd probably not lose it. This time. Despair shrunk her heart. She had no money -- men always covered for her. Like...

Money. Even if Selene let her, how could she work at Curly Girls? Cosmetology was intimate -- talk, confessions, dreams.

Footsteps approached. Torie held her breath and waited for the nurse to leave. She turned her chair to the wall, as though facing it and seeing nothing but the green paint would hide her shame. Punching numbers into the phone, Torie willed Lucy to be home -- or if the number she called belonged to Lucy and not the governor's office or a dog-grooming salon in Coxsackie.

"Hey, Luce, it's Torie. Sorry to call so early, but--"

"This is too funny. I was just thinking about you. Can I make an appointment for a mani and pedi?"

Words fled. Lucy's simple request reminded Torie of everything she lost. Everything she ruined.

She ruined. Not Selene. Not Trey.

"Torie, are you there?

Torie nodded and winced. Lucy wouldn't see a nod. "I'm sure we have appointments. It is Sunday morning, not quite eight, and I'm not at Curly Girls." She barreled on before Lucy turned the conversation back to her own life. "I've got a problem. Had a bit of an accident. Do you think you can pick me up at the hospital?"

"When?"

"Right now. I'm going home even though they insist I stay, but my car's wrecked."

Silence greeted her.

Seconds ticked by. They felt like minutes until Lucy found her excuse. "I'd love to, but, you know, um, I need to shower. Then Howie's coming over..."

Without a word, Torie returned the phone to the cradle. Her hand lingered on it like a mamma tucking a baby into bed. Babies. Another train of thought she couldn't follow.

She dropped her hand onto the table. The paper of the yellow phone book felt cool to her touch. The tiptoeing nurse anticipated her need. Torie mouthed a thank you and called Heather Vanderslew. Sweet Heather would pick her up.

Fifteen minutes later, Heather's minivan pulled into the patient pick-up area. With five days to go before her C-section, Heather already picked out the van -- the most awful sky-blue Torie ever saw. Heather coordinated everything, and baby blue was the color for a boy. The infant seat had been installed by the local fire department -- probably the same guys who pried her out of her tuna can last night.

"So what happened?" Heather asked. Perkiness permeated her voice, peaked through her smile.

"Trey and I had a fight." Torie shrugged and stared out the window. "I overcorrected on a curve. Concussion." She pointed at her head.

"I'm so sorry, hon. Shouldn't you still be in the hospital?" Heather's forehead creased, her blue eyes glistened with tears.

"Nah. I'm good."

Heather's smile chased the worry lines away. "Tell me, Torie, how bad was it in the hospital?" Heather ran her hand over her distended belly. "I'm so scared. Wish Mom was here right now."

Torie shook her head. "Can't help you there. The techs only x-rayed me. They won't radiate you. When's your mom coming?"

"Thursday." Heather rambled on about how she wished her mother and she could have shopped together for baby clothes. "Mom's bringing a *whole* suitcase from the girls in her office. She crocheted four layette sets." Heather waved the appropriate number of fingers in Torie's direction. "One in yellow before Mom knew she'd have a grandson. Then two in blue and one in green, for variety." Heather grinned at Torie. "You gotta see them. So cute."

"I'm sure." Torie looked out the window -- anything to avoid seeing bubbly, optimistic Heather. Torie rubbed her belly. *No! What am I doing? I look like Heather.* With her hands now clasped in her lap, Torie stared at the passing scenery and struggled not to think of babies. *Not* thinking about them made it harder to forget.

Heather chatted, and her happiness filtered through Torie's self-absorption. Moaning as she shifted in her seat, Torie faced Heather. Her blonde hair, backlit by the sun-soaked window, accented her innocence. Torie reached over and patted Heather's arm. "Don't worry. You have a mother who adores you. A husband you love. Friends. Your baby will be perfect."

She and Selene used to mock Heather's annoying perky sunniness. For the first time, Torie longed for Heather's lightness in her own life.

In fifteen minutes, Torie found herself at 478 Burnt Hollow Road, outside the colonial she shared with Selene. Trey's Mustang sat in the driveway.

Chapter Four

"Yea, mine own familiar friend, in whom I trusted, which did eat of my bread, hath lifted up his heel against me." Psalm 41:9

Torie stood in the doorway and studied Trey and Selene. They cuddled on the couch facing the fireplace, sipping coffee, their legs braided together. Torie's own legs wilted beneath her. Her arms hung at her side. The couple didn't see her, just as they hadn't heard her keys rattling in the door.

With a step, a board creaked. Selene jumped off the couch and spun around. "Torie. You scared me."

Torie shrugged, the small movement jarred. She opened her mouth to speak, then closed it like a gasping, mute fish.

Trey reached up and took Selene's hand, held it, possessed it. Selene ogled Trey.

Torie knew the look. Lust. Her own eyes had hungered for Trey from the moment they met. She'd been cutting his rich, chocolate hair. She cut it slow, fingered the silk, and relished the thickness. His face reflected in the salon's mirror showed his eyes latched onto her, exploring her body. They were the color of hazelnuts streaked with gold. When they peered at her from beneath thick brows, they saw through her, to everything that had happened in her life. Her stomach tingled and her knees weakened. No man ever made her weak before. She should've taken warning, should've seen she'd lost control.

With men, loss of control spelled trouble.

A year later, Selene looked at him with the same hunger.

This morning, he leveled his eyes at her and smiled. Not the large smile displaying his even teeth. The closed lip, smarmy smile. He cocked his head.

Selene took a step forward. "I'm sorry, Torie." She shrugged. "No one can control love."

Torie closed her eyes. Her head threatened to pound her to powder. She should've listened to the nurses. At least she'd have a place to stay tonight because right now it was clear, she couldn't live here.

"You can stay here."

Had Selene read her mind?

"Until you find another place. You living here won't work out with me and Trey, of course."

Torie held up her hand, spun around and wobbled to the stairs, her hand against the wall to keep her balance.

Collapsing flat on her bed, Torie put her hands over her eyes. No phone, no car, no home. With no home, the last, dim hope for working at Curly Girls evaporated like steam off a curling iron.

A shower would wash off the hospital stink, but despair crushed her to the bed.

What to do?

Minutes ticked away until determination stiffened her backbone. She would get out. Now. Hoisting herself off the bed, Torie climbed to the attic and found her Coach overnight bag. She'd come back for her stuff on Tuesday when the salon opened and customers swamped Selene.

She threw in toiletries, medicine -- lots of Tylenol. Several hot irons, her blow-dryer, and underwear. A nightshirt was the last thing the bag could hold. Heather'd come and get her.

Tossing her soiled jeans and camisole on the bed, Torie dug out a denim skirt, pink tank top, and flip-flops. The shower would wait.

With the strap to the overnight bag over her shoulder, Torie hobbled down the stairs, grasping the handrail. Bypassing the living area, Torie found a phone in the salon. Heather's answering machine picked up. Leaving brief directions about the route she'd walk, Torie hung up. Then as her world twirled around her, she ran to the bathroom, knelt over the toilet while dry heaves racked her. Each wave sent earthquakes through her chest. Nothing Darren ever did to her hurt so much.

She lifted her head and stared at the wall adjoining the living room. Selene may have topped Darren's treachery.

The world settled as Torie propped herself against the wall. She rummaged through her purse, found her prescription, and popped a Percocet. The pill gagged her, and she spit it into her hand -- needed something to wash it down. Clawing her way back onto her feet, Torie searched out the wine in the backroom. Her clients seeking the full-spa treatment always got a glass of merlot. She unscrewed the top, plunked the Percocet back into her mouth, and took a swig.

The bottle needed to be replaced on the shelf. Then, almost by itself, it wiggled its way into her overnight bag. The zipper refused to close, and the bottle's neck poked out. No worries. Easy access. Couldn't get a DUI walking.

Torie didn't bother to lock the door to the salon.

*****

19

After helping Pop climb out of the tub, Adam handed him a towel and left the bathroom. He leaned against the wall next to the door which wouldn't stay latched. Everything in the old farmhouse needed fixing. Their one bathroom, upstairs, sported a claw-foot tub with a hand-held shower. Most times, Pop settled for sponge baths and the commode in the dining room.

A small bath in a downstairs closet would give Pop a little dignity and privacy. He'd have to ask Stephenson how to go about it. Or at the least, who to hire.

The bathroom door creaked open. Adam helped Pop down the stairs and tucked him into the hospital bed in the dining room. Neema excused herself for a nap.

Standing on the porch, Adam studied the quilt stretched on Neema's quilting frame. A piece of art. Dramatic. Neema looked like an old-fashioned grandma -- stooped, gray-haired, old house dresses. Her quilts showed something else. Patches of bright pink, pale purple, green brighter than spring grass filled the quilt frame. Neema could name the exact shades. Maizie inherited her trait. Adam would hand her a red crayon, and she'd pout. "I want brick red." She could have been an artist.

Colors? Adam never remembered. He didn't know periwinkle from lavender or orchid from heliotrope.

Neema's embroidery amazed him. No wonder her hands tingled, and her shoulders ached. She owned stock on antacids -- claimed she chomped them for the calcium and a little heartburn. He wished she'd have an EKG -- for Pop, if not for herself.

Or for him.

With nothing to do for now, he headed out.

*****

Heather's blue van never materialized, and the overnight bag slung over Torie's shoulder grew heavier with each step. Her ribcage burned as though she had tried to straighten it with a flat iron. Had she thrown finances to the wind, she'd be lying on a comfy hospital bed, eating pureed green beans the color of army fatigues, living the life rather than walking the five miles to Heather's.

Designer label or not, before she walked another step, Torie had to ditch the overnight bag. Stone walls lined fields and thickets. A wall would give a hiding spot for her stuff.

To get to the rocks, she scooted down an incline. From the road, it looked gradual. As Torie grabbed at roots and rocks to keep from falling, she knew her eyes deceived her. She stashed the bag behind the lopsided corner of the rock fence.

Now Torie faced the mountain she'd slid down. Tears stung her eyes. Never could she climb that.

With a step, her flip flops slipped off. Grabbing them with one hand, she latched on to weeds with the other and hauled herself up. Her ribs screamed. She thought she did, too.

Thanks, Mid-State for narcotics. Torie wished she'd taken two pills. She clawed at more weeds, the dirt embedding itself in her nails. Her crawl back up lasted longer than her eleventh-grade history class.

Feeling like a Special Ops soldier, Torie finally hauled herself to the roadside. After surveying the wooded lot below, Torie saw no sign of her bag. Good thing it was a Coach. Brown. Blended with the jungle. It was a gift from? She scratched her head. From someone she manipulated. The thought dampened her mood even more. How could it be possible?

Up the road a long driveway led to a small house perched on a hill. Could she beg the homeowners for a ride?

A car whizzed by, headed in the opposite direction. Hitching could be an option seeing as exhaustion swamped her, and she still had miles to walk. She crossed the road. When a red pickup approached, she stuck out her thumb. To her delight, the truck stopped.

Scurrying to the truck, Torie yanked the door open.

"Long time no see, Victoria. Didn't expect to meet up with you begging a ride." The good looking driver grinned her way. "Hop in. I'm more than happy to give you a lift."

She recoiled and bumped against the open door. Slammed it and ran.

Darren.

*****

Adam sped along 443, thought he'd stop by Stephenson's picnic and apologize for missing church. Maybe he'd ask about building Pop's bathroom. As he neared Westfield, a woman sat by the side of the road, in the middle of nowhere. With her back against a tree, legs curled under her and head bowed, she looked distressed. He pulled over.

She raised her head. The drunk from the night before -- Glory, if he remembered right.

Her eyes widened. Even across the road, they spoke of horror. Glory stumbled to her feet, grasped her ribs, and turned toward the woods.

"You okay, Glory?"

She glanced over her shoulder.

"Your name's Glory, right?"

The girl stopped and shook her head. The frightened-rabbit look faded. "Do I know you?"

"I took you to Mid-State last night."

She shrugged. "Don't remember much about the ride. You the ambulance driver?" She approached the road.

He smiled. Common mistake. "I'm a paramedic. I didn't think you'd be out of the hospital so soon. You suffered a pretty nasty blow to the head. You've got a great shiner there."

The tiny woman grimaced. She was thin, but not anorexic scrawny. Her arms in a pink tank top were well muscled. "Your truck looked like someone else's."

"It's mine. I promise. Can I give you a lift?"

Her face lit up. "Would you? I need to get into Westfield. Thought I could make it on my own." Her closed-lipped smile defined strong cheekbones beneath dark eyes and a swollen nose. Her brown hair looked no better than the night before. The bandage spotted blood. Stitches peaked from behind it and ran into her hairline. Flecks of blood clung to the strands pulled tight into a ponytail.

"Climb in." He hopped out, opened the door for her, and gave her a hand up.

"Could you stop by that fence?" She pointed down the road from where he came. "I stashed a bag there."

"No problem."

She glanced away, and bit the cuticle of her index finger. Something in the gesture jogged a memory. Adam peered at her as he climbed into the driver's seat. Strong features defined her, belied her petite stature. Her eyes, though, looked young, and scared. He knew her from someplace other than the accident. "So if you're not Glory, what is your name? If you don't mind my asking."

"Torie." She sat up straighter. "Right there." She pointed. "See where the wall forms a corner. I thought if I stashed the bag there, no one would notice."

Adam pulled over. "Stay here. I'll get it."

He dashed down the slope and found her bag stuffed behind the rock. A bottle of wine poked out. He shook his head. At least she wasn't driving this morning. He returned to the truck and took a moment to study the woman sitting there. She had propped her elbow on the console, a finger to her lips. Instead of looking vulnerable, she looked calculating. Vicious. Then it hit him.

Vicious Vicky sat in his truck.

Chapter Five

"Every saint has a past and every sinner has a future." Oscar Wilde

Silence settled in the cab. A red-hot quiet threatened to burn Adam's nerves. Vicky laid her head against the headrest, her eyes closed. He ground his teeth. She didn't deserve compassion, but still, it bubbled to the surface. Someone else's pain always resurrected his pity.

At the Westfield town limits, he turned to her. "Where to?" His question galled. It would force Vicky to talk. He'd have to hear her vicious voice once more.

Vicky stifled a groan as she shifted forward.

Adam winced. "Shouldn't you be in the hospital?"

"There." She pointed to an apartment building with faded blue clapboards and peeling shutters. It sat wedged into a row of three-story buildings across the street from The Stadium, the most popular restaurant in the county.

He pulled into the restaurant's parking lot. "You need any help?"

Vicky shook her head. "Thank you. I can make it from here." She struggled down the steep step off the truck. In her effort, she looked fragile and defenseless, smaller than she was. "I appreciate the lift." She looked up at him and smiled. "I'm sorry. I never asked your name."

He didn't turn toward her, and she didn't move. At last, he twisted in his seat and met her eyes. They gazed at him waiting for his response. "Adam." He didn't smile.

"Thank you, Adam. For the second time, you saved my life."

The moment the door slammed, he peeled out, and headed west. Within a minute, Adam pulled into Hookskill's picnic area.

People crowded the wooden tables. The rumble of the waterfalls, a short space into the preserve, mingled with the laughter.

Merriment sounded good -- he needed it.

With the ignition off, he rubbed his eyes with two fingers. Behind his closed lids, he saw Cody Lasky. His own sister. Vicky. *So many years of torment, and she didn't know my name.*

A rap on his window jolted him. Stephenson's laughing face peered through it. He circled his finger to tell Adam to unroll his window. "Glad you got here. Everyone's stuffed, but there's enough food to feed all of Westfield."

Adam climbed out of his truck. "All three of the townsfolk?"

23

"Nah -- nine. They invited their in-laws."

He slapped Stephenson on the back and headed to their picnic table. "Make it ten people. Maya's here."

*****

Torie rapped on Heather's door. The sky-blue van sat out front, three stories down. Only one cerulean vehicle existed in the world, so Heather had to be home. She knocked louder. "Heather? It's Torie."

Soft mutters echoed somewhere inside. Heather had to be there. If not? Torie leaned against the wall on the narrow landing and studied the three flights she just slogged up, too tired to descend. The ambulance guy reminded her of someone, but she didn't know from where. It was his hair. Even though he cropped it, the tight curls were growing out. The sandy blond hair must have been the color of sunshine in his youth.

The door opened, and all musing ceased. Standing with her hand on the small of her back, Heather scowled. "Torie, what are you doing here? I thought you needed rest."

A clock ticked inside. The murmur of a TV mingled with the odors from the apartments -- onions and the faint whiff of incense. Torie thought she'd smell dinner from The Stadium across the street, but cheap apartment scents lingered.

Heather didn't ask her in.

"I need a place to stay."

Heather's eyes widened.

"Not for long. Just until your mother gets here." How could she convince Heather to let her stay? She couldn't be homeless. "Please." The plea in her voice grated almost worse than the pain in her head and ribs.

"Bobby."

Torie studied her friend, understood Heather's worry, and turned to go.

"Forget Bobby." Heather's voice regained its usual cheerfulness." Come in. Of course, you can stay." Heather's warm hand held Torie's forearm.

Relief sagged Torie's shoulders and stiffness fled as she followed Heather who waddled to the couch. Torie perched on the edge of a cushion.

"Trey." She licked her lips. She'd never had such a problem with men before. Wasn't used to this pain closing off her throat and choking her. "He's moving in with Selene. I can't live there."

Heather jerked forward. "Oh, you poor thing."

"I'll stay a day or two. Until I find an apartment."

"Bobby won't be happy. He didn't want Mom to come because the place is so tiny. With no motels for miles, she has to stay here." She held her hands up in question.

"I promise. I'll get out of the house when he's here."

Heather reached out and brushed the edge of Torie's bandage. "You look like you took up boxing."

Torie offered a small smile, and offer was all she could do. "I promise I'll have another place by Thursday." There had to be an empty apartment in town.

"You can stay if I can convince Bobby. He should be back soon." Heather stood and turned toward the teeny kitchenette in the corner. "I'm getting ice water. Want some?"

Torie shook her head.

"Make yourself at home." Heather's voice mumbled as she fumbled with the ice trays in the freezer.

The filth Torie ignored at Selene's overwhelmed her now. "Mind if I shower?" If Heather was going to throw her out, Torie, at least, wanted to wash the blood from her hair and Trey from her mind.

"Go ahead." Heather pointed to the bathroom. "We're having macaroni tonight -- an easy meal to stretch, so at least, you've got dinner."

Torie lugged her overnight bag to the tiny bathroom. Among the wires and irons in her suitcase, she discovered she'd packed no clean clothes, just a nightshirt and underwear -- and not much of them. At least she could fix her hair.

Priorities.

Think I need to figure out what's important. First lesson learned -- clean clothes trumped straight hair. She'd have to convince Bobby to gather her stuff later tonight.

In the shower, the hot water washed off the dust from her hike. It rinsed Trey and Selene from her skin. Left her almost feeling good.

As she toweled off, hushed voices drifted through the door. Torie closed her eyes and strained to hear. No words were necessary. Bobby's tone told her all. What would she do if Bobby threw her out?

Heather was on her side. She'd flatter her husband's machismo.

Torie rubbed her pulsing temples. It'd been a couple of hours since she took the Percocet -- way too soon for another. In the bottom of her overnight, Tylenol nestled next to the bottle of merlot. Popping two, Torie washed them down with a slug of wine.

With a deep breath, a hot poker jarred. Westfield had no pharmacy, so her prescription would soon be gone unless someone drove her to the drugstore in Burnt Hollow. Torie rubbed her head. *I wish this jackhammer would quit.*

Torie leaned in toward the mirror, her hands on the sink. Beneath wet hair, the angry bruise mocked her. She yearned to get drunk, to forget her messed-up life. Instead, she brushed her teeth. Under the cabinet, Torie found a bottle of Listerine. She gargled and hoped it was enough to hide the scent of wine, which was sure to make Bobby furious. As though Heather's lush of a husband had the right to call her a drunk. She closed her eyes once more and saw Adam. A vague familiarity floated in her mind.

Probably someone she took advantage of years ago.

Chapter Six

"...(T)hey measuring themselves by themselves, and comparing themselves among themselves, are not wise." 2 Cor. 10:12

Maya Vitale sat with legs wedged under the weathered picnic table. Justine Stephenson had just bolted after her toddler, leaving Maya to soak up the sun and the silence alone. It felt wonderful. If only her parents savored this small-town, country peace. Then they'd understand her need to be here. She scrunched her eyes and turned her head to the sun. *Feel the peace, Mom. Daddy. Feel.* Her attempt to transmit her feelings to her folks made her giggle.

"Maya, grab your pie. I want you to meet someone." Justine's yell startled Maya out of her reverie, and her giggle turned into a chortle.

Her best friend's children trailed Justine like three goslings. Justine turned to her kids. "Scoot. I've got to talk to Maya. I think Daddy needs more people on his team. Micah, take Isaiah." She handed him off to her eldest, and the two boys raced to the ball field.

"Mommy, push me on the swings." Little Hannah yanked on her mother's t-shirt.

"In a moment." Justine shooed the five-year-old away. Hannah returned and wrapped her arms around her mother's leg. Justine took a step closer to Maya. Hannah clung to her like gum to the underside of a desk.

Maya used her friend's distraction to check out Justine's mating match. The man settled at the Stephensons' picnic table -- the prized octagonal table nestled beneath an ancient weeping willow. Its branches formed a romantic and cool canopy. A handsome blond man tickled one of the Stephenson tribe. Their laughter rang above the voices of the other picnickers.

"Hurry," Justine said.

"No rush. If he can plow through all the food you gave him before I get there, I don't think I'd want him."

Justine continued to tug.

Before Maya could step over the picnic bench, she stumbled. "Ouch." She shook her hand.

"What happened?"

"I got a splinter."

"Perfect." A grin split Justine's face as though Maya had won the

Trifecta. "He's a paramedic." Justine pried one of her daughter's arms loose. No sooner had she extricated herself, than Hannah wrapped another limb around her leg. "Hannah, take Henry, and I'll meet you over there." Justine rounded up her youngest son, handed him to Hannah and pointed to the playground. She grabbed Maya's hand again.

Justine tripped over her daughter, but never loosened her grip on Maya. Justine shooed Hannah and Henry away with one hand, all the while tugging Maya with the other.

"Careful. You'll make this an upside-down pie if you keep pulling. No one would eat it. Not even your husband."

By the way she continued to yank, Justine hadn't heard her. Or ignored her.

Maya felt like the tail end of the snap-the-whip game her first-graders played. She tumbled into Adam as he clambered over his picnic bench.

"Maya's got a splinter." Justine turned toward her kids. "I'll race you to the swings." She ran off.

"Not too obvious, is she?" Maya asked.

Adam smiled. Lips like the curve of Cupid's bow -- shot straight toward her.

"Justine wouldn't know about the pie." She slid it on the table. "It's my first one ever, and it hasn't been cut."

"It looks delicious." Adam glanced at the pastry, then turned back to Maya. "Let me see the splinter."

Maya pulled the hem of the shirt's long sleeve over the heel of her palm, then offered Adam her hand.

He turned it over and inspected the offending sliver. "Easy removal. Be right back."

Maya studied Adam who walked to his truck with surprisingly long strides for a short man. She gnawed her skin at the edge of the splinter. He had to be five foot seven? Eight maybe?

Nipping the splinter with her teeth, it slid from her finger.

"Here we go." Adam returned brandishing a small first-aid kit.

"Sorry. I got it out." Maya turned her head. Everyone had fled.

"Here I thought I'd be your hero."

Heat crept up Maya's face. She lifted a hand to her cheek. Was she blushing?

"Sorry. Didn't mean to embarrass you." He waved his hand toward his table. "Keep me company, would you?" Adam sat.

Maya ducked her head and clambered over the bench.

"Justine and Stephenson thought I was going to starve to death." Adam lifted a half-empty bottle of wine. "Want a glass of the

Stephenson's finest?"

"I don't drink."

His lips curved into a beatific smile. "Good. Neither do I. However, I haven't kicked the eating habit."

"In case you didn't have enough to sustain life -- Justine wants you to be my guinea pig." She centered the pie which sat too close to the edge of the table. "Before you starve, can I entice you to try it?" She turned the pastry on the table like a prized jewel. "Justine taught me how to make crust people will fight over."

"What kind?"

"Of crust?"

"Pie. What kind?" Adam leaned forward.

Maya took a chance to peek into his eyes. Blue. Subtle blue -- almost gray. "Apple."

Leaning over the pie, Adam breathed in the earthy, tangy aroma. "If I resemble my namesake at all, I understand why Adam gave in to Eve's temptation. Who can resist anything apple?" He winked.

Warmth flowed from the pit of Maya's stomach. She fumbled for a knife and sliced into the pie.

He groaned.

She startled. "Is something wrong?"

Adam shook his head. "That's one beautiful specimen." He reached for the plate. "The only thing wrong is I haven't eaten it yet." Picking up a fork, he lifted a bite and studied it.

"Afraid to eat it?"

A half-smile lit his face. He bit in. With closed eyes, he moaned -- delight obvious in the tilt of his lips.

"You like it?" Maya clasped her hands in front of her chin.

"Love it." He put down his fork and wiped his hands on his jeans. His gray eyes sparkled like the play of light in the shadows.

Eyes didn't lie.

*****

A song bubbled up as Adam pulled out of Hookskill. He hadn't felt the urge to sing since Jennifer had moved in with him a year ago, but meeting Maya signaled a change. He switched on the truck's radio. A stupid ballad whimpered from the speakers. Adam had no stomach for it today.

He switched to a sixties station. The Beatles proclaimed, she loved you. With a lusty relish, he joined their yeah, yeahs and inserted a few extra of his own. Who would have thought meeting a woman could change his mood so quickly? Of course, Maya was chunkier than Jennifer -- who wouldn't be? Jennifer ate dry salad and sprouts -- more greens than a rabbit tolerated. Maya's weight rounded her in all the right places. Her warm, hazel eyes and shyness captivated him, made him want to protect, to shelter her from the darkness of the world. Her cute little nose crinkled when she smiled. It seemed Maya always smiled. He imagined her in his arms and his stomach warmed. He shook the thoughts away -- he was driving, after all.

At least she wasn't as heavy as Justine. But after babies?

Again. He couldn't imagine baby making and stay on the road at the same time.

Maya's thick, long hair, his weakness, after the more feminine parts, enticed him. Half the time together, he'd wanted to free it from its elastic band and let it flow.

Yet, more than her sensuality, her compassion drew him in. She loved others in a capacity greater than Jennifer ever showed. From what he'd seen, Maya loved others more than Jennifer loved herself. Maya even understood why he wanted to be a paramedic and not a doctor even though doctors made boatloads of money. Definitely not like Jennifer.

He could love her, yeah, yeah.

Ten minutes later, he pulled his F-150 up to the plain back wall of his cabin which faced a one lane, dead-end road. He loped around the cabin to the porch facing the valley. Backwards, Jennifer called it, but he built it this way to see what mattered most in the world.

The evening cooled. He threw kindling into his patio fire-pit, lit it, and pulled up a chair. With legs propped on the porch rail and a Coke in hand, he watched the sunset color the clouds. He let his mind wander.

He'd come a long way since the days of his crazy crush on Vicious Vicky. Braces from Neema and Pop disciplined his wayward teeth. A buzz-cut tamed his willful hair, and he had grown to an acceptable height. With all the lifting and hauling in his job, he'd even developed a decent upper body.

Twelve years since his folks and his sister burned to death, and he moved in with his grandparents. Twelve years since he got out of Burnt Hollow Middle School, transferred to Neema's district in Schoharie. He should be over it. Despite the time lapse, he was still a kid in middle school.

Twelve years and Vicious Vicky showed up.

He tried not to remember, but middle school wormed its way back into his present.

You don't know my father, Boy Scout.

Quit gawking at me, Madam Adam.

The laughter hurt most. Vicky always got the kids sniggering. They pointed fingers behind hands hiding hoots, legs in the aisle, getting pantsed in the parking lot. The worst of everything, one week before the fire...

He gulped air and refused to remember. His good mood faded like the rosy clouds of the sunset. As an adult sitting on his own porch in a setting rivaling Eden, he felt the flush of shame. Middle school still shot the quiver of terror.

He'd never be a victim again.

His phone buzzed with a text. Maya.

Loved meeting you. Can't wait 2 Fday.

What was wrong with this woman? She was his age, single and liked him.

Chapter Seven

"There are two ways to be fooled. One is to believe what isn't true; the other is to refuse to believe what is true." Søren Kierkegaard

Adam inventoried the meds in his rig.

"You're eager, Garfinkle." Stephenson sat on the bench in the back of the ambulance with crossed legs. He leaned against the sidewall and took a slug of coffee. "It's not even six and you're all set for the day."

Adam didn't bother to look up. "Nope. Not ready. Almost."

"Relax. We're supposed to hate working, should crave the weekend. Drink a cuppa joe with me and quit being a Boy Scout."

Adam grinned at his partner. "Not a Boy Scout. If I'm busy, the day will fly by."

"Would a certain young hazel-eyed woman with killer apple pie have anything to do with your good mood?"

"Nope. Just a good paramedic. And if you were a decent partner, you'd shut up and give me a hand instead of supervising."

Stephenson slapped Adam's shoulder and hopped off the rig. "Justine tells me Maya's smitten with you like a fly to a cow barn."

Adam quit inventorying his meds. "*Justine* said that?"

"I'm not going to repeat her exact words. I'm not a pansy using her meta-whatevers."

"You're an idiot--"

"Rig twenty-seven, code three," the intercom interrupted Adam's retort. "Comatose woman. Third floor. Two-twenty-nine Main. Westfield."

Duty hadn't officially begun, and they were off. Stephenson flipped on the lights and raced the rural roads from Schoharie in silence.

Within five minutes, the rig pulled up outside the three-story apartment across from The Stadium.

Adam clenched his jaw. It could be anyone -- a diabetic or epileptic or a drunk. Yep. Another drunk. He hoped not *that* drunk.

Until yesterday, he had laid his past to rest and was certain he'd reached a state of pure contentment. One encounter with his middle-school bully showed him how he lied to himself.

Adam threw the green bag with O2 over his shoulder, grabbed the med box, and jogged into the apartment building ahead of Stevenson. At the bottom of the steps, he stopped and stared at the three flights.

Straight up. At least if Vicky were the vic, she'd be light. Easy to carry down.

With a deep inhale, Adam raced up. At the second landing, he turned to see if Stephenson followed. He was right behind him. Adam was glad he checked here because if he looked down from the top landing he would have tumbled to the ground floor. He felt like he was climbing Jacob's ladder right into the heavenlies.

At the third floor, the door flung open. A very pregnant woman waved them in. "Hurry. She shouldn't of left the hospital. Torie totaled her car the other night. Me and Bobby can't wake her up." The woman scurried over to her unconscious friend and took her hand. "It's gonna be okay, Torie. The ambulance drivers are here."

The woman's husband pulled her away. "Is she dead?" He held his wife in his arms and sidled against the counter in the kitchen that opened into the tiny space. Adam squeezed around the pull-out couch. With it unfolded, he had almost no room to unload his equipment. He knelt at the bedside.

The man pointed to Vicky. "Heather tried to wake her, so we could move around a bit, but she won't get up. I didn't wanna let her in here -- what with Heather due this Friday -- but--"

Adam took Vicky's pulse. It was slow and bounding. Checked her eyes -- unequal. Could he have missed something the other night?

"Is she gonna die?" the man asked. "Torie's nothin' if she ain't trouble. Still, I don't want her to die. Not with Heather and the baby--"

"Bobby, stop." His wife pulled away from him and edged closer to the couch.

Adam grabbed his BP cuff and the D5W tubing. He tossed the tubing to the end of the bed. Stephenson nabbed it and began the setup.

"Any vomiting?" Adam asked.

Heather shook her head.

"Headaches?"

She nodded.

Adam sighed. *Not good.* "Drugs?"

"She better not of," Bobby snarled. "I laid down the law when Torie showed up at our door."

"Her pain meds," Heather said.

"What was she taking?" Adam asked.

Heather shook her head. "Don't know. She should've stayed in the hospital. Medicaid or something would've paid. We pay taxes for those things."

She should have. "Can you check her bags for her medicine?" Adam asked.

Heather knelt by the couch and rummaged through an overnight bag.

"Let's get her packaged. Need a line of D5W." Adam stood. *Please don't let it be what it looks like.* He checked her glucose. They needed to run fast -- get her to Mid-State. He slipped the non-rebreather mask over Vicky's mouth and nose and got a line going to keep the vein open for meds.

Heather handed him a vial of Percocet. He checked the dosage and the number of pills left. He cocked his head. *Vicky hadn't been overusing?*

Strapping her into the stair chair, Adam and Stephenson maneuvered her out of the tiny apartment into the narrow hall. The tight quarters made movement difficult and more time consuming than he wanted.

Without jarring her, they finally stowed her in the ambulance. Stephenson added sirens to the lights and took off as fast as the narrow streets allowed. Adam steadied himself in the back, set up the EKG, and straddled the cot to check Vicky's face. "You were every boy's fantasy, Vicky." Adam took his knuckles and rubbed them over her sternum.

She groaned and grabbed his hand.

"Good girl." He grinned. A reaction to pain. His tension ebbed making him feel weightless -- like an astronaut in zero gravity. With her sensing discomfort, he could stop the stimuli. The lack of consciousness might be temporary, after all. Adam studied her heart rhythm on the EKG. "Lord, if you are merciful, please let her live. Please, no brain damage."

"You okay back there, Garfinkle?"

"Yep."

"Talking to yourself?"

"I'm an interesting conversationalist. Unlike you." Adam studied Vicky's face and whispered, "Just between you and me, Vicky, we can't let Stephenson know I'm praying -- especially for you. I'd never hear the end of it. And BTW -- glad you hurt with the stimuli -- but not in the way I daydreamed of hurting you."

By the time they arrived at Mid-State, she was semi-conscious. As they handed her off, Adam prayed for the rest of his day to be quiet.

And for Vicky.

Weird.

*****

Maya watched the hall monitor lead her gleeful charges off to lunch. Pizza day at Delmar Elementary always proved popular. She leaned against the cool tiles of the wall and stared into the distance even long after her students were out of sight.

Justine's monologue from the morning commute droned in her head.

Adam's got faith. Dormant. It's there.

Adam's done with the super-model type.

Adam knows you're adorable. Not the clunk you think you are.

Adam needs you.

Adam...

Shaking her head to chase the cobwebs away, Maya returned to her desk. Twenty minutes of the lunch break remained. She chomped into her PB&J sandwich and tapped her phone. Maybe Adam texted.

She dreamed again. Something about the man cloyed at her. More than his looks -- every action of his screamed he cared. Concern for others determined his desire to be the best paramedic he could. Adam saw beyond the surface of his patients' symptoms, even the hypochondriacs. When she gazed into those eyes, all she pictured was...

Oh, she couldn't think of that and teach first graders.

She remembered the phone in her hand.

Indeed, a new text arrived.

From her mother.

Being a glutton for punishment, or a dutiful daughter, Maya opened the message.

Call me. Important.

Call her? The classroom clock ticked reminding her time was running down. Although, having less time would shorten the conversation. She hit her mother's number, then took a huge bite of sticky peanut butter.

"Vitale and Vitale."

Peanut butter gummed her mouth. "Is Viola there?" Maya hoped the secretary understood her mumbles.

"Whom may I say is calling?"

"Her daughter." The secretary should know her voice by now.

"Oh Maya, sorry. You sounded like you had a mouth full of marbles. Must have a bad connection. Let me see if Ms. Vitale's available."

Maya sipped her water while music played.

Played some more.

Finished with her lunch, she tossed her wrappings.

Voices twittered in the hall accompanied by shuffling feet. Maya clicked off the phone.

Her mother. When would she ever learn?

Chapter Eight

Torie sat in the chair beside her hospital bed and rubbed her neck. She needed another ride. Heather promised to find someone but had never gotten back about who would be here.

The nurse claimed it was Wednesday, so Torie had one more day before Heather's mom arrived. One day to find an apartment.

Two nights in the hospital worked better than any spa treatment. They gave her enough pain meds to make the ribs bearable. The headache now pulsed below the surface rather than pounding like a drum in a military parade. She stopped forgetting things. At least, if she remembered correctly, she quit forgetting.

Her unemployment taunted her. Jobless and broke. No place to live after tomorrow. If only Westfield had a shelter. Seeing as it didn't have a grocery store, finding a shelter was improbable.

It did have a food pantry. The church in the old school had one. The church with the weird name. Maranatha? They gave out food a couple of times a month. Maybe this week was the dole-out time.

With no job holding her in town, she could move to Albany. The city offered plenty of work along with easy access to stores. Getting there would be problematic. Without a car, it was a mite too far to walk. Once she got there, she'd find a homeless shelter. A big city like Albany had to have one, didn't it? Her mushrooming tension fled with her joke. Looking on the good side of things helped.

The positive side? Heather and Bobby had gone to Selene's, and packed a suitcase full of Torie's clothes and a few essentials. They offered a home with them.

Tonight.

She nestled a pillow under her arm. Her heavy eyes refused to stay open.

The voices woke her.

No. Heather wouldn't have.

Unmistakably, Jean's voice echoed in the corridor, and her mother blew into the room two steps behind her perfume. At Torie's doorway, Jean turned and called to the nurses. "I've *got* to send you flowers. My baby girl looks fabulous."

How could Jean tell? Her mother never even glanced at her own daughter.

Jean flipped her hair over her shoulder and propped her sunglasses on top of her head. At last, her mother looked at her daughter. For a second.

Torie forced a smile. "You're a blonde now." Stifling a groan, she pushed herself off the chair.

"I see your accident didn't hurt your eyes."

Jean's smile had evaporated, but her voice could entice rattlesnakes. "Victoria, sweetheart, I'm sure the wonderful staff here gave you enough medication to keep you out of pain. Quit your belly-aching and get a move on. I'm meeting a friend."

A friend. Male, of course.

Torie's nurse entered the room. "Here are the discharge papers." She turned to Jean as though Torie were a child, too young to care for herself. "If the headache gets worse, make sure your daughter sees her primary care doctor."

"I'll be sure to. I don't want anything worse to happen to my baby." Jean's eyes shot fire at Torie. They screamed -- *Make it look so.* Jean turned back to the nurse who'd been reviewing the discharge notes, oblivious of Jean's indifference.

"...no unnecessary exertion. Call if--"

"Thank you," Torie interrupted. "Jean suffers from dyslexia and doesn't know up from down."

"Victoria Elizabeth Sullivan, I don't have any disease. You know better."

Torie glanced at Jean. "And ADD. She'll be gone within five minutes after dropping me off and not even remember she left me behind."

Her mother pitched the papers the nurse had handed her onto the bed. "See what my daughter's like?" She put on her sunglasses, and with another toss of her over-bleached hair, stormed out of the room. "I'll meet you downstairs, Victoria."

"It's Torie." Her mother was well out of hearing range, but still Torie whispered. "I'm Torie, now. Remember?" She gathered the papers her mother had lobbed onto the bed and the plastic bag containing her hospital toiletries.

The nurse helped her into a wheelchair. From the patient pick-up area, Torie spotted Jean flouncing across the parking lot, hips swaying, and her shoulders back.

No.

Jean climbed into a red Ford truck.

Torie's heart banged hard enough to break another rib. Darren Brown's? Back with her mother? How could she?

The truck door slammed shut and the engine turned over.

Torie stared at the truck as it rumbled to the pick-up. She considered running, but her mother had climbed into the driver's seat. No one else was there. *It'll just take a few minutes.* She inhaled, and winced at the deepness of her breath.

Jean leaned on the horn and waved furiously. Torie shuffled to the truck, threw her toiletries in the back seat, and clambered up.

Before Torie closed her door, Jean peeled out of the spot. "This is the *last* time you interfere with my life, Victoria. You're old enough to not need your mommy."

"This wasn't my idea." Torie stared out the window at nothing.

"You're always trouble. Not like Robin and Crystal. I wish I'd never met your father."

"At least *you* got to meet him." The heat of Jean's anger melted Torie's skin, but they finished the ride in silence. She pointed to Heather's apartment. "Right there."

Torie climbed out and slammed the door. Then she remembered her hospital toiletries. Before she could reach for the door handle, Jean pulled away, splaying gravel which pinged against Torie's bare leg.

"Love you, too, Mom." Torie waved to the fading exhaust fumes of the red truck.

*****

It took Viola Vitale two days to return Maya's call. On Wednesday Mom texted.

Is this man you're seeing going to become a doctor?

No.

Maya refrained from texting more. If Mom cared, she'd call. Maya waited.

Nothing.

Maya pulled the sleeves of her shirt over her wrists.

Chapter Nine

"Kindness is in our power, even when fondness is not." Samuel Johnson

Torie yanked on the window to open it. "Yeow!" The stupid thing was painted shut. She wrapped her arms around her chest and fought to keep herself from doubling over. Raising the blinds would have to do for sunlight.

The scene below remained the same -- empty restaurant lot, parked cars, and nothing else. Neither had the stuffiness of the apartment changed. The minute hand on the clock seemed stuck. Were the batteries dead?

She eased herself back onto the couch, picked up Heather's laptop, and checked the apartment listings. Nothing had appeared in the last five minutes, and no one offered a job.

The days in the hospital were sort of okay, seeing as she slept a lot, but now that her ribs and head didn't threaten to kill her, Torie needed to do something. Maybe someone posted an apartment for rent along the streets -- were too cheap to list it online.

In the bathroom, Torie washed her face and brushed her teeth. Bracing her arms on the vanity, she leaned forward, closed her eyes, and willed her tension away. There had to be a way to relax, to get a light buzz, and take the edge off, but the merlot was gone.

Mouthwash. Heather had a bottle and with its taste, Listerine had to have a lot of alcohol. Fishing under the cabinet, she found the bottle of yellow liquid and held it to the light. Her nose wrinkled. "You look like pee." She unscrewed the lid and sniffed. "But you smell like whiskey. I'll pretend." A nip made her gag. The next one didn't. Just one more would do it. She wasn't an alky like Darren, after all.

The stuff lost its nastiness after the third swig. Fortified and with fresh breath, Torie headed out the door into the gentle spring breezes, cool, but pleasant after the apartment and the overheated hospital. Out on the sidewalk, she lifted her face to the wind and the sunshine. As she opened her eyes, a white Bronco pulled into the parking lot of The Stadium.

Collin.

He stepped out of his SUV and waved her over.

"How're you doing?" He grinned. "Heather said you had a tough go of it."

"Doing good. Ribs hurt, yet." She rubbed her forehead, careful to avoid the stitches. "My head feels like a hangover."

"Next time you'll listen to me?"

She couldn't take offense at his mini-lecture. "Yep."

He smiled.

"I hit rock bottom." She rushed the words. No way did she want to hear *I told you so.* "Gonna change."

"Can I do anything?"

The ground became fascinating. Studying it avoided seeing Collin's kind and gentle eyes. She dared to peek up at him. "Collin, you wouldn't need a waitress, would you?"

He crossed his arms and stared. "Do you have any experience?"

Hope niggled when he didn't say no, and her belly fluttered. "Plenty of experience taking orders." She giggled. "Did it all the time."

"What about your ribs? Your headache?"

"I have a *big* tolerance for pain."

His brows puckered. His lips pinched, probably in search of an excuse not to hire her. He had to see otherwise.

"I'm your biggest fan. Trey and I know your menu cold. We're familiar with the local places you buy your ingredients." Her eyes caught his, and wouldn't let him look away. She reached over and brushed his arm with her hand. "If not a waitress, I'll bus tables. Wash dishes or tend bar. I *do* know something about liquor." Torie fluttered her eyelashes and let her hand linger on his arm. No man ever resisted these moves.

He tried to look away.

Shifting closer, her torso brushed against him and her gaze wouldn't break eye contact. *Please. A job. All I'm asking for is a chance.*

"One of my girls needs to be out of town. I'll try you out. As a sub. See how it works. Can you come in tomorrow?"

Torie's troubles evaporated with the fumes of her mouthwash. A job. With a foot in the door, she'd do anything to make it permanent.

"However. There's a stipulation."

Torie held her breath. Should've known Collin would have conditions. Conditions she couldn't fill.

"You've got to come in at lunch tomorrow for training. You work for tips."

She looked away, clenched her teeth to keep from crying. *Unpaid won't pay bills.* Catching his eyes once more, Torie nodded. *Anything to get started.*

"Then, if you do well, we'll try you out. Linda called in with an emergency. Otherwise, there'd be no chance."

Tomorrow unpaid.

"We will give you lunch."

Lunch? She'd do it. A paycheck would arrive at one point. She'd do anything to avoid welfare. Even take charity from friends.

Now if an apartment materialized, life would be okay. With a lighter heart, Torie explored the short length of Main Street, and the gods were with her. On the brick-faced building next to the library hung a sign. Its red letters proclaimed a ground-floor apartment for rent and to call after five.

She peered into the window, but blinds shut out any view. Judging from Heather's place and the uniformity of these buildings, it wouldn't be big. Who needed big? A room would do. She scribbled down the number.

Torie shrugged in delight and grinned. The warmth of self-sufficiency filled her. A job and a home.

She now savored the warm spring day. Her lost iPhone lay out of town a mile or two. If she rambled toward her accident site, she could look for it. Taking it slow, a couple of miles wouldn't hurt, would it?

Her ribs didn't wait long to nag her. Minutes later, they screamed. Walking a mile or two was out of the question. The tenth of a mile to the Ready Mart around the curve just outside of town wasn't even feasible.

The picnic benches at the entrance to Hookskill Preserve beckoned her. She found an octagonal one under a fine-looking weeping willow, its leaves still more yellow than green.

Torie plopped down at the table and rubbed her ribs, quieting now that she sat. The background sound of water tumbling down a waterfall lulled her. After five minutes, though, the time dragged. The picnic area sported nothing but splintered tables and a couple of families barbequing early dinners while their kids tossed baseballs or swung on the swing set. The call of falling water, no more than a few hundred feet beyond the picnic area, summoned her. She could sit at a table splattered with bird waste and watch strangers relish their family time or find a rock ledge near the falls and enjoy the sights and sounds in privacy.

She got up and explored.

The last time Torie had investigated the waterfall was during a fifth-grade field trip. She'd hidden behind a rock ledge and hoped her teacher would forget about her and not send her home. Living in the forest with the whitetail deer and bunnies beat life with mother. Unfortunately, her teacher found her, and Torie lost recess privileges for the rest of the school year.

Where was her fifth-grade ledge?

The trail wandered uphill and the tree cover grew dense. Trillium poked through winter's leaves, and the trees displayed an unfathomable number of shades of green. Benches dotted the base of the falls and begged her to sit, but it wouldn't be long before a crazy lady with a walker came along and wanted to make small talk. Torie didn't mind the old coots. She preferred them to people her own age, but today she wanted to be alone.

Alone. A giggle caught in her throat. What a lie. Never in her life had she wanted to be alone. It left too much time to think.

Today, solitude offered solace -- an escape from the happy lives in the village. It made her believe she had something to do.

The trail to the upper falls promised privacy.

It was farther than she thought, but Torie had nothing better to do. She crawled along the path, like a crazy old lady with a walker. Flip-flops were not helpful with mountain climbing.

Above the falls stretched a footbridge. At its middle, she leaned against the rails and gazed downward. Water without end tumbled over the rock ledges in white foam. Spray caught the late afternoon sun and painted the air in rainbows.

A family with a wet dog passed her, their children's laughter rivaled birdsong. The homey sounds soothed, but Torie needed the quiet, so she wandered. Why did she ever look at this place as sticks in the sticks? Wildflowers, streams, and the smell of old leaves beneath her feet offered peace. Collin was right. Her snotty attitude ruined everything.

The path curled left, then right. It rose and descended, and -- it had to be fifty miles in -- it flattened out. To the left, Livingstone Pond sparkled bright blue in the spring sun. She ambled to the shore.

How could this be a pond? It had to be over a mile long and a half-mile wide. Several yards out, a finger of land poked into it. The peninsula covered in trees divided this end of the pond. She bent over and scooped water. It was warmer than she expected. With the ice thawing completely just a month ago, she thought it would be frigid. The main road, where her iPhone lay, curled along the far side of the pond. No one would know a road lay hidden behind the trees if it weren't for the rumble of an occasional truck or car.

Halfway down the far side, white sand of the swimming hole glinted. She should return to Heather's and call about the apartment -- but nothing waited for her there -- nothing but Heather's happiness and her own loneliness. She couldn't go back.

Defying her exhaustion, Torie followed a trail behind her.

The track became rougher, and her ribs protested as the mouthwash and Percocet wore off. Then half hidden in the shrubs sat a lean-to.

Easing herself onto its raised platform, Torie sat and thought of nothing but the woods and its early spring scents until dusk settled over the park.

With twilight, little light penetrated the trees. She'd never find her way in pitch black. No one could stay here overnight. At least no one in her right mind. No way would she ever remain here once the sun set.

She picked her way along the darkening path. Her eyes darted in the dark trying to make out forms along the path. In the distance, a dog howled.

A shiver scurried up her back. Was it a dog? Dogs barked. Wolves howled. Did Hookskill harbor wolves or coydogs? This was what homelessness looked like.

Not for her. Ever.

The instant she hit Heather's, she'd check her account balances and get the apartment.

She shuffled along the paths, afraid to lift her feet or move too quickly. Her eyes adapted to the darkening woods. The last gray of the sky faded quickly. Stumbling down the incline, Torie knew she'd never be out here after dark again.

Fifteen minutes later, Torie hit Main Street. The closeness of Heather's urged her to run, but pain and exhaustion made her waddle like a decrepit crone.

After slogging up the mountain of stairs, Torie eased herself into the apartment, brewed a cup of coffee, and logged on to her bank account. Glee shivered up from her belly. Her account held the total of seven hundred dollars and change -- enough to rent the place next to the library. Being so close to the library would mean she wouldn't have to buy internet service. She'd dovetail into theirs.

Plus, the library sported an old table out front where people left their overabundance of zucchini and green beans or lettuce. She and Selene used to mock the welfare stand. Now? Free food would help her budget without having to turn to food stamps. Plus working for Collin would provide some meals. She'd have no need for the freebie table after all.

She called the number for the apartment and made an appointment to see it.

She didn't bother to open the couch to sleep. Heather and Bobby would be in late and didn't need to stumble over her.

Tomorrow she'd change her life.

*****

The Stadium lunch crowd had been slow. Torie gulped more pain meds than she wanted to, but her aching ribs could get her fired before Collin officially hired her.

She filled water, took orders, bused tables.

Gritting her teeth helped to hoist overloaded trays without moaning. Her shoulders squared. With her head held high, the world would see her at her best.

"Hey, Torie. Take a break," Collin called. "You're past lunch time. Order anything you like."

"Anything?"

"As long as it's alcohol free."

Her stomach rumbled and her usual salads wouldn't satisfy it. Prime rib should appease her own ribs.

The succulent steak set before her made her drool. Literally. Torie ducked her head and wiped her mouth, then glanced around to see who may have noticed.

All was good. She cut into the meat and red juices flowed. Her stomach growled. Oh, to shove her face into the plate and devour the whole, luscious meal. Tomorrow, though? If she didn't save half of this, she'd have to go dumpster-diving.

She headed back to work before her break officially ended. Work soothed more than sitting around.

The afternoon morphed into the early bird rush. "Here you go." She offered takeout boxes to an old couple. "Looks like you have enough for two more meals."

"Appetite's not what it used to be." The man handed her two twenties. "Keep the change." He winked, and his wife swatted him.

Torie laughed with the couple, then headed toward the kitchen. She almost bumped into Collin who stood with arms crossed.

"What'd I do?"

"Stayed way too long. Go home. Get some rest. Come back tomorrow at three."

The urge to kiss Collin smack on the kisser overwhelmed Torie. Instead, she squared her shoulders and grinned. Life was good.

Outside The Stadium, traffic clogged the Main Street. The pair of old folks who'd left her a great tip edged their car out of the parking lot. A truck blared its horn. The couple backed up. Another car approached.

Torie shook her head. Why didn't people show a little decency? She strode into the middle of the road, stopped an oncoming car, and waved the old guys out.

A little after seven, Torie knocked on her future apartment's door.

The landlord scowled. "You're late."

"Sorry. Work ran over."

"Don't care. Here's the place. Five hundred dollars a month."

It didn't take long to explore the studio. A mini-fridge, a cook-top. The one room made Heather's look like a villa. On the positive side, it was clean and beat the Hookskill lean-to. She had no other option.

She took out her checkbook. "Five hundred?"

"Plus one month's rent in advance."

"I have seven hundred. Can I give you that and pay the extra each month until I'm caught up?"

The landlord shook his head.

"Look," she turned on her most charming grin. In school, no boy ever resisted her smile. Trey never withstood it until Selene dug her claws into him. "It'll sit empty. This way you'll be making--"

"You also need a month's rent to cover damages."

"I haven't damaged anything."

"You welfare slobs always wreck stuff."

"Welfare? I'm not on--"

"It's fifteen hundred bucks down. Five hundred every month thereafter. Due by the first. Not after. You want it?"

Torie stuffed her checkbook back into her purse, then a bright idea hit. "You take credit cards?"

The man scowled.

Torie was homeless.

She trudged back to Heather's. The darkening sky only hinted at her mood. Tomorrow morning she had to be out.

The house phone rang. Its caller ID showed Heather's cell number.

"Torie, hon, I'm so glad you picked up. It's Heather."

As though anyone else could sound so perky.

"We're staying over in Albany. Mom will be in the apartment once the baby's born. So you have an extra day."

A small smile lifted Torie's mood.

"You there, hon?"

She nodded. "Yes. Thank you."

Torie had a home until Friday sometime.

Then she'd be officially homeless.

Chapter Ten

"The thing that hath been, it is that which shall be; and that which is done is that which shall be done: and there is no new thing under the sun." Eccl. 1:9.

Maya stood on tippy-toes and studied her back in the bathroom mirror. Too fat. Would another pair of Dockers work? The stretchy material of the next pair of khakis felt better but made her look like her mother, and her mother was five inches shorter and three inches rounder. She went back to the first pair then checked the clock.

With a half-hour before Adam arrived, Maya rummaged through her shirts. The off-white one with pale blue flowers and long sleeves had darts running down the bodice, so it didn't hang like a sack.

She slipped it on and studied her reflection.

Mirrors didn't lie. The short shirt poofed over her stomach, and the two pockets drew too much attention to her chest.

With a toss, it landed on the ever growing pile of discarded clothing. She picked out another blouse.

This ecru shirt blended with her slacks, and Kat Leppert -- TV's fashionista -- would claim the monochromatic colors elongated her torso, and slimmed her down. With the approval, albeit an imaginary one, of her favorite reality show -- the only fashion diva she could name -- Maya moved on to her hair. With the brush half-way to her head, she paused and stared at her reflection. When she met Adam five days ago, she'd worn this shirt. With a sigh, she trudged back to the bedroom, tossed the offending article of clothing onto her bed, and searched for another blouse.

She settled for a lime green number she'd have to tuck in. The loose cotton fabric camouflaged what needed camouflaging, and the sleeves angled out over her wrists. It would have to do even though she'd have to be careful to keep the sleeves from sliding up.

Now to fuss with the blow dryer. Shaving her head sounded good. People would believe it showed solidarity with cancer patients. Or perhaps she wanted to look like Denai Gurira or Demi Moore?

Tay Diggs?

Her bone structure would never pull it off.

Blown dry, her hair had the body to frame her face and soften her features, so Maya left it loose. While fussing with her makeup drawer, the hair fell back into her face. She tucked it behind her ear. By the time she looked in the mirror, it swung back over her eye and cheek.

Mascara and gloss took less time than buttoning a shirt, and Maya still had ten minutes. Outside, Mr. Harrigan, her landlord, stopped the rototiller. Talking to him appealed to her more than clearing her bed of her rejected outfits.

The cold seeped through her bare feet on the back porch of the Victorian housing her apartment. Maybe it would be best to wear a pair of shoes. Scurrying back into her bedroom, she slipped her bare toes into a pair of brown loafers.

Would Adam figure out how green she was at this dating game?

*****

Adam stepped onto Maya's tiny porch. Bare vines clung to the lattice promising rich green shade in a few weeks' time. A white wicker loveseat with blue flowered cushions bordered the lattice offering a private nook to cuddle.

He felt her in his arms. Tasted her lips.

He knocked on her door but got no answer. Adam wiped his sweaty palms on his jeans. Running into Vicky had resurrected everything, and had shoved him back into sixth grade.

Curtains obscured the kitchen. He could sit and wait, but the old fears rose and sweat beaded on his forehead.

Maya had to be here. He'd parked next to her car, and she lived too far out in the country to leave without it. He turned and stepped off the porch. Maybe fifty yards away, by a huge garden, Maya chatted with a middle-aged man. A bear of a dog lay near her feet. His muscles relaxed, and he strolled toward her.

Before taking more than five steps, the behemoth canine rose and bounded toward him. Its tongue lolled, and drool dripped. It looked like a Bernese mountain dog. Fresh mud caked its paws.

Maya turned, a beautiful smile framed her face. "Don't worry, Buff's a baby and too big to leap on you. Although you'll soon find out, he thinks he's a lap dog." She patted her leg. "Buff, come." The dog lumbered back to the garden. She pointed to the ground. It settled down.

Wind caught her long, heavy hair and blew strands behind her. Sunlight caught the light brown, and it shimmered gold.

"Look what Mr. Harrigan gave me." She nodded to an armful of asparagus, held like a scepter. "Would you like some?"

He crinkled his lips "Sorry. I'm a meatatarian. Venison. Wild turkey. Bear. You do realize vegetables have rights, too?"

Her laughter rivaled a bubbling brook.

"Give those green daggers to some homeless person."

His shoulder brushed Maya's, and she leaned into him as they ambled to the house. Electricity zinged. Oh to grab this girl and kiss her.

In the kitchen, Maya stuck a fistful of spears upright in a cup of water and stashed them in the refrigerator. The rest she threw into a plastic grocery bag and stuffed it in her purse. "Ready?"

"I think the restaurant is going to feed you. It's not covered dish."

Maya tossed her head back, her hair bouncing in the action as a full-bodied laugh belied the reserve she'd shown so far. So unlike Jennifer who struggled to make her face serene and lineless -- to prevent wrinkles. "You told me to give them to a homeless person."

"Are we headed for a shelter?" They stepped out onto the porch.

"No, silly. The Stadium's across from the library."

"Library? It now loans vegetables?"

"The freebie table out front? I used it before I rented Harrigan's apartment. Even the worst gardeners can't use their stockpile of vegetables. They leave them there for us non-gardeners. Better than a food pantry."

"I'll use the library table when they stock it with their excess bacon." He hurried ahead of her and opened the truck's passenger door. "What happened to your car?" He pointed to the unpainted back fender of her Honda.

"A colleague's car slid on some ice and rammed into it. Her husband replaced the fender. We have to get our summer checks before he can paint it."

Taking her arm, Adam helped her step up into the truck. Maya slipped and he caught her under her arm. He pulled her to him, and she stiffened.

Too much too soon? He loosened his grip, but she turned, her arm on his shoulder and gave him a smile that would taunt cupid.

"I better help you up," he said, "before I forget about dinner."

A blush crept up her cheek, and she ducked her head and hoisted herself into the cab. "I love your truck."

Me, too, especially when you slip. "Just got it. Saved like Shylock and wrangled like a fish wife. I did get a good deal, though."

Maya sniffed and smiled as she snapped on her seatbelt. "Smells new. My goal in life is to buy a car with a new-car smell. One I can get without an air freshener from Yankee Candle."

They chuckled.

"Did you know, this thing's got roll-stability control?"

He caught her glance. It looked lost.

"Our church is down there." She pointed behind her as he turned toward Westfield. "Our food bank's having trouble keeping up with the demand."

"You work there often?"

"Every other Saturday."

"Do you like it? Do you kayak?"

"Never been."

"I think you'd love it. Oh, and our department is having a chicken-biscuit dinner..."

Before he knew it, he was pulling into the town limits.

"Stop!"

Adam slammed the brakes. "What's wrong?" Had he not seen an animal in the road? A person? He pulled over.

Her shoulders hunched, and she grinned. Pink colored her cheeks. "Sorry. Didn't mean to scream." Maya hauled out the plastic bag of asparagus from her purse. "Give me a minute." She dashed across the street and dropped the bag on the library's wooden table then clambered back into the truck. "Good thing we stopped. The cupboard was bare."

He drove the remaining few yards to the restaurant. After parking close to the entrance, Adam scurried around the truck. Unfortunately, Maya had already gotten down and he couldn't use his chivalry as an excuse to hold her.

Taking her hand, he led her inside. The hostess seated them by the front window behind the entryway in a little alcove hinting at intimacy. Adam held out the chair. Maya beamed up at him, and heat crept up his neck. Her skin glowed. A rosy blush marked her cheeks. Make-up? It didn't look like it.

Her lips tilted up in a chronic smile and made him forget she wasn't a waif, wasn't flawless like Jennifer. He pushed the chair in, and longed to bend over, kiss her hair. He never wanted a super-model woman again.

If Maya ever donned a bangle -- he'd cut and run. His private joke forced him to smile.

"What brought on your grin?" Maya gazed at him across the table.

He bit his lip and gulped. "Good day at work." It wasn't a lie, and it'd change the subject.

Maya leaned in, candlelight dancing in her eyes. "You love your job."

"More than my truck."

Her rich laugh rivaled the candlelight.

"Why are you a paramedic?"

Here it comes. Why not be a real doctor? He shrugged. Didn't need to hear the lecture.

"Did I say something wrong?" Her eyes held his. "I teach because I love kids, love to see the light of understanding dawn in their eyes. Their *joie de vivre* is contagious. My folks, though, would prefer I be a lawyer, like them. Or a politician. Or caped-crusader." Her smile tipped her lips. Half-hearted. One more of apology than joy. "Nothing beats children and their purity of spirit. So why do you do your job? Like that baby who died in the fire -- the heartbreak's got to be unbearable."

A heaviness settled over Adam. This evening with Maya had pushed away thoughts of Cody Lasky. His other... failures. Her question though?

"I'm sorry. I seem to be asking all the wrong questions."

Her rich voice broke the dark mood like popping bubbles. He shook his head. "No, your questions are fine. With my job, the inability to save someone is the hard part."

"From what Levi tells me, you don't work for the money."

He laughed. "You know Stephenson's an EMT and *not* a paramedic?"

She cocked her head. "I know the difference between EMTs, paramedics, *and* ambulance drivers."

His muscles relaxed, and he settled back in the chair. She wasn't going to lecture him about his supposed lack of ambition. "No, not the pay." Adam settled into his second favorite subject. "Mostly things are routine. A broken bone. Chest pains that half the time prove to be indigestion. Picking up drunks who got bit by what they thought was a male cat, but turned out to be a skunk. Those are good. Easy. I get along with my co-workers, but then the serious things happen." He paused and looked down at his silverware, and the moments ticked away.

Silence hovered. Adam wondered if Maya's attention flagged. Was she as empty-headed as Jennifer? He prayed for a distraction, anything to block his memories of fires and dying children.

"Hi. I'm Torie. I'll be your server tonight."

The unexpected arrival of the waitress startled him, and Adam struggled to regain composure, but tension infused his muscles. Like an answer to prayer, the waitress had arrived and provided a diversion. Yet, typical of God, it was the last person he wanted to see. Vicky.

"Hi, Torie." Maya's voice regained its whole exuberance. "I'll have raspberry ice tea."

Vicky's eyes lit up as she turned toward Adam. "I'm so happy you're my first customer." She paused, grasped her order pad. "I've been let loose after a day of training and non-stop coaching." She looked over her shoulder and nodded at Trish. "I wouldn't be here without you. You

51

didn't by any chance take me back to the hospital on Monday?"

He nodded curtly. *He had no time for small talk with Vicky.*

"I learned my lesson. Not walking across the state again." Vicky chuckled, grabbed her abdomen and winced. "Sorry. Need more time before the ribs quit complaining."

"A Coke, Vicky."

Her eyebrows arched. "No one's called me Vicky since middle school."

"Knew you then. Thank you. We'll look at the menus now." He buried his head in the menu and flicked his wrist toward Vicky. *Get out of my life. You ruined it once already. You're not getting another chance at it.*

She turned to get their drinks. When Adam looked up, he caught Maya's frown.

"What?"

"Why were you so mean?"

"I wasn't mean."

"Rude."

He shrugged. *Drop it, Maya.*

"I don't know you well, Adam Benedict, but your behavior doesn't match what I've seen. Or what Levi and Justine tell me."

"Let's change the subject."

They studied their dinner choices in silence. Adam saw nothing. He had made Maya angry. Vicky, whose name should've been Penny -- Bad Penny -- showed up everywhere.

"Why do you call her Vicky? She said her name's--"

"Enough." He glared across the table. Maya's head jerked, and her eyes clouded. Even her smile thinned. He hid his head in the menu.

His crazy crush on Vicky resurrected. Memories of her treachery -- the laughter of her friends. The terror in the stench of their cigarette smoke. The hours alone before a janitor found him.

Worse than his panic in the locker, a week later, her father burned up his family.

At last, he sought Maya's eyes. "Forgive me." Shame prevented him saying more. He, a rational man, became stupid around Vicky. This attitude needed to stop.

Vicky returned. Her hand brushed her jeans. "I forgot to tell you the specials."

"I don't need to know," Maya said.

"Just give me what she's having."

"Better rethink your choice, Adam. I'm ordering the spring veggie polenta."

"Um," he looked up at Vicky. "What are the specials?"

Vicky looked baffled as though she forgot.

"I remember. Adam Benedict..." Her hand ran over her stomach, and she blanched. "Not my most shining moment."

"Don't say a word." His intensity shocked him as he flung up his hand in the signal to stop.

Vicky stumbled a step back. "Sorry."

"Is there a problem here?" Another waitress hurried over. "This is Torie's first day and..." She whispered to Vicky and handed her the order pad. Vicky scurried back to the kitchen.

"No. There is no problem," Adam said.

"I'll be glad to wait your table. Do you need a few moments?"

Adam nodded, and buried his head in the menu. The words printed there wouldn't focus until a movement across from him reclaimed his attention.

Maya scowled and stood. She tossed her rumpled napkin on the table. "Take me home."

"No, Maya." Adam rose -- his eyes level with hers, and took her hand. "Please sit. I'm sorry." His soft words almost drowned in the restaurant clatter.

She shook her head. "You're different than I expected." Her gaze drifted to the door. "The first snide remarks I brushed off, but I don't want to start a relationship with someone who holds bitterness like you. It's toxic."

"Please. Sit." Adam glanced at the kitchen as though Vicky stood there. The thought of her mocking him once more raked his nerves. His attention drifted back to Maya. Something deeper than pride worked inside him. He used to feel this conviction when he went to church regularly. "I'll change my attitude. It's too raw to talk about right now. I'll tell you, though. Soon."

Maya swayed, and edged back into her chair.

Adam leaned forward and stiffened. He swallowed once, and then again. When he found his voice, his words came out in a swoosh. "I never knew *how* raw until this week's traumas. Like wounds I thought healed have been ripped apart. Trust me?" He reached across the table. "I'll spend this evening showing you the real me."

She didn't take his hand.

*****

"Except for one disgruntled customer at the beginning, you did a wonderful job, Torie."

"Thanks, Collin." With her head ducked, she swept the floor.

Collin took the broom. "It's late." He pointed at the floor. "You've already cleaned this. Go home."

She handed off the broom. Little did he know. She had no home. By staying in The Stadium, she wouldn't be out on the streets. Alone. Those dogs -- or hyenas -- at Hookskill haunted her. Her heart skipped a beat.

"I'll call you again."

With a wave goodbye, Torie stepped outside. A late-season frost settled on the lawns. Crystals of ice coated the windshields of the cars. Home? Tonight she had none. She wrapped her arms around her to ward off the chill and peered up at Heather's dark apartment. Heather's mom had returned from the hospital with news of baby Robert and a safe delivery. She now laid claim to Torie's couch.

Torie walked. From time to time, ice crystals caught the light sifting through the trees from the streetlights and glimmered like stars. Could've been pretty. With her hands shoved into her coat pocket, she fingered the dollars and coins collected in tips.

Over a hundred bucks. Tips were instant dollars. At the Ready Mart, Torie picked up a hot coffee to get her through the night. By being careful with her pay, she'd rent an apartment soon.

Or buy a car. A car would be a two-fer. A home *and* a vehicle. A way out of town.

The Ready Mart sold disposable cell phones. They weren't iPhones -- but with a cell and a twenty-five dollar phone card, she could reconnect with the world. This store even had a circular display rack sporting flashlights of all sizes. The deepness of the dark begged her to splurge on one. She picked the cheapest, along with a package of batteries, then counted the money left over. The Stadium had fed her. Work meant free food.

Wine coolers would ward off the freezing night after the coffee cooled. Torie picked up a four-pack of Horton's Hooch, paid for her purchases and wandered out into Westfield's streets.

Wonderful evening, except for Adam. He had changed. A lot. Became a handsome man. Beautiful smile. The same blue eyes. The same fuzzy hair. A curse she could fix. But his personality? Something warped there.

It'd been twelve years. Right in the midst of Darren's heat. Just before her step-father turned his attention to Crystal, and Torie had freed her sisters of him. Her act to save her family incurred her mother's permanent wrath -- along with both of her sisters'.

At the bench next to her soon-to-be-apartment, Torie sat and pulled her coat tight around her. For now, home would have to be outside this apartment, but not for long.

Someone had left asparagus on the freebie table. She loved them roasted with a little olive oil. Uncooked, they'd fill her stomach if Collin didn't hire her back. Maybe she could find some sticks and roast them on the grills at Hookskill? She stuffed the whole bunch into her plastic sack from the Ready Mart along with her empty coffee cup. She tucked her legs under her and shivered. The darkness exposed her. Left her cold.

Even with no traffic whizzing through Main Street, and almost every light in the apartments off, the streetlights spotlighted her. She pulled out a cooler and her pain meds and sipped. Felt warmed. By the end of the first bottle, her ribs no longer ached, and Hookskill Preserve didn't scare her. It was private. She could hide there if she didn't freeze to death.

Maybe she'd find the lean-to.

Hope propelled her to the park.

Her plan proved to be an illusion. The black of evening stopped her at the picnic grounds. Nothing penetrated Hookskill's darkness. Her new flashlight barely pierced it. Sitting at the picnic table under the willow, those coyotes yipped again. They *were* coyotes. Barking.

Something swooped over her head. Torie screamed, leaped, and grabbed her ribs. Five weeks until complete healing couldn't come soon enough. She doubled over in pain as another monstrous shadow swirled. And another.

Bats.

Someone, please help me. She scrambled under the picnic table and finished her second cooler.

*****

Sleep dodged Adam. He dragged Neema's quilt to the Adirondack chair on his porch and savored the sounds of the last of the spring peepers. Seasons were changing. The warm rains would end the chorus of these little frogs and bring in the warmth of love.

With his eyes closed, he felt Maya in his arms. After promising to show her his true self, his real nature, Maya softened once more. The evening fled in the delight of discovering each other.

He'd do anything for Maya.

Adam never wanted anyone more than he wanted her. Not Jennifer. Not Vicious Vicky. No one.

God had heard his plea for a woman he could love forever.

The bitterness of his youth would die.

If he could only figure out how.

Chapter Eleven

"Behold, I will do a new thing; now it shall spring forth; shall ye not know it? I will even make a way in the wilderness, and rivers in the desert." Isaiah 43:19

Seven a.m. Torie stood in the hallway and knocked at Heather's door. No one answered. Her friend wasn't a stickler for locking the apartment, and the door opened with a swoosh of warm air. Heather's mom was gone -- probably back to the hospital.

The silence of the apartment soothed. No bats circled, no rabid wolves howled. No one would begrudge her one more morning's handouts. The first freebie? To shower off, not only the dirt from under the picnic table where she dozed after startling at every noise and crunch in the night, but the bat guano that had to have fallen from the sky. The heat of the water warmed bones frozen in the frost.

In clean clothes in front of the mirror, Torie blew dry her curls. The play of hair in her hands pleased her and settled her shattered nerves more than the hot water. In her earliest memory, she skipped out of the bathroom with a brush in order to comb her mother's mop -- even back then dry and over-processed.

It was the one time Torie didn't blame her mother for her fit. Of course *her* mommy would find it inconvenient for her child play beautician, but using the toilet brush? Torie giggled. *Gross -- but appropriate.*

Her sisters never cared what she used -- doll combs, dog brush. Crystal let her braid her hair or curl it or straighten it. Once she let Torie color it with food dye. When the puce color wouldn't wash out of Crystal's hair or the furniture, she got grounded for a week. Her mother made Torie scrub the entire carpet and sofa. The one time the house was clean.

Robin? What Torie wouldn't give to have her hair. Curls? Snap your fingers, there they were. Straight? A puff of air, and it laid the way it should. Her color? A rich mahogany, no chemicals needed. Jean didn't much like Torie the day she buzzed Robin's hair with the dog clippers.

What did Robin do nowadays? Multi-dyed mohawk. Gelled into peaks rivalling the Catskills, and she lived with a meth-head.

After her arrest, where had Crystal disappeared to?
My help came too late.

She shook the depressing vision of her sisters away. The hour or two of luxury wouldn't be wasted.

Working her flat iron, Torie thought about styling her long hair in a lean-to with no electricity. It would never be sleek and sexy after this morning. Ponytails would have to do.

She pulled her hair back. Ugly black threads like railroad tracks ran into her hairline. For a few more days, Torie'd have to hide them.

Bangs would camouflage them. She dug out scissors from her suitcase stored in the living room, and cut her hair.

When finished, a toddler with a battered eye peered out of the mirror. The bruise had spread over her cheek, and now a yellowish-green in its last hoorah. At least it would vanish in a day or two.

Torie smoothed on her foundation to hide the yellowing bruise and added blush and mascara.

The mirror revealed her artistry. Or, rather, her lack of it. With the bangs, she now looked like a two-year-old in a beauty pageant.

She shrugged. No one would see her tucked away in the forest, anyway.

With her supplies shoved back in her bag, Torie microwaved a packet of oatmeal. While eating, she painted her nails -- toes and fingers. The pink polish was bright enough to light up her evening in the lean-to.

Civilization. One day away from it, and she'd missed it more than a good Chardonnay.

When she had her own salon, Heather could have free cuts for the rest of her life. Small payment for all her help.

After washing and drying the dishes, Torie opened the door to the corridor. Cool air flushed away the heat in the apartment. It'd be cold again tonight.

One week of hard luck made her appreciate little things. Made her cringe at the recollection her past -- her family, school, and her foster homes couldn't be changed. Couldn't be blamed for her choices. She was the one who used her friends for parties, free drinks, their boyfriends. Then when Selene did the same to her? It crushed more than her ribs.

Bile rose with the familiar hatred. The good mood the few hours' peace had given her evaporated.

How did one change? How did changes last forever?

In the bottom of Heather's linen closet, under a pile of old sheets, Torie found a ratty blanket and a worn throw pillow. She took both and left Heather a note with her new phone number.

Time to hit the road. Torie yanked up her suitcase and doubled over. A stupid dragon stomped on her ribcage, scorched it with its breath. She dropped her bag and fished out her Percocet. Two pills remained. She took one.

Using her feet, she shuffled the suitcase into a corner. For now, she'd have to haul her stuff bit-by-bit or con Bobby into doing it.

Then he'd discover her living arrangements.

Bad plan.

In the cupboards, Torie found a large, black garbage bag, and tucked the pillow and blanket into it. From her suitcase, she selected jeans and the fresh Red Sox T-shirt and the baseball cap. Should she get another gig at The Stadium, she'd need her uniform.

She shoved yoga pants, a skirt, and flip-flops into her overnight bag. A couple of shirts and underwear completed her wardrobe.

Mud and rocks and weeds littered the path she crawled up the other day, so she put her sneakers on -- became quite the yuppie with a skirt and sneaks.

With her sleeping gear slung over one shoulder like a homeless Santa Claus, and her Coach bag over the other, Torie snaked her way to Hookskill.

At the park entrance, she scanned the trees for bats. Didn't see any swooping around looking to bite her neck. One of her teachers said they only came out at night. No fear. Why should little gerbils with wings terrify her anyway? The bats didn't kill her last night. They wouldn't tonight. How long did it take for bat rabies to manifest?

She'd worry about it when she foamed at the mouth.

Torie squared her shoulders and marched into Hookskill.

Something swooped overhead. She screamed. Ducked.

A bird.

She had to get a grip.

Once out of the picnic area, the pine needles, leaves, and bark along the unpaved trail threatened to trip her dragging feet. Each breath beat her ribs. Why couldn't the hospital have put her into a cast? Why couldn't she have been in a coma until the ribs healed? She would've woken up refreshed and ready to be a Girl Scout. She smiled. *Me? A Girl Scout?*

A picture of a goofy Boy Scout floated through her head. Teeth angling all different ways, staring at her with eyes like Darren's -- blue, soulful, yearning. Lustful. Her stomach lurched.

She kicked a rock out of her way, stomped along the dirt track. One Grizzly Adams' crew dressed in flannels passed her. A soaking lab bounded after Torie and jumped. His claws scratched her bare legs.

"We're so sorry." The Grizzlies apologized, but their eyes focused on her black garbage sack and overnight bag.

"It's okay."

"Can we give you a hand?" They pointed to her bags.

Torie shook her head. "No, thanks." *Please, no. What if they follow me?*

"You sure?"

Torie smiled. "I'm good." She watched them hike away, their conversation punctuated by laughter. When was the last time she felt so carefree?

Turning right at Livingstone Pond, Torie wandered down Haverset Trail. A few minutes later, she arrived home.

Plopping down on the raised platform of the lean-to, Torie surveyed her neighborhood. Her treasures couldn't stay out in the open, ready to be pilfered by the next Bear Grylls.

The back of her lean-to stood six inches above the ground on small stumps. By digging it out a little, she could slip the overnight bag under it, and cover it with leaves. Torie pulled at her ear as worry gnawed her gut. It was a Coach bag -- expensive even at outlet prices. Would the dirt and worms ruin it? What about her fresh manicure?

Did she have a choice?

Fumbling through her stuff, Torie dug out a pair of socks and pulled them over her hands.

She dug, but the ground was made out of cement. After five minutes and a broken nail, her fingers ached. Sitting back on her heels, Torie studied the ground. A solid chunk of bark lay under a nearby pine. She nipped the wood and dug.

Tools were a good invention, and the bark hollowed out a hole for her goods. She stowed her bags, covered them with leaves and sticks, and stood to survey her handiwork. No one would find her treasures. It looked like only dirt hid under the lean-to.

Despite having put socks on her hands, filth coated them. Torie headed to the pond to wash her hands and knees and the asparagus from the library. A lone kayaker fished near the other side -- a bright yellow speck on the gray water. Her stomach grumbled. One packet of instant oatmeal didn't sustain one forever. She lifted her hand to the fisherman. "If you want to get rid of your fish, I'm awfully fond of sushi."

He disappeared behind a tiny clump of trees -- hardly big enough to be called an island.

"Please come back," she whispered to the vanished fisherman. "I can't live like this."

*****

Adam tied his yellow kayak in the back of his truck. Water dripped, caught the sunlight, and splintered into light. Kayaking and Maya. Life

59

was good.

On Livingstone Pond Road, he fished out his cell phone, hit the speed-dial, and before it rang twice, Neema answered.

"Hey, Nee--"

"Adam!" His grandma's cry started his heart racing. "Your grandfather fell. I think his leg's broke."

"I'm on my way. Why didn't you call rescue?"

"Adam. It's your grandfather."

"I know--"

She'd hung up.

Adam pressed down on the gas. He should've called them *before* hitting the pond.

He swerved into their yard and jogged up the steps. In the living room, Pop sat on the floor, his back against a pillow propped against the wall. The deep coughs rattling his body jarred his leg which rested on another stack of pillows.

"How're you doing?" Adam knelt beside him and placed a hand on his grandfather's forehead. "You've got a fever."

"Jus' my bronchitis. The leg's the problem."

"Not so, Pop. You're sick."

"Yer grandma didn' call you about a little cough. I jist can't git up and git anywhere. It's gittin' to be a habit."

Biting back a chuckle, Adam palpated the leg. It wouldn't do to let Pop know his grandson found him cute. The swollen ankle felt hot, more than likely not broken. He looked at his grandfather. Peaked, eyes lackluster. He caught Neema's attention. "How long has he been sick?"

"Bronchitis started a day or two ago. The fever this morning," Neema said.

"You should've called me sooner."

"Grace gave me stuff," Pop said. "Give me more water than a camel kin handle. You don't gotta worry."

"We're going to the hospital." He peered up at his grandmother. "Bring the Lincoln out front." Adam scooped up his grandfather, light like a bundle of kindling. His lanky frame, drooping from Adam's arms, threw him off balance as he hurried from the room.

"Put me down. I ain't a girl."

Pop wriggled like a two-year-old wanting to be a big boy. The squirming gave Adam no choice. He had to either put him down or drop him. Once Pop's feet hit the floor, Adam draped his grandfather's arm around his shoulder and together they hobbled out of the house.

Long minutes later, they shuffled down the steps. It took so long, Neema had the car idling in the yard. With each step, Pop clenched his teeth. Adam could hear them grinding. His ragged gasps punctuated each step.

Fears about Pop's failing health assaulted Adam. *What if he passed? How would I survive?* Adam tucked Pop into the front seat, helped Neema climb into the back. His once vigorous grandparents were now like leaves in autumn. Frail. Thin. Dried out.

Chapter Twelve

"Change is not made without inconvenience, even from worse to better." Richard Hooker

Dressed and ready for work, Torie sat on the bench outside of the library and watched for Collin. When the familiar white Bronco drove by, she hoisted herself up, grateful her last pain pill had kicked in, crossed the street, and hurried to the parking lot.

"Hey, Collin."

"Torie." His face lit up, and the heaviness in Torie's chest lifted. "I called Heather's, but her mother said you moved out. Where're you living?"

"Down the road." She hiked her purse back onto her shoulder. "So is Linda back?"

"No. Want to work again?"

Her grin gave the answer. She headed toward the restaurant.

"You start in two hours."

Torie called over her shoulder. "I'll get ready now."

"I'm not paying for the early start."

"It's okay." Work without pay trumped living in a lean-to.

The night was busy, from the moment Torie started prep-work with Trish until the first dinner customers arrived. The bar, set in the back of the main dining room, buzzed with patrons. Passing it to get into the kitchen, made her wonder if being a bartender wasn't even better than being a hairdresser. Bartenders listened to everyone's life stories, gave them advice, and sent them on their way with a pleasant buzz. Barkeeps made life a whole lot better.

Four hours later, Torie strode out of the kitchen with an order. A new couple sat at a round table on her side of the restaurant with their backs to her -- the man's tall, well-muscled frame familiar. He sported short hair without an ounce of coarseness. Silk. Next to him, nearly on top of him, a plump redhead -- hair sculpted, sleek, fire engine red -- played with his shirt sleeve. Trey and Selene. In her section. Switching sides in a panic was not an option. A grown-up should be capable of facing anything -- even Trey and Selene. Becoming gutless was not in her DNA -- at least not since she was twelve.

On the bar to her right, a glass, half filled with some kind of amber booze sat in a puddle of condensation. Collin and Trish were nowhere to be seen.

She licked her lips, snagged the glass, chugged it. The whiskey burned and gave her a coughing fit. With an inhale, Torie thanked her stars for the last Percocet. It masked her pain. Fortified, she delivered the order to a middle-aged couple, then marched off to meet her enemies.

"Can I get you anything to drink?" Torie handed the couple a drink list and their menus.

"Oh how the mighty have fallen." Selene ran her hand down Trey's arm, contempt in her eyes trained on Torie.

Torie smiled. It was her job to be nice. "Did you see the spec--"

Moving closer to Trey, Selene kissed him full on the mouth.

Torie choked -- the pain of Selene's kiss worse than the one stabbing her ribs.

Upon meeting Trey, she knew she had landed the love of her life. From a rich family, he was a soon-to-be lawyer, interning for the lobbyists at Stone-Creek Strategies, Trey would be her ticket out of Burnt Hollow and into the bright life in Albany.

Although broke right now, Trey wouldn't be poor forever. When his clients in energy and gambling recognized his skills, the money would pile up. Torie was supposed to climb the status ladder. Not fall off it.

How'd she let herself be used again?

A customer waved for Torie. "I'll be back."

"No," Selene purred. "We're ready."

Torie took out her order pad.

"Hmm." Selene batted her eyes at Trey. "What do you suggest, babe?"

"I'll let you think." Torie turned away.

"A Blue Moon," Trey said.

"And you?" Torie asked Selene.

"Let me see." Selene gazed up at Trey, lust oozing from her eyes.

The man signaled for Torie once more. He was now scowling. She stepped away.

"A red wine," Selene said.

"Which one?"

Selene tapped her lips with her index finger. "Hmm. Any suggestions?"

Torie shoved the order book into her apron and smiled at Selene and Trey. "There's so much to choose from. I'll give you a moment to figure out more ways to torment me." She headed to the other customer.

"Excuse me?" Trey bellowed after her.

Torie turned her attention to the man who'd signaled her. "I'm so sorry. Those guys can't decide. What can I do for you?"

"Water. And more bread."

Torie smiled her practiced, pacifying grin, refilled his water, and brought more bread. "It just came out of the oven. Careful. It's hot." She delivered the Blue Moon to Trey, and looked at Selene. "So what can I get you?"

"A zinfandel." Selene didn't look at Torie. She caressed Trey's cheek with a finger.

Torie gritted her teeth and smiled like a professional, unsure whether her heart would break in pain or anger. She took a few shallow breaths, then attended a customer at the far end of her section.

"Oh, Torie." Selene half raised herself from her chair. "You've got mail. From State Police. I'd guess it's about your DUI."

Torie tensed, and her hands shook as she scurried to the kitchen. With a white-knuckled grip on the stainless steel counter, her lungs sucked in body-racking gulps of air. Could things get worse?

Back in the dining room, Torie found Collin talking to the couple. Anger showed in Trey's gesticulating arms, his pointing finger. Collin looked somber, nodded. Said something.

Her breath hitched. There went her job.

*****

"Neema, you've got to go home and get some rest."

His grandmother wouldn't look away from her sleeping husband. She slumped more than usual, her grey skin defined her exhaustion.

Adam looped his arm over her shoulders. "You're too tired. You need to take care of yourself."

"How can I when he's back in the hospital?"

Adam glanced at the clock. After midnight. If she didn't rest, she'd be hospitalized next. He had to be sly as a serpent, as his father used to say. Neema wouldn't think of herself -- but others? Always.

"I've got to get you home, so I can get some sleep. I promised Maya I'd go to church with her."

She pulled her attention away from her husband. The blue of her eyes faded like well-worn jeans, but a smile crinkled the corners and made them sparkle, and a flush reddened her cheeks. "You going back to church? I like this girl." She leaned over her husband and kissed his forehead. "Be back later, Harold."

He waved a hand. "'Bout time."

"Guess you're not sleeping," Adam said.

He tiptoed out of the room with his grandmother and drove home in silence. At the farm, Adam hurried around the car, but Neema had already swung the door open.

"I can get out of my own car." She brushed aside his arm.

"You can't tell me Pop's the stubborn one." Adam chuckled. "See your doctor for a check-up."

His grandmother offered him the same off-handed wave Pop had given.

"I'm serious." He took her elbow and helped her up the dark steps. "As the caregiver, you're under a lot of stress. What if--"

"I'm fine." She craned her neck and pecked Adam on the cheek. "Now go home and let me get the rest you insist I need."

When his grandmother used *that* tone, everyone complied -- his grandfather, himself, the mailman, the dogcatcher.

As he drove to his cabin, Adam's mind churned from one bad scenario to another. Pop's mind functioned as keenly as ever, but his body betrayed him more each day. How much longer did he have to live?

Could he survive without this man?

His grandmother? Just as stubborn as her husband. She withered in front of Adam's eyes. How could he stop time? Keep them forever?

Once in bed, sleep proved elusive. It neared dawn, and Adam figured he could stress out in bed or unwind for an hour or two with his kayak.

Chapter Thirteen

"Eye for eye, tooth for tooth, hand for hand, foot for foot, burning for burning, wound for wound, stripe for stripe." Ex. 21:24-25

The lean-to proved to be almost as uncomfortable as sleeping under the picnic table. The hard, wood floor bruised every bone in Torie's body, mashed each muscle.

While night still dyed the sky black, the birds raised a ruckus. Weren't they supposed to start their chattering *after* sunrise?

She sat up, leaned against her wall, and pulled up the blanket to ward off the morning chill. Its thinness didn't protect much against the frosty air. Her teeth chattered.

Her stomach rumbled.

She wanted orange juice. And coffee. And pain to cease. All pain.

More than all of that, Torie wanted a home. She lifted her eyes to the graying sky. "I don't care what kind of hovel I sleep in -- anywhere but here." One night in her lean-to was too many.

At least Collin didn't fire her.

"I would've belted them," he had said about Trey and Selene. "You did the right thing. This time."

She'd watched him walk away. The words *this time* made her heart tremble.

Within moments of uttering "this time", Collin turned back to her. "Want to be a permanent sub? I need more workers like you."

Recalling the compliment, Torie hugged herself and grinned. She did well. Didn't murder the duo.

After she had gotten old-man Symonds, her seventh-grade math teacher who should have been retired years earlier, to listen to her, no one ever took advantage of her again. He helped settle the issues with Darren but couldn't do anything about the baby...

Happy thoughts. Think happy things.

The relief about being able to work drifted away with the morning's darkness. *I wish I felt better. Inside more than out.*

Coffee would help. She wished she had bought a coffee pot. Her joke shifted her mood. Life in the jungle could be good if the Ready Mart sold air mattresses and a cheval mirror, and orange juice.

OJ?

Torie sort of had orange juice. The Hooch she'd picked up last night was orange. Three wine coolers remained. She popped the lid off one and sipped. It soothed her throbbing ribs. She popped two Advil -- extra-strength. The Percocet was gone. Not having them was okay. She wasn't gonna be an addict.

After downing a second Hooch, Torie emptied her tips from her purse, and counted over a hundred and twenty bucks.

At the Ready Mart, she had also bought a box of Fruit Loops, extra batteries for her flashlight, and dish detergent. Frugal. She had to be a penny-pincher, an old Scrooge. A small bottle of dish soap was a lot cheaper than laundry soap, and if it washed dishes, it would clean her clothes. Especially her jeans after she dumped spaghetti sauce all over them. Unfortunately, they'd never dry in this weather. She should've invested in an umbrella -- a heavy mist mimicked rain.

Fortunately -- or not -- she was off tonight. Guaranteed. And on Monday and Tuesday when Collin closed The Stadium, unless he was catering something special. Nothing special happened out in the boonies.

Her stomach rumbled. She could open the cereal. Instead, she popped the lid off her last wine cooler. *How can it be so damp and not actually rain?*

Coffee. I wish I had Selene's Keurig. Or a Dunkin' Donuts at the neighboring penthouse. The stench of fried food clinging to her clothes wafted over her.

She rummaged through her belongings. The warmest clothes she brought were capris and a short-sleeved shirt. The yoga pants and sweatshirt she'd slept in would have to do. Her style wouldn't worry the birds. She wandered down the shadowed path to the lake and scanned the water. Gray light worked its way over the horizon.

So early and too quiet. A peace settled as the mist rose and danced over the pond. She shivered in the chill. As she squared her shoulders, her resolve strengthened. She'd accept her lot, and do what had to be done to survive. If she learned anything, it was how to survive..

No fisherman boated on the water, so she stripped and waded into Livingstone Pond.

A scream strangled in her throat. How could she have thought it was warm yesterday? Goosebumps jitter-bugged down her legs. She dove under the water before she lost her nerve, and scurried back to shore to get her shampoo. Standing wet in the morning breezes froze her more than being under water. She waded into a deeper section, soaped her hair, dunked herself.

No wonder homeless bums stunk. Who wanted to bathe like this?

The cold worked like an ice pack and numbed her aches. She dunked once more to rinse the last of the shampoo from her hair. As she surfaced, her splashing echoed in the morning's quiet.

Fish? By its sound, the fish was a whale. She didn't think coyotes or bats swam. She listened. Heard nothing. Had to have been her own splashing. Then a yellow kayak rounded the spit of land jutting into Livingstone Pond.

*****

Adam negotiated the promontory in the pond. The best fishing lay on the other side where the rocky shore slanted into shallower water and offered the fish good hiding spaces. A shadow caught his eye. Someone swimming in this chill?

He sat up straight. Recognized the bather.

What was *she* doing out here?

Vicky screamed and ducked beneath the water. It didn't take long until her head, like a fishing bobber, peered above the surface. Her dark hair and delicate features froze in fear -- and in cold.

He laughed. For once in his life, he'd let the bully experience the disgrace of being the victim.

"So who do we have skinny dipping so early in the morning?" He dipped his paddle into the water, and the kayak glided closer. "I wouldn't have taken you for a nature lover." The bitter tease didn't taste good. Yet the momentum of his cruelty pushed him on like the dip of his paddle propelled his kayak.

"Adam. I didn't expect--

"I also didn't take you as a morning person." He lifted his head and peered into the water -- the sweetness of vengeance. Vicky clasped her hands over her chest and sunk deeper, obscuring the pale skin in the brown water. "It's chilly, isn't it?" He softened his voice, tried to sound sympathetic.

"Yes. I'd like to get out--"

"Don't let me stop you."

The surprise in her face fired his resolve. He picked up the paddle he had laid across the kayak and, instead of moving away as he knew she'd hoped, he paddled closer. Would get a good view of Vicky in all her glory.

One stroke closer and Vicky took another step back. To maintain any modesty, she had to slink lower in the water. Before too long, though, she'd run out of water and have to expose herself for what she was. Adam knew the joy Vicky had to have felt when she connived Dylan into trapping him in his locker. Adam heard, once more, his high-pitched pleas to stop. Heard the click of the lock. Felt his pants hot and wet. Saw light seeping into the locker vent and smelled their cigarette smoke.

He heard Vicky banging on the door before she left him alone. Four hours alone. Her voice, squeaky, contemptuous. "Don't you *ever* flirt with me, Boy Scout."

He hated her.

Adam dipped his paddle back into the water and leered.

*****

Closer? Torie should've known. Men wanted one thing. The shore lay a good distance away. Lots of shallow water lined with sharp rocks stood between her and her clothes. She'd freeze to death if she didn't get out of this ice cube soon, but she wasn't going to give this creep the satisfaction. Torie inched closer to the shore, ducked further beneath the surface. Her teeth chattered, as much from the cold as the sudden thought of what Adam, as a man, was capable of doing.

That would never happen again.

How did little, mousy Adam Benedict have become a bully? The man in the kayak changed from the timid little thing he had been. Still small, his shoulders had broadened as though he worked out. The quilted vest he wore this morning added layers to his chest, puffed him up -- like his ego.

A little testosterone and several years transformed all men. She understood their brains. Or lack of brains -- like mating praying mantises -- copulating with no heads.

She inched closer to the shore. Another stroke of the paddle. He closed in. The kayak glided after he brought up the paddle. Torie took a long step toward shore and bent her knees so the water came to her chin. He glided closer. She hoped fishing gear sunk. Hopefully, it was expensive enough to make Adam want to save it.

She faked one more step away. He approached. She stepped forward. Straightening her legs, Torie caught the kayak broadside with the heel of her hands and propelled herself upward. His weight, the surprise, and the lightness of his kayak served her purpose. She bit back the searing pain in her side, refused to give him the satisfaction of yelping as he went over -- away from her.

She scurried out of the pond. On the shore, she scooped her clothes and disappeared into the bushes.

*****

The cold water swallowed Adam and soaked through his down vest. He surfaced. A flurry on the shore caused bushes to ruffle after it. The motion of his spill sent his gear off toward the outlet. He sloshed through the water, nabbed it, stuffed it into his kayak then hauled his sodden body to shore.

The wind blew, and the cold water iced him. The down vest weighted him, his jeans chaffed.

What a fool. He shook his head as shame shuddered through him. "Touché, Vicky," he called toward the direction she took. A grin formed despite his discomfort. Disquiet filtered into his psyche. He shivered. Vicky in the woods at dawn didn't make sense.

He wrapped his arms around himself and walked in the direction Vicky had run until he came to the trail marker. Wind rattled the branches over him. He didn't have time to chase a naked girl through the woods. He'd promised to meet Maya in church.

Church?

What was he becoming?

Chapter Fourteen

"Anyone who is to find Christ must first find the church. How could anyone know where Christ is and what faith is in him unless he knew where his believers are?" Martin Luther

Torie's yoga pants tangled as she shoved her legs into them. Her head resisted the neckline of the sweatshirt. Adam's terrifying leer meant one thing. All men thought alike.

She scooped clothes into the overnight bag lying on her lean-to floor and kept her eyes on the trail. With no time to bury them, they had to come with her. Now.

Since Adam could see her on the well-worn Haverset trail, Torie ducked into the thick woods and ran. In the undergrowth, tree branches grabbed her like talons of a hawk. A stand of brambles blocked her way, forcing Torie to zigzag. Every stick and fern and blueberry bush delayed escape. Fleeing exhausted her.

As panic fled, her chest screamed at the bag's weight, begged her to stop.

Drained, she surveyed her surroundings and plopped down on a large log. Though her pounding heart settled a little, her headache thumped. Was Adam crashing through the bushes after her?

Once her breathing calmed, Torie stood and hoisted her overnight bag. It'd be safe to go home.

Home. One night at the lean-to, and now it's home?

Ten minutes later, she stumbled onto an unfamiliar path. *Which way?* She turned right and followed the track as it narrowed and ended in a clump of sumacs overrunning the path.

Sumacs. During the Darren years, he loved to take her into the patch behind their house. His rapes made them the only trees she could identify, and now she was lost in a clump of them. Lost. In a jungle.

At least this jungle didn't sport alligators, but it did have snakes. Spiders lurked under leaves. Bats at night. A violent shiver racked her ribs.

She rubbed her eyes with two fingers. Straightened her shoulders. Pity served no purpose.

Since the end of this trail led nowhere, she'd turn around. The other way had to end up somewhere. Her torso protested against lugging all her luggage. In the thickest clump of sumacs, Torie stashed her junk. Her purse with her phone and credit cards, her comb and mirror would stay with her. Funny how misery reduced the importance of stuff.

Refusing to be lost again, Torie shoved sticks into the soft forest soil where footpaths merged.

Down the path, nothing looked familiar.

Before long, her trail exited to a main road. Which road? Should she turn back into the jungle and hope to find the lean-to?

No.

Was this the Schoharie-Westfield two-lane? The one with the Stewart's Shop. Which way should she go? Woods lined each side of the highway, and no familiar building peeked through the tangle of foliage. Turning right onto the path in the woods brought her to a dead-end. Might as well switch it up. Head left.

The cold mist now falling needled her head and penetrated each pore of her skin. She slowed. Ten minutes later, the gas pumps of Stewart's came into view.

Inside the shop, warmth seeped into her skin, but not until her second cup of coffee. With hands cupped around the cardboard mug, her fingers thawed. She stared out the window. Motor oil rainbows splashed along the parking lot and rippled from the spray of vehicles flying past. She had a whole day with nowhere to go. Nothing to do.

The manager would ask her to leave soon. Before another indignity slathered her, Torie stood, found a rack of umbrellas and bought one. Why didn't Stewart's have a twirly rack of socks? Her feet, in flip-flops, hadn't defrosted from her trek here.

Westfield had nothing. Not even a Wal-Mart or a Dollar Store. Burnt Hollow offered more -- not much, but more -- a hardware store, a Laundromat. Useless businesses like those. Westfield? Only a restaurant, the Ready Mart, and a minuscule library.

She walked the way she had come. And walked. Walked some more. Wished her sweatshirt had a hood. Wished she'd packed mittens and Uggs and a fur coat. Mink. Definitely mink.

Fine mist worked its way under her umbrella and froze her.

Since every path into Hookskill looked the same, she turned in at every one. All of them dead-ended or circled back to the road. Exhaustion showered her along with the rain's mist.

A marquee announced Maranatha Church. Torie stopped. *I guess I didn't find every path.*

Its huge sign said services would start in a half-an-hour, yet the lot stood filled with cars. Churches were supposed to welcome everyone, and this was the one with a food pantry. It'd be warm. No one would know her. Maybe they'd give her a can of beans from their surplus. She'd become a bona fide hobo.

At the least, she'd sit for a while and listen to the geeks sing their boring songs. What else did she have to do? Or to lose?

She entered the lobby right behind a man who looked like a biker dude in a do-rag covering long, grey hair.

*****

The car engine just turned over when Maya's phone played "Onward Christian Soldier." She leaned her head against the headrest. "Hey, Mom."

"Did I catch you at a good time?"

Viola Vitale always called after mass on Sunday. The time varied from week to week, but when Maya hoped to get to service early, she was guaranteed a call.

Maya didn't answer since she knew Mom would correct herself.

"Oh, of course." Mom's laugh didn't disguise her disappointment that Maya chose not to follow in the family religion. Maya had to give her mother credit. She did try to accept Maya's faith. At least, Mom only nagged once a month instead of four times. "This will take a minute. I keep forgetting you Protestants only have one late mass. Anyway, Daddy and I are sitting in Denny's for our brunch. He came across an article he thought might interest you. Here. I'll put him on."

"Hey, Baby Doll." Sal Vitale's voice belied his size. Slight, sinewy, and smaller than his daughter, it boomed as though browbeating a jury.

"Daddy." She tried hard to not whine his name. "Can I call you back? I'm on my way--"

"I won't be as long winded as Mom."

A thump and a yelp from her father made Maya smile in spite of herself. Mom had walloped him. No one crossed Viola. Maya turned off her engine and resigned herself to being late.

"It's late in the season, but Albany County will have two vacancies for legislators."

"I'm not interested in politics, Daddy."

"So you've said, but you have our heart for the downtrodden, ergo, you'd find this a great niche --you know, do something useful after you pay your bills."

"My job does more than pay the bills. It shapes the minds--"

"All right, already. You give me the same spiel each week. You do know we support your altruism?"

Maya checked her watch. Adam would be waiting for her, and she didn't want to stand him up. She loved his compassion for those in need, his devotion to his family. Justine said his faith smoldered and promised a service or two at Maranatha would provide the kindling to reignite it.

"You've got the Vitale social fervor, so what do you say? I'll text the link?"

Dad's questions shook her back to the present. She stared ahead but saw nothing as the windshield glazed with rain.

"Send it." A text could be ignored. "I'll call you later. I'm late." She started the car.

"Of course. You're always prompt -- nothing you learned from us." He laughed at the standard joke. Her mother and father never arrived anywhere on time. Court trained them in delays. "Mom and I love you, Baby Doll."

"I love you, too." She pulled the phone away from her ear to disconnect, but her father's resonant voice continued.

"Mother wants to speak to you."

"Is everything okay?" Mom asked.

Why wouldn't it?

"Maya, sweetie?"

"I'm here."

"Answer me."

"Of course."

"You didn't call last Monday when I texted."

"I did."

"I never got it."

"You were busy. I left a message."

"You should have called again."

"Mom. I'm late." Maya glanced at the clock on the dash. Ten minutes until service. She scrunched her forehead, and opened her mouth. No words formed. Wanted to be snarky -- six days later Mom calls back because she was so worried? "Things are good. Talk to you during the week." Maya clicked off before her mother responded. Why did God invent mothers? If she turned out like Mom, she'd willingly hand her kids over to a commune -- just to save their sanity.

*****

Torie slipped into the church, kept her head down and her eyes averted. No need to invite conversation. Across the foyer stood a table loaded with coffee and tea and donuts. *A third cup?* She made a dash for it hoping it was free.

She almost made it to the table when an old woman with a divine silver tint in hair permed to perfection offered her hand. "Hello. I'm

Celeste." She cocked her head. Her eyes held Torie's, and a half-smile froze on her lips.

Torie forced a smile. The interrogation about her injuries would soon begin. "Glad to meet you." She avoided completing the introductions.

"Your name?"

Torie pulled on her bangs, straightened them across the bandage. "Torie."

"Is this your first time here? I haven't seen you before."

Torie nodded and relaxed. Aside from innocent questions, this lady asked nothing embarrassing, nothing Torie didn't want to answer. People as old as Mr. Symonds proved themselves safe.

"You here with anyone?"

She shook her head.

"Well you are now. Come, sit with Angela and me. Service's about to start." Celeste took Torie's arm. Then her eyes narrowed, and she cocked her head.

Torie *knew* this lady itched to say something about her injuries.

"Sorry. I've got to ask--"

Here it comes.

"I interrupted your trajectory to the coffee. You want a cup?"

"Trajecto-what?"

"I can recognize the signs for java. Ol' joe is a friend to people like us." She pointed to the table.

"Didn't you say service would start?"

Celeste nodded. "Get your cup and come on. Angela will be sending out an APB soon."

Torie wasn't going to argue. After Torie doctored her coffee, Celeste linked her arm in hers and led her into the sanctuary.

It felt good to be dragged down the aisle. Someone else made decisions and took care of her.

They shuffled through a row of chairs on the right side of the church and found a seat next to another silver-haired lady.

"Are you guys twins?" Torie asked.

Celeste forgot she was in church as her laughter rattled the rafters. "Heavens no. If I got a nickel every time someone asked if we were twins, I'd be worshipping my Savior in the Caribbean instead of upstate New York. This county ain't never heard of spring. Angela's my *older* sister."

Angela hugged Torie who stiffened. *What are their motives?* She pulled away.

"Don't let my sister give a bad impression of Maranatha," Angela said. "We're not all dingbats here. Come. Sit. We're almost ready to start."

"I've never been in a church before," Torie whispered.

"What?" Angela asked.

"This is the first time I ever--"

"Speak up," Angela yelled. "We don't hear so good."

"How does church work?"

Celeste and Angela patted her arm. "Any way God wants it to." Celeste's merry laughter echoed throughout the sanctuary.

*****

Worry nagged Adam as he pulled into the packed church lot. He wished Neema would've let him stay with her, but knowing he'd be in church? If she were on her deathbed, she'd make him go.

The cool morning air chilled him as he opened the truck door. Images of Vicky flashed in his mind, and his face heated. He was a hypocrite heading off to church after what he did to her. Of course, he wouldn't have been indecent -- but tormenting the freezing woman the way he did? God wouldn't approve.

Nor would He think highly of his going to church to pick up a pretty woman. Shame niggled. *Forgive me, God.* The rusty prayer whisked away the last of his guilt. Warmed him.

Inside, he scanned the sanctuary. No Maya.

They hadn't made arrangements to meet anywhere except church -- somewhere in this building. He hadn't expected the place to be packed. In the sea of heads bobbing in front him, he couldn't identify Maya.

He found a seat near the center back, took out his phone and texted.

At Maranatha -- can't find you. I'm in back. Meet in lobby later.

He silenced the phone.

A large-screen monitor displayed the song lyrics, and Adam found the melody easy to follow. He settled in. To his surprise, the song comforted. He'd harbored bitterness about his parents and his school years so long, he only allowed himself to remember stodgy old hymns like the ones Neema and Pop loved. The songs he used to love at First Baptist.

The music compelled Adam to lift his arm in praise. Warmth permeated his spirit -- and his side. He grinned and turned his head.

"Sorry I'm late," Maya whispered as she slipped into the chair next to him. "Will explain later."

Maybe God was good after all.

With two more ballads sung, Adam dared to hope this church had expunged all the old anthems, but his luck ran out. Before the offertory, one of Neema's favorite songs began. He grew restless as it crawled through each verse. Instead of singing the dreadful chorus, he studied the members of Maya's church.

Then he saw *her*.

*****

Torie loved the music. Although her clothes were damp, and her hair curled in the wetness, and her feet froze, warmth filled her. Why hadn't Jean ever told her God *really* existed? All these people acted like He did, and with the comfort she got from the bad singing, she knew there was a God 'cause no one here was gonna make *The Voice*.

Tension released her shoulders and back, her head tingled like the beginning of a buzz. The singing intoxicated her but didn't impair her senses. Joy filled her for the first time since...? First grade?

The mood of the service shifted as a slow song started. "I come to the garden alone..."

The melody wasn't as easy as the other songs, so she closed her eyes and listened. Judging from their singing, Celeste and Angela loved it more than the other songs. Their voices harmonized over Torie's head as each crooned with zest. Their fervor made their yodeling pleasant.

"He walks with me and He talks to me..."

Talks with me?

Now there was a thought. Would God talk to her? How would she hear him? He didn't speak in voices like those a schizophrenic heard, did He?

"Though the night around me be falling..."

Night? Her long, cold night at the lean-to made her shiver. Thoughts of bats and werewolves howling in the forest.

"He bids me go; through the voice of woe, His voice to me is calling..."

Then Torie lost control of her body. Her arm lifted by its own accord, and she waved it over her head like she did in concerts.

Embarrassed, she lowered it and looked around. She hadn't been out of place. Others did the same. This place felt homey. She felt God.

*****

Maya's doubts floated away. She found Adam, thanks to his text, and she studied him from the foyer before making her way to the vacant seat next to him.

He appeared lost in worship. His arm raised, his head swaying in beat with the music. Her heart warmed. She'd let go and trust Justine's judgment. When she slipped in beside him, his face beamed. Beatific.

"In The Garden" started.

Adam's mood shifted, and it appeared he lost interest and looked around the sanctuary. He took her hand and held it by his side as she sang. She felt weightless and leaned closer to him.

Then he squeezed. More than an affectionate squeeze -- more like something was wrong. His face glared toward the front of the church. Maya searched for what bothered him and found nothing. She turned her attention back to the service, and in the corner of her eye, she caught sight of the waitress from The Stadium.

She jolted. Looked at Adam. *Was he still angry at her?*

Chapter Fifteen

"The greatest enemy to human souls is the self-righteous spirit which makes men look to themselves for salvation." Charles Spurgeon

The preacher had everyone open to the Gospel of St. John, chapter eight. In the warmth of the sanctuary, Torie's eyes grew heavy. Her head bobbed, and she jerked upright, glanced around the church. No one appeared to notice, so she hadn't snored. Wriggling upright, Torie swallowed hard, squared her shoulders, and determined to listen. Her eyes drooped again, and she slumped against the cushioned seat.

The priest-guy who took the podium read, "The teachers of the law and the Pharisees brought in a woman caught in adultery. They made her stand before the group and said to Jesus, 'Teacher, this woman was caught in the act of adultery. In the Law Moses commanded us to stone such women. Now what do you say?'"

They were going to stone her? Torie's drooping eyes popped open, and she sat upright, unable to believe the words. *Because the woman was in love, those men wanted to kill her?*

Had the lady been with a married man? The preacher did say adultery. So she hooked up with someone already taken by another woman. Just like Selene. Torie'd love to stone her.

She smiled and ducked her head. Probably wasn't a good idea to smirk in church.

"The Pharisees knew the law. Adultery was punishable by death," the preacher continued. "All sins have consequences."

Torie understood consequences. She lived them. But what about the guy the woman had slept with? Didn't the law apply to him?

Things never changed. Even back in the olden days, men ruled everything.

"We can't throw stones," the preacher said. "Everyone sins, even those goody-two-shoe teachers of the law."

Torie giggled.

"What's so funny?" Celeste leaned over and whispered.

"Did he call them goody-two-shoes?"

Celeste patted Torie's hand and nodded. "They were a buncha prudes."

Torie smiled at the thought.

The minister went on, "Because of Jesus's love, everyone can be free from sin's punishment. Preachers--"

A smattering of applause stunned Torie. People smiled and nudged each other. She felt like someone left out of a joke.

The pastor held up his hands, grinning a goofy smile. "Preachers and drunks." Giggles echoed. "Teachers and lawyers. Boy Scouts and dropouts. DPW workers and sex workers. All have sinned. Everyone is forgiven if they acknowledge their sin and accept the price Jesus paid on Calvary. Everyone can erase the sins of their past and start anew."

A tingle started in her chest, spread to her toes, radiated to her head. Her body trembled. Everyone would include her. *Me? Boy Scouts in kayaks who hated me because of my past?* Her heart pounded. *Can I start over?*

She blinked away memories of Darren and the baby. *Oh, Jesus, be real.*

Forgiven? Me?

She blinked again, a few tears slid down her cheeks. She dashed them away. *No crying. You're not drunk.* Booze created tears. Not religion. *I'm forgiven?*

The tears came faster. Her nose ran. Biting her lips did nothing to stop her fit, and her crying bordered on sobbing. Her hand didn't sop up the tears and digging through her purse produced no tissues. Resigned to using her sleeve, Torie discovered a packet of tissues on her lap. To her right, Celeste stared straight ahead, riveted on the preacher. On the left, Angela scribbled notes in an illegible scrawl.

"Our past will be washed away if we accept that no one is too great a sinner to be forgiven. Lies, lust, or drunkenness. Anger, pride, murder..."

Torie heard no more. Her past choked her with sobs which pounded ribs numbed by Advil. Something inside, quiet but insistent, repeated the word forgiven. Doubling over, Torie sobbed.

*****

Adam saw himself tormenting Torie earlier in the morning. Shame crept up his neck and heated his face. The law offered a statute of limitations on many crimes. Shouldn't his vengeance have a statute? Shouldn't shame?

As the pastor spoke, questions arose and Adam's mind couldn't grasp onto peace. Rubbing his eyes didn't erase the visions of his crude actions.

Maya clasped his free hand. Her smile focused on him, and he shuddered. If he didn't forgive Torie for things she did twelve years ago, or for something her father did, he'd lose his chance with Maya.

Worse. I'd lose myself.

"Those preachers used the letter of the law to condemn," the minister said.

Didn't God create those laws? Why did Jesus condemn those men for doing what He commanded?

He tried not to listen further. Still, every attempt to think of kayaking or fishing brought Adam back to the words from the pulpit. Pastor Arendsen spoke of how the legalists strained at a gnat and swallowed a camel, how they bound heavy laws on the populace so no one could enter the kingdom of heaven.

Adam's jaw strained as he clenched it. Every word the minister spoke speared him. He found no reason to ask what Maya thought about his lack of forgiveness. He knew.

*****

Prosecutors -- even in Jesus's time -- were legalistic, adherents of the law. Maya's parents taught her to dislike them. As defense lawyers, the Vitales demanded compassion.

So was their love for her pity?

Buried fears wormed their way back into her soul. She'd been drunk on Parents' Weekend her freshman year. Had that made her suicidal? Or did her genes hold her captive?

Her parents didn't judge her.

She snuck a peek at Adam. *Lord, help him see how he judges Torie --* the prayer stuttered in her mind. *Who's the Pharisee now?*

*****

"Anyone who wants liberty--"

Torie didn't hear the rest of the statement. Somehow she found herself stumbling over Angela. *I'll take it. Let me.*

Freedom beckoned her forward. She nearly tumbled to her knees at the altar. Nothing penetrated her consciousness but the conviction that God had removed her past. He'd freed her from all she did wrong.

Warmth seeping through both of Torie's shoulders refocused her. Turning her head, she smiled up at Angela on her left side and Celeste to her right. Old folks were wonderful. They expected nothing. Gave everything. Played no games if they got a little love.

"Is it true?" Her voice barely whispered.

Celeste's bowed head touched Torie's. "You'll never know the half

81

of it, darling."

Torie's head bowed at the knowledge. Every heartbeat declared it. Every breath confirmed the fact. She could start all over.

Chapter Sixteen

"I have always found that mercy bears richer fruits than strict justice." Abraham Lincoln

It took a lot of doing to shake off Angela and Celeste. Torie wanted to go home. Finger this new life in private. Besides, no one could see her shame living in the woods.

She wandered up the road, the umbrella close to turning inside out with the wind. At last, the trail marker for Haverset appeared.

On the path, Torie folded the useless umbrella. Rain blew in from every direction, and what didn't rain down on her, rained up. The brush along the path held more water than the clouds. Chilled through and shivering, she found a stick pointing to the left. To her clothes. She turned, hoping her overnight bag was waterproof enough to give her dry duds. Ten minutes later, another stick marked a path. A trail to her right.

Circles. She just walked an endless, pathetic circle. A merry-go-round loop.

Another route dead-ended. The next returned her to Schoharie-Westfield Road. None led to her sumacs. None to her clothes.

She was not only homeless but naked.

Life couldn't get worse.

The preacher-priest had lied. God was punishing her for the sins of the past. Torie shoved her hands into the pockets of her sweatshirt and fingered the slim New Testament Celeste had given her. Outside of church, Torie found no joy or peace that her prayers at the altar had given. Maybe God only existed inside the building.

Or maybe He didn't exist after all. Look what happened by trusting Trey. Was the experience in Maranatha simply a mob mentality, like jumping into a mosh pit? Getting high at a party?

She stomped her foot. He *had* to be real. Then she'd never be alone. Never be guilty of being a...

A dog. A witch. An outlaw.

Or naked.

Surely God frowned on her running around without clothes. Living as a nudist wasn't on her bucket list, either. The image made her smile. If God were real, He'd find her clothes.

It neared four o'clock when she rounded a bend in the path and found her lean-to.

"Well, well, well, look who made it home."

Torie jumped. "What are you doing here?" Fear rooted her feet to the ground. They refused to run. Adam hated her, but he wouldn't kill her, would he? She gasped for air. Not kill, but worse. Death was preferable to rape.

Adam remained seated in her lean-to with his back against the wall and her pillow cushioning him. Her blanket covered his legs stretched out before him.

The world whirled and black spots danced in front of Torie's eyes. Shaking her head to release her terror, she stood her ground. "You look cozy." Her voice squeaked. Gulping swallowed her fear. "Made yourself at home I see." Breathing came easier now. She sounded in control once more.

"It is a little drafty."

"How'd you know I stayed here?"

He picked up an empty four-pack of Horton's Hooch. "I recognized the décor. Rather minimalist." He shoved the carton aside. "Oh, and you left this." He held up a pair of shorts. "Not a big wardrobe."

"Guess I won't go naked. Or be broke. Those are my deposits." Torie pointed to the empties. "Twenty-cents should keep me from being a convicted vagrant." Her legs ached, and she wanted to snatch her blanket from him, curl up in a ball, and sulk the night away.

He tossed the shorts on top of the empties.

"Why are you here?" Torie asked.

"Curiosity, I guess. I never took you to be the nature lover -- swimming au natural, camping out. Wondered why you were out here."

Torie stared at the ground and pushed the pine needles with her toe. No home. No car. No clothes. She glared at Adam. One tear slipped. She dashed it away.

The hard lines of Adam's mouth melted.

Before the tears humiliated her, Torie pivoted and stomped down the trail. Curses gurgled in her throat, but anger and self-pity choked her voice. She became the Torie of kindergarten who won student of the week. When she got home and told her mother, Jean smacked her. Said her boyfriend had moved out, and it was all Torie's fault. He didn't want no kids -- stupid or smart.

It didn't take Jean long to move Mike in. To cause Mike, the only man she ever called Daddy, to leave. Her fault, too. Darren, his friends and their STDs. Her fault. Trey. Her fault.

Adam grabbed her.

Screaming, Torie twisted, her ribs wrenched and caused her knees to buckle, dropping her to the pine-covered path.

"I'm not going to hurt you." Adam's soft voice sounded sincere. He lifted her to her feet, clasped both her arms. "I'm sorry. I came here to help, not be a jerk. Guess old habits die hard." The last words contained an edge as though forced. He led her to the shelter where they sat against the back wall in silence.

She shivered.

Slipping off his denim jacket, Adam draped it over her shoulders, tucked the blanket around her.

Torie glared at Adam, and studied every movement. If he tried anything...

She had no defense. Couldn't catch her breath, let alone fight him off.

He glanced toward her empties. "With the concussion you had, it's not safe for you to be drinking. Or to be out here." He huffed a sardonic chuckle. "What's going on, Torie?"

Her name. She looked at him. "Torie?"

"It's your name." His statement of fact sounded like an accusation.

"Not Vicky?"

"As you can see, I am a Pharisee and a keeper of the law. I can change."

"You were in church?"

"Even Boy Scouts need to repent."

His smile warmed her.

"Why are you here with nothing but bottle returns?"

Torie ducked her head. Could she tell Adam? Emotions warred. Why not? She looked him in the eyes. "I lost my clothes."

"You what?" He snorted.

"It's not funny." Her snigger betrayed her attitude. "It's all your fault."

"My fault?" He laughed outright and shifted further away from her. "Sorry. Not fun--"

"No. Not funny." She crossed her arms and gave him her meanest scowl.

He laughed louder. "Quit the pout. You can't look scary."

"Well, you are. You terrified me this morning -- I figured you had..." *What is the word?* "I thought you had ulterior motives, so I grabbed my bag. It was a Coach bag, mind you, not cheap." She grinned. "I ran. Once I got clothes on."

"Do you make a habit of camping with designer luggage?"

She ignored his jibe. "I kept it buried behind this thing, but it was out because I needed to dress, and most people don't take walks in the dark and the rain, or go sailing in tippy boats. I was afraid you'd take it.

When it got too heavy, I stashed it on a dead-end trail in a clump of sumac. Now I can't find it."

"You can't stay here alone."

"I have so far." She might as well confess. Life was getting too complicated. "Well, one night here and one under a picnic table."

"With no clothes, you'll be naked."

"I have shorts." She held them out, winked, then tossed aside.

His lips quirked as though hiding a grin. "It's not safe."

"What do you suggest?"

Adam shook his head.

"I thought so." Torie expected him to get up and go, but he sat with head bowed. Silence filled her chalet.

"Come stay with me for a night. Until we figure something out."

Torie clambered half-way to her feet. *Should've known.*

Adam grabbed her arm and pulled. Torie winced and crumpled.

"I'm not suggesting we sleep together."

Her shoulders relaxed.

"I have two bedrooms. Both have locks. On the inside. It's a small place. It'll work for a few days. Maybe my friends Levi and Justine can help. They have four kids. What's one more person?"

A shower. A bed. She closed her eyes and imagined the warmth of a house and a bed. "I can't put you out." Despite her refusal, and her attempt to make it no-nonsense, Torie's heart leaped in hope. "I don't make enough money to pay rent."

"No rent, and as far as putting me out -- I've got to get to the hospital tonight and help my grandmother. Then I work a lot of doubles. Tomorrow I start at five a.m. That's in the morning." His eyes sparkled.

Tori pouted at him. "I may only have a GED, but I know what a.m. means." She examined the floor boards then peered back at Adam. His eyes studied her without blinking. Gray-blue like the overcast skies.

"Torie, you can trust me. I won't beat you. Won't rape you. You'll be safe with me until Justine and Levi can take you in."

She licked her lips and studied her toes. Could she trust him?

What choice did she have?

Chapter Seventeen

"For outward show is a wonderful perverter of the reason."
Marcus Aurelius, *Meditations*

After throwing the folded blanket and pillow on the landing, Torie banged on the locked door. Locked? Heather never locked it. From the interior, a radio hummed.

"Heather? Bobby? I've got a place to stay for a bit. I need a minute to get my suitcase." Torie put her ear to the door but heard no movement even though soft, indistinguishable music played inside. Someone had to be home.

She hammered on the door.

Kicked it.

Adam's warm hand held her shoulder and pulled her back. "Easy. You're in no shape to blow the house down, Ms. Wolf. No one's home. Or they're not answering."

"My stuff."

"Let me pick up a few things you need -- a toothbrush and whatnot. I've got soap and toothpaste and other sundries."

"I can buy my own." She forced a grin and shoved her hand into her pocket. "I may be destitute, but I'm not penniless." She pulled out the dimes from her bottle returns.

Adam didn't laugh.

*****

Adam sat in the truck, staring at the doors to Grocery*World. Torie had insisted she could manage her few packages herself. Told him to wait. *How much longer, God?* The wait dragged longer than at the Ready Mart, more than the dithering at Heather's. The moments ticked by, ticking him off. He tapped his fingers on the dash. *Why, God, did You suck me back into her world?*

Starting the truck, Adam backed out of the parking space. Then he pictured Torie in the lean-to. Not a safe place. Cold. Inhumane. He could handle her at his cabin for a day or two. Pulling back into the space, Adam turned off the ignition and headed into the store.

Lines crowded the registers, so he turned down the first empty aisle. *Where is she?* With his eyes searching for Torie, he ran smack-dab

87

into some lady painting lipstick on her hand.

"Sorry." He tried not to stare at her odd behavior.

Her outlandish outfit made *not* staring impossible. The lady wore leggings and a tight, pink t-shirt with a black bra underneath -- an outfit more suitable for a teen -- not appropriate, but more suitable. Piercings lined her ears, and tattoos dotted her forearm.

Biting her lower lip, the lady dipped her head. The action made her look like someone else he knew. The lines around her eyes and mouth suggested she was as old enough to be his mother.

Flirting with me?

Nah. He had to be mistaken.

"You never can tell by the color chart how the lipstick will look." She held up her hand to him. "Which looks best?" She fluttered long lashes.

"Sorry." He shook his head and scooted around her.

At the back of the aisle, he spotted Torie -- pressed against the milk cooler. A muscular, square-jawed man pinned her shoulder to the glass door. His bristly chin twitched. Torie's chin jutted toward the man. A picture of defiance.

What'd she do now?

He wanted to turn away. Let her duke it out herself, but his feet pushed him forward.

"Torie?"

The man released her shoulder with a rib-bruising jolt. He stabbed his index finger inches from her nose and hissed something, but all Adam could make out were the staccato expletives.

And the look in Torie's eyes?

He'd seen it in a countless number of patients, in pain and terror -- heart attack or stroke or impending birth of a breech baby, in victims of car wrecks or bicycle accidents, all who understood their lives were in critical danger.

"Torie." He loped toward her.

The square-jawed man hoisted his twelve-pack off the floor and strutted in Adam's direction. He puffed out his chest clad in a stained, gray *Blud Thirsty* t-shirt. The front sported a skull logo with the dagger piercing its eye.

Torie stared after the man, her chest heaving. After a minute, her large brown eyes found Adam's and offered an apology.

With her mouth set in a grim line, she reached down for the red plastic basket holding her purchases. A paltry few things -- no need to see if she qualified for the express line. Her shopping didn't explain her delay.

"Let's go." He thought she'd hurry toward the check-out. Instead, she stopped by the dairy creamer.

"Do you prefer flavored creamer or plain half and half?"

Haven't you dawdled enough? Biting back the retort, he raised his eyebrows.

"For your coffee?" she clarified.

"I use the dry stuff."

She smiled her Torie smile, lips slightly parted, ends tipped up -- the one he fell in love with in fifth grade. It continued its torment into sixth. The perplexing tip to her lips seemed sad. "You'll have the good stuff as long as you're putting up with me. I got you coffee, too." She glanced down at the basket. On the top lay the Starbucks blonde blend.

She shouldn't be spending her money on him. He said nothing.

Torie stood in line. Adam wanted air. "Meet you outside." The electronic door swooshed opened, and he stopped. The evening breeze wafted the stench of gas and car exhaust from the parking lot. Smelled hostile. He stepped back into the store. As the door shut, he caught sight of the man who had confronted Torie, climbing into a red truck.

Adam sat on the ledge in front of the plate-glass windows and studied the truck pulling out of its space. In the passenger seat sat the woman he'd bumped into in the make-up aisle. He turned to watch Torie inch along the check-out. He didn't know what Torie had done to the man, but Adam had taken Torie in to keep her safe, and this altercation confirmed his decision.

*****

Torie didn't dare glance at Adam. She hadn't meant to be rude, to make him wait, but staying at his place already put him out. She wanted to have juice and coffee and English muffins, so she wouldn't eat his.

Then Darren stalked her. Shouldn't she have grown out of his age preferences? Jean should've been too old for him for sure. Or maybe her mother was his cover. Sleeping with Jean with no kids in the house proved he'd been rehabilitated. He preferred grown women.

She shouldn't have mouthed off to her mother about letting Darren move back in. Orders of protection didn't work when Darren wanted his vengeance.

"You know what they did to me in jail because of you?" he had hissed. "All your fault with your parading around in your underwear. Tempting grown men. You've always been a tramp."

How had he expected her to react?

He and Jean believed she ruined their lives?

89

When Adam got home, she'd shower and lock herself in the room. Never come out. Not until they carried her out in a body bag.

Darren just threatened to make her death come sooner rather than later.

Chapter Eighteen

"Wisdom comes only through suffering." Aeschylus, Agamemnon

"Torie Sullivan's living with you?" Stephenson laughed so hard he yanked the ambulance over the middle line on their first pick-up the next morning.

"Easy there. We're going to transport not be transported. Keep your mind on your driving."

Stephenson saluted. "What brought on this altruism?"

"Altru what? Speak English."

"Why so helpful."

"Church. The preacher put noble ideas in my brain. I understand why they used to stone people." Adam spoke in a falsetto. "Stop here. Stop there. In Grocery*World, she ticks off some guy so bad, he assaults her. At least, she locked herself in her room all night. Once the hot water in the shower ran out."

The smirk strained the corners of Stephenson's lips. "You and Vicious Vicky. Wait until Maya hears you're living with another woman." He winked.

Adam slapped his fist into his palm and forced a scowl at his friend. He'd thought a streak of good luck hit him when he got to work with Stephenson three weeks in a row. Now he doubted it. "Pay attention to your driving, or the next call will be for my knuckles on the side of your head."

"Like I'm scared of your girlie hands." His partner threw back his head and laughed.

"You trying to kill us? Concentrate on your driving."

"What? You'll punch me for laughing?" He wiped tears from his eyes. "You've never hit a soul. Never will. Even if she's a five-foot she-devil from grade school."

"Middle."

"Middle what?"

"Middle school. Not grade school. Now drive."

They continued on to Mid-State. A comatose man needed transport to Albany. As the man was stable and unconscious, he wouldn't occupy Adam much. It would give Stephenson ample time to tease.

"Come on, Garfinkle. You've got to see the humor in it. If it was anyone but Vicious Vicky, I'd caution you about having her in the same house." Stephenson laughed once more. His genial nature was as refreshing as the crisp morning air -- clear and promising a beautiful day. Even when he aimed his jokes at Adam.

Adam chuckled. "I'm not laughing with you. If God is, indeed, merciful -- you and Justine will pick her up this evening and hide her among your brood. One more person won't matter."

"You know Justine would take Torie in if she could, but she stripped all the wallpaper out of the nursery. Says we're done with kids. The furniture's stuffed in the spare room and boxes line the living room wall. Of course she starts this at the end of the school year with tests, portfolios, and report cards. Then she gets panicked parents who decide now's a good time to take an interest in their kids' work. It'll be a mess until the Second Coming." Stephenson chuckled. "With this timing, God may be learnin' ya a lesson or two. Torie might live with you forever."

Forever? There were moments Adam hated Stevenson's sense of humor.

The next call offered no relief. A woman complained of chest pains. She refused treatment when they arrived at Mid-State. They attended to an alcoholic with tremors, a mother whose child had a headache, and one fender-bender. Those were the interesting calls.

The day dragged.

At six, he visited Pop, brought Neema dinner and nagged her -- fruitlessly -- to go home. By seven, he pulled up to his cabin.

A dim light shone in the spare bedroom -- nowhere else. At least he'd have a little quiet. He'd grab a bag of chips, a bottle of Coke, and catch up on his back issues of *Field and Stream*.

He steeled himself for the discomfort of sharing his life with Torie and pushed open the door to a quiet cabin.

His roommate had squirreled herself away in her room, and the house lay in silence.

The nightlight glowed in the kitchen and a full pot of coffee sat in the carafe. It smelled fresh -- not burnt like the stuff at the station after sitting all day.

Adam poured a cup and grabbed his Cremora. Then he remembered Torie had bought a quart of half and half. He yanked open the refrigerator. There, swathed in plastic wrap, sat a plate heaped with spaghetti and meatballs. A note lay on top. *Microwave for two minutes.*

Like I haven't lived on nuked food since becoming a paramedic.

He heard nothing from her room. Maybe she went out and left a light on.

The food, homemade and basic, tasted wonderful. He cleared his plate, stuck it in the dishwasher, and went in to shower.

Her underwear, sweatpants, and shirt, hung over the shower rod and dripped in his tiny stall. He'd have to tell her she could use his laundry -- even for her few items. With everything dripping wet, Torie had nothing to wear but the pajama pants and t-shirt he loaned her last night. He tossed her clothes in the dryer.

Maybe living with her would be easy.

He grinned. *Easy? Torie? I guess God still worked miracles.*

Chapter Nineteen

"Our life dreams the Utopia. Our death achieves the Ideal." Victor
Hugo

"So how'd your evening with your girlfriend go?" Stephenson
shoved over a box of donuts.
Say nothing. Say--
"Well?"
This was going to be a *long* day.
"Didn't see Maya."
"Maya?" Stevenson opened his mouth, then shut it.
"You said *girlfriend*. Who else could you be referring to?"
"Vicious Vicky, of course."
Adam rolled his eyes. Stephenson would continue his jibes until
someone needed his attention. Five minutes later, two cars collided
outside Schoharie. They hopped in the truck and took off with lights and
sirens as needed. Adam studied the scenery. Like dealing with a vicious
dog, he avoided all eye contact with Stephenson. Gave nothing to bait
him, to keep him teasing.
Once they arrived on the scene, gawkers crowded the EMS workers.
With only a single lane open, traffic backed up. The EMTs had already
packaged the victims who suffered from back and neck pain.
Stevenson and Adam chatted a moment or two with the fire chief,
eased around the wrecks, and headed for the intersection of Route 443
and 30A -- a good central point for incoming calls.
"So how's your grandfather?"
Adam glanced at the dash clock. "Says he won't use his new cane."
"Sounds like Harold. When's he coming home?"
"Around noon. My grandmother called late last night. Said all was a
go."
"Grace better take care of herself."
Adam shuddered as the breeze blew through his open window -- he
wished Stephenson would tease him. Not talk about Neema.

*****

Torie stared at the phone. "How stupid are you?" she whispered to
Bobby. She put the phone back to her ear. "I promise, this will be the last

time I beg for help." Torie struggled to keep the desperation out of her voice. "I know you just got home yesterday. I've got to get my stuff, or I'll be naked."

In the background Torie heard a baby cry -- sounded like a cat in pain. Its noise made her palms itch. Did Adam stock something to drink? A little help to calm her down?

God. I can ask Him. Celeste said I can ask Him anything. She rummaged through cabinets while she strained to make out the words of Heather's higher-pitched voice in the background. "...Be nice...my friend...get out of my hair."

The cabin held no booze. Adam had drunk it all.

God probably thought shelter at Adam's would be enough to lift her stress, but she couldn't let her guard down. Darren taught her to never get too comfortable. The other night proved it. He'd approached her, ran his arm over Jean, draped it around her shoulder, dropped it toward her chest.

Darren leered at Torie like he used to. He chatted like an old friend until Torie told Jean how she disgusted her for taking up with the sleaze-ball.

Her old vocabulary clogged her throat. Torie used the terms disgusting and revolting and slimy instead.

Those words made him nearly re-break her ribs, and how did mommy-dearest defend her? Left her alone with Darren like she hadn't learned how effective the tactic had been in the past.

Torie wandered around Adam's tiny home as Bobby argued with Heather. He hadn't hung up, so he might still have a sliver of mercy.

"Hey, Torie, what's going on, hon?" Heather's sweet voice gave Torie hope.

"How's the..." She couldn't say the b word. "Bobby? The new Bobby?"

Heather's laugh settled Torie's stomach. "He's an angel. Just wait until you have your own. It's heaven."

Torie forced a smile, but Heather couldn't hear her grin. Yet words wouldn't come.

"Mom's a dream. Bobby'll get you. It'll get him out of Mom's hair. Her and Bobby don't get along so good." She laughed again. "Big Bobby. Should've thought about the confusion of two Bobbies when we named our little Pooh-Bear. Where are you?"

How could Torie answer?

*****

95

The radio crackled. "Benedict, Stephenson, you guys in the area of Stewart's on the Schoharie-Westfield Road?"

"Affirmative," Stephenson responded.

"Code three. Woman down in the store. Apparent cardiac arrest."

Stephenson turned on the lights. "Hang on, Benedict." He made a U-turn in a gas station parking lot.

"Are you going to head back through the traffic jam?" Adam asked. "The gawkers will still be looking for gore."

Stephenson shook his head. "I know the shortcuts." He hit the sirens. "That's why I'm the driver and you're just a paramedic." He swerved up a side road and hit a bump so hard, Adam bounced in his seat.

"Good thing I'm not starting a line. I'd amputate the arm with this driving."

"Not you. Besides, I'm easy when I gotta be."

Within five minutes, they pulled up to Stewart's, ahead of the fire trucks. The lot stood empty except for two cars.

Adam's stomach flip-flopped. One of the vehicles was a black Lincoln. Impeccably kept. He shuddered. *Lots of black Lincolns.* Grabbing his bag, the O2, and the heart monitor, he and Stephenson raced the gurney toward the store.

Sale signs covered the plate glass. Adam couldn't take in a preliminary assessment.

Stephenson swung the door open. Now the cot and his partner blocked Adam's view.

Between the register and the candy shelves, a woman lay on her back on the floor. The store manager straddled her body. His torso blocked the patient's face as his arms pumped like a superhero on the latest medical drama.

Adam didn't need to see the victim's face. He recognized the shoes. Sturdy. Cushioned. Tied orthopedic shoes worn with a dress. Neema always wore dresses. His mouth dried. He couldn't swallow. Or breathe.

No.

Not her.

"You're going to be okay." A woman hovering near his grandmother stepped away as Adam and Stephenson scooted into position. "EMS is here. So you're going be okay, ma'am."

"I've got it now. Thanks." Inhaling to quiet his racing heart, Adam nudged the store manager aside. No time to think of himself -- to worry. He knelt and studied Neema's blue lips. Moisture coated her gray skin as though she'd just been pulled out of a pool. He checked her pulse. Irregular, but strong enough.

"Adam." His grandmother's voice was thready. Barely a whisper.

"Shh, Neema, no talking now." He placed the non-rebreather over her face set at fifteen liters per minute. "We'll get you to the hospital. Let you bunk in the same room as Pop."

"Pop. Need to pick him..." Her eyes closed, and her voice came out in wisps, almost inaudible over the hiss of oxygen.

"Shhh. Let me work. Any pain?"

Her hand fluttered to her chest. "Like. Harold. Was. Sitting." Her eyes belied her attempted humor. They told him she knew.

"On a scale of one to ten? Ten the worst. How bad's the pain?"

"Eleven."

A fire truck roared into the lot, sirens blaring.

The volunteers would be careening in soon. He loosened her blouse, wiped her damp skin with gauze while Stephenson fastened the blood-pressure cuff, and placed the stethoscope to his ears.

Adam attached the EKG patches and swallowed hard as he read the results. PVC's. He guessed ten to twelve a minute. *Couplets. Bad, bad, bad.*

He pushed the button to run a strip. Heart attack. No doubt. Not a small one.

"One-oh-five over fifty." Stephenson removed the stethoscope.

"Okay. Not great." Adam slipped a nitro tablet under her tongue and glanced at the clock. Ten-oh-five. He scribbled the time of the dosage on his hand. "Any headache, Neema?"

She nodded.

"Ready to go?" a volunteer asked.

"Going to start a line first." Adam grabbed his tubing. Worked by instinct. His grandmother's skin was as thin as a dried flower petal. Her veins rolled. With the first prick, he nabbed a vein. "Lidocaine!"

One of the EMTs handed it to him. He infused it into the line.

Radios crackled. EMTs stood at the ready. Some assisted. Others stood prepared to work. "You okay?" "I got the doors." "All packaged?" Their questions swirled, but they had arrived too late.

He had been too late.

"Let's go." Adam stood.

Together, Stephenson and he lifted his grandmother onto the gurney. She had withered away over the last twelve years. Had never recovered from the loss of her only child and his family. Had wanted a house full of grandchildren and happy voices. Had to settle for one.

"You're coming with me," Adam called to the two EMTs who locked the gurney into the rig.

She wouldn't crash. Couldn't die. Wouldn't. Just in case, he needed the men.

The front door opened. Slammed. The engine engaged. Sirens wailed. They raced full throttle.

Adam ran the D5W into the IV while another EMT checked her pressure.

He took his grandmother's hand and studied the monitor. The heartbeats were uncontrolled. He infused more Lidocaine.

"Don't worry. I'm ready." Neema's voice was softer than before.

He looked at her and inhaled to steady his breathing. "Don't say that." He studied the monitor. Triplets. The PVCs were wide and tall. Came too fast.

"Promise me." The words came in gasps between clenched teeth.

"Anything." He bit his lip as tears blurred his eyes. He wouldn't lose control. Couldn't. She knew he'd take care of Pop. She didn't need to ask. "Get back to the Lord."

He jolted upright.

"Promise?"

He nodded. He'd do anything, say anything to keep her alive. "I do."

They screamed into the ambulance bay. The EMTs swung the rig's door open, and the firemen unloaded the cot, the monitor stowed between Neema's legs. As they raced through the ER doors, Adam ran another strip. The gurney clacked between firemen. Nurses swarmed. He briefed them. They took over. A doctor arrived within seconds.

"She had three nitro." Adam jogged alongside, updated them with the latest BP, handed them the EKG strips. They disappeared into the exam room.

He now stood. Her life out of his hands. He'd hoped to have saved her. It was his job -- to save her. Even as he answered their questions, he knew he had failed. He didn't get her here in time.

Didn't need to be a doctor to know it.

Adam glanced at Stephenson. "I've got to file the PCRs."

"How can you do paperwork now?"

"How can I not? They've got to know what I did. They won't let me in with her. I'll keep busy. Wait for good news I can take to Pop." Adam turned and hoped the minutiae of record keeping would make him not think.

He stared at the forms. The lines blurred together. He clicked his pen open. Clicked it shut. Looked at the door.

"Harold still in the hospital?"

Adam nodded. "Supposed to come home." He looked at the clock. "Now."

"He can't stay alone, can he?"

"For a while -- my grandmother never left him for long."

"How long?"

"Hour or so." He wrote. Clicked the pen. Wanted to punch the wall.

"I'll phone Justine. We'll get the prayer line going for Grace."

Adam closed his eyes, sucked in a breath. He hoped prayer would work, but he had treated Neema. He knew.

Chapter Twenty

"Every man must do two things alone; he must do his own believing and his own dying." Martin Luther

Torie now stood on the deck, phone to her ear. "Bobby, I told you, I don't know the address. There's no mailbox on the porch or cabin or anywhere. Not even another house. Let me look around the back." The spring sunshine spotlighted her, should have gladdened her. Instead, it melted her into the porch. Stupid boondocks.

She wandered toward the driveway, inspected every inch of the cabin's siding for the house number. In the earpiece Baby Bobby squalled. "We're on a hill between Burnt Hollow and Westfield. I think on Baitsholts Road."

"You're no help."

"Robert Vanderslew, I am *not* deaf. Can't you simply drive down the road and get me?"

His string of curses hurt her ears. Made her glad she gave up cursing -- since Sunday.

"Quit being a jerk and give me a minute." She stepped onto the driveway and flicked at a speck on her hand. Tiny. With legs. Torie screamed, dropping the phone as she danced across the roadway. "A tick. A tick." She slapped her arm and imagined herself dying of Lyme's. The dance of terror ended when she hit the grass on the far side of the narrow roadway. Venturing off the pavement would shove her deeper into tick territory. She inspected her arm. The bug was gone. Fortunately, her yoga pants covered her legs, but flip-flops exposed her toes.

She examined every inch of her bare feet, then her arms in the t-shirt Adam lent her to sleep in. Assured no tick stuck to her, Torie picked up the phone. Bobby had hung up.

Great.

Picking her way back to the cabin, Torie tiptoed across the low grass, her eyes trained on the green blades hoping to see a tick or a spider or a mouse or a bear before it attacked her. Adam's place was only one step better than the lean-to.

As though to punctuate her revulsion, she walked into a spider web.

Swiping her face, she dashed up the porch steps and into the cabin. Safely indoors, she wanted to slam the door, lock it behind her and barricade it.

Bobby'd never find her burrowed in her bed. Instead, Torie nabbed her Kate Spade purse and house keys, exited and tiptoed across the grass. Down the driveway -- about fifty miles away -- and out to the street, someone had to have an address.

Once on the road, she called Bobby and read the address off the mailbox. Plopping down on the edge of the blacktop -- off the tick-grass -- Torie filed her nails.

With one hand manicured, she wandered into the middle of the road. No truck headed her way. She sat back down. Filed the other hand. Two cars passed. No Bobby. Another phone call produced voicemail.

A half-an-hour later, Bobby showed up.

"Glad you found me." Torie hoped to add a little humor as she climbed into the truck.

Bobby turned on the radio.

"You turn left at Route 443."

"Ain't stupid."

Why'd she pick jerks for friends? She thought of herself and bit her lip. Hopefully, God would change her like Celeste promised He would.

Within five minutes, Bobby pulled into Selene's empty driveway.

Empty? But it was Tuesday.

Trey would be at work. Curly Girls only closed on Sunday and Monday.

Maybe Selene had an emergency shopping trip.

Selene. Her betrayal hurt the most. Darren taught her how to handle men once their hormones caught on fire. Tease enough, promise what you didn't intend to deliver, they were putty in your hands.

Women? Selene was her sole female friend. Except for Heather, but Heather loved everyone. Torie had loved Selene more than her own sisters -- sisters she had given everything for.

God, it hurts.

Her silent plea startled her. Somehow, she understood God knew betrayal, and the thought comforted.

"You getting out or did I drive you here so you could sit in the truck all day?"

Torie startled, but she didn't look Bobby's way. She climbed out, fished through her purse for her keys, and approached the house like a soldier to battle.

No one answered her knock. Or the bell. The silence confirmed what the empty driveway had shown her.

She wiggled a key into the lock. It didn't turn. She checked her key ring. She, indeed, held the gold key labeled home. *Selene changed the locks.*

My stuff's in there, and she changed the stupid locks.

The weight of Selene's treachery weakened her knees, and Torie leaned against the door.

The salon? Hope fluttered as Torie scurried to the salon doors. Tried the locks. The same thing.

She looked over her shoulder at Bobby and lifted her arms in question.

He got out of the truck and slammed the door, but didn't approach. "What now?" he yelled.

Why sweet Heather liked this guy, she didn't know. Opposites. "I'm locked out."

"Well get back in the truck. Let's go."

"Wait."

Bobby rolled his eyes, crossed his arms, and leaned against his pickup.

Ignoring his temper tantrum, Torie walked to the back of the house and tried the kitchen door. Locked, too. She peered through the door's glass and saw no one. The kitchen window was open, though.

She hurried to the side of the house and waved to Bobby who, aside from lighting a cigarette, hadn't moved. "Come here."

With hands in jeans, and cigarette clenched between his lips, he sauntered around the corner and stood beside her.

"Give me a boost."

"A what?"

"A boost. Look, you're over six foot. I'm a smidge over five. I don't weigh a hundred pounds. Do this." She laced her fingers together, palms up. "This screen always falls out. Trey promised to fix it. Never did."

"With your ribs?"

"They're getting better."

"Forget it."

Torie crossed her arms and scowled as Bobby stomped away.

"I'm not going down for a B and E," he growled without looking at her. "If you want in, do it yourself, and I'll be long gone."

"It's not a break-in. I paid rent."

Bobby had already disappeared.

Torie gnawed her cuticle. Climbing through a window was a stupid idea. She eyed the back door.

Windows broke.

In the backyard, an ancient tree had shed a hefty limb. Torie hoisted it, poised it like a baseball bat, and funneled her fury at the back window. The resulting spiky shards like the teeth of a Sesame Street monster could be picked out.

"Torie! What did you--" Bobby rounded the corner of the house as she began her dentistry, extracting those jagged teeth from the back door window.

"Shut up. It's my house until June first. I'll leave her twenty bucks to get the window fixed. I'm heading to the kitchen."

She reached through the broken pane, unbolted the deadlock, opened the door, and stepped into the kitchen. Rifling through her purse, she dug out a rumpled twenty and waved it in front of Bobby who had trailed behind her. "Happy?" She slapped it on the counter.

Although Torie'd been gone a little over a week, her home felt foreign. Selene's Fiestaware still sat in orderly rows behind glass-door cupboards, the Corian countertops gleamed as they always had, and the stainless steel appliances stood without a smudge. All as she had left them. None hers to use. She licked her lips and longed to be here, cooking with Selene and Trey.

Selene and she would stay up half the night watching The Cooking Network or studying recipes online. They'd bought every spice God ever created. Selene stuck to the ordinary -- garlic or sage. Torie loved the less common --tarragon or saffron. Trey loved her cooking.

Too bad he loved to cook up more than food with Selene.

"You gonna stand around all day?" Bobby startled her.

Without turning, Torie shook her head and hit the stairs.

Nothing had changed in her room, either. Her bloody clothes lay on her bed. The closet stood open. First, she had to get out of her ratty clothes. She slipped on a denim skirt and tank top. Thought about the spiders and ticks in Adam's yard, Torie dug out her ballerina flats.

"Hurry it up!" Bobby yelled from the bottom of the stairs.

Torie took her time, and stripped the pillowcases from her pillows, and stuffed them with as many clothes as they would hold. "Take these to the truck," she yelled down to him and left the bags on the landing.

Bobby, who despite his protests about being an accomplice, stomped up the stairs.

"These your things?"

"I'm not a crook, Robert."

He clomped back down.

From the bathroom closet, Torie nabbed a few more pillowcases and filled them with the last of her toiletries, careful to take only her own. She'd done a lot of stuff in her life, but would not be accused of thievery. Pilfering was her mother's M.O. She hauled the cases out to the truck where Bobby sat, fiddling with his phone.

"You think you could've come back and helped?"

He glared for an instant and returned his attention to his phone.

"Get in."

"Got to get my hair stuff."

He snarled something -- probably obscene.

Back in the salon, Torie studied her supplies. Selene had made good use of them in the week Torie slept in the hospital and the woods. Her stock had dwindled, and her hot irons and straightners jumbled together, their wires a rat's nest.

She shoved curling irons, blow driers, her container of scissors into a plastic crate and hauled them out to Bobby.

"You ready yet?" He blew out a stream of cigarette smoke mingled with whiffs of beer he had open on the console.

Torie squinted and studied him. The thought of flattering this fool's ego churned her stomach. He had the rugged, square jaw like Darren's, but lacked the lecher's brilliant blue eyes. Bobby's unshaven chin needed to be groomed. It was growing out into a disheveled beard like a crazy hermit's. His brown eyes narrowed in anger. His face already took on the haggard look of an alcoholic.

She turned back to the house. "Need my mail."

In her mail would be her court date. She had to buy a car. Had to pay her fine, or she'd never be allowed to buy a car. *Didn't cops send APOs or APBs or AP somethings out to dealerships? Will I have to buy a car with an alcohol blow-pipe thing in the ignition?* They'd cost a bundle. *I gotta live cheap.*

She rifled through the salon desk for business mail. Then thought better of it. Selene had used her stuff. Torie no longer had a job here. None of these bills were her responsibility.

In the main living room, Torie pulled open a desk drawer and sifted through a pile of opened bills.

The door rattled, and Selene stormed into the room with Trey trailing her. "What are you doing here?"

Torie bit off a chuckle at her friend's self-righteous outrage. "What do you think?" She turned back to the desk and yanked open another drawer. "Do lawyers get lots of vacation days, Mr. Trey Currey, Esquire?" Torie injected all the venom poisoning her blood into her words. She refused to look up from her quest.

"This is breaking and entering, Torie. Call the cops, babe," Selene said to Trey.

"The police number is 5200." Torie shuffled through envelopes. "Seeing as it isn't the end of the month, I live here. I only took my stuff -- unlike you who used my products in the salon. I won't call the cops on you." She slammed the drawer shut, winced as the action jarred her ribs and turned empty-handed.

Her eyes caught Trey's. He looked haggard, his skin pasty and his luscious hair disheveled. His arms hung at his sides. One hand gripped his cell phone. "I'm going to lie down." He tossed the phone on the couch and left.

Torie turned her head and watched as he lumbered out of the room. "Hungover?"

"None of your business." Selene scooped up the phone and pressed in numbers.

"Where's my mail? Stealing another's mail is a crime."

Selene quit dialing and stuffed the phone into her back pocket.

"Coupled with locking me out of my paid-up apartment, stealing my products, looks like you're in big..." Torie hesitated, thought about the stones she was throwing. "Never mind."

Selene pushed her aside and stormed into the kitchen with Torie close behind. Selene yanked open a cupboard, snagged a stack of mail, catalogs, and magazines bound with a rubber band. She slapped it into Torie's hands. "Change your address."

"Done."

"Now get out."

Torie narrowed her eyes. Her heart expanded to bursting. Her hands balled under the pile of mail. She wanted to toss it down, grab Selene by the hair, and slap her.

Two days ago, God had forgiven her. Her -- and all the petty things she did her whole life. According to the preacher who prayed with her once the sanctuary cleared, even the big things Torie had done had been washed away in the blood of Jesus. Blood? Yuck. Someday she'd understand the gory image. Having been given mercy, didn't Selene deserve the same?

Still, forgiving hurt. Whacking Selene's face or pulling her hair would satisfy more.

Instead, Torie squared her shoulders, looked Selene in the eyes. "It's my pleasure. After you give me my cooking spices."

"Your what?" Selene sputtered.

Torie opened the spice cabinet and pulled out her supplies.

"What did *you* do!" Selene's bellow was not a question.

Torie looked where Selene had pointed. "I'm not a vandal." She pointed to the money on the counter. "Take it out of the rent you owe me if it comes to more. Have Trey make himself useful and fix the glass."

"He's been sick. Been having killer headaches."

Torie twirled her finger. "Stop being drunks." She slammed the cabinet shut. "Next time, use the legal process to evict someone."

She stuffed the spices into a plastic bag, tied it into a knot, and took a slow, dignified step to the kitchen door. Took a second. Then another. It required all her restraint not to run to Bobby, throw herself into him, and beat his chest in frustration -- even though he hadn't bothered to come to her aid. It didn't matter if he hated her. Once he held her, he'd turn male and want to protect.

Instead, she opened the truck door, climbed into the passenger seat. Eased the door shut and strapped herself in.

"I have one last favor, Bobby."

He ground his teeth loud enough for her to hear.

Leaning into him, Torie softened her voice. "You've been so good to me. Such a..." She let her voice drift, lowered her lashes, and felt his muscles relax under her hand. All men were the same. "Would you drive me to the post office so I can change my address? Afterward, I can walk wherever I need."

She hoped it'd be to The Stadium -- for work *and* pleasure. She deserved a drink for listening to God.

*****

Adam approached his grandparents' porch, his legs heavy, holding Pop's new cane -- which he refused to use. With his hand on Pop's back, Adam helped him up the rickety steps. The undertaker had taken Neema away. Pop had been discharged. Now, the new life hovered in the shadows.

The empty life.

The porch door clanged shut behind him, bounced once and settled. His grandfather lost his balance and stumbled.

"Pop!" Adam grasped his arm. His farmer's arm. At one time it had been muscled. Now? Skinny and wasted. "Let me help you."

His grandfather shrugged him off, settled into his chair on the porch and began a long, slow rocking. He stared out the side screen. "Was supposed to be me." He looked at Adam with eyes clouded with tears.

No words formed. He could do nothing but sit opposite Pop, and stare into his eyes. In their depths, Adam saw death, and pain. Loss. Sobs choked Adam as he struggled for composure.

Pop gasped.

"You okay?"

"Just can't catch a breath to sigh. It's hard not to be able to sigh." Adam leaned in to hear the soft words, and Pop's tears wet his own cheek. "I'm pretty selfish, ain't I?"

Adam shook his head. "How so?"

106

"Wantin' ta go first. Be spared the sorrow of losing yer reason for life."

Sorrow choked Adam. He scooted his chair close to Pop. They sat in silence and stifled their tears.

Adam studied the floorboard, felt as though Lidocaine flowed through his arteries -- numbed his nerves with each pulse. Helplessness paralyzed him.

At last, Pop spoke. "God's been merciful to us, so far. Won't desert me now."

Again the talk of a merciful God. God showed no mercy. He took the caregiver and left Pop alone to fend for himself. Neither of them could survive without Neema.

Chapter Twenty-One

"For he shall have judgment without mercy, that hath shewed no mercy; and mercy rejoiceth against judgment." James 2:13

At a stainless steel table in the post office, Torie rifled through her mail to find the DUI ticket, marked the guilty plea and wrote out a check for two-hundred-fifty bucks. After subtracting the funds from her seven-hundred-dollar balance, she turned to the window. The line snaked through the Burnt Hollow post office. Everyone had multiple packages and special delivery letters. If Torie didn't get in line now, she'd never blow this joint.

The rest of the mail could wait.

Her turn at the window came. "I need a post office box."

The clerk stamped forms and hauled away an oversized package from the last customer. Had he heard her? She opened her mouth to speak.

"Thirty-four dollars -- a half-a-year." The clerk never looked at Torie.

Relief loosened her muscles, and she bit back a smile. Not too bad a price. She forked over the money and her envelope holding her guilty plea, and asked for the change of address form.

Back at the stainless steel table, she filled out the paperwork and shuffled through the rest of her mail. The renewal for her hairdresser license and a towing bill mingled in the stack. She couldn't pay it all. Not right now. She needed to work, and would rather do hair than wait tables. Some salon job would come up, so she wrote out a forty-dollar check for her license. The tow company could keep her car.

In the pile came a notice needing her signature. Torie had to hit the line once more and sign for whatever so-called important document awaited her. Probably an arrest warrant.

Tossing her bills into the mail slot, and the junk into the recycle bin, Torie once more took her place at the end of the line. She counted ceiling tiles as it snaked forward. Bored with counting, Torie checked her watch. Five minutes? She shook her head.

The legal notification she had to sign for had come from the DA. She stepped off the line and tore open the envelope. It told her half of what she already knew. Darren was out of jail and living in Westerlo.

Eight miles away. At least she wouldn't run into him every day.

Time to hit the parking lot. Bobby had to be having conniption fits after all this time.

Outside, no pickup. She strode around the lot, glanced down the street. She threw up her hands. Men. She paced the lot for five minutes and checked the road. Bobby must've run an errand.

Nothing.

And nothing to do but call Heather.

Heather picked up on the fourth ring. "Hey, hon. What's up?"

"Bobby drove off." Torie ground her teeth, then breathed in as much air as her ribs would allow in order to calm her voice. "Do you know where he is?"

"No, sweetie. I'll call him." Heather clicked off.

Torie looked up at the sky, and opened her mouth to scream. Shut it. The sunshine mocked her. "This is a day for porch sitting with a glass of wine," it said. Instead, Torie slumped against the brick post office, stranded in downtown Burnt Hollow.

Ten minutes later, her phone rang.

"Torie, honey, Bobby just pulled in. He said you only wanted to be dropped off. I need him to help with the baby. Is there someone else you can call?" Baby Bobby wailed in the background.

"Wanted to be dropped off? How was I supposed to get home?" *The stupid pinhead.* She ran her hand through her hair. "Where's my stuff?"

"I'm sure he left it at your place." The baby now screeched like a victim in a slasher movie. "I gotta go."

Torie hung up, counted to ten then slammed her palm against the brick wall of the building and let loose a string of salty language. Words as bad as those she had condemned Bobby for using. No solace came from her crudeness. Instead, her language salted her wounds. Torie shivered and leaned her head against the rough brick of the post office.

A car pulled into the lot, but no one else milled about, so no one heard her cussing. *Please, God, help me.*

"Excuse me."

Torie jumped.

"Sorry. I didn't mean to scare you." A tall woman with a wide grin and a swinging ponytail approached.

Torie shook her head. "Didn't see you."

"Aren't you, Torie? From The Stadium?"

The woman looked familiar -- Torie would never forget her thick hair. With the proper color enhancement and the right cut, she'd have a mane to kill for. *How do I know you?* "Adam Benedict's date?"

"Good memory. I'm Maya."

"I never forget gorgeous hair."

Maya's head jerked, and her eyes squinted. She pulled the ponytail. "This?"

Torie nodded.

"If you say so." Her grin widened and revealed beautiful, white, straight teeth. A rosy blush colored her cheeks, made Torie want to open her spa -- become a fairy godmother and transform every woman into a princess. With the good bones of this woman, the job would be a snap.

Torie shifted her weight, lifted her hand in farewell and crossed the street to a mini mart. Maybe they had an ATM, and she could find out if she was going to be arrested for bad checks when the ones she just wrote had cleared.

She inserted her card and crossed her fingers, hoping the machine wouldn't swallow it and shred the card or set off an alarm or whatever these things did when the customer was overdrawn.

She exhaled hard. No drama from the money machine. Buoyed with hope, she punched the button to check her balance.

Her shoulders sagged, and she bit her lips. She had enough to cover the bills and a hundred and fifty left over. She took a hundred. *God, can You get me work? Soon.*

With cash in hand, Torie needed something guaranteed to soothe. Wandering the aisles, she searched out a four-pack of Horton's Hooch. This time strawberry.

At the front desk, the clerk bagged the carton for her. No sense looking like an alky as she tried to find her way home.

Back on the road, Torie wandered down Main Street. So many buildings stood boarded up -- if the owners cared enough to board them. Other buildings sat with broken, dirty windows. Downtown Burnt Hollow matched its name -- blackened with decay, a hollowed out town empty of almost everything like the rest of rural Albany County.

Kind of like her.

The last of her energy fled. Fatigue and pain weakened her legs. A bench sat outside an open hardware store. Torie eased herself down and buried her head in her hands.

Lord, help me.

"Hey." A car pulled to the curb. "Torie, you okay?"

Torie jerked her head up.

Maya leaned across the passenger seat and called out the window. "Can I give you a ride?"

Her heart picked up its tempo. *A ride?* "It's a distance."

"If you need to get somewhere, I've got time."

Torie's heart froze. It wouldn't sound right if she asked to be taken to Adam's. Nothing went on between her and Boy Scout, but Maya couldn't think Torie was moving in *with* Adam, as in the hot-sex fashion. No way would she make Maya believe she'd been two-timed. Being cheated on ripped a person apart. Torie knew.

"Baitsholts Road. Do you know where it is?"

Maya squinted. A smile bloomed like a morning glory. "Adam's road."

Not knowing what to say, Torie nodded.

The door lock clicked. "Climb in, and let's get you home."

They drove in silence past Grocery*World and turned up Route 443. Farms and fields and hip-roofed barns with huge double doors dotted the countryside. Houses lay scattered like children's forgotten toys.

"So do you live near Adam?" Maya asked.

Licking her lips, Torie turned her attention out the Honda's window. "It's pretty out."

"He's so sweet," Maya said, "but sometimes he's too dark. You know what I mean?"

"Dark?" She turned and studied Maya.

"Broods about..." An awkward silence filled the car.

"About me?"

Maya nodded and turned down Baitsholts Road. "And about God."

God? "Does he know God exists?"

Maya laughed. "Of course. Doesn't everyone?"

"I didn't until the other day."

"For real?"

"My family are devout degenerates. Too wasted to think about anything but themselves. In church I *knew*--" Torie clamped her mouth shut. "It was weird."

"I know what you mean." Maya's face took on a dreamy expression. "Faith is simply knowing. You *feel* God."

Torie sighed, and her body relaxed against the seat. Again, the simple thought of a God she didn't know a few days ago forced her tension to disappear. She cleared her throat. "About Adam..." Her mouth dried. Maya had to see his goodness. "He does reach out to people, even those he doesn't like. Underneath it all, he cares."

"How so?" Maya glanced at Torie.

"He took me in."

The car jerked. Maya stared at Torie, and the Honda wove across the lane. She pulled to the side of the road, and tree limbs raked the car. Maya shifted into park. "What do you mean, took you in?"

"I was..." The word homeless choked her. "I needed a place to stay." She shuffled the bag at her feet against the door. "He offered his spare room."

After a moment of silence, Maya pulled back onto the road. Her hands clenched the steering wheel.

Something compelled Torie to assure Maya about Adam's innocence and kindness. "My life had crumbled. He offered help." No need to give Maya the sleazy details. Ahead, a pile of trash bags, stuffed pillowcases, and a milk crate lay half in the road, half in the drainage ditch. Torie pointed. "See how my so-called friends helped me. Adam hates me, but he showed me more compassion than the people I hang with."

Maya turned into Adam's driveway and got out of the Civic with Torie. In silence, they stashed the belongings into the trunk and backseat, climbed back into the car, and drove the quarter mile to the cabin. She turned off the ignition and reached a hand to Torie. "God is true."

Torie fished for an answer, and her face must have shown her confusion.

Maya giggled. "With new faith, the devil will fight to make you doubt. Don't ever do it."

"I'll never forget--"

Maya squeezed Torie's hand. "You made me jealous. Insecure. Living here with Adam. God showed me *my* misjudgment. I'm proud of Adam. Not jealous. But..." She licked her lips. "Careful living in such close quarters with my hunk."

"Lunk, you mean?" Torie laughed, but Maya raised her eyebrows. "I'm not interested in him. Don't worry. My best friend..." She swallowed and decided God wouldn't want her to throw stones. "I know what living with someone can do. I promise, you have nothing to worry about."

They stepped out of the car, and Maya popped the trunk. She hauled out a milk crate.

"Just leave it here." Torie pointed to the grass and hoped no ticks would burrow into her belongings. "I'll take it in bit by bit."

"Don't be silly." Maya dragged out two pillowcases full of clothes. "Two people will halve the work."

They rounded the corner of the cabin, and Torie opened the door. "My room's to the left." She nodded to the closed door. "I double lock it at night."

*****

After loading the last of Torie's belongings onto her bed, Maya took off. Like rubbing alcohol, her initial jealousy evaporated. Quickly.

112

Coolly. Torie acted and talk rough. Blunt. Still, something underneath begged for love and understanding. Showed the capacity to love.

Adam? Her shoulders lifted in delight. Taking Torie in showed a character trait confirming her assessment of him. True religion gave to the fatherless, the widows -- and the homeless hairdressers.

On the other hand, she had to be realistic. The two of them alone in the same tiny house would lead to trouble, especially with someone as lively and exotic as Torie.

And as cute as Adam.

She shook the thought away.

Unbidden, her nerves tingled and warmth rose through her torso. Then a shiver trembled up her back as she recalled his lips on hers. Wouldn't do to let her fantasy rove while she drove. Unwinding the car's windows, the sweet smell of the countryside drifted over her. She was a Vitale, and Vitales overcame the world.

Then Torie's image rose before her. The beautiful waitress. A striking little thing. A goldfinch to her crow. A teacup poodle to Bernese mountain dog. Sensually dark, vivacious and striking.

And she was living with Adam.

Maya didn't have a prayer for keeping him.

All things are possible with God.

Refusing to fight for herself nearly ended her life. Had scarred her childhood. She glanced at her hands on the steering wheels. Time to put the gloves on and start fighting.

*****

Thanks, God, for rescuing me again. Torie pulled her hair out of the clip reigning in her curls and shook it out. She checked her image in her bedroom mirror. Despite the bangs, a gypsy stared back at her.

She dug out her gold hoop earrings. *Might as well play the part.* She grinned at the image, making her stitches pull. *Wait. I've got manicure scissors!* After grabbing them from her toiletries, Torie pulled the end of a black stitch, wiggled the scissors under it, snippd and inched the thread.

"Oww." She winced as the stitch crawled through her skin. Yanking fast like peeling off a Band-Aid didn't lessen the sting which lingered on her skin like a burn. One stitch out. This would take a lifetime and kill her in the meantime.

Something had to numb the pain. Twisting the cap off a cooler, Torie took a sip, then swigged a mouthful. More booze would work like an anesthetic.

Reinforced, she plucked another stitch. "Yeow." *What'm I going to do?*

The first time her friends had pierced their ears, they'd numbed their lobes with ice. Torie scooped a few cubes from the freezer, held them to her forehead, and swigged another drink while waiting for her skin to deaden. Once frozen, she yanked out a stitch.

Nothing but a tiny tug.

The formula works. Torie iced, chugged, and pulled. After one-and-a-half bottles of Hooch, little pink lines ran up her forehead like a zipper. Tilting her head, angling it from side to side, Torie studied the scar. Pink, teeny lines would heal.

Thanks, God. With a third cooler, Torie stepped out onto the porch, took a swig, and settled into a large, weathered Adirondack chair, one in need of a good sanding and a little paint. *Now if you could make Collin call and say I have a job.*

With her head leaning back against the chair, the warm May sunshine bathed her face. Thinking of new skin forming on her forehead and getting sunburned, she pulled off her headband, dropped it on the ground, and fluffed her bangs in place. No sooner had she resettled herself, than her phone rang.

"Torie? Collin here. Can you work Thursday through Saturday? Linda's mom's not doing well, yet."

If Torie's ribs would have allowed it, she'd have done a jig across the porch like people did at Maranatha. "Yes. Yes, yes, yes." She gulped. Didn't mean to sound so over-eager.

"Be here between three-thirty and four. You're an answer to prayer."

Torie grinned. *Me? An answer to prayer?* She squared her shoulders and puffed her chest.

Prayer gave you power. Snap your fingers get a home, a ride, and a job. If Jean had known about this prayer stuff, she would've become a Billie-Jean Graham.

She took another sip of Hooch, then jolted forward. Torie winced as she stood and ran her fingers through her hair and paced the tiny deck.

Who was she to wrap God around her fingers? She didn't know a whole lot about Him, but church had warmed her like a massage with heated rose oil. Sitting in the service, her life had dissolved. It had transported her somewhere else. Then when she gave her life to Christ?

Heaven.

Leaning against the deck railing, Torie stared at the bottle in her hand. What was she doing? Turning into a drunk like Jean and Darren? Raising her bottle high over the porch rail, she dumped the contents out like Hookskill's waterfall.

The last cooler from the pack sat by the chair. It needed to go, too.

Grabbing the cap to twist, Torie paused. With no booze hanging around, her decision to not drink would be because of circumstance -- no way to get it. If she kept some lying around and didn't touch it? It'd prove her willpower, show God's work in her life.

Taking the last bottle inside, Torie tucked the Hooch in the bottom drawer of her dresser and smoothed out her clothes over it. Scouring out her other empties, she went outside and buried them in the large trash container under other bags of garbage. It wouldn't do for Adam to find them.

Back in her bedroom, Torie lay on the bed with a magazine and crossed her leg on her knee.

Yuck. All the hair on her legs? *I'm a monkey.*

Until today she had no razors, gel, or hot water. Couldn't do much about hairy legs, before. Now? How could she show up in public wearing legs that would shame an orangutan?

Fishing in her dresser drawer for her razor, her fingers grazed the stashed bottle of booze.

Before shaving, she'd head down to the creek and drink the last bottle. It'd be out of her life. Then she'd quit for good.

Honest, God.

Chapter Twenty-Two

"For every man shall bear his own burden." Gal. 6:5

On an antique mahogany dresser in Pop's bedroom, faded photographs sat in frames -- Mom and Dad and Maizie and him. Adam picked one up, ran his hand over the glass -- pristine and clear. In this group picture, he smiled tight-lipped. His folks had just started the process for braces. Poor Maizie displayed an ear-splitting grin, unaware her baby teeth were not super-model straight or her hair was as wayward as aerosol whipped cream. Her eyes sparkled with joy which mimicked his mother's.

His folks were a handsome couple. Blond. Blue eyed. Short in stature but big on character. *Why wasn't I more like Dad? Or Mom?*

Maybe he was a little. A homeless, drunken Sullivan lived with him, too. A smile forced itself through his ache.

Sullivan -- the man who claimed to be Torie's real father. Ted or Tom or Terry Sullivan? T-something. Funny. Sullivan changed his life forever, and he couldn't recall his first name, had always called him Mr. Sullivan. He had struggled during the year he lived with the Benedicts. Went to AA. To church. Smoked like a forest fire and more than once fell asleep with a fresh cigarette between his fingers. Despite his problems, Adam's folks believed in him. Nothing proved what caused the fire. Maybe it wasn't Sullivan.

Adam set the picture back on the lace runner, another of Neema's intricate pieces of needlework. He pulled out a dresser drawer. Women's undergarments filled it. He closed it, leaned forward, his hands on the dresser top, and bit back tears. Reminded himself about his task. He'd have to find clothes for Neema to be buried in. Not now, though. Later. He pinched the bridge of his nose and closed his eyes, and wished the shock of Neema's sudden passing wouldn't wear thin. Would keep his keening hurt at bay.

As Adam turned toward the second dresser, his phone vibrated. A text arrived.

Gave Torie a ride to your place. Be careful. Proud of you.

Maya.
He needed to tell her.

Fingering the cell, Adam sank onto his grandparents' bed, covered in an old quilt. His weight on the spread sent up whiffs of lavender and mothballs. The scent spirited away the thoughts of Maya. Instead, he saw Neema sitting on the sunny porch, sewing colorful quilts stretched out on the frame. Her clothes emitted traces of the lavender gathered from her herb garden. He ran his hands over the blue and white circles of the quilt. This one she brought out each May in honor of her wedding. For sixty years, it covered her bed every summer.

Maizie would jump on this bed when they visited. Mom cringed, paddled her bum, but Neema laughed and folded down the quilt and told Maizie to jump until she hit the ceiling.

One time Neema even joined Maizie and threw out her back. Neema was laid up for a week.

Maizie never hurt herself here. Her head never grazed the ceiling, but she did break the bed boards. Pop would fix them, and next time Maizie would jump again. Never outgrew it. Didn't have the chance to mature out of it.

The cell phone slipped out of his hands. He bent to retrieve it and remembered the text. He needed Maya. Needed to hear her voice. Her wisdom. The joy of her character. He punched in her number.

"Hey," Maya said.

Even a one-word greeting sounded cheerful.

"Adam?"

His throat ached, and his lungs couldn't expel the air for him to speak.

"What's wrong, Adam?"

He squeezed the bridge of his nose -- stopped the tears.

"Adam? You're scaring me."

He drew in a breath. *Lord, give me the words.* "Neema--"

"Is she okay?"

He pinched his nose once more, but this time it didn't stop the tears.

"No." Her voice lowered in despair. "What can I do for you?"

The tears overcame him.

Maya said nothing.

"Just come to the wake. Okay?"

"Of course, I'll be there."

He gripped the phone to his ear and said nothing. Squeezing the phone was as close as he could get to hugging her. A poor substitute.

"Oh, Adam, my heart is breaking for you. Do you want someone with you now?"

He shook his head. He couldn't inconvenience Maya. "No. We're good for now."

"When are you making funeral arrangements?"

"Tomorrow."

"I'll call school and use one of my personal days. I'll be there with you."

He wanted to object. She didn't need to take time off from work to console a man she just met. He didn't protest.

With half-hearted good-byes, he disconnected his call.

He threw a suitcase on the bed, yanked open a drawer, and tossed in what he thought Pop needed -- boxers, t-shirts, jeans, flannel shirts, and socks. Enough for a few days. They didn't live so far apart. Just needed something until he figured out how to care for Pop, and keep his own sanity. Clothes until they buried...

He snapped the suitcase shut and descended the stairs. "Ready, Pop?"

"Told you. Ain't goin' no place but here."

Adam crossed his arms and scowled. "Not going to happen."

"Don't need no babysitting."

"Never said you did, but you can't stay alone."

"So you stay here."

Adam dropped the suitcase, his arms dangling. Awkward. Pop had sacrificed for him for years. Could he stay here? "I can't, Pop. I..."

"Then why'd you ask like I had a choice?" His grandfather crossed his arms. Trouble brewed. Pop looked out the side screen. Adam could hear his thoughts. *Growed man. Farmed my whole life.* He could grumble all he wanted. Neema wouldn't dream of leaving him alone overnight, and Pop knew it. Adam should stay here. Give Pop comfort as Pop had given him.

But his scanner. His clothes. Emergency equipment. Familiarity lived at his own home. What about his grandfather's needs? "Tell you what, Pop, you'll stay with me a day or two, a week at most. Let me square things away at work, figure it out. Then we'll decide where to live. For now, the guest room--" The guest room? Torie lived there. He didn't trust her to live at Neema's, unsupervised. He couldn't send her back to the lean-to.

What was he going to do?

Didn't matter. He *had* to be home.

Fishing out his cell, he texted Maya.

Can you help find a place for Torie to live?

"Let's go."

Pop stood.

Adam handed him his new quad cane. With the way Pop glared, you'd have thought Adam had handed him a snake.

In the Lincoln the silence weighted. Pop stared out the window.

His grandfather's pain tore Adam's heart. *Only a week. I'll take him home then, God. I need a few days.* His stomach roiled and heat flooded his face. Adam gripped the steering wheel.

From the curtained guest bedroom window of his cabin, light spilled over Adam's driveway. He parked behind the cabin.

Another text arrived.

Checked with Mr. H. She can stay here.

Tossing his head against the headrest, Adam closed his eyes. *Thank you, God, for Maya.*

"You goin' to sit there and sleep?" Pop fumbled with the door.

"Wait!" Adam loped around the car and took Pop's arm to help him out. Pop shook it off. Adam grabbed it.

"I kin walk. Ain't crippled."

Adam threw up his hands. Living with Vicious Vicky sounded lots better at the moment.

Pop maneuvered his cane toward the cabin. At least he used it now without arguing. Thankfully his pneumonia responded well to the antibiotics.

"The ground's uneven, and it's dark. Let me lead you until the motion lights blink on."

Pop growled -- a low rumble. Too bad. His grandfather was sure to fall and break a hip. In his condition, a fracture would be a death sentence.

They'd just stepped into the cabin when the door to the guest room popped open. Torie took one step into the living room and stopped. "What's wrong?"

Pop lowered himself onto the couch and eyed Adam's new roommate.

"My grandmother." Adam gulped. "She passed." Would he ever be able to speak those words, the real words not the euphemism, without stuttering? Without knowing his world had died, too?

Torie raced forward and threw her arms around him. "I'm so sorry. When?"

He stumbled at the unexpected embrace and stepped away. Torie dropped her arms, but her hug had comforted and made the next words a little easier. "This afternoon. I've got a problem."

Torie looked at Pop who studied her. "Are you Adam's

119

grandfather?"

"Yep. Name's Harold Benedict. Adam told me you was here. Good grandson."

"I'm so sorry about your wife." She bent over and hugged him. "Let me clean out my stuff so you have a place to sleep." She glanced at Adam. "Can I stay on the couch for tonight? Where are your sheets? I'll change--"

"Don't change nothin'. Adam's taking me home in the morning." Pop stared at his hands. His lips tightened as he rolled his fingers as though turning a pill between them. Red flags of his distress.

"No, I'm not," Adam said.

Pop raised his arm in protest.

"We don't have to worry about it now, Mr. Benedict--"

"Harold. Not Mister. My grandson will take me home in the morning. You ain't sleeping on no couch. You're in the guest room and stayin' there. What's my grandson gonna do? Throw you out on the street?"

"I wouldn't," Adam protested.

"'Course ya wouldn't. You're a Benedict." He turned his attention to Torie. "I kin sleep here." He patted the couch.

"Pop, just for tonight. Maya offered Torie a room."

Torie jerked her head in his direction; her lips parted, but she said nothing.

"Sorry, Torie," Adam said. "This place..."

"No problem." Torie sat next to Pop and slipped her hand onto his arm. "Thanks, Harold, for the offer of the bedroom." She licked her lips and tilted her head toward him. "I'd be so much more comfortable here. That bed's too hard for me."

Pop said nothing, but Adam could see Torie could charm even the old guys, and lie as she had in her school days.

"I tossed and turned all night. Got a wicked crick." She rubbed her neck and stretched as though to prove her point. She almost convinced Adam.

Pop smiled. "So you'd rather *I* wrench my neck?"

She chuckled. "Yep."

"Then I best help the lady. I'll sleep in there for one night. My grandson ain't kicking you out. From what he says, you'd been a gypsy."

"Not a homeless one, now. I like Maya. Besides, it'd look more proper me staying with another woman rather than with a man."

Pop studied Torie's face, his head nodding -- whether from tremors or thoughts, Adam couldn't tell. "I like you, Torie. You're good people."

"Like recognizes like." Torie glanced at Adam.

"Thank you," he mouthed.

*****

The smell of cinnamon and maple woke Adam at dawn the next morning. His cabin felt warm and humid, and light seeped under his bedroom door. Slipping on his robe, Adam left his room.

Pop sat at the table by the window, his back to Adam's door. Torie stood at the stove turning a slice of french toast.

The aroma of maple-cured bacon sizzling in the frying pan along with the scent of coffee made his stomach rumble.

After flipping the toast onto a plate, Torie scooped some bacon next to it, and turned to his grandfather. "Here you go. Special recipe Selene and I invented. If you don't like it, you have the taste buds of a toddler." She smiled.

Torie wore Adam's pajamas. With her sweatshirt over his tee, no make-up and hair rumpled from sleep, she looked innocent and fresh. Sexy and hot. Everything rolled into one. His body warmed, and heart pounded.

Their eyes met.

Torie scooted back to the stove. "Want some french toast?" Her tone had changed -- all business.

"Smells good." Adam shuffled through a cupboard for a coffee cup.

"Cardamom's the secret -- and a touch of ginger." Torie filled another plate with a tangle of bacon and a couple of slices of toast. She had cooked it to a delicate brown, the sprinkling of the copper-colored cinnamon perfectly spaced on bread tinted yellow from the eggs.

After doctoring his coffee, Adam took the dish from the counter and almost drooled. "Thank you."

Long lashes swept over eyes. She looked so shy and sweet when she smiled. So painfully sexy. Did she know what she was doing?

Of course. This was Vicky.

"Quit gawking like you ain't never lived with a woman before," Pop grumbled. "Sit down and eat."

Adam stumbled on the braided rug as he tried to hide the heat rolling up into his chest and neck. "We *ain't* living together."

"Then act like it. Your grandma wouldn't..." Harold raised his coffee cup, and ducked his head.

Adam looked away. Knew the grief filling Pop's chest, and turned his attention to the feast before him. He buttered the toast and poured amber maple syrup over it. Sensual thoughts of Torie fled as his mouth watered, and he chewed. Closing his eyes, Adam savored the flavors.

121

With Torie lost in her work at the stove, Adam studied her. Her high cheekbones, and full, defined lips and skin, like the gypsy her wandering life imitated. It intensified her sensuality. Yet her face, distracted with the cooking, looked angelic. He saw her in the woods -- naked in the water, huddled in a lean-to. Once more he sensed her vulnerability, and he yearned to hold her. Protect her.

Chapter Twenty-Three

"Through wisdom is an house builded; and by understanding it is established: And by knowledge shall the chambers be filled with all precious and pleasant riches." Prov. 24:3-4

Maya zipped along the Schoharie-Westfield Road. "I'm sorry I have to run as soon as I drop you off." She glanced at Torie who studied the scenery as though she had never seen a field before.

"I'm a big girl -- can take care of myself."

Torie sounded petulant, but perhaps being dumped after having a home plagued her.

"I'm not implying anything," Maya said. "It seems rude to drop you off and run."

Torie didn't answer. She shouldn't be angry, not with a home to go to. Was she sad?

Torie straightened in her seat but kept her eyes averted. "Where do you live anyway?"

"A couple of miles more. We're almost there." As if to illustrate the point, she turned right onto Soapstone Road.

"I've got to get to work at four. Do you think I can walk it?"

"To The Stadium?" She shook her head. "If you like walking. I'm five miles out."

"Maybe you can drop me off there when you head back to town."

"What will you do all day?"

"Visit. Go to the library."

Library? Maya couldn't picture Torie perusing books.

"Yeah, thought I'd take out some vegetables. Got killer asparagus a few days ago."

Maya laughed at God's irony.

"There's no need to hang out for veggies -- my landlord overloads me with them. I should be back in plenty of time. I'll drive you, unless you want to hang out all day and panhandle for vegetables. It's what?" She glanced at the dashboard clock. "Only ten."

They drove in silence, took the right where the road split into a V and turned into Craig-Hill Road.

Torie stiffened. "You don't live close to this place, do you?" She pointed at the run down trailer surrounded by sumacs and wedged between the two roads.

"Not far. A mile or two down the road."

Torie's shoulders slumped, and she leaned her head against the headrest.

At last, they turned right into a long, gravel driveway.

"We're around back." Maya parked her car next to her porch. "Come on." She hopped out and popped up the driver's seat to haul Torie's belongings.

Torie grabbed a bag and trailed her to the house.

"Here's the guest room." Maya pointed to a tiny room off the kitchen, but she talked to the air. "Torie?" Maya found her on the porch.

"It's peaceful here." Torie sat on the wicker love seat. "I like the blue pattern. Is it Vera Bradley?" She ran her hands over the cushions. "Adam's furniture could use pillows."

"I made them."

Torie's head jerked upright. Her eyebrows rose in question. "Get out of here."

"It's easy." She settled next to Torie who squished over to make room. "I can teach you."

"I doubt it." Torie stared off into the distance. "It's a cozy porch."

"When the vines grow on the lattice, it's shaded and private."

"Doesn't seem you need more privacy out here." Pushing herself up, and gritting her teeth, Torie looked at Maya. "You need to get going. Where do you want me to stash myself?"

"Stash yourself?" Maya stood. "You're not a piece of luggage." She led Torie into the minuscule kitchen and pointed to the open door off to the left. "It's microscopic. I think it used to be a pantry."

"Why?" Torie paused.

"Why what?" Maya bristled a little. Torie wouldn't complain about cramped quarters? Then she remembered her misjudgment about the library. She *wouldn't* assume the worst. Her parents had shown her so many times how misconceptions -- profiling they called it -- ruined lives. They understood their clients, their motives, the reasons for behavior.

"Would anyone imagine this as a bedroom?" Torie asked.

This woman kept the insults coming, but Maya figured she'd make a joke of it. "Keeps company scarce."

"I wouldn't have imagined it as one. It's adorable, and it works."

Maya dropped the pillowcase of clothes on the bed, and turned and grinned at Torie. "I'm going to love having you here."

"I hope it's a bit longer than Adam kept me. Or my home before his." She plopped down next to the clothes, looked up and grinned. "That one was literally in the sticks." She patted the bed. "It's comfy."

"When we pull out the trundle bed, we can hardly fit a human in here. You have to climb over one bed to get to the other. You can't open the dresser. You have to keep your suitcase in the trunk of your car. Makes dressing difficult. My folks never complain, though." Maya laughed.

"What's so funny?"

"You're supposed to ask me why they never complain."

"Because they don't visit?"

"Oh, they visit, but they stay at the Capitol Arms Bed and Breakfast in Albany. Come on. I'll give you the grand tour. It'll last one minute." Maya led her guest through the kitchen into a small living room and opened the bathroom door. "The apartment's tiny, but it's got everything I need except a washer and dryer. Got to hit the Laundromat in Burnt Hollow for clean clothes."

*****

Torie returned to her room. Maya's bedroom was slightly larger than the one she had offered Torie. An odd array of American Girl dolls adorned an armoire. Aside from them, the bedroom was sophisticated and simple and small. The apartment was a dollhouse, but immaculate and tastefully decorated with repurposed furniture painted white and stenciled in light blue Pennsylvania Dutch motifs.

For now, Torie wanted to make believe she had a home. She shut the door and sank onto the daybed. This room was homey. Like Maya.

An inexpensive scarf draped across a worn antique dresser painted in reversed colors from the living room. The dresser blue, the stencils white. Its mirror, flecked with age, distorted nothing.

Lace curtains hung at the window. A crocheted cover in ripples of blues -- midnight, royal, and aqua -- covered the bed. Torie thought if Maya stood in the middle of the room and extended her arms, she could touch both walls at the same time. Torie kicked off her shoes, curled up on the bed, and pulled the afghan over her. The soft yarn was luxurious compared to the scratchy blanket she had borrowed from Heather.

Maya knocked at the door and popped it opened. Torie jumped. She must've dozed.

"I called Adam. He needs help getting his truck back to his cabin. Doesn't want to drive the Lincoln like an old lady, so he's going to pick me up." She turned to go.

"Can he drive me to Westfield?"

Maya didn't walk away. She didn't turn. With her head bent, it looked like she studied the floor. At last, she faced Torie. "My car's in rough shape, but it's all I have. If you promise not to drink, you can

125

borrow it. I'll leave the keys on the table." The door clicked behind Maya.

Maya's letting me use her car?

It made no sense. She deserved none of Maya's... Torie fished for a word to define her new friend's generosity.

Grace. This had to be grace.

Chapter Twenty-Four

"There is none who does not lie hourly in the respect he pays to false appearance." Henry David Thoreau

Pop exhaled in a ragged gasp, clenched the arms of his rocker, and lowered himself to the seat. "Get the blue one. The one yer grandma wore on Easter."

Adam grasped Maya's hand. Its warmth percolated up his arm. Without another word, they left Pop rocking on the porch and entered the house.

"And the..." Pop's labored breath, his Parkinson's and the closed door swallowed the last of his words.

Adam popped back out. "What?"

"The lace collar. The one she attaches to her dresses to gussy 'em up."

"Sure." He turned.

"The one she wore to your folks' funeral."

Adam didn't recall what she wore. "We'll find it." He shut the door.

"And..."

Adam returned.

Pop now stared out into the side yard.

"Pop?"

He didn't turn.

Maya's hand touched Adam's shoulder, and he stepped aside. She knelt before Pop's rocker. "Tell you what. Adam and I will find everything Grace possibly needs, then show you. While we're upstairs, why don't you write down what you think of? Then we can get whatever we missed." She looked up at Adam. "Do you have some paper?"

"Keep the stuff right here." Pop pointed to a frayed wicker magazine holder. "Kin talk to me. I ain't deaf."

Adam clenched his teeth.

Maya handed Pop the writing implements and a worn Bible to rest them on. No sign of offense clouded her face or posture.

Adam's jaw relaxed.

Single file, they climbed the stairs.

Adam opened the door to his grandmother's room and the scent of lavender hit his face like a wall of memories. He wanted to crawl under the quilt and sleep until he no longer remembered. Could no longer feel.

Instead, he stood inside the doorway and stared into the room. Where to start?

The dress would be easy to find. He opened the closet. The stench of mothballs overpowered the tiny space. Neema's dresses and skirts stood color coordinated, grouped by type, and easy to search. She had no more than seven or eight. Those and Pop's one suit and dress shirt were all the closet held. He laid the blue dress on the bed.

Turning to shut the closet door, his downcast eyes noted the shoes. Caskets hid feet, but Pop would want her in shoes. "She'll need stockings, Maya." He picked up a pair of dressy shoes, then thought better of it. Neema was all practicality despite the fact she wore dresses or skirts, even when she farmed, but she liked comfortable feet. He wouldn't let her spend her life in heaven wearing heels and buckles and straps. He put down the shoes he held and chose a brown pair with laces.

After closing the closet door, Adam turned. Maya knelt with her back to him rummaging through a dresser drawer. Even as she shuffled things around, Maya moved them as though she prayed over each. The dignity in her posture contradicted the fact she had never met his grandmother.

Adam touched her shoulder.

Although her eyes showed her sorrow, her lips smiled as Maya peered up at him. "Haven't found the collar. I put undergarments with the dress. Not sure they're needed, but your grandfather wouldn't feel right if they buried Grace without them."

Adam sat near the pile of clothes, amazed at Maya's understanding of his grandfather.

"Tah-dah." Maya held up the handmade collar. "This is beautiful." She sat on the floor and draped it across one hand, and fingered the stitches with the other. "Your grandmother crocheted this?"

Adam nodded. To speak of Neema would cause his tears to flood.

"I wish I had known her. I'd make her teach me these lost arts. Grace probably even knew how to tat. I never learned that skill -- along with baking. I can write a tort, but can't bake one. I love to sew and paint. Something my folks never appreciated." She scrambled up, and her smile vanished. "Where's your iron?" Her voice turned all businesslike. "I'll wash the collar and press it."

"Downstairs." Without another word, Adam led Maya to the kitchen.

*****

The sweet scent of wet cotton steaming beneath the iron made Maya wonder why she never ironed anymore. The action soothed and delineated the lace pattern of the collar. Maya connected with Grace through the homely action.

It tied her to Adam, too.

She pictured his standing close to her in the bedroom. The heat of his skin warming her. Smelled his shampoo. How she had wanted to kiss him.

Wouldn't follow *that* train of thought. Instead, she studied each cluster of stitches as they pressed into their proper patterns. This outdated fashion needed to revive. Society lost too much in modernity.

With the collar dried and blocked and wrinkle free, Maya ran the iron over it with a few more passes. Wished to maintain the peace the simple chore provided.

After stowing the cooling iron, Maya left the kitchen and walked out onto the porch.

"Pop, you won't be able to see her yet." Despite the whispered tone, Adam's voice sounded desperate.

"I'll be near her."

"You're sick."

"Ain't dead yet, son--"

"Adam?" Maya stepped onto the porch and latched the screen behind her.

Adam jolted upright, and Harold twisted his head in her direction.

Maya took a step forward. "There'd be no harm letting your grandfather come."

"He needs his rest."

"One of my students," Maya said, "has severe spina bifida and is confined to a wheelchair."

Adam opened his mouth to say something, but Maya held up her hand. He closed his mouth.

"Nelson can't play kickball during recess but loves to go and watch, be a part of the group. He always feels better afterward. Sometimes he has to go to PT." She shrugged.

"This has nothing--"

"I ain't no--"

The men spoke simultaneously. Maya laughed. "Shh, silly boys. Let me finish."

Harold settled back on his chair.

Adam leaned against the wall.

"They figure PT gives him the exercise recess can't, so it shouldn't matter if he misses it. When Nelson misses playtime, even though he's

129

been with people, been the center of attention, his learning process flags. His academics falter."

"We're not talking about playtime," Adam said.

"The point is, health is more than the physical being. If we meet Harold's psychological needs, his health will improve. Let him come."

Before she turned away, Pop stood. "Get my hat." He toddled to the screen door.

*****

"I want to see her." Pop crossed his arms and glared at the assistant funeral director.

"Don't be difficult." Adam grasped his grandfather's arm. Pop shook it off. "She's in the middle of being prepped. You heard Mr. McCarty." Adam ground his teeth and figured at the rate he milled them, he'd need dentures before the funeral began.

"I ain't going home 'til I see her."

Maya looped her arm around Pop's stooped shoulders. "Mr. McCarty, how long until the mortician finishes?"

"Another couple of hours."

"Do you think Mr. Benedict can see his wife then?"

"Of course."

She turned toward Pop. "Let's get something to eat."

"Ain't hungry."

"I am." She winked at Adam. "At least keep me company."

Harold grinned.

Adam's tension flowed out his bones, and his cheeks relaxed. *Lunch? Peace with Pop?*

Sounded perfect.

130

Chapter Twenty-Five

"Don't be over self-confident with your first impressions of people."
A Chinese proverb

After removing the towel from her shampooed hair, Torie studied her bangs.

Gross.

She lifted them off her forehead and examined her scar. Of course the stitches hadn't faded much. Brushing her hair to the side of her head made her look a little older. Something had to be done with her stupid appearance.

Her comb raked through the snarls. Long hair. Yuck. Trey loved it, said it camouflaged her chin -- too sharp, he claimed. She had grown out her bob to please him. Now, with the comb tangled in her mane, Torie grinned. No Trey anymore. No reason to listen to his whims.

She dug out her scissors and decided to play up the bangs. Cutting with abandon, Torie added layers. Hair rained over Maya's floor as sassy angles took shape. They played up Torie's high cheekbones, displayed her small ears.

Studying her reflection, Torie angled the last layer toward her chin. "How do you like me now, Trey Currey?" With a wink at her reflection, Torie ruffled her hair. Something wasn't right.

Color. Something screaming freedom.

Torie rummaged through her supplies and grabbed the red. After mixing it, she coated a large swath of hair with the dye. No blending. Nothing natural. Just pure vixen.

Forty-five minutes later, she needed to show off the new Torie -- the bold woman no longer mourning the loss of a two-timing man. A grown-up, hot woman.

Making matters better -- she had a car.

Torie stowed her hair supplies in her closet and picked up the keys from the dresser. For an hour or two, she had a ticket to independence. She tucked the keys into her jeans then looked for her purse and stopped. Should she use the car?

Freedom flirted with her, called to her from the driveway. Life in the boonies irritated like caterpillars crawling under her skin. A shudder rippled down her spine.

Maya must have some errands.

In the kitchen, Torie opened cupboards to check for groceries, but everything was well stocked. All except for coffee. Pointless with no coffee maker in the house.

With no needed shopping, how could she kill the time before work? Or justify using the car?

Torie stepped onto the porch. She'd love to shop, get something for Heather and Maya -- but where?

Supermarkets sold gift cards. An Amazon card for Heather? Moms were always buying junk for babies, and Amazon sold everything.

For Maya? Something to brazen her up a bit. Maybe a gift for a massage?

The idea of giving and expecting nothing back made her grin.

Then Torie pouted. God was giving more than she gave because if she didn't get out of this cramped apartment, those caterpillars crawling under her skin would morph into butterflies and carry her sanity south to Mexico.

She floated to the car. At the end of the driveway, Torie signaled to turn left -- the way Maya had come. She cringed. Her hands grasped the wheel. No more than a mile down stood her childhood home. What if Darren were there? Turning right, the backroads would take her to liberty.

*****

"Dina's looks empty." Adam pulled into the Grocery*World lot where Dina's Diner sat at the far end. Since it neared closing time, the popular café had no patrons and plenty of parking spaces. Adam and Pop and Maya took a booth by the windows facing the strip mall containing Burnt Hollow's one grocer. After ordering, silence settled over them, and Adam stared out the window.

Shoppers jockeyed for parking spots closer to the supermarket. A blue Honda Civic approached. It stopped at the end of a row, waited for traffic to pass. Adam straightened in his chair. No. He had to be mistaken. The Civic turned left and displayed a gray rear fender. He wasn't wrong.

Some people never changed.

*****

Maya leaned across the table to better hear Harold who regaled her with the tale of how he and Grace had met.

"Babe. I haven't seen you in ages. How're you doing?"

Maya jerked up and peered at the speaker. The woman, looked like a super-model, wore straight-legged jeans with high-heeled, leather slouch boots and a form-fitting sweater which swept below narrow hips. It accentuated every curve in every right place. The sun shining through the plate glass window highlighted her blonde hair -- strands of it like spun gold. Beautiful.

"It's been a month," Adam said.

The woman scooted onto the bench next to Harold. "You look like you haven't been doing well, Harold." She leaned toward Adam's grandfather who picked invisible lint from his flannel shirt. She smoothed the side of his hair. Harold swatted the hand away.

"My grandmother died."

"Oh, Adam." The woman reached across the table and took his hand. Bangles clicked on the table. "What happened?"

"Heart attack." Adam pulled his hand away.

The slow movement looked reluctant. Heat tightened Maya's heart. Her breath came hard.

"Jennifer, this is Maya."

Maya forced herself to meet Jennifer's eyes. Romance-novel green eyes. Maya's hand moved to her hair. She caught herself mimicking Jennifer, twirling it. Maya dropped her hands to her lap.

Jennifer glanced in her direction. "Adam and I go way back. I always loved Gracie."

Harold grumbled.

"What, Harold?" Maya asked.

"Oh, it's just the Parkinson's." Jennifer spoke as though Harold were incapable of answering for himself. "Sometimes he mumbles."

Harold's lips thinned -- two tight, straight lines, and muttered. "Name's Grace. Not Gracie."

Maya fussed with the cuffs of her blouse while Jennifer toyed with her bangles. They caught the light and glinted while she grilled Adam about the funeral. Whenever she assumed Jennifer wouldn't notice, Maya studied the woman. Brightness radiated from Jennifer's eyes. Adam stared back at her. Did he still love her?

She turned her attention back to Harold. He now focused on the activity outside the window, but his fingers drummed the table, not oblivious to Jennifer's prattle, his irritation palpable. At least Adam's grandfather was unhappy with her presence.

Adam leaned back and crossed his arms. "Thanks for stopping by. Our food should be here soon."

As though he signaled, the waitress bustled to the table with a tray loaded with hamburgers and french fries.

Jennifer stood. "Harold, you shouldn't be eating grease." Her eyes scolded Adam. "Nor you. French fries?" She pursed her lips, then, as though resigned to the will of a two-year-old, her shoulders relaxed. "Never could teach you guys." She turned to Maya. "You should try the spinach salad here. Divine, and almost no calories." She waved. "I'll be sure to make the wake."

"Whatever you like," Adam said.

No calories? Maya looked at her plate of food. One of those fry orders was hers.

She watched Jennifer scoop salad from the bar into a takeout box. Her gaze followed her as she paid, and her appetite traipsed out the door with Jennifer.

*****

Neema looked like she slept. Looked comfortable for the first time since Adam's parents died. He stood back and held Maya's hand while Pop fussed with Neema's hair. "She don't like this style." He ruffled the part. "Said a part showed her bald spot."

"We can straighten it out, Mr. Benedict," Mr. McCarty said.

Pop fussed with his wife's hair, as though he hadn't heard. Adam wanted to make Pop stop, and make him sit. If honesty had its way, he was the one who wanted to run. Hiding would make this funeral go away.

"Did you know she always wanted red hair?" Pop didn't look up at Adam or the undertaker. "I never let her."

Adam scrolled through his brain for something to say. He squeezed Maya's hand and fought the tears threatening to erupt.

"What woulda been wrong letting her color it? I used to complain. 'You wanna run around looking like a rooster?' What would it've hurt?"

"Grace understood." Maya released Adam's hand to step forward, but Adam refused to let it drop, and his arm held her back. She re-tightened her grip and stood behind Pop.

"How kin she die and leave me living?" His gaze never left his wife's face.

Maya caressed Pop's shoulder, but his grandfather shrugged it off.

Losing his balance, he grasped the casket with one hand and held the other up to fend off help. "I ain't as strong as her. I shoulda told her. If I had, she wouldn't of died. How could she?"

Adam gulped. His throat closed off, and he choked. His nose ran. Pulling his hand away from Maya's, he snagged a tissue from a box on a neighboring table.

None of them were as strong as Neema. None of them.

*****

Maya's legs ached and a smile teased at her mouth as she stood with Harold. She bit her lips and tried to look more solemn, but she found it funny. She was almost twenty-four, and she wanted to sit. Adam already succumbed to the need and took a chair in the back of the room. Harold, the weak one, stood, staring at his wife.

Harold's face told the story of his love. At times his lips twitched in smiles, and at others, they quivered. Memories of their lives, their victories and losses had to be playing out. He'd let go of the coffin for a moment and run his hand over one of his wife's features. He wobble, then grasp the casket edge once more. His other hand never let go of his wife's.

If I knew what to say. She peeked over to Adam, wished he'd tell her how to comfort. *Lord, help me.*

Harold glanced at her, then back at his wife. "Good-bye, Grace. I'll see you on Sunday." He bent over and kissed the impassive face. His lips lingered. When he turned to Maya, his eyes glittered. He patted her hand. "You *know* how to comfort. My grandson better not let you get away."

What did I do? His pale eyes showed no jest, but she had done nothing but be present.

Harold was wrong. He, not she, knew how to comfort.

They trundled off to the Lincoln. Inside, the car's atmosphere held a grief Maya breathed in. Adam rubbed her hand, and the gentleness erased pictures of Jennifer. Harold didn't like Adam's ex. He had made it clear. In an emotion transcending jealousy, Maya didn't like her either.

A pulse jumped along Adam's jaw, and his eyes looked glassy. Maya shifted her hand from under his and opened her mouth to speak, but the inanity of words couldn't tell him how much she cared about him. Words didn't erase the pain of losing someone he loved. It was a pain she'd never faced.

She studied her arms, the scarred skin flowing under her sleeves. Self-pity was a sin, not just against herself but against God. She bit back her words of repentance once more. God already forgave her. But what if Adam found out? What would he think? Self-absorbed? Ungrateful? Her parents had saved her from a broken life, after all.

No. She wouldn't think of *her* past.

She squeezed Adam's hand and felt it relax beneath her grip.

Then he slid it away and stared out his side window as they passed

Westfield's Ready Mart.

*****

Adam relished Maya's silence. Most women he knew would chatter and fill the space with meaningless babble. He needed quiet. Hoped he'd make it back to her apartment without his heart erupting.

Pop, too, sat in silence and kept his eyes glued on the passing scenery.

In downtown Westfield, a blue Civic sat in the Ready Mart lot making Adam's nerves crackle like electricity in a thunder storm. *That woman.*

*****

Torie walked up one aisle of the Ready Mart and down the next. Where did the store stash baby formula?

After her third or fourth pass down the aisle, she found it tucked between diapers and face wipes. *Twenty bucks?* She gasped and scanned the shelves looking for something cheaper.

Nothing.

Heather better appreciate this. Tips didn't cover much. By the time she hauled herself back to Heather's, Baby Bobby was screaming and squirming in Heather's arms.

"Torie, hon, hold Bobby for me. He's hungry. I gotta fix this." Heather handed off the red-faced, squirming bundle and took the plastic bag holding the formula.

Torie grasped the baby in stiff arms. They wouldn't curl around the child. Refused to relax. She forgot to breathe and cursed her friend. Heather could've at least waited until she sat. What if she dropped the kid?

Bobby yowled like a mating cat as Torie sunk onto the edge of the couch. His little eyes, squeezed almost shut, looked like those of a cat's newborn offspring. His mouth pursed in an angry scowl. *Is he gonna pass out?* Terror twined its tentacles throughout her.

She twisted around to check Heather's progress, but her friend had her back to her. Torie's stomach churned. She had told everyone she hated babies, but, for some reason, wanted to make this angry, squirming creature, happy, while not dreaming of what would never be.

She stuck the tip of her finger in his mouth. The silence it caused made her smile, but it didn't take long for Bobby to figure out the finger didn't produce food. He grimaced. Then caterwauled. His cry could

136

wake Adam's grandmother.

"Jeepers, Heather. What are you doing? Milking a cow?"

"Torie, hon, it takes time to get the formula right. I've got to run cool water over it. I nuked it too long."

"How do I get him to stop his yowling?"

"Bounce him. Walk around. Come on. Work with me."

On stiff legs, Torie hoisted herself up. The infant rooted at her chest, and she panicked. Before she dropped the baby, she placed him against the back of the couch, grabbed some throw pillows, and put them between the kid and the sofa's edge. "Don't fall off," she whispered.

"What are you doing? Building a fort?" Heather brushed away the pillows. "He won't roll anyplace. Go get me a beer, will you, hon?"

Finally a command she could follow. Nabbing two, Torie settled across from Heather to better view the kitchen clock. Work couldn't come soon enough.

The beer calmed her nerves, and Bobby quieted for real. Heather leaned back on the couch, her eyes fixed on the now contented baby, her open can of beer forgotten. "Just wait until you have your own son. There's nothing like it."

Chapter Twenty-Six

"The secret of happiness is freedom. The secret of freedom is courage."
Thucydides

Torie grabbed a pile of napkins and plopped down at Trish's table. "Wait a minute." Collin stood with his mouth open, and eyes wide.

"What's wrong?" Torie smiled at him.

"Your hair."

She grabbed for it, then remembered the new cut. "You don't like it?"

He shut his mouth and tilted his head. "Wow. If I didn't love my wife so much, Victoria..." He shook his head as though chasing away his fantasy.

"So, you do?"

"Don't you adore the red?" Trish looked up from rolling silverware. "Can I hire you to do mine?"

"I'd love to." Torie picked up a new set of utensils. "Since I quit Selene's, I'd have to do it at your place."

"I like that better. I always wanted a stylist to come to my house." Collin hovered.

"We got this wrapping stuff down." Torie peered up at Collin.

He coughed. "Sorry, you mesmerized me."

"Mesmerized? Speak English," Torie tossed the rolled set of flatware into the bin and reached for more.

"Shut-up or I won't offer you Linda's job."

Torie jerked her head up, and the utensils she held tumbled to the table. "Are you serious?"

"Linda has to quit. Since her mom can't be left alone any longer, she's moving. Can you work regular hours?"

Torie leaped up, threw herself at Collin and hugged him.

"I guess you're hired." He untwined her arms. "You've got extra hours on Monday morning. I've got a funeral reception."

"I'd love to." Torie slapped her hand over her mouth and dropped back to her chair. "I don't love funerals. I mean--" Words wouldn't form. No one could know her needs -- at least not when she was sober.

"And brunch this Sunday," Collin said.

"You're turning us into slaves." Trish laughed at her joke. "No. Worse than that. You'd have to raise our pay to make us qualify as slaves."

"Get to work." He smirked and walked back to the bar.

As the women wrapped cutlery in silence, Torie dreamed of the possibilities. After counting up hours, tips, and paychecks, Torie anticipated the rent Maya would want. Food. Clothes. Full-time work would let her get a car. A car meant transportation, a home and, she glanced at Trish, a business. She wouldn't need a salon -- she'd use other people's homes.

"Trish?" Collin called from the bar. "While you guys wrap, fill Torie in on the prep needed Sunday night."

Trish grimaced as Collin turned his back.

"I saw you," he said.

Torie glanced at Collin and back to Trish. "How'd he notice?"

Trish waved her hand. "He knows, what he calls, my idiot-synchracies. If you haven't noticed, he sees everything."

"How does a reception work as opposed to a regular shift?"

"After Sunday's work stint, we wrap a billion of these." She held up a rolled napkin. "Then early Monday -- hope you're a morning person?"

Torie shook her head.

"After Sunday and Monday's untimely start, you will be."

Torie groaned, knowing Trish expected it, but inside she was willing to get up before the birds and work thirteen-hour days. Get out of the mess Selene got her into.

Trish hadn't noticed she wasn't listening.

"...Then we keep bins piled with food, and pitchers full of water." Trish plopped another pile of napkins on the table.

"Not bad." Torie preferred activity outside the house. She could paint her toenails only so many times.

"Of course you'd think so. You wouldn't if you had listened."

Torie ducked her head. Trish *had* noticed her daydreaming.

"Receptions stink." No trace of resentment colored her voice. "Despite our constant running, no one realizes the waitresses work. So no tips -- other than what had been already added to the meal."

Finished, they stashed the silverware and grabbed a soda. Before Torie finished her drink, the first customers entered. An elderly couple settled on the left side of the restaurant near the bar.

"The early birds have started their dinner migration. Not good tippers. Your section tonight. I call it."

Although tips were teeny, the slow Thursday evening gave Torie plenty of time to dream about starting 'Cut-N-Run', her traveling salon. Humming, she dawdled over an empty table -- slow and easy. A conflict-free evening.

Two hours later, with a loaded tray, Torie pushed through the kitchen door and froze. The door swung back and bumped her. The overloaded platter wobbled. Stepping back into the kitchen, she laid the tray on the counter, closed her eyes, and inhaled.

Near the bar, on *her* side of the restaurant, sat Darren and Jean.

"Torie, get moving before the food gets cold, and I have to re-cook it."

Forcing a smile, Torie glanced at Cook. Two choices faced her: the lean-to and bathing in a pond of ice cubes, or facing her foes.

Squaring her shoulders and taking a deep breath, Torie strode into the dining room as though she owned it.

Trish had already gotten the deadbeat-duo drinks -- a Corona and lime for him. Margarita for her. Predictable.

Hot anger melted Torie's fear. Darren wasn't allowed to be here. Her order of protection lasted five years after his release. His parole ensured no contact between him and her. He could move back in with Jean but had to stay away from her.

When she passed their table, Darren smiled. His chin jutted as he slugged down his beer. He winked.

Her back stiffened. Torie tried not to look their way. She failed. Contempt etched itself in the straight line of Jean's lips, the narrowing of her eyes.

Darren's eyes? No mistaking their intent. They bored into her, hot and lust-filled.

With a smile, Torie delivered the meals to her waiting customers, checked to see if they needed anything.

"Victoria, sweetheart, can you get us the menus?" Jean's voice cooed the words.

It's Torie. Ducking her head, she stepped to the menu rack. Her palms sweated, and the menus slipped to the floor. Torie stooped to scoop them up and froze. *Stop it, Torie. You're not a victim any longer.* She straightened.

Her job? Collin would fire her if she didn't wait on them.

"Come on, Vicky," Darren boomed. "We're gonna starve before you even get us our menus."

Torie pivoted to face her enemies. "You better leave, or I'll call the cops."

Darren leaned back in the chair and stretched his legs. "Why? We haven't finished our drinks, let alone ordered dinner." He signaled with the wave of his fingers. "Get over here and recite the specials. We're hungry."

"You're not allowed to be around me." Torie kept her voice low and glanced to see if Collin noticed. Even if he did, she'd stand her ground. Her tension eased. Collin hadn't returned from the kitchen.

"It didn't stop you from approaching me Sunday night. *You* accosted me, so your protection-piece of legal gobbedy-gook is meaningless."

"'Sides, sweetheart," her mother sounded as though they'd gotten a head start on the drinking, "how was we to know you worked here? This's the only restaurant in Westfield." Jean sipped her margarita and gazed at the lecher. After another slug, Jean stared at Torie. "Your false complaints have forced Darren to live as a registered sex offender. Do you realize how humiliated Darren is? Not to mention what they did to him in prison." She leaned over and stroked his cheek, her eyes soft with pity. Empathy Jean had never given her own daughter.

"Should've thought of consequences before he messed around with a kid."

"Now, Victoria, don't cause a scene." Jean ran her finger around the rim of the glass and sucked the salt off. It looked provocative.

Clenching her fist, Torie held her breath and counted until her hands relaxed.

"Lighten up," Darren said. "The other waitress can wait our table." He pointed toward Trish who turned and caught his eye. He winked, making Torie's stomach churn like a waterwheel. "Where else can we go?"

"To where the devil tangos for all I care. Go get drunk in Schoharie." Her voice rose and fury stomped through her veins. Darren had destroyed her past, ruined her future. He was going to leave her present alone. "Too bad you didn't know I worked here." She clamped her jaw to keep from screeching. "Leave. Now." Her voice came out in a hiss, like the snakes under her lean-to.

"Too bad, sweetheart." He reached over and took Jean's hand. Her mother's face flushed, and her lips parted.

Bile rose and burned in Torie's chest. Stiffening her back, and with as much pride as Torie could collect, she forced herself to walk, not stomp, toward the bar. Urged gentleness into her feet. The duo would not have the satisfaction of seeing what boiled inside of her.

At the bar, Torie picked up the phone to call the cops, keeping her back to the restaurant. Like a child hiding under a blanket, if she didn't see Darren and Jean, they didn't exist.

The phone rang once. The interval before the second ring lasted forever. Shouldn't the cops pick up immediately? What if someone were being murdered? Not a bad outcome for Darren. He needed to be hauled back to his boyfriends at Fishkill Correctional. Before anyone answered, the warmth of a hand on her shoulder made her lift her head.

"They're gone. No need." Collin's warm eyes doused the rage burning Torie.

With his hand on her shoulder, she scanned the restaurant. Empty drinks stood in a ring of condensation at the vacant table. A twenty-dollar bill sopped up the wet. At least he paid.

And tipped.

Torie sank against the bar. Resolve and nerve puddled at her feet. Her hands trembled. She scrubbed her itchy palms on the side of her apron. Wine sounded good.

Chugging a quick slug of something would make her like Jean.

She'd never be.

Normal, uneventful work resumed. Despite the slow night, it took an hour to settle her nerves.

Nine o'clock approached. Torie took advantage of the lull to rest at the bar, but if someone didn't come in soon, she'd fall asleep and look like a common drunk.

"Here you go." Collin slid a Corona and lime across the bar. "Shouldn't encourage you to drink and drive -- but one beer won't hurt. Then go home."

Torie glanced at her watch. "It's an hour 'til closing and the bar--"

"You can stay if you like -- but Trish and I will be gone. The kitchen staff has almost finished cleaning. They can't wait to get out of here."

Torie sipped her beer. Its bitterness warmed her stomach and sweetened her mood. She leaned back in the chair.

"I'll finish up here," Trish said. "You worked like two of us. You need your rest."

Torie shook her head. "No. I'll pull my weight."

Collin laughed. "Seeing as you're a hundred pounds after being marinated in olive oil -- you've already pulled it. I need you tomorrow. If you don't take care of yourself, I'll be looking for a third waitress in two weeks. Go home."

Her protest rose to her throat, but silence answered. Fatigue nagged. She nodded her assent and took another sip of beer. Trish and Collin would be repaid.

Repaid? What's gotten into me? She never owed anyone. Yet, giving to Heather, holding Baby Bobby, once her terror subsided? Being generous when no one asked thrilled her in a way her old attitude never had. Life was funny. Kindness freed her.

"What's so funny?" Collin jolted her out of her reverie.

She shook her head. "Nothing. Why do you ask?"

"Your grin, Li'l Miss Sunshine."

"You wouldn't understand."

*****

Torie pulled up Maya's driveway and parked next to Adam's truck. A soft light glowed from both Maya's bedroom and the kitchen. She grinned. Adam was getting a little comfort. Hopefully, her shower wouldn't disturb the lovers.

She stepped into the kitchen.

"You're home early."

Adam's unexpected voice knocked her back a step. "You scared me."

"What'd you expect? Couldn't see my truck?"

His sarcasm slapped her face. Adam plunged on. "You were in town this afternoon."

Torie glared. "What's gnawing your skivvies?" Her voice deepened an octave.

"Now you're drinking and driving."

Her head jerked. "I'm--"

"You smell like a brewery." He waved his hand in front of his face.

Without answering, she stiffened and clamped her mouth shut and walked into her bedroom. Once inside, Torie threw her purse on the bed and turned to the dresser to grab her pajamas and shower supplies. Adam stood in the doorway. She jumped.

"You're going to scare my hair straight, Adam." She stepped back, bumped into the bed and plopped down. "What's got your dandruff itching tonight?"

"You had no business driving to Grocery*World."

"What--?"

"Or to the Ready Mart." His eyes were crystal bullets.

Movement behind him caught Torie's attention. "Adam, Maya is--"

"Maya wouldn't let a drunk drive her car, and she doesn't need to be used. I know you. From here on out, if you need a ride anywhere -- find one of your friends to dig you out of trouble." The words steamed from his lips. Torie scooted back onto the mattress and sat cross-legged. This was going to be fun.

*****

"Do not talk to my friend that way."

Adam jerked and turned toward Maya who stood in the kitchen, fists on her hips, and her eyes so narrowed nothing but shadows showed.

143

"Your friend?" He stepped into the kitchen. "You've known her less than a week."

"Don't tell me how long I have to know people before they become friends. Didn't know you much longer."

"I'm looking out for you."

"I've managed to look out for myself just fine." She swiveled and stomped out of the kitchen.

"Maya, you don't understand." He took a few steps to follow when she pivoted and stood nose to nose with him.

"I think you better leave before I say something I regret." She pointed toward the door. "You're a bully."

"Me?" He sputtered. *Me?*

She strode to her bedroom while Adam scurried after her like a scolded dog. Her door slammed, just missing him. *Women. Temper tantrums.* He grabbed his jacket in the kitchen knocking over the chair it hung on. *Why weren't women like Neema?* He stormed out of the apartment not caring to right the chair. The screen door slammed behind him.

On the porch, the chilly evening enveloped him, and Maya's accusations reverberated. *Bully?*

Smoke from someone's woodstove filtered through the breezes. The last of winter's fuel -- welcoming. Soothing.

Unlike cigarette smoke.

Or house fires.

He wasn't a bully. Never took advantage of a person in his life, unlike Mr. Sullivan. Or his daughter.

Chapter Twenty-Seven

"I hate and I love. Perhaps you ask why I do so. I do not know, but I feel it, and am in agony." Gaius Valerius Catullus

Silence woke Adam on Saturday morning. He stumbled into the living room to find Pop staring out the window.

"Morning."

Not a tremor shuddered from Pop.

Did he hear? Adam raised his voice. "How about we spend the day at the farm?" If Pop hadn't stiffened, Adam would have sworn he hadn't heard. "I thought you'd like--"

With a back-handed wave, Pop shifted.

Adam stomped back to his room. The door clanked closed. He winced at its clamor. *What's gotten into me?*

After throwing himself on his bed, he nabbed his cell and texted Maya. He stared at the phone and waited.

Nothing.

He tried two more times but heard nothing.

An hour later, Adam drove to the farm for clothes and medicines.

It was a little after ten, and already, enough casseroles and cakes and Jell-O salads to feed all of Westfield sat on the porch. Adam hauled them into the kitchen. As many as he could freeze, he wrapped and stashed in the freezer. The rest he piled into an empty box and lugged to his truck.

Will my fridge hold all this?

If not -- there was always the food bank.

For the fourth time, he texted Maya and studied his phone. If he stared, she'd have to answer.

Had he irritated her so much she wouldn't accept his apology?

He pulled out a lasagna, still warm, and an apple crisp, two of Pop's favorites. After hauling them to his truck, Adam stuck his keys in the ignition.

With the radio off, he returned to the solitude of his own home.

He had thought the actual funeral would be the worst part.

*****

Since fighting with Adam Friday night, nothing lifted Maya's spirits. Yesterday's work at the food pantry didn't even help.

This morning, she squirmed in her seat in Maranatha as Pastor Arendsen babbled on about stewardship and tithing. Blah.

She rummaged through her purse for her cell and frowned. *Where is it? School?*

What if Adam thinks I don't ever want to talk to him again?

Her house phone. She slumped in her seat, ducked her head, and rubbed her forehead. *Could've found his number and called.*

"So Abraham gave Melchizedek..."

Maya crossed her legs, and curled her toes inside her shoes. *If he only has a cell, there'd be no listing.* She uncrossed her legs. *Should've thought about trying anyway.* Maya shifted.

Pastor couldn't seem to find the end of his sermon.

After noon, and at home and unable to find Adam's cell number online, her nerves danced a jig.

Why did she need Adam to like her? He was self-righteous and cruel.

She pulled the cushions off the sofa for the fourth time. No phone.

In despair, Maya plopped down on the cushionless couch, memories of their brief courtship flitting through her restless mind. Adam had cried when he lost Cody Lasky. His heart broke over his grandfather. He took in a homeless woman he hated. This was the real Adam -- the man she loved.

Loved? She smiled. Yes. She did love him.

Two-fifteen crawled around. Time to get Torie and head to the wake.

Nabbing her keys, Maya drove toward The Stadium.

Nearing the V in the road a mile down, the flap, flap, flap of a flat tire forced her to pull over.

She got out and inspected the wheel. Flatter than an open can of soda. More deflated than a burst balloon. Than her hopes for Adam.

Ducking her head into the trunk, Maya searched for the jack. *How do I change a tire?*

"Need a hand?"

She jumped and bumped her head on the trunk. "Ouch." Rubbing the injury, Maya turned to face the stranger loping from the manufactured home wedged into the V of the road.

He put out a hand. Its warmth penetrated her arm. "Sorry. Didn't mean to startle you." The charming man grinned a sexy, wry smile. "I got this." He took the jack from her. "No need to dirty those pretty hands."

She tugged on her shirt sleeves. "Umm." She glanced away. Strangers who weren't six-years-old kept her speechless.

He wedged the jack under the car. His Blud Thirsty t-shirt strained against a well-muscled chest as he pumped. A rugged profile and well-defined chin sporting a stubble spoke of fashion, not laziness. Classic Roman features.

"Be done in a minute. Let you get on your way to some sweet man."

Maya felt her face flush. "No man. A funeral."

He looked up, his eyes, so blue in this light she thought of tranquil, cloudless skies. They spoke of trust. Of peace.

"So very sorry." He lowered the car and gave a final twist to the lug nuts. The man stepped back and stumbled over the tire iron. "Oops. I'll get it in a minute." He reached out. With the gallantry of a knight, and his hand on the small of her back, the helpful stranger guided Maya toward the car. "If you ever needed that fender painted, I used to do it all the time. Can do it cheap."

"Thanks." His hand warm on her back released her worries. Someone cared. The sensation last ten seconds. It then repulsed. It was too intimate.

He leaned into the window. "If I can do *anything* for you, don't be a stranger."

Tongue-tied, Maya waved and sped off.

*****

The cloying stench of carnations intensified the stuffiness of the packed funeral home. Adam chatted with the mourners who stood in lines queueing out the door. More often, he had to comfort them as sobs welled up or they choked them back.

And Pop? He sat motionless in an armchair facing the open coffin, ignoring most of the people. A neighbor would say something, and he'd answer in abrupt sentences, making little eye contact. With his hands folded in his lap, Pop kept his gaze glued to the casket.

"I'm so sorry for your loss."

Adam refocused on the man in front of him and smiled. Shook hands. Thanked the man for coming. Repeated the process. The conversations were genial, and laughter punctuated the condolences as much as tears.

He checked his watch. Three. An hour more. They'd gather again tonight. If the wake was torture, what would happen when they buried Neema? He shook his head to chase the thought away.

In the action, Adam caught sight of Jennifer.

Before he could stop her, she threw her arms around him. He inhaled the sour-apple shampoo in her hair, the scent of Chanel, the mint of her breath. Her familiarity became a refuge in the hollow spaces strangers, acquaintances, and neighbors couldn't fill.

Fighting with Maya had created a wound, and Jennifer's presence became its temporary salve.

Maya. Thoughts of her reminded him of what Jennifer was. All show. Bleached hair, hours in front of a mirror, constant make-up checks, endless shopping, and the omnipresent bangles. The cost of his trophy. The proof he no longer was the middle school geek.

Middle school? Maya was right. He needed to grow up.

"Let's step outside for a minute, Jennifer."

"I'll say hello to Harold, first. Peek at Gracie." She dabbed her eyes with care, always cautious about her mascara.

Five minutes later they exited into warm sunshine.

*****

Maya didn't need to talk as Torie regaled her with tales about her customers. Her sarcasm, shocking but funny, took her mind off Adam's possible reaction to their arrival at the wake.

She parked across the street from the funeral home and shoved open her car door.

"Wait, Maya. Look." Torie wiggled her hand between the driver's seat and the console. "You owe me." Torie waved a slim Galaxy in the air as Maya grabbed for it. With a laugh, Torie handed it over.

"You're my good luck charm." Maya glanced at the phone's screen. "Or maybe not. It's dead as a..." She was going to say corpse, but considering her mission, her joke sounded hollow. "No wonder we couldn't find it when Justine phoned. Dead phones don't ring." Maya shoved it into her purse. It'd get charged at home. Who needed to see the billion missed calls from Justine or her home phone trying to locate this dead one?

Maya slipped out of her Honda. A line of passing cars rooted her in place, but it didn't matter. She couldn't move. Across the street stood Adam with the woman from the restaurant. *Jennifer?*

The couple stood on the lawn facing each other, inches apart. Adam's hand rested on the small of her back. She wore a tight black dress belted at the waist. Gold bangles glinted in the sunlight. Jennifer threw back her head and laughed. Model-perfect hair swung with sass. A Ken and Barbie.

What would she and Adam have been?

A Lucy and Ricky?

Their argument over Torie had to be God telling her he was the wrong man.

"You coming or are you going to stand there until a semi hits you?" Torie grabbed her arm.

They dodged cars to cross the street. She'd interrupt Adam for a minute, give her condolences, and find Harold. Maya opened her mouth to speak as Adam ducked his head, and his arm pulled Jennifer closer. Her arms looped around his neck as they pulled together -- two magnets, inseparable. Maya pivoted and took the steps into the funeral home two at a time.

Forget him. Harold will tell Adam I was here. Or not tell him. Who cares?

The heat inside suffocated. Maya signed the guest register next to the window in the foyer and gazed through the lace curtains. Adam had disappeared. She reminded herself she didn't care. Harold was the reason for her mission.

Silence swathed the receiving line. The lady in front of her looked forward. Torie said nothing. In the awkwardness of the quiet, Maya straightened her long sleeves and studied her legs clad in khaki Dockers. No style. A dress or something in black would have been more appropriate. Something like Jennifer's.

If only she could wear sassy bangles.

No chance.

I shouldn't have come. Shouldn't forget that some people never find love.

After ten minutes that crawled like a crab in quicksand, Maya stood in front of Adam's grandfather. "Harold?"

His eyes lit up. He reached out and grasped Maya's hand as he clambered to his feet.

"I'm so sorry. Losing someone you adore..." Tears choked off her words. She'd known Harold for only a little bit, and had never met his wife, but loss and sorrow and pain were a trio she understood. Seeing it in anyone, even on a dumb TV show, always made her cry.

He hugged her, then turned to Torie. "My little chef." He fingered her hair. "How is life with this wonderful woman?"

"Better than I ever believed, Mr. Benedict."

Dipping his head, Harold glared. He waggled a shaky finger in Torie's direction.

"Sorry," Torie said. "I'll never be polite to you again." She tilted her head. "Harold."

"Come and see my Grace. I wish you ladies coulda known her." He took their hands.

Flanking Harold, they stood in front of the coffin. Maya studied her companions -- Harold lost in Grace's world, Torie now clasped his arm and murmured. A softness Maya didn't expect from Torie given Harold's age and health. Another misjudgment on her part.

Harold laughed at something Torie said. "My Grace woulda liked your spunk. And your hair. She loved red."

"Do you?" Torie asked.

He studied her, and Maya wondered if he had heard. She was about to speak again when he nodded. "Takes some gittin' used to, but I do like it." He turned to Maya. "Grace would have loved your character."

Maya's heart hiccupped. She wished Grace would have loved *her* spunk. *Her* looks. Character was better. Really.

"I've got to get back to The Stadium," Torie said. "Seems some family is demanding a big shindig tomorrow. It's making a slave out of me." She winked. "As your servant, I'll make sure no one messes with you."

Harold patted her hand where it lingered on his arm, and a small smile played about his lips. He said nothing.

Maya's stomach compressed. If only she could offer the easy comfort like Torie.

In the lobby, Maya stopped short. Adam.

Jennifer was nowhere to be seen. She had no choice but to face him.

They took a step, and Torie peered up at her -- her mouth set in a thin line. She looped her arm in Maya's and pulled her forward. "So tell me about the little girl with dyslexia." Torie kept her voice soft, almost a whisper.

The action forced Maya to bend toward her. They neared Adam, and Maya realized what her friend was doing.

"How the heck do you convince her letter *d* is a *b* or a *p* is a *q*?" Torie's plan didn't work.

Another hand grabbed her. "You showed up." Adam's voice came soft and breathless.

"Sorry we can't linger," Torie said. "Work calls, and we're late. Don't worry, Mr. Benedict. Maya's driving me there. Trish is taking me home. I won't upset your sensibilities."

"Whoa." Adam held out his hand to stop Torie. "What'd I do?"

Torie opened her mouth, Maya's grasped her arm. "I've got to get her to work."

"Come back to the wake tonight. Please."

"You want me to?"

Adam nodded.

Maya lifted her chin. "Sh...sure." She glanced at Torie. "Can you--"

"Is this what you want?" Torie's gaze nailed Maya in place.

She nodded.

Torie's smile looked forced. "Of course. Trish will bring me home."

Is she gritting her teeth?

"No sweat."

As they headed to the car, Maya twisted her neck and gazed back at the funeral.

"You and I are going to have a long talk, Miss Maya." Torie's voice refocused her.

*****

School work couldn't occupy Maya as she counted the minutes until the wake resumed.

At six-thirty, she climbed into her car, started it, and backed up. Breaking, she looked at the console. Too eager.

She pulled forward, got out and checked the garden. Not much poked its head up -- rhubarb, asparagus, and spinach.

At seven, she gathered her keys and headed out, smiling at her self-control, at being stylishly late.

The funeral home looked different at night. The darkened windows and low lights intensified her insecurity. Torie was right. Desperation made people rash. She should have stayed at home.

Crowds further obscured her vision. If she left, Adam would never know. With an exhale, Maya decided to leave when she saw him.

Adam sat in a green velvet chair, leaned in toward an elderly woman, his ear turned toward her mouth as though to better hear. He laughed. Then Adam turned his head back toward the woman. His gaze held hers. The lamplight glinted.

Adam grabbed a tissue and handed it to the woman. They stood, and he hugged her. Instead of being consoled, he comforted.

He gave.

He always did.

Flaws marred him like scars on a wrist. Sin ate at all of them.

Maya's heart raced. This was the real Adam Benedict, and she loved him.

*****

After work, Torie nestled on Maya's porch. With her head back, Torie pulled her afghan over herself and savored the Sunday evening quiet. Buff snuggled on her feet and a soft breeze ruffled her hair. After the evening at The Stadium, the crisp air felt good.

An old fashion phone rang. *A landline?* The ringing continued as she tried to free her feet from the hundred-pound Bernese mountain dog.

She nabbed the phone on the fifth ring. "Hello, Curl--" Phones like these demanded formal greetings. "Sorry, force of habit. Can I help you?"

"I must have dialed the wrong number," the woman said.

"Looking for Maya?"

"Yes."

"She's getting out of the shower. Can I take a message?"

"With whom am I speaking?"

How could she describe herself? Friend? Charity case? Homeless woman? "Her roommate." The term sounded odd, but it was closest to the truth.

"My daughter has a roommate? Since when?"

The woman sounded like a mother. Cold. How could anyone be hard on Maya? "A few days."

"Does my daughter need money?"

"I don't think so." Maya hadn't asked for rent, but Torie would give her something.

"Don't ask. I'll pop a check in the mail."

The shower curtain screeched.

"She should be out in a sec. Want me to call her?" Torie didn't wait for an answer. With her palm covering the mouthpiece, she craned her neck and shouted. "Your mother's on the phone. Want to take it now or later?"

"Be right out." Maya's muffled call sounded like she had her head wrapped in a towel. Probably because she was wrapping her head in a towel.

"She'll be here in a moment, Mrs. Vitale, and no, it wasn't money making her take me in. It was charity."

"My girl."

Torie heard the pride in Mrs. Vitale's voice and pictured the smile like Maya's. The crinkle of the nose making her look like a bunny rabbit. Cute and innocent and kind. Torie had never met a proud mother.

A hand reached for the phone. "Thanks, Torie."

In the second it took to pass the phone, she recognized Maya's scars. Not simple cutting.

Torie ducked into her room and changed into her PJs. By keeping the door open a fraction, the conversation would drift into the room. Laughter rang and stabbed her with envy. When had she last felt happy about her mother? Before--?

She was going to say Darren, but her joy vanished long before he arrived. Lost it in the closet, when her mom got drunk and forgot to unlock it. Or when they ran out of food and she had to wait until school lunch was served. When Burnt Hollow Elementary started serving breakfast, she was one happy little girl.

The conversation didn't last long, and in the silence of the house, Torie wished she'd been as good as Maya who grew up in a Brady Bunch family. Yet, if her life was perfect, why had she slit her wrists?

Maya knocked at Torie's door and poked her head into the room. "Guess I need to charge my cell. Mom never calls on the house phone -- no answering machine, no way to nag if she doesn't catch me." Maya dangled the portable charger. "Do you remember where I stashed my phone? Can't even call it to find it."

"This afternoon, you had tucked it into your purse. How can you survive without the phone? You lost it Friday." She followed Maya into the kitchen.

Maya shrugged and rummaged through her pocketbook. "Just forgot. Prefer things the old-fashioned way, anyway."

"You and Adam make up?"

Maya ducked her head, but the crinkle of her nose and flush of her skin gave her away.

"A shower in the evening? Must have been some great make-up sex."

Maya's head jolted, and the flush turned crimson. "No. I don't believe in premarital sex."

It was Torie's turn to be startled. "Why? Are you a lesbian?"

Maya laughed, and joy sparkled in her eyes, all trace of embarrassment gone. "Not in the least. It's Biblical."

"What's Biblical?"

"No premarital sex."

"You mean you never..."

"Here. I'll show you." Maya got her Bible and flipped through pages.

If guys didn't get a little, Christian or not, they'd run off. Maybe sex was why Adam kept the Jennifer-hussy on the side.

Torie didn't listen to Maya's lecture. Instead, she studied Maya's wrists as she ran her fingers along the text.

Maya had secrets, too.

153

Chapter Twenty-Eight

"What is food to one man is bitter poison to others." Lucretius

The sunrise had turned the parking lot pink when Maya dropped Torie off at The Stadium. "You sure you're going to be okay?"

"Of course. My life in the jungles prepared me for this."

"For *one* day, Victoria."

Torie pointed a finger at her. "You call me Victoria, and I'll move out. One day is as a thousand -- or so you said once." She laughed. "Besides, it was *two* days there. One in the lean-to and one under a picnic table."

"It's not even six a.m. I wish I didn't have to drop off my sub plans. Should've thought ahead."

"You didn't know until yesterday -- like it wasn't obvious Adam would want you around today. Quit worrying. It works out best 'cause Collin needs me early." She stepped out of the car and waved until it disappeared down the road. Collin wouldn't be in until nine, so instead of heading to work, Torie wandered to the Ready Mart. After picking up a pack of Coronas and a lime, she'd crash at Heather's.

Once she was sure they were awake.

Sipping a beer, Torie wandered to the bench outside the library. The brew warmed her, and the self-consciousness about wandering Westfield before the crows even woke up evaporated. She curled her legs onto the bench and studied her feet, followed by the few frozen leaves of kale on the produce table, and the passing traffic -- the whole of two cars and a pickup.

Minutes crawled. At last, whether ready for her or not, Torie headed to Heather's.

"Torie." Bobby blocked the door. "Do you know what time it is?"

Torie held up the carton.

"It's seven a.m." The sight of the Coronas didn't soften his mood.

"Then I'll drink it myself. I've got to be to work, but I had to get a glimpse of the baby."

"Hon, let her in. It's okay."

No sooner had Torie entered the apartment, than Heather plopped her kid into Torie's arms. "Don't worry. I get to hold him enough. I don't mind sharing." She giggled. "Just as long as I get him back." She rubbed her nose against the baby's.

Heather didn't have to worry about not getting him back. With stiff arms and a raging desire for another Corona, Torie settled on the sofa with Baby Bobby and Heather.

"Let me show you this video." Heather grabbed her iPhone and fiddled with the apps. She scrolled through the phone until a video of Baby Bobby sucking on a bottle came on. "Isn't he a doll? Look." Her finger jabbed at the video obscuring the image. "See his dimples."

"Cute."

Big Bobby twisted off a cap from the beer he claimed it was too early for and flipped on his Xbox. He threw himself on the couch, his hip touching Torie's. She wiggled away. After settling the sleeping infant in her lap, Torie nabbed a beer from the carton at her feet. Heather, unaware of Torie's inattention, played another video, this one of Baby Bobby's bath. The infant squalled in the movie as though Heather was killing him.

Torie handed the baby back to his mother and twisted off the bottle top and took a swig. The tedium became tolerable until Heather scrolled through her phone for another video.

The loneliness of the library bench looked good.

At nine, she peeked out the window. Collin's SUV sat by the back entrance of The Stadium.

Torie turned to Heather. "Collin's here. Time to work."

"Before you do, can you take Bobby?" Heather didn't wait for a response. She handed off her infant and hurried into the bathroom.

The baby squirmed and fussed. Big Bobby hadn't succeeded in overcoming the Templars, or whatever he hunted in *Assassin's Creed*. For the past two hours, his attention never wavered from the TV screen.

Torie looked from the infant to his father. This kid wasn't her responsibility. "Bobby?"

He didn't respond.

"Bobby." She called louder, but still got no reaction. Torie walked in front of him, and plopped the baby on his lap.

"What are you doing? I was just going to--"

"It's a game. Get over it. I've got to go to work."

Without waiting for Heather to return, Torie strode out of the apartment and jogged across the street. Never did work look so good.

After tying her apron and adjusting her Red Sox cap, Torie pried open the Sterno cans, hauled out the baskets of flatware, and arranged the tiny vases of flowers in the back room where the reception was to take place. The details of setting up made the rest of Torie's life vanish.

"You're ambitious."

She smiled up at Collin. "Trish taught me well."

"She won't be in for another hour -- like a normal employee. I'm not paying you to come in early."

"No need to. I'm a denture servant."

Collin cocked his head. "Indentured? Your education needs updating."

Torie giggled and swatted him as he left.

A half-hour later, Trish arrived. She scanned the room. "Collin should've hired you years ago. There's nothing left to do but wait for the guests. Let's grab a Coke."

At the bar, Torie leaned back in the chair and swiveled, sipping her diet cola through a tiny swizzle stick. She scraped her tongue against her teeth. "Aspartame tastes like chemicals."

"Because it is a chemical," Trish said.

"Too bad I can't avoid calories with something with flavor." Torie didn't look over at Trish. Instead, she surveyed the bottles lining the mirror in front of her. *Rum would hide the aftertaste.*

"Trish? Can you come back here a sec?" Collin leaned out from the kitchen and waved.

Trish disappeared behind the swinging kitchen door, and Torie returned her attention to the bottles lining the shelves. It was like God had heard her. She scooted around the bar and grabbed the rum. A splash in the Coke would go unnoticed, and it would boost the fading buzz from the Coronas.

A little before one, the first of the mourners arrived. Torie bustled back and forth keeping the crudités stocked, and checking on drinks.

"Trish," she asked during a kitchen foray. "Have you got any Advil or something?" She rubbed her ribs. If they continued aching, she wouldn't make it another hour let alone six.

"Back here." Cook pointed to a cabinet.

Torie grabbed a couple of pills, popped them into her mouth, and headed back to the dining hall. She tried to swallow, but the sweet coating dissolved. Bitterness filled her mouth. Torie glanced around, nabbed a glass, and pulled the handle of the draft beer. Just a small swig to get them down.

"Torie. Can I see you a minute?"

Her back stiffened. *Great timing, Collin.* Torie gave him a sultry smile, "Anytime, big guy."

"In my office."

She swallowed. And followed.

Collin shut the door behind her. His office was little more than a closet with a desk cluttered with papers. Broken cooking utensils piled up on chairs, and beneath the tiny window sat well-worn bar guides.

Torie would use the close space to her advantage. She scooted up on his desk, crossed her legs, and leaned forward. "So why all the privacy?" She batted her lashes, turned her statement into innuendo like men craved.

"You're a good worker." His cold compliment told her sweet-talking wouldn't change the tone of this conversation. "You're fun. Reliable. But if you *ever* drink on the job again, you're fired. Do you understand?"

Torie held his eyes. "I'd never--"

His eyes narrowed, and Torie read the anger. "The rum I overlooked. Drinking *while* you're working?" He inhaled then drummed his fingers against his desk. "You've got a drinking problem, and it's poisoning your life."

She bristled and straightened "I don't--"

"I'm not kidding."

"You think I'm an alky?" She hopped off the desk and took a step toward Collin. He put out his hand and stopped her.

"Find an AA meeting." He opened the office door.

She slid by. Shame crawled over her skin like maggots. Why? Because Collin was unreasonable?

*****

Harold clung to Maya's arm as the funeral director handed each person a white rose. He took a step and Maya guided him over the uneven ground. Adam laid his hands at his grandfather's back and helped Pop as he laid his flower on the coffin, bent and kissed the casket. Adam grasped Pop's arm, but he shook it off and walked away without either of them.

Maya laid her rose next to Harold's and turned. Adam's grandfather was halfway to the Lincoln.

Adam took a giant step toward him.

She grabbed his arm. "Let him be."

"But he's--"

"A man who knows his mind. Don't treat him like a baby."

"I need--"

"I?" Maya dropped her hands to her hips. "Stop the I-s, Adam. You can't force a grown man to live according to your dictates."

"He's frail. He's hurting--"

"Then let him heal."

"Look, he's my grandfather. He needs care." He strode off and arrived at the Lincoln before Harold. Adam yanked open the front passenger door.

157

Harold stopped, and opened the back door.

Touché, Harold. Maya bit her lips to keep from grinning. "I told you so," she said to Adam who stood holding the door open. She slid into the front seat.

They drove in silence.

Chapter Twenty-Nine

"Character is like a tree and reputation is its shadow." Abraham
Lincoln

Ten minutes later, Adam pulled up to The Stadium. Cars packed the parking lot. He maneuvered the Lincoln into the last handicapped spot. Hopping out of the car, he bounded around it and opened the door for Pop.

His grandfather shifted to the other side. Shoved open the door himself.

Right, Maya, he's a grown up. He rounded the car once more, took Pop's arm and ushered him inside. "Maya?" He turned to ask her to find seating for them when he noticed she wasn't at his side.

He'd deal with her later.

In the back room, he found a round table for twelve, reserved for family. His now consisted of two. He glanced at Pop. Soon to be a family of one. *Where are you, Maya? I need you.* He held out a chair, and his grandfather slid into it. "What can I get you to eat?"

Pop stared at the serving line. "You gotta be in control of everything. You figure it out."

Adam held his breath until his anger seeped away. To the count of five, he exhaled and headed to the buffet line. En route, his grandfather's neighbor Mark LaValley and his wife, Margaret, stopped him. They chatted for a few minutes, then Adam grabbed a plate. Another neighbor interrupted, grabbed his arm, and offered the condolences everyone gave all morning long.

After the neighbor moved on, Adam scooped out mashed potatoes, talked to another well-wisher, piled on fried chicken legs, talked some more, found green beans in butter sauce, and grabbed a roll and butter. With his plate piled with more food than he could eat, he returned to the table and caught Torie pouring Pop a cup of coffee.

"You want some?" She held up the carafe.

He nodded to the water glass already on the table. "The water's good. Thanks." He slid the plate in front of Pop. "Is this okay?"

Pop nodded.

Still unseated, Adam scanned the dining room. He grabbed Torie's arm as she passed. "Have you seen Maya?"

Torie shook her head.

Have I been so awful that Maya won't even join me? Adam threw his napkin on the table. With his appetite vanished, he headed out to the parking lot. Maybe she was outside?

*****

"There you are." Torie poked her head into the restroom. "I didn't see you come in."

"Came through the patio door." Maya dipped her head in the general direction of the courtyard. On warm summer days, Collin threw open the door at the end of this corridor, and many patrons ate al fresco.

Maya fussed with her hair, twisting it up in a ponytail.

"Leave it down. Looks better."

Maya wrapped her arms across her chest. Her eyes were distant and looked right through Torie.

After bending over to check the stalls, Torie leaned against the bathroom door. "What's up?"

Maya turned her face back to the mirror. "I need you to give me a haircut."

"Anytime." Torie sought Maya's gaze in the mirror. "You haven't answered my question."

"I better go see to Harold." Maya turned away from the mirror, but she didn't take a step toward the door.

"You act like you'd rather go home."

Maya's nose crinkled, and her eyes sparkled. "So you are a gypsy after all."

"Read minds all the time. Only way to get what you want." She stepped forward, lowered her voice. "You and Adam have a fight?"

Maya turned back toward the mirror and tucked a stray strand of hair into the ponytail

"I thought you saw the compassion and gentleness in him last night?"

Maya shrugged.

"Look. The boy is gaga over you. I don't know what went on, but ignore his ogre-side, and bask in his Adam-side."

Maya raised her brows.

"In middle school, he was so good. Raised his hand to answer *every* question, did his homework -- including the bonus questions. Who does more than necessary, anyway? He helped the teachers. Joined the science club. He was the perfect mark for bullies like Dylan Moser and Brad Duquette."

"And?" Maya's eyes twinkled.

160

"Didn't I hear you once say something about our sinful stuff being forgotten?" She winked. "Even now, he works to save people, and he's plagued when he loses them. Adam took me in even when he had every reason to leave me to the lions and tigers and bears in Hookskill for nights on end."

Maya held up one finger.

Torie held up two. "When he drags *you* into the boonies for a camping trip, you'll see I've never exaggerated." She paused, and Maya turned from the mirror and leaned against the sink. "I know he likes you. A lot. When I give you your new-do, I'll teach you how to flirt. Then you'll always have the upper hand."

The bathroom door swung open. "Torie," Trish said. "You better get back to work. Your extra hours before customers will *not* make up for letting them starve."

The door swung shut, and Torie straightened. "Here." She fished in her back pocket and took out a tube of lipstick. "Give me your lips."

Maya jerked her head away.

"Come on. I've already used your toothbrush, so you've got my germs." The horror on Maya's face made Torie bark a laugh. "Just kidding. I don't want your cooties." She opened the door. "After today, you go *nowhere* without make-up. Go out there. Chug a glass of wine and let life take over."

"I don't drink."

"Don't...?" Torie shook her head. "You are weird."

A grin crinkled Maya's nose.

"Don't worry, though, so's Adam." She tossed Maya the lipstick. "Put this on your lips and leave it on Adam's."

*****

Maya stood at the entrance to the reception. Her heart hammered. Mom and Daddy would own this room, prance in and command it like brigadier generals. Why didn't they nurture the confidence skill into her? What resided in her genes that she always felt like a lump? It came from none of the parents she knew.

Harold waved Maya over. Her shoulders relaxed, and a slow smile eased the tension in her face.

"Go git yourself some food. I saved you a spot." He patted an empty seat next to him. To the right of the empty place sat a plate with fried chicken and shrimp -- the pile undisturbed. Harold pointed at the food. "My grandson's being the gracious host for me. Don't know where he's off to now."

161

Maya scanned the room. No Adam. She found a plate at the head of the empty serving line and doled out some roasted chicken and asparagus and spinach salad sprinkled with chives. Jennifer wouldn't approve of the chives, but she'd like the spinach.

"What're you eating?" Adam laughed as came up behind her, his lips close to her ears. "Where's the red meat? Or at least the fried?"

Warmth nestled through Maya. She hoped for a kiss. For Adam to nibble her ear. She could almost feel it.

"Been looking all over for you." His arm looped over her shoulders as he ushered her to the next food warmer.

Been looking? A smile spread and her cheeks warmed.

"Just remind me with every meal we have why you like those green things." He pointed to the buttered beans. "Green means mold."

"Blue, silly. Mold is blue."

With his hand touching, they slid into the two chairs next to Harold.

Harold said something Maya couldn't hear. As she bent toward him, she grinned at Torie's thumbs up.

"What church do you go to?" Harold asked.

The large round tables, designed for communal dining, made it hard to talk to anyone but *one* immediate neighbor. Maya strained to hear. "Maranatha."

"The wild one out on the Schoharie-Westfield Road?"

"Not so wild."

"Don't they sing them rock-n-roll songs?"

"Rock's a bit of an exaggeration. We like upbeat, but we sing hymns. Hear preaching. Reach out to the poor."

"Believe in Jesus?"

She cocked her head. "Mr. Benedict--"

He raised a finger in admonishment, and Maya clasped it and pushed his hand back to the table.

"You talk foolishness, you get called Mister. Of course, we do."

His brows drew together in a scowl, and his lips puckered.

"Quit acting like a curmudgeon."

"Use English. What the heck's a curmudgeon? Some kinda fish?" His smile told her he teased.

Maya reached for a water glass. Adam had disappeared again, his food untouched. She scanned the room, caught sight of Jennifer heading out of the dining room. *Coincidence?*

"Maya." Justine pulled up the chair Adam had vacated.

"Hey there." Levi centered another seat between the two women. "Benedict says he'll make show-n-tell Friday."

Maya excused herself from Harold and turned her chair to face

Levi.

"I thought he'd cancel given the circumstances," she said.

"Nah. Said Harold could stay alone for a couple hours." He leaned toward Harold and raised his voice. "Right, Harold?"

"Don't shout, boy." Harold waved him off and continued his conversation with the man to his left.

"Adam wants to get back to work. Needs to find someone to care for his grandfather. So tell me. How much time you giving us for our demonstration? Couple of hours?"

"All day if you like. Less work for us."

As they chattered, Maya surveyed the crowd to be sure Harold was okay. He picked at his food while his neighbor chatted. Adam now stood at the far end of the room. She turned her attention back to her friends. Laughter came easy, and thoughts about Adam drifted away.

"Missed you at school this morning," Justine said. "Must be nice getting a whole day off."

"Oh yeah. Come in early to get sub plans ready. Attend a funeral. Tomorrow I get to figure out what the sub did or didn't do."

"True. More work to be out than prepping for a sub," Justine said.

"I missed driving in with you, missed the weekend gossip. How was Sunday school yesterday?"

"It was a hoot," Justine said.

Torie came by with a carafe of coffee and filled their cups. "Didn't forget." She placed a glass carafe of hot water and a tea bag next to Maya. "I need to buy you a coffee pot, and convert you to the serious brew."

"Making me your own little Pygmalion, are you?"

"Pig? No."

The women laughed at Torie's confusion.

"The original *My Fair Lady*," Justine said.

"Quit talking above my head." Torie winked. "Careful. The java's super-hot." She moved on to another guest.

Levi grabbed his coffee, took a slug and sputtered, spitting some of the liquid. "Whoa. Hot." He balanced the cup on his knee.

"Didn't Torie warn you?" Justine dabbed his lips with a napkin. "Be careful from here on out, Hot Stuff." She threw a play punch at his arm.

"Coffee here." He lifted the cup in warning. In the action, he flipped his arm and sent the scalding brew flying.

It splattered Maya's khakis. A huge, brown stain spread along her thigh. She jumped out of her chair, pulling the hot cloth away from her leg.

"Sorry!" Levi shouted, and bounded up to grab a napkin. "Did I burn you?"

"No, but I better clean my pants."

Levi scrubbed the napkin over Maya's leg, then yanked his arm away as though burned. He handed her the napkin. "More appropriate if you do the honors. I'll clean up the rest of the mess."

Maya excused herself and headed to the ladies' room.

As she pushed on the bathroom door, she caught a glimpse of a couple outside. Jennifer, no mistaking her, had her arms looped around Adam who stood with his back to Maya, his hands on Jennifer's waist. No mistaking their pose, either.

Should never have listened to Torie.

As she scrubbed the stains with a wet paper towel, the door opened. Jennifer stepped in. Her stare made Maya feel like a stink bug.

With a pout, Jennifer leaned over the sink and reapplied lipstick to her already pinked lips. "You don't stand a chance with him." She spoke to Maya's reflection. "You're not his type."

Maya stared at the floor, gulped air, then straightened. She turned to Jennifer and cocked her head. "The delusions of the shallow." Mustering all the grace she could, she strolled out of the room.

She was a Vitale, after all.

Chapter Thirty

"Belief in the truth commences with doubting all those "truths" we once believed." Friedrich Nietzsche

Later that evening, car door slammed, and Maya scuttled to her feet, struggling to bridle her smile. She had to look like a carnival clown. A happy one.

Stopping herself from throwing open the door and blathering everything to Torie before she hit the porch, Maya sat by her Cricut machine once more. The seconds Torie took to march into the apartment took hours. Dipping her head to hide her ridiculous joy, Maya slipped the mat from the die-cut feed and picked at the purple magnolia clinging to the sticky mat with its death-grip on the paper.

The door rattled, and Maya clasped the flower to her chest, crinkling it beyond use.

"I hope I'm not disturbing you," Torie said.

"Nope."

"You look like the cat who chowed down on Tweety-Pie."

Maya opened her mouth to speak.

"Tired tonight." Torie sank into a chair and picked up one bright pink tulip and a light blue one from the scattered die-cuts on the table. "These are math problems?"

Maya nodded. "Guess--"

Torie's eyes narrowed as she studied the worksheet. "You're doing each one different? Why don't you photocopy 'em? My lazy teachers Xeroxed 'em. Didn't put them on any pretty paper, either."

"This is more fun for the kids. More challenging."

"If my sour-puss teachers gave me worksheets like this, I might've liked school." She placed it back on the pile of flowers and picked up a yellow daffodil. Torie's eyes turned toward Maya, and her eyes widened, a small smile tipped the corners of her lips. "Doesn't look like you want to talk school. What's up?"

"Guess what?" It took all of Maya's strength not to squeal and jump up and down.

Torie dropped the construction paper, leaned her elbows on the table. Her eyes shone.

"Adam and I--" Maya bit her lip and hesitated. "It's serious."

"The boy figured out what was good for him?" The tug of a smile

165

blossomed into a full-fledged grin.

"With Jennifer around, I worried."

Torie shook her head and leaned back. "Jennifer's the one who's hot to trot. He's not interested in the least."

"How do you know?"

"Have you seen the way he *doesn't* look at her? Pushes her away? The way he avoids her?"

"I saw them on the patio."

"If it looked like the time Jennifer hung all over him while you were sulking in the bathroom, his hands weren't hormonal. He was pushing her away. His eyes didn't show a speck of lust. More like disgust." She laughed. "Hey, I'm a poet." Torie's lips curved up like a cat licking her chops. "I've got to teach you how to read men. Believe me, it's one thing I'm good at -- aside from hair. I told him he was a jerk if he lost you."

"You didn't?" Even without Torie's answer, Maya knew the moxie of her friend and heard the lecture Torie had given Adam.

"So you figured out he likes you more than Ms. Anorexia."

"She's so pretty."

"Have you looked in the mirror?"

"Me? I'm fat. My hair's dull. My clothes are boring."

"First, you aren't fat. You gotta meet Selene. *She's* big. Didn't matter since my ex-friend got the hottest guy in town. I can tell you, I was better--" Torie's mouth tightened, then twisted to the side before she grinned. "S'rry. Trish and I kicked back after work. It looshed -- um, loosened my tongue too much."

The imp wink through Torie's smile.

"Your clothes are dull. Need to fix 'em up -- shorter sleeves, and something other than tan. Teal? Pink?" Torie paused. "Pink -- with your coloring and your cute little nose, pink's your color. Or a sunny yellow."

Maya tugged her sleeves. The heat flooded her face, probably making it as pink as the clothes Torie wanted to dress her in.

"Wanna talk 'bout it?"

"Talk about what?"

Torie took her arm.

Maya yanked it back. It was none of Torie's business.

"Like I said, I chilled-out with Trish. Too much. If Collin saw me now, he'd give me another lecture about..." She shook her head. "Do you think God minds a drink or two?"

Maya ducked her head and licked her lips. She needed to answer honestly. "One or two's okay. Never to get drunk."

Torie stood. "Tomorrow night, I'm off. We'll talk as I do your hair."

"Do my hair?"

"Didn't you say it was too dull? You can't refuse me a good time. Your hair's got lovely highlights already, but I can brighten the ash-blonde, enrich the brown. Dress you up, and Jennifer will look like the la-de-da idiot she is. I'll search the supplies I rescued from Curly Girls." She turned to go.

"Torie?"

She faced Maya.

"It's Justine's turn to drive to work. If you promise not to drink and drive, feel free to use my car."

Torie's brows pulled together as she glanced away.

"What, no smile? No effusive thank yous?"

"Effusive? Isn't ef..." Torie bit her lip, "something like refuse?"

Maya hooted so loudly she snorted. "Not effluent." She covered her mouth, but her laughter erupted. She fanned her face. "Sorry. It's not you. It's..."

Torie's smile stiffened. Her eyes held no sparkle.

"Please forgive me."

"Nothing to forgive." Torie hesitated at her bedroom door. "Why are you doing this?"

"What?"

"Letting me crash here. Loaning your car."

"You need help. I like you."

"No angle?"

Maya shook her head.

Torie pushed open her door and turned. "Tomorrow we talk." She sliced a finger across her wrist, and with a soft click, closed the door.

Maya pulled on her sleeves and her mirth vaporized. She stared at her wrists. Who else had noticed? Given the advantages life as a Vitale offered, who would ever understand?

*****

Without bothering to undress, Torie lay on the bed and stared at the spinning ceiling. Like a stutter, words from the first sermon she heard returned to her. The more she tried to push them away, the more they repeated themselves. The laughter from the congregation when Pastor Arendsen spoke about the forgiven drunk echoed. Collin told her she had a drinking problem. Maya mentioned it two times. If her ceiling told the truth, she was beyond tipsy.

She wasn't a drunk.

She did smash her car.

The crash was Trey's fault. Actually, Selene's doing. The fat witch.

167

She needed to shower, but the twirling room and her busy brain welded her to the bed.

When Adam had rescued her from the cold and rain and wild animals of Hookskill, he had commented on her empty wine coolers. A whole four of them.

She had to keep warm somehow.

Her mouth felt like cotton. She sat up, wanted water or to brush her teeth or mouthwash.

Mouthwash?

She saw herself at Heather's, swigging the swill.

Pain had overcome her, so what could she do? She was supposed to have been in the hospital, but who could afford the luxury except welfare rats like Jean.

Wasn't she a welfare rat now? Living off of Maya. Giving nothing for what she got?

Living here was temporary. She'd pay Maya back.

She twitched her lips. Everyone drank. Well, not Maya. She didn't count. Maya wouldn't even chug coffee. Aside from her, Torie didn't know a single person who didn't overindulge. Even Collin. How could a bartender not? She'd prove to everyone who pointed fingers at her she controlled her drinking. *God, I won't have one drink until the weekend. If I do? I'll go to an AA meeting and prove I'm not as bad as those alkies.*

Chapter Thirty-One

"In failing to confess, Lord, I would only hide You from myself, not myself from You." Saint Augustine

Maya waved off Justine, and turned to her apartment, to emptiness. Her car was gone, and her home quiet. A heaviness settled in her chest. No Torie. Maya needed her, her sarcasm, her attitude, and her love of a good time. They were complete opposites, but complements. Her spirit craved the luxury of Torie's vivacity.

Torie's door stood open, and Maya peeked into the room as though she couldn't see its entirety from the kitchen. Her shoulders slumped, and her book bag slid to the floor. No Torie.

As her stomach rumbled, Maya rummaged in the fridge for food. Before she decided which yogurt she'd devour, her phone summoned her. Her mother, and not on the weekend?

With her cell wedged between her ear and shoulder, Maya peeled the cover from the yogurt. "Everything okay, Mom? It's not Sunday morning."

"Don't be fresh, sweetheart. I need to let you know, I won't be calling Sunday because Daddy and I will be away."

"Didn't you just get back from Vienna?"

"A month ago, darling. It doesn't mean we can't hit Albany and bring a gift to our favorite daughter."

"Your only. When will you be here?"

"Friday late. Just a minute."

She got a crick listening to nothing but the background chatter, the ringing of phones -- the clatter of her parents' law office. Maya put the phone on speaker and set it on the table.

As she dumped the empty yogurt container in the trash, her mom picked up. "I'm sorry, sweetheart. I've got to take care of this. Interruptions are why I call on Sundays. We reserved a room at the Capitol Arms. Excelsior is already reserved for you. See you Friday night."

Before Maya responded, her mother hung up.

Tires grinding the gravel driveway kept Maya from dwelling on the call and its demand. Within seconds, Torie bounded into the kitchen holding aloft a bulging, pink paper bag from *Hair Chez Iz.*

"Hope you don't mind, but I took the car to Albany. Don't worry.

It's got a full tank of gas." She plopped the bag on the table. "Izzy's got the best hair products this side of France -- if you've got to order local." Torie pulled out a chair and plopped down across from Maya.

Maya studied the table, half listening. She didn't want to spend the weekend in Albany, but no one argued with Viola or Sal Vitale. Especially with Viola.

"Don't fret. You'll be gorgeous. I promise." She blew across the table. "I'm stone cold sober."

Maya shook her head. "Knew you would be."

Torie said nothing, only lifted her eyebrows.

"My mother called with demands."

"No need to say more." Torie stood. "Tonight, girlfriend, you're gonna be smokin'." She left the room. Within seconds she returned. "And we will talk." Torie shut her door, leaving Maya alone once more.

As she cooked dinner, Maya shed her fears for both the hair and talk. However, once the dishes were dried and stashed, dread shivered through her. She clenched her jaw. Never had she uttered a word about her attempted suicide to anyone other than her counselor.

And Justine.

After the dinner dishes had been stashed, Torie laid her hair supplies on the table like a surgeon preparing for the operating theater, or an executioner readying her implements.

"All set?"

Maya shook her head. "You sure about this?"

Torie nodded. "Trust me. You'll be so hot, tomorrow you'll be begging to go to Crossgates Mall to buy new duds to match the do. Adam will never think of Jennifer again."

Within minutes, cold dye slathered Maya's head and the stench of ammonia permeated the kitchen. Torie wrapped minuscule quantities of hair in tin foil and nattered about Trish and Collin and Selene and Trey and a host of other people Maya knew nothing about. When Torie shifted her conversations to actresses and singers, Maya relaxed under strong, confident fingers and released the fear of confession.

"You're a quiet one, aren't you?" Torie asked.

Maya nodded.

"Done wrapping. Now we gotta let you cook." Torie left the kitchen, then poked her head out of her room. "Remember. No peeking."

Maya glanced at the window and caught a ghost of a reflection of an alien Rastafarian. This one wore old-fashioned floppy disks stuck to her hair. In aluminum. Torie left no hand mirror on the table, and it wasn't worth tiptoeing to the bathroom to check. She'd see nothing but foil. Maya needed to know what Torie did to her. She stood.

"Hey." Torie emerged from her room waving a hand mirror. "You'll use this when we're done." She placed it face down on the table, out of reach. "You've got about fifteen minutes left." She sat at the table, and Maya faced her. "So now's when we talk. Why'd you try to kill yourself?"

The house creaked. A breeze from the open kitchen door mingled the scent of lilies-of-the-valley with the stench of ammonia. Like her life -- sweet and acrid. She ran her finger along the crack of the table leaf. Torie made no sound. Maya took a deep breath and met Torie's eyes examining her own. "I'd rather not talk about it."

"Yesterday's poison will still kill us if we keep drinking it."

"But, it hurts to talk about it."

Torie nodded. "I understand. My step-father used to molest me. Took a long time before I told anyone. Then no one believed me. Worse, he used to pimp me out to his friends for drug money. Then he knocked me up."

Maya shivered and twisted in her seat. "Torie, I had no idea. How can you talk so matter-of-factly about it?"

"Can't do anything about it. The talk makes it easier. Most of it."

"Makes my self-pity sound pathetic and self-absorbed."

"Time to rinse."

A reprieve. *Maybe she'll forget.*

Torie slipped the aluminum from her hair. They fell into the sink with little clacks. "Time to rinse." Maya stuck her head under the faucet. Every muscle in her back tensed. Torie massaged Maya's scalp in sure strokes, petted her head as though she, not Maya, got the benefits from the coddling.

"What happened to your baby?" Maya asked.

"Here, wrap this around your head." Torie wound an old towel over her hair. "We'll get to the fun part."

Had she aborted? Maya glanced at her roommate, but her face wore an indifferent expression.

Torie picked up a comb and teased out the tangles. "You don't look Italian. You adopted or something?"

"Yes."

"Not a bad thing. Your folks chose you. Jean got stuck with me."

"My folks always said they *cherry-picked* me. 'A cute little button-fruit' in their words." She glanced at Torie. "I didn't use to think of it as something special -- more like no one else would have me." The apple scent of the hair products and Torie's contented attention swathed Maya in a peace she didn't expect given the impending confession.

"So, why did you try to kill yourself?"

"You're frank."

171

"Nah. Torie." She offered her hand as though to shake. "Thought you knew my name."

Maya puzzled out Torie's joke -- then got it. The giggles washed away the last of Maya's reserve. Like a priest or psychiatrist, hairdressers' comforts forced one to confess. "Don't tell *anyone.* Do you swear?"

"Hey, the hairdresser's chair is as sacred as a lawyer's office."

With Torie standing behind her, and in the intimacy of her playing with her hair, Maya felt the burden lift even before she opened her mouth.

"My biological mother was an addicted hooker and got arrested in a vice sweep. She ended up as one of my mother's pro bono cases. Mom got her off, got her into rehab. She left it after six months. Three months later, she showed up in my folks' office with a baby."

"You?"

Maya nodded. "Fortunately, she stayed clean throughout rehab, so I escaped addiction." Maya shifted and bowed her head.

"Hey, quit wiggling unless you want to be as bald as an eagle." Torie continued cutting.

"Right after ditching me, she jumped off the Queensboro Bridge."

"Ouch!" Torie stood back and stared down into Maya's eyes. "You got good folks who wanted you. Why did you want to kill yourself? I mean, my mother's a drunk, does drugs, and might as well have been a working lady with her string of men. Jean had no clue where my father ran off to, and I never met him. You got good folks."

"Good folks who had no time for me. Got talked into taking me."

"Are you sure?"

Maya dropped her gaze and pulled at her sleeves.

"Did they leave you alone for hours on end?" Torie asked.

Maya startled.

"Easy, there, Maya." Torie clicked the shears in the air.

"They wouldn't dream of it. My nanny, Anita, either came to my house or took me home with her when my folks were late. I was a kid. They wouldn't leave me alone."

"My mother did. I remember skipping school lots of times in second grade 'cause she forgot to come home. Someone had to watch my sisters."

"Now I feel worse about my self-pity. My folks had no clue who my father was, nor did my biological mother. From my looks, white, Anglo-Saxon."

Torie leaned back and studied Maya's face. "German would be my guess. My last name's Irish, but sometimes I think I look Indian -- not the

172

American ones. The guys overseas who seem to always be our 'customer representatives.'"

The ladies giggled.

"I used to want to be Guatemalan like my nanny. She taught me to cook paches and chuchitos wrapped in corn husks. I learned to love spicy foods. My folks eat pure Italian." Maya settled back into her chair, but guilt rattled up her spine. She forgot how good she had it. "My folks made sure I had the best of everything. They sent me to the finest private schools from kindergarten on. I owned about a million American Girl dolls."

"I noticed the stash in your room."

"I haven't grown up, yet." She offered a weak laugh. "They were always my best friends. My babies. I didn't get to care for real children like you."

Torie said nothing.

"I know I had a good life. My parents love me." Maya brushed away an errant tear. "Knowing my ingratitude hurts the most. With my folks' vocation, I understood people lived with your type of life. Still, I convinced myself..." She hitched a breath as the scissors sawed at her hair, little hisses and clips.

"This ain't about me. Go on."

Did she want to?

Maya closed her eyes and placed her palm on her chest. *Lord, give me courage.* After a moment's pause, she answered. "Mom and Daddy worked seventy-hour weeks and would come home after I was asleep. I saw them at breakfast -- until they shipped me to boarding school. I never did well enough for them. I was third in my class at St. Martin's, a prestigious prep school where most students headed off to Harvard or Princeton or Stanford. I wanted to go to Albany State and be a teacher. They wanted me to join their law firm, but the law bored me. Especially defense work."

"Those guys are slime buckets."

"My folks weren't--"

"Sorry, but they are. You'd say the same if you heard Darren's defense blame me for his rutting problems. Go on."

Maya clamped her mouth shut. Her folks weren't bottom feeders. She opened her mouth to protest. She shut it. *I want to defend them for once?* Maybe she needed to forgive as much as Torie did. "Most of my folks' pro-bono clients are like Darren."

"Got many of them?"

"They can only handle so many. The big-shots pay the bills." She chuckled. "The paying clients aren't much better than the freeloaders,

173

and not all those guys are wicked. My parents believe one is innocent until proven guilty. Sometimes businesses are falsely accused because of others' greed. Good guys sometimes end up on the wrong side of the law. They needed to ensure everyone's constitutional rights. When the cops arrested my birth mother, they sent the john home to his wife and kids, even though both parties broke the law."

"Of course cops would free the hormonal male," Torie murmured. Sorrow, not sarcasm, tinged her voice.

"When I decided to be a teacher, they argued. Teaching was for those who weren't brilliant. Teachers were people who didn't excel, so they had no recourse but to teach. They claimed I was raised to 'give to the downtrodden'. They didn't see teaching as giving to others.

"I went to Yale for pre-law, as they wanted. Being away from them, I had some control. My freshman year I partied a lot. Too much."

"Is that why you don't touch booze?"

She nodded. "They missed Parents' Weekend that year. My friends were out with their folks or boyfriends. I'd never had a boyfriend. I knew I meant nothing to anyone. I drank a half-bottle of wine, then I cut my wrists."

At last, the blow-dryer whirred, and Torie tugged on her hair with a circular brush. The noise and the action prevented more conversation. Maya relaxed. Perhaps she wouldn't have to say anything else.

Torie now worked a flat iron through Maya's hair in blissful silence.

The iron clunked onto the table. The clack of metal against wood signaled the end of the stylist chair.

Torie grinned and held up a hand mirror.

"Go ahead. You might as well see yourself now, after the queen of cosmetology finished. I ain't doing your hair every morning, my dear."

She made no reference to Maya's confession. Had Torie heard a word she said?

Chapter Thirty-Two

"Truth is the highest thing that man may keep." Geoffrey Chaucer

Maya put the mirror down. This wasn't her hairstyle, her personality. Not only had Torie not listened, she had no clue about Maya's comfort level.

She tugged at her hair, and wouldn't look at Torie.

"Do you like it?"

Lies bubbled up. Maya picked up the mirror and studied her reflection, and pulled her hair back as though to shove it into a ponytail. A few tendrils escaped.

"Don't worry. You can pull it back."

Maya glanced at Torie, who looked like the proverbial canary-chomping cat, then studied her reflection. Aside from her hair's natural hue, she counted three other colors. Her ash blonde sparkled like the dry sand out at the Hamptons. The other colors enhanced it. So subtle yet dramatic.

"I love it." As she said the words, she knew she had spoken the truth. She couldn't take her eyes off her reflection. A wave of mahogany -- almost auburn -- wove between the blonde and blended into a deep brown and to a dark umber.

Hair swept across her forehead, like grown-out bangs. Layers angled at her chin and flowed past her shoulders. She fluffed her hair and leaned closer to the mirror. She remembered to close her mouth.

Torie stepped back, hands on hips, head cocked. An artist admiring her work.

Maya stared at herself once more. Her cheekbones looked higher, her skin tone bronzed. Her dark and arched eyebrows -- brows like Brooke Shields' -- no longer made her think of fuzzy caterpillars, but something sexy. Was this a good thing?

"With a little eyebrow pencil, you'll be as hot as Audrey Hepburn. *My* fair lady. I've got the perfect lipstick and mascara for your skin tone." She paused and put out a hand as though to silence a protest Maya wasn't about to make. "Don't fret. Bought it for you. Still in its shrink wrap." She left the kitchen, and Maya fluffed her hair.

"It's an easy do with your mane's natural body." Torie returned to the kitchen.

Maya jolted. "Torie, make some noise, and quit reading my mind."

Torie grinned -- the first genuine smile Maya had seen from her roommate. "Just toss your head upside down after showering and blow dry. Since we've done a partial color, you won't need to redo it often." She took the mirror out of Maya's hand. "Now for the makeover."

Torie tilted Maya's chin and with short strokes, colored her brows.

"Aren't they thick and dark enough?"

"Shush or I'll be tattooing your forehead." With deft strokes Torie colored. Next, she picked up mascara.

Maya struggled not to blink as the wand approached her eyes.

The tube clacked on the table, and Torie grabbed the lipstick. "Tomorrow we go find sexy sundresses."

"I won't wear sundresses."

Torie applied lipstick, its faint oily scent reminded Maya of the hours in her attic playroom with her mother's makeup. She'd spend half the day applying it to herself and all her American Girl dolls. She spent the rest of the day trying to clean it up. Her mother noticed when, on the rare occasions she used the stuff, she found her pulverized powder or smeared lipstick tubes. The next day, Maya had a gift of age-appropriate makeup. Boring, unnoticeable cosmetics.

In silence, Torie ran blush over Maya's cheeks. "My masterpiece." Torie handed Maya the mirror and stood back. Her friend bit her cheeks, but the action didn't repress her smile.

Maya licked her lips, and studied herself in the mirror.

She gulped, and caught her breath. If she walked out of the house like this, people would stare. What would Adam think? He had said he didn't like the Barbie doll/pageant queen types of women. He said he liked down-to-earth, real ladies. Would this be good or bad?

"Like it?"

Maya set the mirror down. How could she answer? Yes. She liked it, but felt silly. Lifting her chin, she inhaled. It was time to put the old Maya away. The need to change nagged her. Maya wanted to let Adam love her, but more than his adoration, she wanted to love herself as Jesus did.

"It'll grow on you. Trust me."

"I know." Even Maya heard the uncertainty in her voice. She stood.

"Wait a minute." Torie motioned with a finger for Maya to sit once more.

She turned and questioned with her eyes.

"Finish your story."

Maya filled her lungs, let out the air in one long swoosh, and plopped back onto the chair. A moment ago she was furious because Torie hadn't listened. Now it flustered her because she had.

Torie held out her hand to stop the words. "*I* know the benefit of getting the story out. It won't undo the past, but if someone cares, like my math teacher cared about me, you can live with it."

"I've lived with it fine."

"Long sleeves on hot spring days, tell me otherwise -- which, by the way, it's time for you to wear tank tops. Be the vixen you should be."

"I'm too fat for strapless shirts."

Torie rolled her eyes. "They've got straps."

Maya snuck one more peek at the mirror lying face up on the table and caught her reflection. The dramatic change made her see herself not as Maya Vitale, but as a stranger, a woman she would pass on the street and admire. Dream she could be like. Time to believe someone. Why not Torie?

"What about..." Maya held her wrists up as though Torie could see the scars through the long sleeves of her blouse.

"Bangles, elastic bracelets, charm bracelets. Wear them. People will see the bling, not the blemish."

"I don't know."

"I'll show you tomorrow when we shop. Now talk." Torie's tone brooked no argument.

"Is this the hairdresser's confession?" She studied the table then peeked up at Torie. Her friend's eyes told her it was safe to tell her the truth. Not Adam. If he ever found out...

Torie nodded. She held up her hand, palm out, and crossed the other arm over her heart. "I swear upon my flat irons."

Maya chuckled.

"Your smile," Torie said, "it's natural to you. Even when you're not interacting with anyone, you smile. And your cute nose? You make me so stinking mad because you make me happy just looking at you."

"You make no sense."

"Set yourself free, and tell me what happened."

Maya played with her hands resting in her lap. She raised her eyes and studied Torie who sat, legs crossed, arms leaning on the table. Eyes expectant.

Maya's mouth twitched. The comment about her smile made her self-conscious, and she knew a big grin was coming. She tried to rein it in. It grew. A solemn, stupid act shouldn't make her want to laugh.

As though standing on the edge of a pool, she dove in. "As I said, all my friends were out celebrating Parents' Weekend. My folks cancelled last minute, and Trudy, my roommate, went partying with her boyfriend. I was a freshman and no one loved me. I knew my roots -- daughter of a hooker and unknown john. Mom and Daddy told me nothing about her, I imagine client-lawyer confidentiality, even though she had thrown herself off a bridge. What kind of scum was my father?"

"I understand."

Self-pity heated Maya's face. "I had everything given to me. Despite everything, I believed I was worthless."

Torie stiffened. She opened her mouth to say something, but settled back, no longer in her relaxed posture. Expectant.

Her bearing catapulted Maya. "I knew I needed warm water to keep the blood from clotting. People usually sat in bathtubs, but all we had were shower stalls. I took a razor, and fully clothed -- didn't want anyone to find me naked -- stepped into the shower. The water comforted. I knew I was doing the right thing. I tilted my head back, let the warmth cascade around me." She tore her eyes away from Torie. If she didn't look at her, she could tell the tale.

"I picked up the razor. Slit." Shame shivered through her.

Torie took one of Maya's wrists, and Maya tugged it back, but Torie had a strong grasp. "No. Face it. If you do, you'll accept it." Maya's hand relaxed as Torie studied the wrist. "As I said, the scars aren't bad."

"A good plastic surgeon."

"How'd you survive?"

"Fortunately, and this is the one time I'd ever called the prank fortunate, we had a trick we called toweling. Our showers had an outer chamber where we changed, then the stall itself. Each compartment was closed off by a curtain. When someone took a shower, we'd sneak in and slip our hands into the changing cubicle and steal all the clothes and the towel leaving the poor victim naked and sopping wet. It was hysterical for the pranksters, not the prankees.

"Trudy's boyfriend had gotten sick, so she came home early, heard the shower going and figured it was me. When Trudy slipped into my stall, she found no towel or night clothes. Just me, unconscious."

Silence filled the room. Not even breathing disturbed the quiet.

"The best part. My parents let me transfer to Albany State. Let me become a teacher."

Fire lit Torie's eyes. "The best part? You lived." Her tone asked Maya why she refused to believe this truth.

Maya studied her friend and smiled thinly. *I will believe.* "To this day, my parents' will reaches into my life and strangles me until I force myself to remember how much they love me. After I found Jesus, I understood pure love. I forgave them for being who they are."

"I'll never forgive Selene and Trey, let alone Darren and Jean."

"You need to."

Torie crossed her arms and looked away. Her mouth worked in a

178

tight line.

"Forgiveness doesn't mean condoning the actions. My parents are too busy for the life *I* want from them, and I can't live the life they want for me. Forgiving them took away *my* pain." She fingered the mirror on the table for a minute and searched Torie's face. "My self-pity pales compared to what you described."

"I'll never forgive them. Ever."

"I've told you everything. However, you never answered my question."

Torie continued gathering her supplies. "What question?"

"You said Darren got you pregnant. What happened to the baby?"

Torie grabbed the last of her hair products and headed to her room. "We'll hit the outlets in Glens Falls. I know it's a work week, but it'd be cool to shock Adam with a new look when he shows up for the field day on Friday."

Chapter Thirty-Three

"The kind of man who always thinks that he is right, that his opinions, his pronouncements, are the final word, when once exposed shows nothing there. But a wise man has much to learn without a loss of dignity." Sophocles

Friday arrived. All week Torie prepped Maya for Adam's promised field trip showing Maya and Justine's classes the workings of a real-live ambulance. Torie couldn't wait to hear how it went. A new yellow sundress, bangles, and a morning hair-dressing, a one-time deal she'd told Maya, and off to school for a love fest. Life was good as a giver.

A sober giver. Torie smirked with pride. She knew how to keep her promises -- no drink *all* week.

Her good mood vanished as she pulled Maya's car into the Laundromat's parking lot. The Laundromat. Who used them, anyway, except losers? Who wanted to put their clothes in a machine a louse-ridden, clap-infected person used? Even Adam owned a washer and dryer, and his cabin made Maya's place look gargantuan.

Torie hauled the laundry basket, overflowing with both their clothes out of Maya's Honda and butted the door closed. No other cars sat in the lot. Hopefully, no one else needed clean clothes today.

The aged door buzzer on the side of the building grated and announced her entrance into the tiny foyer leading into the washing area. The manager ducked his head out of the room containing the dry-cleaner conveyer. He eyed her basket. "If you need anything, hit the bell." He nodded toward a button near the counter. "Noisy back here." He vanished back into the world of chemicals.

The room was as empty as the parking lot promised. She grinned at her good luck. After loading the machines, Torie found a seat near the single window in the front of the dingy joint. Since the view it offered was the stunning vista of one of Burnt Hollow's grimy side streets, she picked up a copy of *People* magazine. With the background music of her washing machines and the grinding of the dry-cleaning conveyer, Torie settled in for the long, boring wait.

Half-way through the magazine, the buzzer announced a new customer.

Darren and Jean strolled through the side door.

She raised the magazine, kept her eyes on the page. *Go away, Darren.*

She peeked over the page. *Where was the manager? Sniffing dry-cleaning fluid?*

Someone had to do something to help her. She couldn't sit here with them around. The magazine dropped to her lap. "You need to come back later." She glared at Darren. Even at this distance, his dilated pupils sent a shiver down her spine.

"It figures you'd show up here, Victoria," Jean said. "Babe, put the clothes there." She pointed toward the two machines running. Torie's machines. "We'll go get something to eat and come back later. Nobody's gonna be bothered--"

"I don't even want your stuff next to mine." Torie cut off her mother's rambling.

"We won't be bothering you, Victoria." Her mother fished out a cigarette.

"No smoking." Torie pointed to sign by the counter. "Chemicals."

Her mother glared. "Oh, lighten up--"

"I think his probation," she nodded at Darren, "states he's not allowed to get high--

"High?" Darren snarled. "Who's high?"

"My orders of protection state--"

"There you go. Orders of protection. Why're you picking a fight?" Darren glanced toward the manager who now made an appearance and scowled in their direction. Darren lowered his voice. "We ain't psychic. How'd we know you were here? Didn't see your car in the lot."

"Well, it's there."

"The one with the bad fender?" Darren glanced at the manager who was tapping his fingers against the counter.

Adrenaline from asserting her rights swelled Torie's courage. "Why aren't you over in Westerlo where you're registered as living instead of mooching off Jean?"

Darren stepped toward Torie, finger pointed, squinted eyes shooting sparks, then stepped away. He smacked his fist into his other palm. "Why don't you drop the attitude? Let bygones be bygones."

Torie stood. The fight, like liquid courage from scotch, fueled her anger. "It's easy for you to let go. You didn't get pimped-out, lose a baby because your buddies infected you with chlamydia--"

"Don't lie, Victoria," her mother hissed. "It was *you* who infected--"

"If Jean hadn't been gutted and spayed, you could have a whole litter of mongrels to molest."

"You little--" Darren took two steps toward Torie.

The manager now strode toward the trio.

"I have an order of protection, sir. My clothes are in the wash. I can't leave."

"Does she have one?" the manager asked Darren and Jean.

"Because she lied. Falsely accused my fiancé." Jean's voice grated and lost its seductive purr.

"Lied?" Torie hissed. "I'm your daughter. You're supposed to protect--"

"Enough." The manager pulled a cell from his pocket. "As far as I can tell, you're all aggravating this altercation. You all have to leave."

Darren swiped his palms on his jeans. "I'm sorry. This..." He cracked his knuckles and lowered his voice. "This woman has a big chip on her shoulder from false memories. Her lies ruined *my* life. Not hers."

The manager punched numbers into the phone. "Yes. This is Burnt Hollow Laundromat on Mill Street. We have an altercation."

"Forget about it." Darren stomped toward his laundry. "I'm outta here -- gonna go to Vorheesville or Schoharie from now on." He turned back to Torie and jabbed a finger at her. "You ain't pushing us around no more."

Torie tilted her head, and gave a tight-lipped smile.

The manager turned toward her. "You can finish your laundry, but you're not welcome here after this."

Darren's eyes sparked daggers before he turned and thrust the door open. Torie knew the look, and her heart stopped. Maya's words flitted through her head. *Forgive him?*

Never.

*****

During the field trip, Maya heard nothing of Adam and Levi's chatter. They led the kids through their ambulance and prattled on about the equipment. All she saw were his covert glances followed by stammered words. Joy made her hug herself with glee.

If they could talk in private.

If she didn't have to spend time with Mom and Daddy this weekend.

If only she made this transformation earlier.

At last, they ushered the kids back into the classroom.

Their students sat cross-legged on the floor, and Adam asked for questions. Hands shot up.

"Well, Stephenson," Adam leaned over toward his buddy, "now you'll see what a natural teacher I am."

"Don't be too sure of yourself," Justine said.

Maya covered her mouth but didn't manage to stifle her laughter.

"Do you get blood all over you?" one little boy asked. A chorus of high-pitched squeals and groans of "gross" or "ew," responded to his question.

"How about puke?" the boy in the wheelchair asked. "What happens when someone barfs or gets--"

"Nelson," Maya admonished. She smiled at the men. "This is what they *really* wanted to know."

Another little boy stood and flapped his arms, and rotated his neck. "D-d-don't y-you g-g-get dizzy from the zooming *amlence?*" He flopped to the floor. Maya stepped forward, pointed to the back of the room. She bit back her smile but prayed the child didn't notice. Without a word, the boy got up and sat in a chair by her desk.

"Do you cry?"

"Do they die?"

"How do you get rid of a dead corpse?"

All the questions revolved around their own scatological or psychological concerns. Almost none pertained to the true nature of the job. Maya shook her head. Adam, hopefully, understood how little these kids grasped.

Justine turned to the kids. "What do you say?"

"Thank you, Mr. Benedict and Mr. Stephenson," the class singsonged.

"My class will stay here for a minute while Ms. Vitale sees our visitors out." Justine smiled at Maya.

They walked in silence -- perhaps being in the hallway made the men hesitant -- other classes were going on, after all. "Thank you," Maya broke the quiet. "The kids loved it."

Levi laughed. "Who knew by being bloody, we'd convert the whole crew. They're going to be ambulance drivers, yet."

Adam shoved him. "Paramedics."

Reserve returned until they got to the lobby.

"I'll wait for you outside." Stephenson headed out.

Adam stared out the front doors. "Do you think they learned anything?"

"Look at me, Adam."

He glanced at Maya, then turned away.

She took his chin and turned it to her. "What's eating you?"

"Don't you have to get back to the kids?"

"I don't believe you!" She shook her head and took several stomping steps toward her classroom. She skittered to a stop, spoke to the air, and refused to look at Adam. "All morning I caught you staring at me -- drooling like a moronic male. Now you say nothing?" She pivoted, expected to see an empty lobby. Adam stood as though stuck to the waxed floor. "You can be insufferable, Benedict." She fisted her hands onto her hips. If this man was going to act like her first graders, she'd be the teacher. "What's eating you?" She didn't move closer.

He stepped toward her but glanced at the office. A teacher left the suite and passed them.

Adam opened his mouth to speak, and she stopped him. He took one step toward her, then stopped.

"Why so quiet?" she asked.

The silence between them felt awkward.

Adam shrugged. "If you let Torie--"

"Torie? This is about Torie?"

"Your hair. The clothes. She's going to make you look like her. A--"

A what? Don't say it. Blood pounded in her temples. "I've had enough. On Sunday we'll talk." She stomped off, then turned. "*Maybe* we'll talk."

*****

With Darren's exit, the manager cast a warning glance at Torie and disappeared once more. While the dryers thumped and clumped and rattled, she visited the ladies' room to fix her hair. She smiled at her image. The scarlet streak in her hair looked sassy, a sign to the world of who *she* was.

After an eternity, the laundry dried. The crisp linen smell of freshly dried clothes made folding them a delight. Giving the laundry sharp creases, Torie lingered over the sorting and stacking. With the last shirt finished, she hauled the basket to her hip and headed toward the door. Her ribs didn't even protest.

Life had healed.

Pushing through the doorway, Torie stopped, the basket too heavy in her arms. Her ribs pounded raw by her heart.

Every window of Maya's car had been smashed like crushed ice.

With the basket of clothes now resting on shards of glass scattered across the car's hood, Torie found her phone. As though she punched Darren, Torie pounded 9-1-1. With arms wrapped across her ribs, she paced the lot while waiting for the cops to show up. Who else could she call? Maya was in the middle of her school day.

Who could pick her up? Where would she haul Maya's car? It couldn't be driven. The windshield was a mosaic of Pabloesque spider webs. She tapped it with her fingernails, hoping glass would rain down. If it did, she'd at least see out the windshield.

How do I get home with this laundry?

Now I have to pay for this.

Once more, she had to pay for Darren and Jean.

After earning enough in tips over her two weeks at The Stadium, hope dared to resurrect. Torie daydreamed about cars and apartments and sales at the outlets. With three make-overs done this week, she even dared to believe she could start a salon someplace.

As she waited for the cops, she called Heather, got the answering machine. Called Lucy. Brooke.

Were they all screening their calls? Her name wouldn't show up from a TracFone, would it?

Ten minutes later, the police arrived.

"Darren Brown and Jean Turcotte did this," she said.

"Did you see them?" The cop pulled out a pad and scribbled Torie's statement.

"No. You can ask the manager." She pointed toward the Laundromat.

"He witnessed it?"

Torie shrugged. "He saw the fight they started when they came inside high as those electrical wires." She waved her hand in the general direction of the power lines. "They were the only ones here."

"But not the only ones on the street. Let's go in."

A half-an-hour later the cops left, supposedly to check out Darren and Jean. Fat chance of anything happening there.

She borrowed the manager's phone directory, called the one tow company in town. After telling the woman who answered what she needed, Torie was put on hold. Music played some boring stuff by dead composers. Halfway through the third song, the woman picked up.

"I see you have an outstanding bill. Until you pay for our last tow, we're not coming out."

"How am I going to get the car out of here?"

"We take Master Card, Visa or Discover."

Torie dug out her card, gave the woman her numbers and waited through two songs.

"Sorry. Your card's been denied. Do you have another?"

Without responding, Torie hung up. She had one last option. Maybe life with Trey softened her friend.

Friend?

Never.

She called Curly Girls. The phone rang.

And rang.

Rang too many times for Selene to be busy with a customer. After

185

ten or twelve rings, the answering machine clicked on. Instead of their funny duet claiming they were Snip and Snap and would you leave a message -- or your hair at the door -- Selene's solemn voice said the salon was closed due to a family emergency.

Family emergency? Selene's family was as close as Jean and Darren were to her. Forget Trey's snobby folks. Could Selene be ill?

She hyperventilated as she dialed Selene's cell.

"Hello?" Selene's voice sounded as winded as Torie felt. Sounded worried.

"It's Torie. What's going on?"

The cold silence transmitted over the phone was better than the red-hot anger of their last contact.

"I'm in a fix at the Laundromat in town. Darren bashed up my friend's car. I need a way home--"

"Call a cab." The phone clicked off.

A cab. Coming from Schoharie, it'd take an hour and would cost her last week's wages.

She called the taxi, then checked her wallet. Needed to hit the ATM if they expected her to pay the fare.

At the market, she made a withdrawal.

With fifty bucks in her wallet, a little of the edge evaporated. Just enough to let despair flood her. She needed to chill, so she could think. A drink would help. She'd been good all week, so something light would be okay. Even she knew Jesus drank wine.

She picked up wine coolers and crossed the street to the post office to see if some unexpected check arrived. Instead of money owed *her*, Torie walked away with a fistful of bills -- most of them medical.

She shuffled through the pile as she wandered back to the Laundromat to find no cab came yet.

Torie stepped behind the building and leaned against the wall. She twisted a lid from the cooler. *It's not a week since I made the promise to not drink.*

Her thoughts startled her. She wouldn't drink the whole bottle, and she'd never do coke like Jean or meth like her sister Robin, let alone, end up in the hoosegow like Crystal. Just enough wine to think straight. Surely God hadn't seen this problem coming when she made the promise to Him to not drink for a week.

Sipping the wine, Torie laughed and looked up at the sky. *I don't make sense, do I?*

She'd already taken a slug. She'd finish the one bottle and not drink until *next* weekend.

A car pulled into the lot.

Got here quick.

She tossed the bottle toward a dumpster and rounded the building. In the lot stood Trey.

Torie's own hands clutched at her chest. *Trey.* She willed her heart to slow, and blinked back her tears. Her attention shifted to Selene, and the unfamiliar hatred of her Judas bubbled up once more. Selene didn't bother to get out of Trey's Mustang. She sat, her lips tight, hands clenching the wheel, and her eyes trained on the parking lot.

"Darren loves you." Trey shook his head as he surveyed the smashed car.

"At least you know who did this. Cops are *investigating.*"

"Hop in. We'll drive you home."

Her eyes moved from Trey back to Selene. Her feet refused to move. Women were nasty creatures. Why did she so crave Selene's friendship? She'd stolen Trey, after all. They'd shared years of gossip, talks about men and hair and food. But she'd taken Trey from her. It made no sense.

"How'd you change her mind?" Torie nodded toward Selene.

"You know her soft side. She's like you -- a pineapple."

Torie arched a brow.

Trey laughed. "All spiny on the outside, but sweet and soft and a teeny bit acidic inside. Let's go, my little pineapple, before her acid tang turns to venom. You make her jealous."

"Jealous? Me?" Her heart, which had quieted, pounded again. Did she dare hope?

"She thinks you're prettier and livelier than she."

"Thinks? Gee, thanks."

Trey chuckled. "She's afraid I'll go back to you."

"Not if I can help it." Yet Torie knew she lied.

"It's funny. You can't help love. I didn't mean to fall for your best bud, but I care about you. As a friend. Come on before Selene changes her mind."

Torie hauled her clothes and the plastic bag of Hooch into the back seat while Trey and Selene sat in the front. Adam would at least have helped carry her stuff, and *he* had a reason to hate her. At one time. Not now, of course.

Torie called the cab company and cancelled her ride. They drove the rest of the way to Maya's in icy silence. Torie studied the back of Trey's head. His brown hair grew long. As lush as always. She wanted to bury her face in it, rub her cheek along the stubble on his face. She glanced at Selene whose jaw worked as though holding back tears. Something bad was happening.

Should I ask?

She bit back her questions and wished it was Adam or Maya driving her home.

They pulled up in Maya's drive. Torie plopped her clothes and supplies on the gravel, careful to avoid the grass which would be crawling with ticks. She turned to close the door and noticed tears in Selene's eyes, her hand on Trey's, her gaze fixed on him. Torie's hatred melted.

"Thank you. I don't know what's wrong, but I'll pray for you."

She shut the door, and asked God to help her forgive.

Chapter Thirty-Four

"Not for ourselves alone are we born." Marcus Tullius Cicero

Adam pulled up to his cabin. *Where's the Lincoln?*

He jogged into the house knowing what he wouldn't find.

"Pop?" In the guest room, his grandfather's bed lay rumpled, but made-up after a fashion. Back in the kitchen, dishes sat dry in the drainer. He dialed the farmhouse. "Pop, pick up the phone. I know you're there."

He pocketed his cell. If Pop went home, he'd be on the porch, and would ignore the phone. Neema was the one who made sure the cordless sat near his rocker.

He hopped into the truck and burned rubber down his driveway.

Five minutes out, flashing lights told him to pull over. As Chad Morgan stepped out of the trooper's car, Adam rummaged in the glove box for his license and registration.

"Hey, Benedict. Haven't seen you since you rescued the drunken pixie from the ditch."

"Afternoon, Morgan."

"Do you know how fast you were going?"

Adam shook his head. He needed to explain his situation. Talk his way out of the ticket, but fear for Pop and worry over the delay his speeding caused froze his excuses.

"Can I see--?"

Adam handed over the documents.

Trooper Morgan gave them a cursory glance. "What's up?"

He swallowed hard. "My grandfather ran off."

Morgan nodded. "Sorry about your grandmother. Look, I'll let this one slide. Grief makes us careless. Be sure to tell your grandfather he's going to kill someone if he drives. Take the keys away."

"We have."

"Next time, lock them in your gun safe."

The men chuckled, and Morgan handed back the documents.

Adam waited until Morgan climbed into his cruiser and pulled into traffic. Shifting into gear, Adam drove the speed limit, tapping his fingers on the steering wheel as he tailed the trooper. Morgan made a U-turn. Once out of sight, Adam pressed down on the accelerator and pushed the curves until he was certain someone would have to fish him out of a ditch.

No telling what trouble Pop could get into, if he hadn't wrecked the car already or fallen or...

He sped by a dented guardrail and pictured his rescue last year of a teen with a two-week-old driver's license. Adam slowed. For a minute. On a straightway, he stepped on the gas, hit a pothole, and bounded across the line. What about Pop? Had he hit this? Seen it?

He pushed more. Saw Pop in the drainage ditch, pictured him racing through the barbed wire -- or worse -- the stone fences.

No. No. No.

After what felt like miles of careening around curving roads and miles of heart pounding, he swerved into Pop's driveway. The Lincoln was parked next to the porch at a cockamamie angle. At least Pop got home.

Adam bounded up the stairs. The porch lay empty. In the house, he found Pop in the kitchen. "What got into you? How could you drive yourself home?"

Pop fussed with the bread wrapper, working the twist tie to open it. Tightened it, instead.

"Give it to me." Adam grabbed the bread, and his grandfather yanked it back.

"I kin do it. Done it longer than you."

"Why'd you run off? What if you killed someone?" Adam swallowed hard, not meaning to sound so harsh, not wanting to condemn his grandfather.

Pop dropped the unopened bread on the counter. "Been gone so long, probably stale anyhow."

Adam's tension ebbed, and he gentled his voice. "Pop?"

His grandfather stared at him, and tottered out of the kitchen.

Adam darted after him. Once more, he sounded like a parent hounding his kid. Not a grandson. Not worried sick.

His grandfather settled on the couch, clutching a quilted pillow in his lap. He ran his hands over the pattern. "Your grandma sure was good with a needle." He smoothed the fabric.

Adam couldn't force eye contact. He knelt in front of Pop. "Your reflexes are too slow. You can't drive."

His grandfather lifted his head, caught Adam's gaze and held it. He licked his lips, opened his mouth, then closed it.

Adam sank next to him. "We'll get some of Neema's needlework and bring them back to the cabin. No more driving. Promise me?"

"I ain't promising nothin' I can't keep. Not like you."

"Me?"

"A few days at your place you said. Been purt near two weeks. I ain't living in no two-by-four cabin."

"Pop, all my stuff's--"

"My stuff's here. Case closed." His grandfather wobbled to his feet. "I'm goin' to lie down. You go get some fresh bread. That stuff," he nodded toward the kitchen, "got mold all over it." He headed out of the living room.

Adam assumed he'd go to the dining room and his hospital bed, but when Pop took a step up the stairs, Adam bolted after him and grabbed his arm.

His grandfather twisted free. "Let me be, son. I ain't no baby. I'm sleeping in my wedding bed tonight."

Adam slunk into the recliner as Pop wobbled up the steep stairs. He wouldn't stay at the cabin any longer. This house wasn't safe for him. Adam had to make it secure. He stood and opened the closet. Assessed where plumbing should go for a half bath.

Could he make it work?

With Stephenson's help.

He stepped back and studied the room. Once more, Pop propped his Winchester beside the kitchen door. He gritted his teeth. Home two minutes and got the stupid gun out. He stomped into the kitchen, nabbed the rifle, and stormed up the stairs.

"Quit throwing yer tantrum." Pop's voice sounded frailer through the closed door of his bedroom.

Adam entered his old room and surveyed the childish mementos, Boy Scout badges, Star Wars Legos -- evidence of who he used to be. He locked the rifle with the other two in the safe. *Fat chance of it staying here. Why'd he need this rifle? With his tremors, he'd hit the ceiling instead of the barn out back.*

Since Adam couldn't lock him up at his cabin like he had locked up the old Winchester, Pop needed full-time care. Adam plopped down at his old desk under the bunk bed.

How would he care for him? Adam couldn't stay home full time. He needed to work. He should've listened to Jennifer, have become a doctor, and earned real money so he could hire in-house help.

Even if he started his studies today, Pop would be dead before he graduated.

Dead.

He rubbed his eyes. He needed help.

*****

191

Justine pulled her battered van up to the Capitol Arms. No black BMW waited in the driveway. What did Maya expect? It was a little after three, not even the normal person's quitting time, let alone the end of the Vitale work day – so much for hope. The year after her suicide attempt, they doted on her.

Work called them in the end.

Maya reached for the door handle. What would it have cost them to sacrifice a little extra time for *their* planned weekend?

She knew the Vitales -- their love for their clients, their dedication to justice, and to constitutional rights.

Forgive me, Lord.

Justine rolled down the window as Maya rounded the front of the van. "Will you be okay? Want me to stay?"

Maya forced a smile. "Not a baby." The phrase made her think of Harold, and a real smile blossomed. "Monday's absence put me behind at work." She yanked open the back door, and grabbed her laptop and her briefcase holding this weekend's math papers. "Got enough to keep me busy until they get here."

"Call if you need anything. If Adam can't get out here on Sunday, I'll come get you."

"Thanks." Maya waved and watched as Justine drove down the shady, residential street. Large maples stretched across the road and made her think she was out in Westfield or Rensselaerville rather than the city of Albany.

Seconds after the bells attached to the front door clanged their greeting, Arianna Thompson, the owner of the B & B, hurried into the foyer. "Maya. So good to see you. As usual." She opened the Queen Anne oak escritoire, the B & B's sign-in desk, and pulled out a key attached to a fob shaped like the state seal of New York. "You know your room -- Excelsior. Sal and Viola are in Justice."

"They wouldn't have it any other way." Maya mustered a smile because she knew what Arianna would tell her next.

"As usual, you've beaten them here." She yelled down the hall. "Ben. Come help Miss Vitale with her--"

Maya grabbed her arm. "No need to bother your son. I imagine he's in the midst of a clan war and needs to upgrade his town hall. I just have this." She pointed at her overnight bag and computer. "By now, I know the routine."

"The usual?"

Maya smiled. Arianna knew how to run a beautiful B & B.

Her folks always reserved the Excelsior for her. Ever upward. Her direction in life. Despite the dig at her lack of ambition, Maya loved the room. She plopped her bag on top of the queen-sized four-poster bed. The bold poppies on the comforter gave the antique bed a contemporary feel. Atop the bedposts, a gauzy canopy fluttered in the breezes from an open window. She breathed in springtime. The mattress was made for the princess who couldn't sleep on a pea -- so high, Arianna should supply footstools to climb up on it, and so soft, it cradled Maya when she slept.

A bottle of wine sat chilling on one of the two matching end tables. Her parents, once more believing her life modeled theirs, forgot her foray into alcohol lasted three months. Maya set up her laptop atop a small desk with Queen Anne legs. A matching antique dresser with bas-relief flowers around the mirror completed the furnishings.

This place always made her feel like a princess.

Once her parents arrived.

She checked her watch. Not time for them to be here, but Maya couldn't stop herself. Dialing her mom's cell, voicemail instantly picked up. Mom's cell wasn't even on. She forced a smile to lighten her voice. "I'm at the Capitol Arms." She paused. Her message sounded too curt. "Can't wait until you get here." By saying the words, the feelings followed.

Shoving her computer aside, Maya slipped off her bangles and tossed them on the bed. Kicking off her shoes, she lay down. Work held no appeal. Only her parents mattered.

Her stomach grumbled. A stroll would take her to Kauffman's Deli. Their staff made the world's best Reuben sandwiches served with kosher dill pickles plucked from a barrel. If Mel, the owner was there, she'd sit at a booth and eat. Before she'd finish grace, he'd be at her side. Would regale her with tales of wayward college kids. She'd splurge and buy chips and linger until her folks arrived.

The bangles clinked as she rose from the bed. Annoying things, but Torie promised she'd get used to them. She lifted one and slipped it on.

Maya studied her wrist. The Yale-New Haven plastic surgeons stitched it well. One scar was slightly raised and redder than the rest, but as a whole, they were faint. If you didn't know what to look for, you could mistake them for something else. What? A fall on barbed wire? A vicious Maine Coon cat? Or perhaps the truth. It was dangerous to believe a lie.

After her confession to Torie, Maya knew she had one more lie to clear up. Would she hurt her parents in healing herself?

Healing.

They all needed one -- her, Torie, and Adam. Maybe a hurt ate at him?

He acted more quiet and distracted today. Sometimes she worried about his change in temper, but Justine loved him. Although not much older than him, she treated him like one of her sons. Levi considered Adam his closest friend. The stress he was under with his grandmother's death and his grandfather's failing health had to be getting to him. Until his mourning ended, she'd take it slow. She didn't need love so badly she'd throw herself at any man. She was a Vitale, after all, not at all like her biological mother.

Slipping the rest of the bracelets back on, Maya headed out the door. On the first step down, her cell rang.

"Maya?"

Torie should be at work, not calling. Was she on her way to The Stadium?

"I waited until you were out of school. Your car..."

Her heart skipped. "Are you okay?" She turned back to her room and fished for her key.

"Yeah. I'm good." Silence filled the line. "Your car's been..."

"Been?"

"Vandalized." As though the dam burst, Torie poured out the story.

Maya clenched her free fist and plopped onto the bed. Counting to ten as Torie rambled slowed her pulse minimally. Maya remembered her family. The Vitales understood the lives of the less advantaged. Anger fled. Understanding filled its void.

"I'll call Justine. She or Levi will figure something out, and they'll get the car home and get you to work. I'll call back if we can't work it out." Maya dialed Justine.

The phone rang twice. Maya hung up. Justine would barely be back in Delmar, let alone Westfield. Levi worked three o'clocks this week.

She called Adam.

Her hunger vanished. Why did trouble dog Torie?

*****

Adam shoved his scanner and laptop into the passenger seat and slammed the door. The bed of the truck held a few suitcases and boxes.

At the end of his driveway, his phone rang Maya's tone.

"Hey." Adam pulled onto the main road, grateful for the Bluetooth so he didn't have to check for Trooper Morgan. "So glad you called. Guess what I'm stuck doing?" He pictured the little crinkle of her nose as she worked on a guess, the tilt of her lips. He imagined the Jennifer-bangles off her now bare arms -- how could bare arms be so sexy? Without the bracelets, all resemblance to the empty-headed beauty

194

would be gone.

He grinned. Jewelry didn't create character. Maya hadn't changed just because she looked as beautiful as Jennifer.

She said nothing.

"Can't see you shrug." He turned onto Route 85. "Pop ran off. I'm going to have to move into my grandparents' place until I can talk sense into him."

"Or him you." Maya sounded sad.

"What's wrong?"

"Torie took my car to the Laundromat."

Adam held his breath as anger churned. He sighed. As though it blew him off-course, he swerved over the double yellow line, corrected, and pulled off the road as Maya explained the predicament.

"Can you tow my car?"

He stifled his frustration. Why'd Maya insist on being involved with Sullivan? Shouldn't Torie suffer the consequences of her own actions?

Her actions, though, always pulled in others. The car was Maya's, and Maya needed help.

"Adam? You still there?"

"Of course."

"First, can you get her to work?"

He sucked in a breath.

"Take her to church on Sunday?" Maya chuckled, a laugh sounding more self-deprecating than humorous. "Get my car, *before* Sunday. My students' inability to sequence events has rubbed off on me."

Words stuck in his craw. He should say something soon before Maya hung up and called again. Why'd Torie come back into his life? "Church?" Adam caught himself before he yelled. "What good will church do her? She's a needy drunk."

"Adam. Without it, what hope do any of us have?"

"Fine."

"You don't have to be so curt."

The truth of her statement slapped his face. "You're right." With the words out of his mouth, he knew he had to change. He'd start right now.

Instead of heading toward Pop's, Adam turned right and up to Maya's. Remembering his resolve to become the person God created him to be, he hopped out of the truck.

Before he could close the door, Torie exited the house. She said nothing as she climbed into the waiting truck, and silence, along with the fumes of alcohol, filled the F-150 as he drove toward The Stadium. He strained to not look at her, studied the scenery as it sped by his window.

"You can drape me--" Torie giggled and put her hand to her mouth.

"Um, drop me off at the Ready Mart. I need to pick up some gum."

He looked at her. Instead of a drunk, a lost child appeared. Adam grabbed her arm as she shoved the truck door open. "Are you okay to work?"

Her eyes, large and brown looked lost. For the first time since he met her, since he had known her, he understood the world of hurt in their depths. Had her pain always been there?

He opened his mouth to offer help.

Torie jerked her arm away. "Quit judging me." She slammed the door, and with the action, pity vanished.

She had to fix her own messes.

Chapter Thirty-Five

"Everybody, sooner or later, sits down to a banquet of consequences."
Robert Louis Stevenson

Customers crowded The Stadium early. It was going to be a long night. Torie slid the T-bone into place. "Anything else?" She turned to go before the man could answer. Picking up the trout from the serving tray, Torie placed it in front of a woman at another table. Without asking if everything was fine, Torie grabbed her tray and headed to the kitchen.

"Excuse me."

Torie turned to the guy with the steak. "This is as desiccated as shoe leather." He poked it with his knife. "Looks mummified to me."

Desiccated? Isn't that what you do to holy stuff?

"I asked for rare."

"Sorry." She picked up the steak, returned to the kitchen and shoved the plate towards Cook. He caught it before it slid off the counter. "The guy changed his mind. He wants it rare." The lie stabbed her conscience, and she blinked as tears threatened.

"You're off your feed tonight," Cook said. "You feeling okay?"

"Yeah. Great." Squaring her shoulders and determined to focus, Torie returned to the restaurant with a carafe of coffee. She stopped short at the bar. Collin was gesturing to the trout lady. Whiffs of their angry words reached her, and her hands shook. This was bad. The couple stormed out of the restaurant.

The pot slipped out of her hands, shattered on the floor, splattering her with steaming coffee. Grabbing a bar rag, Torie bent over to swab the muck. Her head whirled -- throbbed like the bass of a teenager's car radio. She shouldn't have drunk *all* the wine. Or at least not chugged it.

They were wine coolers. Lighter than the real deal. How was she to know it'd make her woozy. Woozy? Her mind whirled like she'd drunk a four-pack of scotch. She smirked. *Should suggest they sell ol' Jim in multi-packs.*

"Torie," Collin said. He nodded toward his office.

She jerked upright, held onto the bar to stop the room from spinning and headed to the office. He wouldn't fire her, would he? She hadn't drunk *on* the job. If he were going to can her, she'd have to talk her way out of it.

Talk her way out of it?

Exhaustion overwhelmed Torie. Her excuses drained. Flirting her way out of messes dirtied her.

Collin held the door open, and she brushed past him. With barely a sound, it clicked shut. Not a good sign.

"Do you realize you could have killed the woman who just stormed out of here?"

"Killed her? Come on. Cook's cooking's not *that* bad." She slumped into a chair to steady herself.

"You gave her the pistachio trout."

"So?" Her rudeness curdled her blood. Her flippant mouth tasted sour. Collin was her boss. Torie squeezed her elbows into her ribcage, wished to become like Alice -- tiny. *What does God think of me?*

"She's got a severe nut allergy. She told you about it as soon as you handed them the menu."

"I forgot."

"They reminded you when they asked for the order."

She opened her mouth to speak. Words wouldn't form.

"I've told you about drinking," Collin said.

Dear God, don't let him can me.

"There's no easy way to say this. You're fired. Now."

"Trish will be alone, and--"

"She's better off working on her own."

Torie couldn't force her eyes to meet Collin's. Shame, something she hadn't felt since first or second grade, flooded her. She couldn't lift her head. Had nothing to say.

"I won't let you drive. Is there someone to call or do you want a cab?"

Torie raised her head, and scrutinized Collin's eyes. Worse than anger or contempt, she read pity in their extended gaze, in the moisture brimming there. He tilted his head and frowned, and took a step toward her.

She rose, lost her balance and bumped into his desk. He reached out to steady her. She threw up her hands. "I'm good."

"Yes. When sober, I couldn't ask for a better waitress. You have the work ethic to run your own business."

"Well, I'm *not* drunk."

Collin crossed his arms.

He *knew.* She'd show him.

Torie stepped slowly, made sure every step was steady. She opened the door, straightened her spine, and walked out of the office. The door clicked shut. Once certain Collin couldn't see her, she scurried down the hallway, untying her apron and tossing it by the coat hooks. On the back patio, the cool, evening breeze did nothing to stop her spinning world. Torie turned up the street and hurried as fast as her feet would take her. If she walked home, she'd be sober by the time she got there.

Her head pounded and her ribs moaned with every footfall. She needed some Motrin or Advil or Aleve or Tylenol or all of the above. The Ready Mart would sell some sort of pain relievers.

Inside the store, Torie ambled up and down the aisles looking for the pain-relievers. On a back counter, the Advil sat next to packages of Aleve. Commercials said she needed two of them. She'd take Aleve. Fewer drugs would prove she wasn't a druggie.

Torie paid for her pills, and in the parking lot, ripped open the carton, pried off the cap, and shook out two. Then she took one more. She wanted to not hurt.

In order to swallow them, she needed water. She returned to the store.

She stumbled to the rear coolers and grabbed a bottle of water, then noticed the price. *A dollar-fifty for a bottle of water? I'm not paying almost two bucks for water. All the manufacturers did was scoop the liquid out of some spring and screw on a top.*

Instead, Torie picked up a can. Light beer. One can.

Once outside, Torie popped the lid, took only two Aleve, seeing as she had some alcohol to help it along, and continued her trek.

*****

Pop moped. He was home like he wanted, but he sulked like a toddler denied a sweet. He wouldn't eat or drink anything, even after Adam bought fresh bread, made tomato soup, brewed a pot of decaf, and brought everything upstairs to Neema's bedroom. Each time Adam coaxed his grandfather, he'd roll away from him. Adam gave up, and pulled the quilt up over Pop. Adam's fingers brushed over his clammy skin, felt his head. Pop hit his hand away.

"How're you feeling?"

Pop shifted to the other side of the bed.

"Any headache?"

Pop said nothing.

"Chest pain? Shortness of breath?" Adam ran down a list of possible causes -- each greeted with silence. "Want to go to the ER?"

Pop growled something.

"I'll be back in an hour," Adam snarled. In the kitchen, he set up his scanner, stowed his emergency bag in the dining room, under the hospital bed, then cleaned up the kitchen and, once more, checked on

Pop who now slept. Adam tiptoed to the bed, felt Pop's skin. Dry. Pinker. Adam's muscles unknotted. His grandfather was doing better.

He had to remember Neema had passed. With more than fifty years together, the separation must burn like a fever.

With nothing to do, Adam switched on the TV. Maya had to be enjoying her rare time with her folks. Stephenson was at work. Adam wished he was there, too.

Nothing but inanities filled the TV. He clicked it off and listened to the scanner instead. Even the scanner was quiet tonight. Maybe tomorrow would be a better day.

Without Maya?

He checked his phone -- no text. Enjoying her folks, Maya wouldn't be rude and text him. He tossed his phone on the counter and went to bed.

He lay in his new room -- the guest room. No way would he crawl up his old bunk bed and be a little boy again. Adam prayed he wouldn't be here long. Then guilt pinged. Neema and Pop had been his whole world. They sacrificed everything for him. Maya would lecture him on his callous, Pharisaic attitude. His parents would cringe, if cringing were possible in heaven, at the uptight, self-righteous man he'd become. Someone who fit into Jennifer's world, not Maya's.

Maya. He never loved someone like her.

*****

At ten, Maya's cell chimed "Onward Christian Soldier".

"Sweetheart," Mom's static-filled voice greeted Maya.

"In the car, aren't you?" Maya asked.

"This Bluetooth stuff doesn't work so great," Mom said.

"Hey, Baby Doll," Daddy said.

"Where are you guys?" Maya hoped they'd say Catskill or at least Poughkeepsie.

"Just hitting the Whitestone," her mom said. "We're a little late. Don't wait up and tomorrow we'll get a prompt start. Love you."

"Love you, too."

They signed off.

The hunger that gnawed at Maya's stomach all evening fled. Was it too late to call Adam?

Adam. He infuriated her half the time. When he agreed to help Torie, he sounded put out. Church -- he'd leave services different -- uplifted -- like a genuine Christian. When planning to go, it was like getting him to the principal's office.

A tear slid down her face.

Adam, the desired child. He had the perfect family. Parents who adored him. They had waited years until he was born. They had longed for him. A sister, eight years younger, who saw the sun and moon in her brother. And grandparents like his? Who could have asked for more?

She swiped another tear and got up for tissues.

Her parents loved her. She knew it, but did they want her? Would they ever understand?

Her biological mother? Was her attempted suicide genetic? Her biological mother jumped off the Queensboro right after she gave Maya away.

Did any parent want *her*? She needed Adam.

She texted. Maya studied her phone's screen. When no text returned, she washed and tried to sleep.

Traffic rumbled outside her window. Counting the cars like sheep, Maya turned to her side. Flipped on her back, and threw off the covers, found her phone, and checked for texts.

None.

Maybe his grandfather was ill.

She tapped out the question. Her words looked too needy. She deleted the text, tucked the phone under her pillow, and closed her eyes. She pictured Adam working overtime, never an ill word to say about anyone -- except Torie. Compassionate.

Conflicted.

Caring.

Confident.

Sometimes too proud.

Just plain human.

Chapter Thirty-Six

"Bitterness poison we drink hoping our enemy will die." Unknown

Blisters bled through Torie's sneakers. *One mile to go.* Might as well be ten. At least the physical pain eased her emotional ache. A pickup sped past splaying her with road dust. A pebble pinged her calf creating a searing sting like she'd been hit with a BB.

The truck pulled up to her old home in the V of the road. Even in the pitch of night, the dreaded sumacs blowing out back mocked Torie. The porch light shone like a warning beacon.

The occupants jumped out, and Jean threw open the front door. Streams of light silhouetted her, making her hair glow like a halo. The men called indistinct greetings while Jean waved. The driver scooted to the truck bed, hauled out a cube of beer, and loped into the house. He hugged Jean, and she left the front door open as they entered.

Music blared out back. As Torie trudged up Maya's road, she could see the party. Chairs circled a fire pit whose blaze leaped and danced as though it heard Blud Thirsty blaring from the stereo. The newest guests now spilled out the back door. Laughter punctuated the night.

The merriment stopped Torie. Jean and Darren partied unaware of her predicament, and unconcerned about how they had left her stranded. Worse, they didn't care they destroyed a sweet woman's vehicle.

Did they ever think of her? Probably not. Yet her life since Darren molested her had been consumed by her hatred of them. Twelve years later, his actions still held her prisoner. It wasn't fair. They got off scot-free. The day she'd turned her life to Jesus, Celeste told her God would make all things new. He'd erase the years destroyed by the locusts. Why didn't He?

Her stomach churned as she watched like a person drawn to an accident. People chugged from beer cans. Punk rock shattered the air. One partier tipped over his chair and went tumbling backwards. Laughter erupted. All drunk. All having a good time.

All alcoholics.

Revulsion rose like heartburn, and she saw herself walking home from the job she lost.

In a drunken depression, she'd driven her Rabbit into a ditch.

Every solution to every problem began with booze. Then the demon created another crisis.

The chorus of accusations people had hurled at her echoed. *You need to stop drinking. You can drive my car as long as you don't drink. If I catch you drinking. Don't become your mother.* She didn't listen to any of them, and what did it get her?

Oh, God. I am my mother. She lifted her eyes to the sky. *Do something. Please.* She lowered her gaze and studied the partiers. *Why did I believe I was better than them because I didn't do drugs?*

God, I'm powerless. Change me. She turned and half ran, half scuttled the rest of the way to Maya's.

In the driveway sat Maya's car, plastic stretched taut on the windows. Not Darren's fault. Hers. Hers alone. She provoked him, got high on asserting her power. Scurrying into the house, Torie bolted the door behind her as though to lock what she had become outside.

In her room, she threw herself on the bed and studied the shadows on the ceiling. Read them like the scrawl of her life.

How could she change?

*****

A 7 a.m. tap at the door interrupted Maya's lesson planning. "Baby Doll, breakfast is ready to be served. I hope you're up." Daddy's cheerful voice bellowed from the hallway.

Last night's unappeased hunger vanished with her hopes for the weekend. When would her parents understand she was as important as their job?

Why didn't she have folks who wanted her like Adam's grandparents doted on him?

Torie's mother? Maya smirked and shook the thought away. Then she reminded herself of her student Julien, a bully with parents who never found time for him. Other kids got PINS petitions. One girl in Justine's class lived in five different foster homes.

She slipped on the light blue sundress Torie insisted she buy for today. The gathered waist would make her look fat she told Torie. Her friend swore Maya erred. Torie said the blue highlighted the blush of her cheeks, and the shirring at the waist hid her tummy -- which Torie denied Maya had. Maya dabbed on some mascara, a little lip gloss, and ran a brush through her hair.

In the dining room, her parents sat at their usual seat.

The usual. Always. Same B & B, same rooms, same bottle of wine. Viola and Sal would have their unvarying breakfast. Maya grinned. She could count on them.

203

"Hey, Baby Doll." Daddy stood, both in greeting and the old-fashioned protocol of rising for a woman. He reached for her chair and stopped. His mouth dropped open.

Mom's eyes grew wide.

"You're beautiful." Daddy found his voice.

"What happened?" her mother asked.

"You make it sound like I was the ugly duckling, and you're shocked I'm a swan." She smiled to assure them she teased, and sat in Daddy's proffered chair.

Mom laughed, reached out and took Maya's hand. "I'm so glad you're out of those dreadful khakis and cotton shirts. Shirts. You're sleeveless -- and a dress. Give me a kiss." Mom lifted her cheek to Maya. Her mother ran her hand along Maya's arm, and let it linger on her wrist.

A carafe of coffee and a pot of herbal tea already sat at the table along with fresh squeezed orange juice. Maya sipped the juice and fought the urge to spit out the pulp. Pushing the glass aside, she opted for a cup of ginger-peach tea.

"How can you get yourself going without coffee?" Mom asked.

Maya forced a smile and looked at Mom. "I do it to annoy you."

Daddy threw back his head, guffawed and slapped his thigh with his hand. When his laughter died, he leaned over and planted a fat, wet kiss on Maya's cheek.

"It wasn't that funny, Dad."

"No. It's a good thing you didn't go into comedy. Comedy's not your strong suit." He sipped his coffee. "It's been a tough week. You should've seen your mother in court. A mamma tiger wouldn't have been fiercer. Plato would've been proud, Margaret Thatcher silenced." He laughed. "Yesterday morning she wrapped up her pro bono case. We waited six hours longer than anticipated and feared we wouldn't be able to leave until this morning. The Iron Lady herself would have been nervous. Not Mom. She was certain deliberation would go our way."

"It didn't?" Maya asked.

"What else is new?" Mom said.

"Filing appeal?"

"What else is new?" Mom sipped her orange juice. "This is good stuff." She nodded toward Maya's half-drunk glass. "Finish yours."

"Thank goodness we have clients who pay us." Daddy chuckled.

Again, the tone sounded harsh, but Maya caught the wink Mom sent Daddy. His lips quirked in a suppressed smile. "It's even better you two didn't go into comedy."

"Oh come on." Mom leaned back as Arianna set spinach quiches and toast at their places. No need to rethink breakfast. "Tell us about your new roommate. Did she do your hair?" Her mother fingered it.

Maya nodded.

"We'll follow you home, and you can introduce us."

"Maybe you can drive me home. It'd do double duty. I would save Adam a trip, and you'll meet my new friend."

"Drive you?" her father asked.

"Torie busted..." No. Maya couldn't phrase it negatively. Her folks had taught her the irrevocability of the misused word. "Her step--" What would you call Darren.

"Come on. Spit it out, Baby Doll. We're your folks. You're not on trial."

Maya eyed both of them. *I'm not?* She bit her lips. Didn't want to be snarky. "Her mother's lover busted all my car windows."

"Here." Her mother bent under the table and hauled out a huge box wrapped in ivory foil. A bow measuring at least a foot in diameter adorned the top.

Had she heard me? Maya bit back the rising hurt, resisted getting up and running back to Excelsior. Then she remembered Torie's admonition. *Everything gets easier once it's out of your system. Speak.*

"We can charge him. We'd do it pro bono."

Maya's head jerked up from studying the gift. "I'm not following your non-sequitur."

Daddy barked his laugh. "We'll sue the life out the car-smashing creature."

Maya grinned. "I'm afraid this creature hasn't got a life worth suing."

"It's a weird gift, but Mom couldn't resist." Daddy nodded at the package crowding the table then bit into his quiche.

Shaking her head, Maya digested the two strains of thought -- charge Darren with vandalism, and a weird gift. *Odd.*

She scrutinized her folks and searched for a sign of an uncharacteristic jest. They both looked at her like her students at Christmas when they stacked her desk with the coffee mugs and chocolate and candles and Starbucks' gift cards they helped their folks pick out. Like her students, her parents' own desires guided their pure hearts.

"Open it, Baby Doll."

Love sparkled in her folks' eyes, and Maya's heart melted. She pulled the ribbon. The bow slipped off. She peeled the wrapping, careful not to tear it. Her kids would love to use this pretty paper for a project.

"Come on." Daddy spoke through another mouthful of quiche. "Tear it off. The paper's not the gift."

Her grin grew. Little did they know. She looked into his eyes, so brown they were almost black. They twinkled. Giving to her -- to others -- was their life. She arrayed the wrapping on the floor; she'd smooth it out later when she had the time to do it right. Maya opened the box.

An American Girl doll sat inside.

Maya touched her lips with her fingers, looked from her mother to her father and back at the doll. *What?* She lifted it from the box. Its long hair matched the wet-sand color of her own before Torie re-decorated it. Its hazel eyes were flecked with green and gold. The doll wore khaki pants and a long sleeve shirt. A chalkboard and ruler sat in the box.

"We would have gotten a sundress had we known. Or some bracelets from Vienna -- Frey Willes -- well, anyway. This is a "Truly Me" doll. We never got it for you when you were little -- I don't know why -- but those catalogs still come in. I was perusing it one morning, and I knew I'd get one just like you--"

"Viola, honey, I think you better breathe." Daddy winked.

Mom quit talking, but her excitement exuded from her grin. She put down her coffee. "When Daddy found it, he *knew*." She shoved the cup away and stood. "So let's go have some serious family time."

The questions bubbling in Maya's heart before breakfast surfaced. Now wasn't the time to bring up her concerns. Yet, if she swallowed her words, she'd be drinking the poison of bitterness. She raised her gaze and focused first on her mother, then her dad. "Before we begin, can you tell me...?" Words sunk back to her stomach.

After thirty seconds, seemed like minutes, Daddy spoke. "Tell you what, Baby Girl?"

She knew the answer but needed to speak.

"Did you want to adopt me or--"

Mom blanched, Daddy's jaw dropped.

"Baby Doll, I thought..." He frowned and rubbed the back of his neck, and he looked toward Mom.

Mom took her hand. "It's about time we put an end to your worries. Rather than shop, let's head to Washington Park. We won't take you home until you understand."

*****

The sun shone through Torie's window and onto her face. It had to be mid-day. Groaning, she pulled the pillow over her head -- her pounding head. Why get up?

The pillow suffocated her. Torie shoved it aside and stared at the ceiling. Even when she wrecked her car, lay in the hospital, when she knew she'd lost Trey to Selene, during that time, she felt better than now.

Jean and Darren created a life together, happy in each other and with their friends. Maya was off with her folks, parents who wanted her and doted on her -- even though Maya didn't see it. Adam had Harold, memories of a grandmother who adored him. Real parents who would love him, yet, if they lived.

She had?

A mess of a world.

The worst of her mess was she crafted it herself.

Not Trey. Not Selene. Not even Darren. Victoria Elizabeth Sullivan created the world she chose to live in.

Throwing off the covers, Torie roamed the house. Why didn't Maya drink coffee? Coffee would get rid of her hangover.

She was a drunk. Was one since she was thirteen when she lost the baby and started partying like a pro. As a kid, her promises of never doing drugs made her feel better than Jean. In the end, Torie became the person she swore she'd never be.

Ducking out of the kitchen and onto the porch, Torie studied the fluffy clouds floating in a pretty blue sky. As kids, she and Robin and Crystal would lie in the backyard and imagine mermaids and unicorns in the clouds. She squinted and studied them. Today they were clouds. Returning to her room, Torie buried herself under the quilt to block out the light.

Quilts. Not even God could piece beauty from the scraps of her life.

Adam and Maya didn't know how good they had it. They hadn't made her mistakes.

*****

Pop sat on the porch listening to NPR. Adam lay on the couch inside. A long, boring day. At home, he'd fiddle with the cabin -- clean, repair the loose board on the porch, mow the lawn, or paint the clapboards.

Or go kayaking.

Were those days done? Was he doomed to be a paramedic on shift and off? A never-ending nurse?

The ungenerous thought increased his despair, and he drew Neema's quilt over his head, wanted to be like Hunter, his old Labrador. If he hid his head, his world would vanish. How could he be so petty? His grandparents had been saints, saviors to his lost life. Neema cared for him in his darkest hours. Her dogged insistence for justice ended the hell school had become.

She'd brought him to her pastor for counseling, threatened the principal with legal action if the bullying didn't stop, hauled him to every Boy Scout meeting, and even went camping as a chaperone -- all while managing the failing farm and battling her own losses. He'd do anything if he could get her back. If he could be like her.

Pop? He worked until the Parkinson's got too bad. Even when sickness bogged him down, he tried.

The loose board on his deck? If not for Pop, Adam would have no clue how to mend it. Now what? Pop needed time to mourn, to accept his loss.

He threw off the quilt and stepped out the back door. Cumulous clouds floated on the slight breeze. Neema loved days like this.

He closed his eyes. Her last moments lying on Stewart's cement floor, having ribs bruised by the well-meaning manager appeared behind the lids. Her last words, "Promise me you'll get back to the Lord."

He did promise.

He would take care of Pop in the manner his grandfather wanted. No. The way he needed.

He would go back to church. God was his sole chance for a changed character.

Chapter Thirty-Seven

"God, grant me the serenity to accept the things I cannot change, The courage to change the things I can, And the wisdom to know the difference."
The Serenity Prayer

At 9 a.m. Sunday, Adam pulled into Maya's driveway. She'd spent the previous day in Washington Park, talked about her adoption, and understood her parents -- her *real* parents -- loved her. Her biological mother had been victimized much like Torie, but it ended poorly. The Vitales *never* regretted adopting Maya. Ever.

And never would.

She must have told him thirty times.

After an hour's talk, they texted. In his endless texts, Adam assured her he wouldn't forget to take Torie to church.

This morning he'd called Torie three times, but Sullivan never answered her phone or the house phone. She had to be here.

He rounded the porch and knocked on the door.

"I'm right here."

Adam jumped. Curled up on the wicker loveseat, almost hidden under an afghan, sat Torie. Her wild hair fluttered in the wind. She wore no make-up, was dressed in some kind of exercise garb. "I didn't see you."

"Obviously."

"I've come to get you for church."

"What's the use?"

"What do you mean, what's the use?"

She shook her head and looked past him. Her gaze became so intent Adam turned to see what caught her attention. Nothing filled the backyard but Mr. Harrigan's garden, still mostly fresh-tilled soil. Beyond it lay fields and woods. No rabbit or deer broke the nondescript view.

"You tell me." Torie focused on him, and her eyes would not release him.

"Didn't you come to Christ a few weeks ago?"

"I thought so. I sensed Him. For two weeks, I believed life would change. Friday night I realized it was another case of smoke and mirrors."

Adam sat on the edge of the loveseat, and Torie moved her legs to make room for him. He settled in, and for the first time, didn't feel awkward at his proximity to her.

"Like my life. I reach for one thing and get something else."

"Like?"

"I got fired Friday."

"I thought Collin liked your work."

"He does. Says I'm the best waitress who ever worked for him. He also claims I'm a drunk." Torie's eyes darkened and shimmered.

I'm a stinking Pharisee hurling stones at a sinner I never understood. Have my sins so poisoned me that I'm killing my future?

"Am I?" she asked.

"Are you what?"

"A drunk?"

How he'd envisioned slicing this woman open and repaying her for being a middle-school tyrant who controlled the other ruffians even when she was put in a foster home in another district. She now gave him the opportunity, but the feelings didn't come.

"You need help. 'Knowing the Difference' would be a good group for you."

They sat in silence for so long, Adam wondered if she had heard him. "Can I ask you a personal question?"

She shrugged.

"What happened to your baby?"

She stiffened. Didn't say anything. At least she didn't bolt.

"I ask the question because I think I have to ask for your forgiveness."

"My forgiveness?" With her glance, a tiny smile struggled to form. She studied Mr. Harrigan's garden again.

"I made up my own opinions, believed them as the truth, and used them to despise you. I can't hate anymore. What happened?"

"I lost it."

"You were showing, so you were past the first trimester, weren't you?"

She nodded. "Four-and-one-half months."

"It's unusual to miscarry in the second trimester. What went wrong?"

She stood, and he grabbed her arm. Adam expected a fight, but Torie surprised him by sitting back down.

"Last week when I gave Maya a makeover, I made her tell me her darkest secrets." She focused her attention on him. Her grin crinkled her eyes which shone, and not from tears. "No, I'm not telling you them. The hairdresser's chair is as confidential as a shrink's." Earnestness replaced her playfulness. She paused as though weighing her words. "I told her by speaking them, the pain would heal. Like when I told my math teacher how Darren molested me--"

"He what?" Adam stiffened, and after a moment, he closed his gaping mouth.

"Didn't you know? How else would I get pregnant?"

"I thought Dylan Moser..."

"In Dylan's dreams. You didn't know?"

He shook his head. He thought of his childish hatred, of her egging Dylan on to torment him because of his wild crush on her. His infatuation made her cruelty harder to bear -- scars he tried to hide with women like Jennifer. By being a hotshot first responder.

"Worse. He used to sell me for drugs--"

Adam sat upright. "Oh, Torie." He drew her to him, expected her to pull away, and she surprised him by moving in closer, by melting into his arms. She buried her head in his chest.

"Don't look at me."

"I won't." He looked down.

"If I don't say this, it'll kill me in the end."

A silence followed. Seconds clicked by. Adam was ready to encourage her to speak.

"He started when I was seven. Then I got too old for him, so he got another use for me. His friend gave me chlamydia. It went undiagnosed. Then Darren got a dose when he thought a pubescent girl would be fun. Those last rapes left me pregnant." Torie pulled away and swiped her eyes. "Jean blamed me, told me *I* seduced *him*. When Darren made moves toward Crystal, I knew I had to get someone to believe me. No one did until old Mr. Symonds..." A moment ticked by before Torie forced a chuckle which turned into a hiccupping cry. Within moments, convulsing sobs racked. She held up her hands. "Sorry. This shouldn't bother me anymore."

Adam pulled the shaking woman back to him. He saw himself. As shallow as Jennifer. As cocky as Caiaphas, as Pop would say. Bitterness, like a brood of vipers, had made its den in his heart.

*****

Torie didn't understand why she agreed to go to church. Maybe because Maya begged Adam? Adam's kindness? Both?

Since it had gotten late, she had just enough time to brush her teeth. If Jesus didn't like her in yoga pants and a sweatshirt, then He wasn't who Maya and Celeste said. In the truck, she pulled down the visor and ran a comb through her hair.

As she climbed out of Adam's truck, she glimpsed the biker dude from her first visit here. He still wore leathers and a do-rag. Something in his jacket squirmed. *A Chihuahua?* She squinted. The mean looking guy tucked a Chihuahua inside his partially zipped jacket.

Weird.

She wandered into the café. Maybe the coffee had made her come. She had no hangover seeing as, along with no coffee, Maya stocked no booze, so her headache came from caffeine withdrawal. After pouring herself a cup, Torie turned to find Adam.

"Torie. Good to see you."

Only two people knew her here, Celeste and Angela. Celeste stood near the sanctuary doors chatting with another woman, but Celeste wasn't looking at her friend. She stared off at Torie who melted inside. Celeste was eager to see *her.* Before she took a half-dozen steps toward her friend, Celeste squeezed Torie in a bear hug.

"You're stronger than I expected." Torie giggled. "But, I'm balancing hot coffee, and if you don't want to wear it, be careful."

Celeste took Torie's free hand and tugged. "Come and sit with us. Angela will be excited to see you."

"I need to tell my friend where I'll be."

"She's welcomed to join us, too."

Torie didn't correct Celeste on her friend's gender. But friend? She bit back a grin. Yes.

"We're about where we sat last time you were here. We like being near the speakers and up front. Our old ears and eyes don't work the way they used to."

Adam had disappeared. Torie took a slug from her cup, and headed back to the café to top it off. Would it be coarse to bring a thermos so she could drink it during the week?

Drink it where? The lean-to? Maya would kick her out when she learned she lost her job and had no means to fix her car, let alone get one of her own.

By the time she doctored a second cup, the introductory music played. In the sanctuary, Adam sat near the aisle, toward the back. Torie snuck up to him, hoping to disturb no one.

"Adam." She tapped his shoulder and whispered. "I'm going to sit with Celeste and Angela."

"I did shower."

She didn't move. *What?* She cocked her head.

His eyes softened and he grinned. "I'm joking. See you in the foyer at the end of service."

The worship began before Torie took a seat, and with the first chorus, the protests and doubts, about believing in God and church being a waste, evaporated. The same feeling came over her as during the first trip here, like someone held her, as though her past was known and forgotten. Nothing else mattered.

This time she didn't cry.

Pastor Arendsen took the pulpit and prayed for the sermon. Torie bowed her head along with the congregation. She wondered what sin the preacher would talk about this time. Did they spotlight one sin to turn away from each week until you were holy?

"Turn to Romans 8:38." The preacher read, "For I am convinced that neither death nor life, neither angels nor demons, neither the present nor the future, nor any powers, neither height nor depth, nor anything else in all creation, will be able to separate us from the love of God that is in Christ Jesus our Lord."

Torie's heart froze. Then pounded. *Nothing?*

She had spent the weekend in tears, knowing everything was ruined and convinced herself God didn't want her. No one did -- not even Maya who loved and forgave everyone. When she'd dried her eyes after her confession to Adam, she swore the tears had dried up forever. An obvious lie. They flowed again -- hot and salty. What Arendsen said was true. Torie knew it like her name or her love for scotch or cooking or playing with hair. She didn't have to worry about what she was or about her past.

Her peace waffled off.

Her thinking had to be wrong. Everything has consequences. Everyone has an ulterior motive. Why not God?

The pastor now talked about a man who'd been involved in a murder as a gang-banger, and spent a stint in jail.

"We all know how his wife waited for him. How his children came to the Lord."

The congregation murmured agreement and looked around for someone.

"Our weirdest deacon--"

The congregation laughed.

"Will be heading to Kenya to be working with the homeless. Before we close, I'd like for us to pray for Lenny."

Now she'd be able to see who this fellow was. She sat straight up. The man in the do-rag came forward. He was the usher who took everyone's money. The one who introduced the services, and wore a Chihuahua under his leathers.

He's forgiven? Murder? He couldn't have been a murderer. He's so nice. If Lenny's so warmhearted and sweet, couldn't God forgive me?

213

Adam squirmed. *Nothing can separate me? But I've become the goody-two-shoes Dylan and Torie accused me of being.*

Sin had separated him from God -- from everything good in life. For years he'd attend church to keep his grandparents happy. When his work shifts fell on Sundays for a full month, he used it to leave church behind.

Then he met Corey. Discovered sex. Jennifer moved him up the status ladder.

What a hypocrite he'd become. He believed Torie was the sinner.

If he didn't change, Maya would be the one to ditch him -- and why hadn't she already?

Why God continued to draw him in baffled him more.

Pastor Arendsen now talked about a mythical sinner, but as the description continued, he realized he referred to Lenny. He and his wife rode bikes whenever they could, the dog in a basket decked out in doggles.

He grinned. He liked Lenny. The goodness and faith flowing out of him always made Adam happy. Adam never murdered anyone. Instead he lived trying to preserve life.

Even took in Torie.

Torie. How could he have been so cruel to her? So hateful?

He bowed his head and heat rose up his neck. He did feel sorry for her when he found her camping in the cold of Hookskill, yet every little annoyance sent him over the top with self-righteous rage. He excused it as protection of Maya, and the need for Torie to reap what she had sown.

What had he sown in his life? Twelve years ago, her bullying ended. His grandparents fought for him. Before their death, he had parents who adored him. He always had a refuge when life sought to destroy him.

Torie's inability to control her own world, a world racked with more pain than his, caused her to harass and intimidate. Yet, at heart, she longed to be good. She fought for her sisters and fretted about Maya's car. Torie was rough, but could have gone down Lenny's road.

Or her mother's.

And him? He had no excuse. He'd become the most hated of all sinners because he chose to become self-righteous.

He looked up to see Lenny and his wife, crying as the congregation prayed. Tears threatened -- both in joy for God's unconditional pardon for these two. He swallowed hard to stop from crying.

If Lenny was forgiven, so was he.

The couple stepped down. The ubiquitous call to salvation was made, along with a reminder about the AA meeting beginning at one. Pastor Arendsen dismissed the congregation. Adam sat alone in his row. *Have I blown my chance to repent?*

He stood. He may not have murdered anyone, but his sins were as monstrous as Judas's. As the congregation filtered out, he knew, whether the leaders were done praying or not, he was not leaving until he got things right. Adam fought the tide and headed to the altar.

*****

I don't want to leave. Torie peeked over her shoulder at the thinning crowd. *Once I leave, life goes nuts.*

Angela touched Torie's arm, and she jumped. "Sorry. Didn't mean to startle you. Would you like to come to lunch with me?"

"I'd go," Celeste said, "but I've missed the last two 'Knowing the Difference' meetings."

Celeste was an alky? Torie's heart hammered. Too many people complained about her drinking. Her long spate of reasons and endless army of excuses always blamed someone else for what she decided to do with her life. *I want to go.* She studied the floor. *How do I ask?*

"Would you rather come to a meeting with me?" Celeste asked.

Torie's head jerked up.

"We drunks can recognize the signs," Celeste said. "Or the fumes on another's breath."

Torie turned her head away. No booze had touched her lips since Friday.

"Admit it." Celeste winked. "Your first day here came after a night of drinking."

Shame silenced Torie. She found herself unable to look at Celeste. After studying the floor for a minute, she shook her head. By going, everyone would know she was a drunk. "Nah. I'm good. Adam will be looking for me."

She hurried to find him in the foyer. A few people milled about. None of them Adam.

Hitting the café, Torie grabbed another cup of coffee before the ladies put it all away. She faced the foyer and studied the few remaining people. Some headed through double doors into the corridors of the old school.

"Sorry I'm late." Torie turned toward Adam who studied the carpet like something interesting lay there, as his foot scuffed the floor. "I, uh, was praying."

"Why are you embarrassed?"

He shrugged. Splotches of red crept above his collar.

Torie searched for Celeste. *Do I want to join an alky meeting?* The desire to attend glued her in place.

By not going with Adam, he'd know she'd be hitting an AA meeting. He'd know he was right, and she was a drunk.

Then, too, how'd she get home?

Celeste would be at the meeting. If Celeste couldn't drive her, she'd walk. Maya's apartment was closer to the church than The Stadium was to Maya's home.

"Torie?"

"No." She swallowed hard. "I'm going to 'Knowing the Difference'."

He grinned. "Then I'll see you later."

A half-hour remained before the meeting. Stewart's was a bit up the road. She'd walk there and pick up a beer -- get a little courage, and one last hurrah.

Chapter Thirty-Eight

"He that is good at making excuses is seldom good for anything else."
Benjamin Franklin

In the parking lot, Torie turned her head to the glistening sunshine. The sweet smell of spring promised life. The purple buds of the rhododendron struggled to free themselves from their tight cocoon. A soft breeze blew pine-scented air. She started up the road.

Five minutes along the way, a deer startled and dashed into the Hookskill woods, vanishing as though it evaporated. She crossed the road hoping to spot the pretty animal. Quiet and trees met her.

About three yards ahead of her, in the ditch, lay a fawn. Tiny and motionless. *Is it dead?* She took a step forward then stopped. *What can I do for a dead deer?* Then its ears twitched, and Torie grinned. *I need to leave and let mamma get back to her kid.*

She froze in place. Torie held her breath and let every nerve feel the moment -- the silence of the woods, the breeze on her neck, and the hardness of the road beneath her feet. The fawn was tiny, perfect, and beautiful. This was why Adam loved the outdoors. She'd never be as nuts as him, but she understood his passion. Once everything settled down in Albany, she'd come slumming to the boonies, and let Adam and Maya show her their world.

If Maya forgave her.

She would fix Maya up for her wedding, be a godmother to her baby.

She rubbed her belly. *Babies? If* I *could.* Torie ground her teeth. Anger tired her. She needed a way to get rid of her bitterness.

The deer's ears twitched, and Torie once more became lost in its world. The fawn was like Heather's little one. Both so helpless. Chance and luck determined their fate.

But...

I want one. Torie squeezed her eyes shut, and stroked her throat. Thought of the possibility. A car swooshed by.

Am I nuts? Darren ruined all possibility with his infections and my blocked tubes. She dug her nails into her palms. It was a good thing she couldn't have kids. They didn't need to grow up with a drunk for a mother.

She looked back at the church then turned to where the fawn lay. It

217

had vanished. Squinting, Torie scanned the ditch until her eyes focused on the deer. Its fur and its spots camouflaged it -- like the trees hid its mother. Wasn't it strange how you struggled to see what was right in front of your eyes?

With a mind of its own, her hand rubbed her belly. Today's doctors did miracles all the time. Could motherhood be possible?

If she did want a baby, she'd have to change. Her child didn't need to be raised by a woman like Jean. It was time to put her and Darren in her past. Not her future.

A drink would take the edge off her nerves, make her quit thinking about children and Darren and Jean. Her past would vanish.

She took a step in Stewart's direction and stopped. Her past would disappear like the fawn -- camouflaged for a moment.

Another step drew her abreast of the tiny deer. It teetered to its feet and ran into the woods -- back to shelter more secure than the ditch, whose sanctuary had been a temporary fix at best.

Temporary fixes. Her drinking was nothing more than a quick remedy. As protective as lying in a ditch.

Adam saw her as a drunk. Torie grinned and stopped. *Like the hidden critter in the ditch, Adam didn't see the real me. Time to prove him wrong.* Torie strutted back to the church.

The foyer stood empty. *Where is the meeting?* Earlier, a few people wandered through double doors leading into the classroom section of the former school. Since no one lingered here, it meant they stowed the drunks back there. Rubbing her sweaty hands against her yoga pants and with her heart jumping rope in her chest, Torie shoved the double doors open.

One clanged against the side wall. Classrooms lined the hallway. Did they label the doors? Hang a big neon sign like those in the bars? "All drunks enter here"?

After a few steps, the double doors behind her clanked.

"Can I help you?"

The speaker held out his hand. "I'm Pastor Arendsen." He smiled, and tension melted out of her back.

He gave a firm handshake, but it wasn't vise-like. "I'm Torie." *Do I ask -- hey, where're the drunks?*

"Are you by any chance looking for 'Knowing the Difference'?"

She stiffened. *Is it so obvious?*

"The church complex can get confusing. I'd be glad to walk you there." He said it matter-of-factly, as though he was heading there himself. Their footsteps clicked against the hallway tile. "I know all our classrooms look the same. We're down a ways because this is a double room. Gives us lots of space if we need it."

They rounded a corner. "Right there." He pointed. "Go on in; help yourself to coffee or juice or heaven forbid, tea. I'll be right back." He turned and hurried off the way they had come.

He'd return? Did he oversee the drunks, too? *Do they have sermons in drunk meetings?*

Coffee? What the heck. She pushed open the door and stopped in the threshold. Celeste would be here. *Could I run?*

"Torie."

So much for the second A in AA.

Celeste grabbed Torie in another bear hug, crushing her more than the morning's clinch in the foyer. "Grab a chair and come sit with me."

Another lady around Jean's age joined Celeste. "Hello, I'm Maureen. I'm so glad you're here. Would you like some literature?"

Torie shook her head.

"How about another cup of coffee?" Celeste asked.

Maureen laughed. "We all substituted caffeine for booze. Come on. I'll introduce you to the gang."

"I'm saving you a seat over there." Celeste pointed front and center.

No way was Torie going to sit up front in a booze-detox meeting. Church was one thing, but all these people would judge her.

At the coffee table, Maureen introduced her to about five different people -- the friendliest group, offering phone numbers and coffee dates and rides to other meetings.

While everyone chatted, a man, in his thirties, not too old, but no spring chicken, stepped up to the podium. "When you find your seats, we'll start the meeting."

People scuttled to their places. As the conversations died, Torie wandered to the corner. She leaned against a wall. Close to twenty people sat on folding chairs scattered about, most clustered in the front. Celeste and one man who'd introduced himself at the coffee table as Mark appeared to be the oldest. Women who appeared to be in their forties sat in a group. A kid who looked like he just hit puberty talked with a twenty-something. A mix of people settled down.

Celeste twisted around in her seat and signaled to Torie.

Torie shook her head. Leaning against the wall would help her flee if needed.

"Let's begin with prayer," the man at the podium said.

Their voices blended together. "God, grant me the serenity to accept the things I cannot change, the courage to change the things I can, and wisdom to know the difference."

An involuntary smile crept across Torie's face as she recognized the meeting's name.

As soon as the last syllable died, he introduced the speaker. "Aiden will tell us a little about his life today."

The pre-pubescent teen stood. Torie would have slunk out of this joint as fast as possible if she'd been called out, but Aiden dashed to the front, grinning like a kid.

"Hi." He waved. "I'm Aiden, and I'm an alcoholic."

"Hi, Aiden," the crowd replied somewhat in unison.

Torie stiffened. Her tightened lips had to betray her surprise. So young. From his voice, he sounded mature, from his size -- not so much. He couldn't have been a drunk for long.

The classroom door opened, and the pastor slipped in.

"I think step one was the hardest for me," Aiden said. "Admitting my life had become unmanageable because alcohol held all the power. Strange, huh?"

People nodded. Some hollered amen as though they were in church.

"It took forever for me to admit a crawfish couldn't sink lower than I." He gulped. Silence saturated the room. Torie didn't even hear a sniffle. No one so much as crossed her legs. "We were fifteen when my best bud got alcohol poisoning."

Torie's head jerked up. *Fifteen? I thought I was bad.*

She slunk against the wall as she heard Adam complain about her empties in the lean-to. Her neck heated recalling both Collin terminating her job and the pity in his eyes.

While Aiden continued his story, the pastor poured a quick cup of coffee, snagged a donut, and took an empty seat near her. His closeness made her heart pound, and she wanted to bolt.

What did he think of all this?

Pastor Arendsen, like everyone else, looked steadily at Aiden. His face somber, and his head nodding.

"My friend died that night. It shoulda stopped me, right?"

Some of the listeners ducked their heads. Others nodded. No one uttered a word.

"It'd never happen to me." Aiden stopped and swiped his eye. After a minute he continued his tale.

His path sounded familiar -- a bad home, a poor choice of friends, and the mystique of partying.

"I did find hope." For the first time Aiden grinned. "When I became a Christian. Jesus didn't make it easy, but He made it possible." He walked away from the podium and sat down.

He popped back up and faced the crowd. "Thanks."

Even from where Torie stood, Aiden's blush was obvious.

The group applauded and half of them made a beeline to Aiden, the others scrambled to the snack table and thus to Torie.

"Torie." Celeste called from the front of the room. "Glad you stayed. Come here and tell me what you thought of the meeting."

"Celeste will never let any of us go unnoticed. I'm looking forward to seeing more of you," a man said.

She turned to the man who spoke. The pastor.

"Will you be our speaker out in Greenville on Thursday?" A man called out to the pastor

He glanced back at Torie. "My supposed anonymous meeting meets in Greenville. They love teasing that a minister's a drunk, too. "He turned to the man who had called.

Torie's jaw dropped. *Him?* She looked around the room. *If all of them, then me.*

Celeste looped her arm through Torie's and yakked the whole way out to her car.

Throughout the ride, Celeste chatted about future meetings and the pastor's fight in overcoming alcohol and anything else flitting through her mind. At last, her tires crunched over Maya's driveway.

Torie straightened. A BMW sat next to Maya's shattered Honda. She stopped listening.

"Are you getting out or going to sit there and wait for more of my babble?" Celeste laughed. "Angela says the good thing about my drinking was it shut me up. I'm a sulky drunk."

Torie pointed at the black car. "Maya's folks must be here." Relief washed over her, and Torie leaned her head against the seat. She sighed. Company would put off the inevitable fight over the smashed windows caused by her own fat mouth.

"Life's getting serious. She brought the folks home to meet you." Celeste chuckled, the laughter making her sound like a teen. "I'll pick you up at noon. You'll have time to look for work in Albany while I catch up with Candace. If you think I talk a lot, wait 'til you meet her. We'll eat at her place or at McDonald's. Don't tell Angela if we hit the fast food joints. Then we'll make the meeting. Hope you can tolerate an old lady all day."

"I'll get distracted and make believe you're not around." Torie tossed her a grin and yanked open the car door.

Celeste threw back her head and laughed. "It never works with Angela."

Torie climbed out of the car and leaned in through the open door. "You'll never know how grateful I'll be to get out of the boonies, even if it means I have to hang with an old coot. I'll endure." She slammed the door, but Celeste unrolled the window.

"One last thing."

"Yes?"

"One day at a time. You've got our numbers, and I'll talk with you anytime."

"Even at two a.m.?"

"Especially then. I can never sleep. Up all night. Even learned how to tweet to pass the time." After blowing a quick kiss, Celeste drove away.

Torie stood in the driveway and relished the seconds before she'd have to face Maya. Long after car fumes and engine noises faded, Torie stared after the vanished car. She turned to the apartment, stiffened her jaw and entered.

"Welcome. You must be Torie." A plump man stood in greeting. "I'm Sal Vitale. Maya's my baby girl."

Maya sat at the table with a cup of tea. She grimaced, and Torie understood her embarrassment. "If you're Sal, this must be Viola?" She offered a hand to Maya's mother.

"I love good deductive reasoning. Sit. Have some wine with us." Viola waved toward a vacant chair.

Torie held up her hands in protest and clenched her teeth. *One day at a time.* "No. I'm good." Pride rippled up her spine and straightened her shoulders. She *would* change. She stepped toward her room.

"Come on and sit." Sal pulled out the chair. "Let us get to know you."

No escape. Torie eyed the glasses of wine on the table.

Viola heaved herself up. Maya hadn't lied about her mother -- short and round and jovial. After fumbling in Maya's cabinet, Viola turned and flourished a wine glass. "Everyone here's rude."

"Mom." Maya stood.

"Oh stop it. You know we're teasing." Viola ran her hand over Maya's hair. Her eyes sparkled with love.

Torie's stomach ached with yearning. To be a mother -- and love a child? What a world she missed.

"My daughter didn't drink the wine at the Capitol Arms, and it's a good pinot noir. I keep forgetting my baby doesn't drink. We got her these glasses, and I think we're the only ones who ever use them. Here." Viola poured wine and plunked the ruby liquid in front of Torie.

"The glass is beautiful." Torie picked it up and studied it. The wine scented the air with notes of spice, of sandalwood. The liquid swirled like scarlet silk. Exotic as the glass. She glanced at Maya who made no movement, or expression that betrayed her thoughts. Maya must be seething, too furious to speak to Torie because of her smashed up car. With justification.

"It's Austrian crystal. We got it..." She turned to Sal. "When, sweetheart?"

"Right after Maya transferred to Albany State."

"Yes. About six years ago."

Torie grasped the stem of the glass and twisted it between her fingers, studied it. *One day at a time.* She looked away from the glass and dropped her hands to her lap. "Did you guys have a good weekend?"

"Wonderful." Viola turned to Maya. "Got our baby girl a baby girl."

Torie raised her brows.

"A 'Truly Me' doll." Viola giggled, then took a large sip of wine. She fanned her face.

Sal patted her hand. "Viola doesn't get flustered, but baby dolls aren't the kind of gifts she gives our daughter." He glanced at Maya, and love poured out of his eyes.

Torie smiled. No jealousy filled her for the first time in years. She looked at Maya. "Another doll?"

Maya shrugged and a small smile played around her lips. Her nose crinkled. "What can I tell you? It was a God-thing."

"A God-thing?" Torie asked

"We started a new era. I'll explain later." Maya's grin bloomed. "I'll introduce you to Truly Me Maya."

"To seal the new life we're going to live," Sal lifted his glass, "a toast."

Viola pointed to Torie's glass, motioned for her to pick it up.

Torie wavered. What harm would one sip do? She lifted her goblet.

"To a long friendship between you and Maya," Viola said.

How Torie wanted to drink to being close to Maya forever.

They clinked glasses, and Maya tipped her china teacup. Sal and Viola sipped.

The delicate rim, regal to the touch, begged for Torie's sip. With the glass to her lips, the wine's aroma smelled more like raspberries than sandalwood. It pleaded with her to be drunk.

Still, a sip would end her new beginning. She was one weekend sober, had a meeting under her belt, and needed to remember one day at a time. Or one minute. *I need to bypass one temptation.*

Plopping down the glass with its untouched wine, Torie studied the table top. "I need to wash up." She paused, then lifted her head and sought out the Vitales' eyes. "I'm sorry, I can't drink your wine, but I'm going to take the first step." Torie stood. "I am powerless over alcohol. I am an alcoholic."

Chapter Thirty-Nine

"If a man's character is to be abused, say what you will, there's nobody like a relative to do the business." William Makepeace Thackeray

"Pop. I've got to go to work." Adam held the porch door open for his grandfather. "Let's go."

"I told ya last night. Ain't going to no babysitter's."

"It's not a babysitter."

"Adult day care. Same thing. Still not going."

"You can't stay here."

The steel of his grandfather's eyes said unless Adam carried him, there was no way he'd get Pop out of the house. Adam looked at his watch. After nine. He ground his teeth. Late and this week he wasn't working with Stephenson who'd understand. Stephenson? He'd be coming off duty in a half an hour. Adam stepped into the yard, out of Pop's hearing and called.

"Thought I ditched you this week, Benedict." Stephenson's good humor coated his sarcasm.

"Can I cash in a favor?"

"Depends." His buddy's chuckle told Adam he solved his problem. "Does it involve pretty women?"

"No. My grandfather."

"It's settled. What do you need?"

Adam explained. He suggested Stephenson catch some shut-eye, do what he needed to do, but to check on Pop from time to time.

"Sleep? You got caffeine out on the farm?"

"You bet."

"Bacon and eggs?"

"All you can eat."

"Nope. No can do." His partner clicked off the call.

Adam loped back up the steps. "Stephenson will be here in a bit. I've got the keys to the Lincoln."

Pop scowled.

Too bad. Act like a baby, and I'll call it babysitting.

He dialed the senior care center as he pulled out onto the roadway.

"Harold Benedict won't be in today," he told a gruff woman who answered his call.

"We'll have to charge you for the day," she said.

"He's never been there and--" He swerved over the yellow line just as Trooper Chad Morgan rounded the curve. Adam righted the truck and gave Morgan a cheery wave.

Morgan didn't seem to notice.

"He'll be in tomorrow. Thanks." Adam clicked off the Bluetooth, pressed on the accelerator seeing as Morgan was out of sight, and drove to work.

An hour later Burnt Hollow High School called. A pole-vaulter misjudged his jump and landed in the plant box. With the call and someone else to worry about, Adam forgot about Pop and the squandered seventy-five dollars owed the adult center. He and Smitty sped to the school.

As Adam knelt over the pole-vaulter, his cell vibrated. He jumped and grabbed his back pocket, then ignored the phone. Stephenson would have made an off-handed joke about ants in his pants or some immature retort. Smitty didn't notice. He handed the longboard to Adam who slipped it under the boy's leg.

Routine.

Divine.

Worry stayed away with people he didn't love.

*****

Tires crunched on gravel. Harrigan's dog, Buff, barked his greeting. Celeste was early. Torie grabbed her purse and scurried out the door, but slid to a stop on the front porch. Instead of Celeste's Buick, a red truck pulled into the drive. *Adam?* It didn't look like his vehicle. She took a step toward it as Buff came barking and bounding around the corner of the house.

Darren.

Torie squinted. "What are you doing here?" She clenched her hands.

Darren leaned out the window. "Seems I run into you everywhere. Doncha worry. I ain't stalking." He held up his hand. "Just gotta return the jack the lady with the Honda left at my place a week or so ago." He eyed Maya's plastic-encased car and pointed. "What happened there?"

"As if you don't know."

A grin strained across his face, but he reined it in. "How should I know? I just figured out where the lady with the flat lived. Had no clue you was freeloading off of her now." He shoved the door open.

Buff growled, and the hair on his neck rose.

Darren closed the door. "It's in the bed." He nodded to the back of the truck. "I'm not getting out with your mongrel snarling."

Torie approached. Buff bared his teeth and continued snarling. "Good boy," she whispered and tapped her leg to keep him beside her. She kept her gaze on Darren's face shadowed by the brim of his baseball cap. No way to read his eyes. He'd shaved and wore a clean, button-down, blue shirt.

"Hurry it up, will you? I'm gonna be late for work. First day at the body shop. Don't want to make a bad impression."

True to his word, the jack lay against the tailgate. Torie hauled it out. She picked up a tire iron lying on the far end of the truck bed. "This Maya's, too?"

"Yep."

"Looks strong enough to smash windows."

"Oh, it would, but I wouldn't. Tell that lady you're living with, my offer stands for a paint job. I'll give her a good deal." With a salute, Darren drove off. Buff gave a half-hearted, barking chase.

Darren knows where I live. Torie gnawed her fingernail.

She placed the jack and tire iron on the porch. Rubbing her itchy palms against her skirt, Torie returned to the kitchen and peered out the side window. Of course, the truck had disappeared.

Last night's wine stood on the counter. Torie salivated and felt the relief a buzz would bring. She was on her way to meeting number two. Two. One day at a time. For Maya. Instead of downing the alcohol, Torie stepped into her room, found her cell, and punched in the number for the trooper barracks. Maybe they could match the damage to the windshield with the tire iron.

*****

With paperwork filed and flirting with nurses finished, Adam remembered his missed call. He retrieved his message. Stephenson. His son Henry had come home from daycare with a hundred-and-two temp. He couldn't take him to Pop's with a fever.

Adam rubbed his neck. What to do now?

In the hospital's ambulance bay, Smitty sat in the truck fiddling with his cell. "Any other calls?" Adam climbed into the rig.

"Nope. Quiet." Smitty started the engine.

"Do you mind running by my grandparents' place? I've got to check on my grandfather."

"Will do."

He returned the call to Stephenson, told him he had it under control -- to take care of Henry. Then they drove to the farmhouse in a silence crawling over Adam's skin like eczema. At the house, he found Pop on the porch, dozing in the rocker. He tiptoed back to the truck, climbed in, took off his cap and scratched his head.

"All okay?" Smitty asked.

Adam refitted his hat and tried to keep from grinding his choppers down to nubs. What to do? In the distance, a tractor growled. Mark LaValley was haying across the road.

"Can you negotiate the track?" Adam pointed to the field's access route.

Without a word, Smitty headed down the rutted pasture, and thirty feet into the field, the ambulance bogged down in mud.

Adam bit back the curse he wanted to spew, but he didn't think he got kudos from God for not using those words. He rocketed the door open. As he leaped from the rig, the radio crackled. An elderly man had fallen and might have fractured his spine. Their call.

An elderly man. Could've been Pop. Time was critical, and they were stuck. He slammed his fist into the ambulance while Smitty answered the call.

Shaking out his aching hand, Adam jogged toward LaValley. Halfway to the farmer, Mark waved. Even from the distance, Adam could see his genial grin.

The tractor lumbered toward Adam.

"Stuck?" LaValley laughed. "Curse of mud season. Got chains in my barn. I'll haul you out."

The tractor crawled toward the road. Adam glanced at Smitty. Time slid through his fingers like quicksilver, breaking into pieces and slipping away the more he tried to grasp it. A life hung in the balance.

As though his driver read his mind, he hopped out of the ambulance and sauntered toward Adam, heedless of time. "Another unit took the call. Already on scene. We don't have to save the day today."

Don't have to save the day.

His anger at Pop, at bogging down, at missing the call turned into disappointment. No. Not disappointment. Frustration. Back to anger.

It clawed his conscience. He heard Torie call him hotshot. Control freak.

Was he?

He cared for Pop by forcing him to live at his cabin. Tried to arrange the funeral his way. Even at work, his perfectionism drove some drivers nuts. If he didn't keep things under control, lives could be lost.

Did he care about others or only his appearance?

His relationships with Jennifer, and Corey before her, answered his question.

The returning tractor rumbled closer and shook away his thoughts. Within a half an hour, LaValley towed the ambulance out of the mud and back on the road. He sent the men off with a promise to check on Pop every few hours.

In Smitty's silence, Adam closed his eyes and leaned against the seatback. Nothing was going right. He could control nothing. Failed at the basics of his job. Couldn't care for Pop. He felt like the Boy Scout in the locker.

*****

Six o'clock. Maya climbed out of Justine's van.

"Sorry," Justine said. "Sub plans took longer than usual."

"No problem. Henry didn't know his mother had nothing planned for the week." Maya slammed the door.

"You're a brat, and you'll pay for your comment."

"Love you. Take care of Henry." Maya waved Justine off. She studied her own car. She had no way to get to school tomorrow. Would Adam loan her the Lincoln? She texted him and stepped into the house.

Her home was too quiet. No Torie.

She dug out a frozen dinner and shoved it in the microwave. The bottle of wine sat on the counter. She picked it up to stash it in the refrigerator, and an envelope wedged behind the bottle flopped onto the counter. She opened it and smiled.

Torie was right. Talking things out led to healing.

*****

Late that evening, not wanting to wake Maya, Torie crept into her room, keeping the light off. Bright, phony light would destroy her mood. How could things have gone so well? Their search in Albany netted her a job. Part-time, but as a hairdresser. Candace offered her a place to live -- all she had to do was to cook the meals while there. Now, she'd have a way out of Westfield with a job in the city. Real life. People. Parties. Dancing.

Best of all, a chance to pay Maya back. Not just to fix her car, or pay for her food, and shelter. For believing in her.

She slipped on her yoga pants and tank top and crawled into bed. Nestled against the headboard, she pulled the quilt up to her chin and hugged herself. Gratitude swelled her heart to bursting.

Maya tapped at the door.

Air filled Torie's lungs. Her ribs no longer destroyed her, but good

229

luck was never in her cards. "Come in."

Soft light spilled in from the kitchen making Maya look like a Madonna. "How'd the day go?" Her voice sounded kind. Happy.

"Good." Torie chewed the inside of her cheek. With every heartbeat, she prayed for God to let her joy last a second more. "Got a job. May be able to find an apartment in Albany now."

Maya blinked. Her happy lips frowned and her nose didn't do its little bunny-rabbit dance. "Congratulations." Her words were kind but hollow. Silence hung between them, and Torie was about to break it when Maya spoke. "I'm going to miss you."

"Miss me?"

"Why do you sound so surprised?"

Torie arched her brows. "Don't know...busted your car, got drunk and fired, been freeloading."

Maya smiled and her nose crinkled. "You've been a problem child, but you taught me a lot."

"*I* taught the teacher?"

Maya nodded. "My folks like you, too. Here." She thrust an envelope toward Torie.

"What's this?"

"Read it."

Torie pointed to the light, and in a moment the room exploded into eye-scrunching brightness. She fumbled with the envelope and pulled out a folded check. Opened it. Dropped her jaw. "A thousand dollars? To me?" She turned the check in her hand and wondered what the catch was. She looked at Maya who now beamed. "For real?"

"Read the note."

Torie scanned the scrawl. *Kind to Maya...changed attitude...admitting your problem to strangers...*

Maya nodded and sat at the foot of the bed.

"I can fix your car. Pay you rent with the rest." Torie grimaced. "If there is anything left over."

"I knew you'd choose the right thing. So did my folks."

"Why?"

"People need a chance to prove who they are."

"I..." What could she say? Every moment had become a struggle. Every choice she made proved wrong. She was an alcoholic. Not much better than a whore, flirting to get her way. Dirty.

"Just before you got home Sunday they told me they wouldn't buy me a brand new car." She grinned.

"You're happy about being stuck with your clunker?"

"Yes. They know I don't want material goods from them. I want

230

them. I want my parents."

"Nice to have parents you can love."

"We're going to take a Scandinavian cruise this summer. Get away from phones and schedules, rid ourselves of distractions. Be a family."

"Nice."

"At first I was sure they'd insist on buying me a car. BMW is their brand. After our weekend, they understood. I should have talked about my insecurities with them at the time of the suicide attempt."

"You didn't?"

Maya shook her head and picked at the quilt. "Only said I wanted to be a teacher. I was afraid of hurting their feelings, so I said nothing else." Maya looked up at Torie. "You changed my life. You make me happy."

"Me? I totaled your car."

"Not totaled. Just busted windows. No, my delight has nothing to do with the car but for not drinking. For telling my folks you were an alcoholic. For realizing you needed to change. For reminding me about a simple truth."

"What truth?"

"Honesty." Maya stood to go. She studied the floor then focused on Torie's eyes. "Where are you working? When will you leave?"

"At a salon in a strip mall on Western Avenue. Weekends. Candace will let me crash at her place if I cook. But why are you trying to get rid of me?"

"I'm not--"

Torie smirked and enjoyed Maya's distress for a beat. "If I go, who'll keep you looking hot? Make sure you and Adam become inseparable. Next on my agenda is teaching *you* how to flirt, but only if you'll teach me how to not to."

Maya clicked the off the light as she left the room. An instant later, she returned. "I forgot to tell you. The cops stopped by. Said they didn't have enough evidence." She paused. "Evidence for what?"

Torie shuddered and flicked her hand as though to brush away nothing. "Yesterday's news."

When Maya left, she pulled Torie's good humor with her.

Chapter Forty

"What walks on four legs in the morning, two legs in the afternoon, three legs at night?" Sophocles

Before the first glimmer of dawn, a soft tap rapped at Torie's bedroom door. Maya stuck her head in. "I'm going to be late getting home. Henry's sick. Adam's coming to get me, so I can use the Lincoln." She looked down, finding her feet interesting. "After work, we're going to get dinner."

Torie sat up and stretched. "So he finds the new you intriguing?"

Her wink and grin hit their mark -- Maya blushed.

"Okay, Ms. Vitale. This evening we're going to resume your femme fatale lessons. Your blush is charming, but sometimes you need to be a vixen if you don't want to get used."

"Adam would never use me." The red of Maya's face deepened.

"How'd Harold like the care center?"

"Wouldn't go. Hopefully today. If he refuses, Levi's got to come and check on him -- but he's afraid he'll get infected with Henry's virus."

"If Harold won't leave the house, have Adam call me. I'll slap the old coot into shape."

"I'll let him know. Just don't be the vixen with Harold." She winked.

Torie opened her mouth to protest as Maya stepped out of the room. Shutting her mouth, Torie understood -- Maya joked. Oh, she was going to make a foxy-lady out of her yet.

A half-hour later, as Torie was stepping out of the shower, her phone rang. Wrapping the towel around her, Torie scurried to her room, and arrived as it quit ringing. With her dripping hair making her shiver, Torie returned to the bathroom, grabbed another towel and wrapped it around her hair.

*****

Adam bit off a groan.

"You've reached Torie, of course not in the manner you desired..."

She flirted in her phone greeting? He shook his head. *Figures.* He waded through the rest of the message which turned mundane. *Sorry, I missed...leave your number...*

Funny. He missed the flirting, the fun that defined Torie.

As he waited, Adam rubbed his eyes which now ached and contemplated skipping work today. Tomorrow he'd have to throw Pop over his shoulder, strap him onto a backboard and haul him to daycare. If Torie couldn't help, what would he do? She was his last hope.

Last hope? He grinned at the thought. Who would've believed twelve years ago he'd be desperate for Vicious Vicky's help.

Finally, the phone signaled him to leave his message. "Hey, Torie. Adam. Maya said..." He hated to grovel. Needed to. Could he twist his words, make his begging sound... Sound what?

The silence of the phone told him he should be recording more than breathing. He stuttered hello, then wanted to hang up. Deal with his problem by himself.

The phone beeped. Call waiting.

Torie.

Now he had to grovel.

*****

Torie lowered her lashes and grinned while she rubbed her hair with the towel.

"You know I wouldn't bother you." He rambled on.

Of course. You need me. It felt good to be playing coy, but it felt a whole lot better to be needed.

"You know, Mr. Benedict, how much I would like to help you, but..." She bit her lip knowing the end of her thought and understanding Adam would misconstrue it.

He did. Adam said nothing.

She couldn't continue. "I'd like to help Harold even more. By the time you get here, I should be ready."

The phone stayed silent. *Did he hang up when I...?* "Adam? You there?"

"Thank you, Torie. We'll get you soon."

Serenity crowded her room. Giving felt better than her booze-buzz.

Fifteen minutes later, Adam's truck pulled up to the apartment, and Torie rushed out. Then stopped.

It wasn't Adam.

"Levi?" Her heart shrunk, and she exhaled.

"Adam was beyond late. You're stuck with me as your chauffeur."

By ten Levi dropped Torie at the farm. "Tell Harold he's too much trouble for me."

His words froze her hand poised to shove the door open. How could Levi be so crass? She turned and searched his eyes.

Laughter.

"You brat. I'll do no such thing." She slapped Levi's arm and climbed out of the van. As she strolled to the house, Torie straightened her skirt and picked at a piece of lint. Before entering, she checked her hair in the window.

"Harold?" The door squawked -- announcing her entrance.

No one answered. It didn't take long to scope out the downstairs. Behind the living room and an old-fashioned parlor, she found what must've been a formal dining room. It now served as Harold's room if the clunky hospital bed was any indication. A nice-sized kitchen equipped with a beautiful farmhouse-style sink, an original, not a modern, stainless steel, state-of-the-art overpriced one, stood to the right of the dining/hospital room. A rifle leaned against the counter by the back door. Torie hoped it was unloaded.

Adam said his grandfather wasn't supposed to go upstairs, but he had to be there.

Torie tiptoed up and creaked open a door to a tiny room. It must've been Adam's childhood one. A quilt displaying scout badges hung on the wall. On a shelf, lay elaborate Lego setups. A loft bed, its mattress adorned with a quilt made up with deer motifs was wedged against the far wall. Beneath it, sat a desk with its dusty surface clear of knickknacks. At the opposite end of the tiny room was a huge safe. The door stood ajar, and another rifle stood inside.

Across the hall, Torie found Harold. He lay on a double bed, his back to her, and a quilt pulled up to his nose as though he breathed in Grace. Traces of lavender drifted in the air. The room spoke of Adam's grandmother, not only in the scent but in the antique furniture covered with crocheted doilies. Lace curtains hung from the windows. A porcelain doll sat on a rocker in the corner. Maya would have loved Grace.

Love.

The idea tugged at Torie, both bitter and sweet. Harold deserved love. It was a shame all of it was fleeting. She clicked the door shut, returned to the kitchen and took inventory. Not much in the cupboards, but she found the ingredients for a chicken soup in the fridge and freezer.

Not her favorite soup. Tomorrow she'd bring her own spices. Harold would have something to savor.

As chicken legs defrosted in the microwave, a scanner, perched on top of it, blared a static-filled message about a car-bike accident in Burnt Hollow. Torie turned the volume down, but not off. She'd forget to turn it back on, and Harold might miss something.

With the oil now heated, the aroma of onions and celery permeated the room. As they sizzled, Torie yearned for someone to cook for.

The stupid scanner issued an alert for a ten-twenty-four something and made her jump. She clutched her chest, her heart hammering like a carpenter on meth.

She turned on the regular radio. Before she added the water to the pot, Harold appeared in the doorway.

"I see my grandson summoned the second-string."

"Not second to anyone." Torie waved the plastic spoon she'd been using to stir the soup beginnings. "He called the best."

"Harrumph." He left the room. The slap of the screen door told Torie where he went.

Men. Was everyone connected with Adam crotchety? She could work her magic with any man, grump or jokester or self-righteous Boy Scout.

She busied herself cleaning as the soup simmered as Harold rocked on the porch. On occasion, Torie checked to make sure he dozed or dreamed. Letting him be would be the best medicine. At noon, she scooped soup into a chipped bowl, found a napkin and saltines, and placed them on a tray.

But it lacked the proper ambiance.

Outside lilies-of-the-valley overran the yard. Their sweet scent brought to her childhood when on a sultry summer day, she and Crystal doused the blue bottle of their cheap cologne over their heads so they could smell like these flowers.

Jean had pitched a fit and hosed them down outside. If she realized how much fun Torie and her sister had frolicking in the water, Jean would've let them stink up the yard.

She still loved lilies-of-the-valley and picked a bunch growing by the back door.

After finding a juice glass, Torie arranged the flowers and brought the tray out front to Harold. "Here you go."

His brows caterpillared together. "Fancy-shmancy."

"Shut up and eat."

He scowled.

"Oh, stop it. I can be cantankerous, too."

He sipped the soup. All traces of ill humor vanished. "You're right."

"About what?"

"Not second string to anyone."

Three days went by with no drama other than the events emanating from the scanner. The plumber finished the powder room in the downstairs closet, so she could yell at Harold every time he hit the stairs. A few friends stopped by for haircuts. Boring. Quiet.

235

At last, her first work weekend arrived.
Her heart sank.

*****

Adam grabbed the venison he'd defrosted, and while the oil heated, studied the kitchen. The tray filled with Torie's hair products on the counter had mushroomed. At first, he thought it was Torie's personal hair care. No big deal. He picked up a curling iron and studied it as though he'd never seen one before. He lifted a container of hair gel. Too many lay on the Formica to be for her own use. Had she set up shop?

"Pop?" Still holding the gel, he found his grandfather on the porch. "Are you starting a beauty parlor?" He lifted the jar. "Don't have enough hair left for this to be yours."

A smile creased Pop's face. "Nope. Them things are my babysitter's stuff. A few ladies came in for haircuts. We're thinking of starting up a salon here. Call it Borrowed Grace in honor of your grandma. We'd be highfalutin."

Old anger rose in Adam's gullet. He couldn't control Pop, let alone Torie. *Lord, I'm not a Pharisee.* He exhaled and with the whoosh of breath, he'd let his anger go.

"We even designed some business cards. Got 'em by the phone." He raised a shaky finger toward the house. "Going to get all the free cuts I kin stand." He chuckled. "Even promised me microdermabrasions. Make me youthful agin." He patted his cheek and chuckled. His eyes twinkled, and Adam caught a glimpse of his old grandfather.

Then Adam's palms itched. In a fleeting moment, he pictured his youthful grandfather teaching him how to dress out the trout they'd caught in the back stream. Saw him smooching Neema when they thought he wasn't around.

In the evening, they sat on the porch for dinner. Minutes crawled by as Pop raised a forkful of venison to his lips. Time stopped while he chewed and chewed and chewed, and with shaky hands, lifted his fork for the next mouthful. Meds controlled the muscle twitching well -- no side-effects. Nevertheless, the Parkinson's slowed Pop down.

It wouldn't be long until another funeral arrived.

Though, it could be years.

Had to be years. With Pop in his own house, with Torie tending to him, Pop would live many more years. Had to.

Torie? He never dreamed the thought of her could comfort him.

Adam shoved his chair aside. "Going to clean up."

His grandfather grunted.

In the kitchen, Adam rubbed his eyes. His temper tantrums over living here, and his desire to keep Torie from helping out convicted him of selfishness. His hatred of her stained his soul. How did he stop his sullenness? He'd become as cantankerous as Pop, without his grandfather's charity.

His cell rang. Maya. His bad mood swirled down the drain with the grease from the night's dinner.

"You're off tomorrow, right?" Maya asked.

"Indeed I am." He thought of taking her kayaking, introducing her to the trails in Hookskill, finding a private lean-to and--

"Do you want me to pick you up for church?"

He'd forgotten about church. Why did resolutions fade so quickly? "No. I'll get you. Would you like to go kayaking afterward?"

"Harold?"

"He's fine for an hour or two. I'll have LaValley or Stephenson check in on him. Don't worry about lunch. I've got it covered."

"Torie and I went shopping. Just wait 'til you see the shorts I got. Shorts. Me? Can you imagine?"

He could imagine, and smiled as he pictured her long legs. Legs hidden by the bow of the kayak. Afterwards?

"She took me to the outlets in Glens Falls. Going to teach me to be sexy."

"Torie's not a good role model."

Maya hung up.

*****

Adam.

The thought of him drove Maya crazy. She was too man-hungry, too hormonally intoxicated or too desperate to be married and have babies. Why did she obsess over this man?

Torie said her feelings were normal.

He sounded more enthusiastic about kayaking in the afternoon than church. Then his snide remark about being careful about Torie's influence. Why was this man so bi-polar? He adored helping those in need, even the people he called frequent flyers who called regularly. Said they called 9-1-1 out of deep emotional needs which could be as critical as the life-threatening ones.

Every time he softened about Torie or his past, something rose up. It was almost like the serpent on the caduceus he wore strangled his good intentions.

He always had to be too in control.

Then she thought about her folks, about her all-absorbing need to be reassured of their love. Change came with one step forward and an inevitable regression.

Chapter Forty-One

"Judge not, that ye be not judged." Matt. 7:1

"Pop, here's some cereal." Adam placed a bowl of oatmeal on the table as he checked his watch. *I don't have time for this. Maya expects me in five minutes.* He focused on Pop. "Eat."

Instead, his grandfather stared at the oatmeal as if it Adam tried to poison him. "Give this glop to the barn cats. You got to git my lil' babysitter to give you cooking lessons." He shoved the bowl across the table. It slid off the edge. Adam grabbed it, and the swill sloshed over his clean jeans.

He gasped and bit back the words he wanted to hurl and squeezed his eyes shut. *He's grieving. Need to give him time.* As Adam mopped up the gooey mess from the floor, his grandfather hoisted himself from the table, then yanked open the refrigerator, and pulled out a carton of eggs and bacon.

"That stuff'll give you a heart attack."

"'S my heart."

Adam stormed toward the stairs.

"Git me my boots."

In the guest room, now his room, Adam changed into dry pants. Making as much noise as he could, he stomped to Neema's.

Not Neema's. Pop's room.

No sense trying to keep Pop downstairs at night. He searched the closet for the work boots his grandfather preferred. Not there. Under the bed, he found them. Next to a rifle. He pulled it out and emptied the chambers. Slamming the bedroom door, he marched to his boyhood room, making his steps as loud as he could. With the gun shoved into the open safe, Adam locked it and turned to go. He'd have to figure out how to change the combination. If not, he'd sell Pop's guns.

Guns. Plural. The safe now held two rifles, his and the one he just locked in there. Should be three.

He shook his head. If Pop wanted to shoot himself or Mark LaValley or Torie, he was old enough to make the decision. He was done being a babysitter.

Grease splattered the stove as Pop shuffled bacon around and tested the eggs. He looked so frail working the simple task. Adam's anger softened like the bacon grease.

"You've got to keep your rifle locked up. It's not safe with your Parkinson's. You're too unstable."

"Don't go jogging with it. Keep it right there." He pointed to the back door.

"Where?"

"'Tween the screen and the door. Keep it out of your view."

"Why was one under your bed?"

"Quicker t'get at night."

"If you leave it lying around, an intruder's going to shoot you."

"Only intruders we got is coydogs. Shot one the other night."

"The other night? In your bedroom?"

Pop glared at him, and Adam clamped his mouth shut.

"You was out sparking with your gal. I scared the varmints outta here. 'S my house. My rules."

"Coydogs don't go upstairs."

Pop didn't respond.

Adam clomped out of the house to get Maya.

At the end of the ten-minute ride, he quit grinding his teeth. He hopped out of his truck and hurried to Maya's door.

It opened before he knocked.

"Sorry I'm late. Pop was a mite uncooperative."

Maya smiled at him, or at least he thought she smiled. She climbed into the truck -- but didn't relax. Seemed to hug the door. *What was wrong? Or should I ask, what did I do now?*

Maya stared out the window.

He swallowed his conversation, turned on the radio, and let the music fill the void until he turned into Maranatha's lot.

A black Fusion pulled in ahead of him, and Adam parked in the neighboring spot just as Torie climbed out of the black car. As Maya bounded out of the truck, she grinned for the first time. "Torie. You didn't tell me you were coming to church this morning." She flung Adam an 'I-told-you-so' look over her shoulder.

"You're getting good with your makeup and hair." Torie threw her arms around Maya.

"I wasn't expecting you until tomorrow."

Torie glanced at the woman who had driven her. "Adam, Maya, this is my weekend-roommate, Candace."

Candace nodded. "Good to meet you." She turned her attention to Torie. "I'm off to find the old fossil who pawned you off on me." She sashayed into the church.

Torie and Maya followed. "Thanks to Candace, I..."

Adam lost the rest of the conversation as the girls wandered into the church, heads together, chatting about what? Him?

What bugged Maya? Did she want him to notice her hair? No. Maya wasn't vain. He saw himself with Pop this morning, and every morning since Neema's passing. Recalled his anger against Torie last night, even after he told Maya he'd repented. Judgment oozed out of him at every turn.

For the first time this morning, he relaxed. He could fix their issue, as it wasn't an issue any longer -- only a habit. Things wouldn't get fixed without help, though.

In the foyer, he caught up with the ladies.

Torie turned to him. "Adam. I have a proposition." She batted her eyes.

Proposition?

"I've got to grab a cup of joe and wedge myself in with the biddies. I'll talk to you later about it." She hurried off.

Adam studied her as she strode to the coffee table. He then recalled the hair products and understood. and looked after Torie who now skipped to the front right of the church. Torie and old people? Odd.

*****

Bad coffee, White Shoulders perfume. Three gray heads in a row. Maybe her own salon? Life couldn't get much better for Torie as she waited for the warmth of worship and preaching to wash over her. If Adam allowed her to start Borrowed Grace at his grandfather's, she could earn her keep as a live-in caretaker, *and* save enough to start her own salon in Albany. She'd keep the name, of course. With closed eyes, Torie whispered a prayer uttered in faith. *Thank you, God, for making Adam agree to our schemes.*

Her mind wandered in her dreams and refused to focus on the song. It went on and on, chorus after chorus -- the never-ending lyric. Boring. Her shoulders sagged. Was this love affair with Jesus over already? He was male, of course, so He'd be fickle. Disappointment weighted her until her favorite chorus -- how could it be in such a short time she'd find a favorite -- began. The song swelled like an ocean's currents and swept over her. Glee wrapped its joy around her. Jesus wasn't a yo-yo, after all.

Announcements, prayer requests -- the interlude stretched endlessly. Ten minutes later, Lenny's replacement, who would give the sermon, spoke. His tone was cultured, not at all like his predecessor's. "A few weeks back, Pastor Arendsen preached about the woman ready to be stoned for adultery. Luke 6:37, today's Scripture continues his thought."

Torie flipped through the pages of her Bible, hungered for more of the healing balm she'd felt with her first experience at church. She read the words before the speaker. Selene's image floated into her consciousness. Torie's blood turned cold, colder than after the walk in the rain during her frosty night out in the forest. 'Forgive, and you will be forgiven.' Didn't God understand? Some people didn't deserve forgiveness.

*****

"Judge not lest you be judged." Adam glanced at Torie. He shivered, then refocused. "Forgive and you will be forgiven."

It was time to quit misjudging her. Or at least, to keep forgiving her mistakes.

Maya showed the most faith of the three of them. After hearing the Scripture, Maya would understand it and accept its truth. He whispered, "I'm sorry. I was wrong about Torie."

Maya tightened her lips, but her nose crinkled. She couldn't act stern. Ever.

She stared ahead, but her hand crept back into his. The warmth penetrated his fingers. Using his Bible as a ploy, he studied her. Beautiful. Her beauty, enhanced with hair color and a touch of make-up, had none of Jennifer's artificiality. He liked the way she changed, not because it made him look hot and lucky, but because it displayed who she was, what he always wanted, even when he had his wild crush on Vicious Vicky. Maya was beautiful but good. Solidly good and just and kind and lovely.

He felt small next to her.

*****

How could she not forgive Adam? Maya glanced at him and pictured his relationship with his grandfather, his attitude toward work. Justine and Levi respected him. Adam wanted to be decent. Strove to be upright. The cruelty of his past made goodness sound bad. Geek. Boy Scout. Goody-two-shoes. The words had become curses rather than blessings.

With a deep intake of air, Maya's love for him warmed her. His weaknesses and strengths, joy and anger.

Why?

One hard spot. *What about my birthmother? My real parents? Myself? We all have at least one stain we can't remove without a lot of work from Jesus.*

She didn't understand the workings of love. It just happened.

Torie claimed love was sex appeal and lust. Could this be?

She glanced at him. His sexy lips were a well-defined Cupid's bow, narrow, but wide and warm and tender. She shook the thought away. She sat in church, so she tried not to lust. The more Maya worked on not drooling over him, the more she imagined his strong nose and sparkling eyes.

And his hair.

He hated it. Called it a white-man's afro. Kept it cropped. Those curls were adorable, though -- made him like a little boy.

The service became a blur.

Three hours later they beached the kayaks on the shore of Livingstone Pond in an area accessible by kayak or canoe. Nothing but the natural world existed in this tiny nook of the pond, and quiet blanketed it. So tranquil she could hear the wind ruffling the trees. Pine, heated by the late spring sun, permeated the air. Water, rippled by the breeze, begged her to soak her feet. She waded in the sandy shallows and watched Adam.

He spread out a gingham tablecloth on the sand and laid out the picnic he insisted on packing himself. Cold chicken. Venison. Hard-boiled eggs. Even a bag of salad for her benefit.

"Can I at least help you set up?" she asked.

"Nope. Enjoy the water. I don't want you to worry about a thing."

Maya studied Adam as he fussed with the food. He looked so earnest. Her eyes must have been palpable as he looked up and blushed.

"Join me," Maya said.

He held up a finger, indicating she should wait, and he wiggled off his boots.

On the bottom of the pond, grasses stretched upward striving to nab the light, and snail shells lay scattered on the sand at her toes. Minnows nibbled her feet. A little ways out, water lilies promised to bloom. She faced the center of the pond. Blue sky and cumulus clouds and sparkling water. Best? Silence.

From behind her, Adam's arms encircled her waist. His hands clasped a small bunch of water iris, and Adam nuzzled her shoulder with his chin. "These will have to do for our centerpiece."

She took the flowers but didn't turn. The warmth of him against her, the puff of his breath against her cheek was a spell she didn't want broken.

"I listened today."

She smiled but didn't turn.

"I've missed church. I'm sorry I drifted away from it. Sometimes I feel so condemned by the sermons. I can be a jerk."

With eyes closed, Maya relaxed back into him. *We all are jerks sometimes.*

When she finally faced him, Adam pulled her to him.

His kiss, like sunlight on water, sparkled against her lips.

She kissed him back.

He strained for a deeper kiss.

She resisted, then lost control. With a passion she didn't know she had, she lost track of herself in the water, in the wilderness, in love.

They broke away.

Torie's flirting counsel flitted into her mind. *Promise, but make him wait. Men are horny and will do anything, say anything if they think they could get a little. Then you can get what you want.*

A cloud passed over the sun and the wind chilled for a moment.

*****

The light disappeared, and the sound of the shower woke Torie. One weekend at the salon, and already she was acting like Celeste and Angela, sleeping her life away. What else was there to do in the boonies?

At least Maya got home.

Torie wanted to hear the juicy details of love in the jungle amongst spiders and bats and coyotes.

She grabbed her nail polish remover and sat on the love seat in the living room. The instant Maya stepped out of the bathroom, Torie'd learn whether her flirting instruction taught Maya anything.

The bathroom door rattled, and Torie dropped her acetone-soaked cotton ball. "Good thing you're not naked."

Maya jumped. "Make some noise, Sullivan. You gave me the vapors."

"The vapors? You dipping into the Vicks?"

"A joke." Maya stuck her tongue out, and continued towel drying her hair and headed toward her bedroom.

"How'd your date go?"

"Good."

"Good?" Torie mimed looking at a watch. "It's ten p.m. Been dark for two hours. How can you kayak in the pitch blackness? Remember, I lived in Hookskill. I know how creepy night gets."

"You didn't live there. You slept there one night."

Torie held up two fingers.

"Okay. Two nights." Two red patches flamed on Maya's cheeks.

Torie *would* be regaled. She patted the sofa. "Sit. Give me the details."

"I'll sit, but there are no details." Maya settled next to Torie and tossed the towel on the ground.

"Wait. You're not going to let your mane dry into a tangled mess." Torie got up, grabbed a comb and sat back down. "Turn around. I'll be the mommy and comb your hair. Then you won't have to look at me as you share the bawdy details of your love life."

"Torie. I told you. I'm waiting until marriage."

"Come on girl. You've known him for almost a month."

"Three weeks."

"Yeah. Yeah. You're young."

"God's ideals don't change because two people have dated for a while."

"With a committed relationship?"

"In the Bible, engagements lasted a year and could only be terminated by divorce. During the long engagement, couples refrained from..." She paused as though fishing for words. "Intercourse."

"Intercourse?" Torie whooped with laughter. "I think that's a name of an Amish town. Come on. Don't you think God understands the times we live in?"

"God's truth doesn't change with the times."

Torie teased the tangles out of Maya's hair. She'd heard this before, but she knew men. God could be standing on their shoulders, and still, they'd try to rut. "Has Adam tried?"

Maya shook her head.

"Is he gay?"

Maya turned. Her face looked like Buff just licked her mouth, a stunt Mr. Harrigan found hilarious.

Torie snickered.

"Do I look horrified?" Maya asked.

Torie nodded. "Now answer me."

"No."

"No, you're not answering?"

"No. He's tried nothing."

Torie leaned back, put the comb on the end table and studied her friend. "Your blush betrays you. Remember what I told you. Make him work for the favors. Men like--"

Maya held up her hands to stop Torie. "Enough. I need to get to bed. Some people have to work tomorrow."

So Boy Scout's not gay, and neither is my friend. Torie grinned.

Then all mirth vanished as fast as money in the mall. What about her life? She loved Maya's innocence, her flushing cheeks, her stammering over any words dealing with sex. When had she herself lost her innocence?

It wasn't just Darren. She had no say in his finagling. How about Dylan, despite her protests to Adam? Trey? How many others?

Only one man ever mattered, and Selene used Torie's own tricks to steal him.

She lifted her head and stared at Maya's closed doors.

"You're right, Maya," she whispered.

Chapter Forty-Two

"A soft answer turneth away wrath: but grievous words stir up anger." Prov. 15:1

Monday morning Torie fussed with the coq au vin stewing in the crock pot for Harold and her. She sniffed the wine as the alcohol bubbled away. Too bad she couldn't sample it before the good part went to waste.

With the lid lifted, Torie studied the backsplash. In the tired white tiles with cracking grout, she saw nothing but her plan simmering like the chicken in the pot.

She would do it.

Running up to the master bedroom, Torie stripped the quilt from the bed, folded it, plopped the two pillows in their shams on top and hauled them downstairs. Laying the queen-sized quilt around the hospital bed, she left one end longer than the other and tucked it under the mattress. The pattern was off-centered, but the effect pleased her. She turned back the shorter edge and fluffed the pillows.

Gnawing her cuticle, Torie studied her handiwork. Something wasn't right. Snapping her fingers, Torie pivoted and hurried to the kitchen and rummaged through the cabinet until she found the open bag of Hershey's kisses. She nicked one, returned to the hospital bed, and placed it on the pillow. Might as well entice Harold with a mite of elegance. Then she jogged back up the stairs.

Hauling down the rocker proved awkward, but apparently, Harold dozed on the porch. He never investigated her racket.

The porcelain doll followed suit and now perched on the rocker in the dining room. Still, something was missing.

Torie inhaled a deep breath. Then it hit her. She loped up the stairs and scavenged through the dressers. In each drawer, she found what she needed. Lavender sachets. She sniffed them. The scent had faded but still existed. The aroma of Grace.

Downstairs, Torie slipped the sachets into secret spots behind the sofa, in the buffet, and on the springs of the hospital bed. On her next shopping foray, she'd find lavender essential oil and scented candles to keep the scent vibrant forever.

Feeling smug, she called Harold.

The scanner came to life in the kitchen.

"Code 3. Unconscious patient. Four-seven-eight Burnt Hollow

Road."

Four-seven-eight? Selene's. A customer? Maybe one of their old ladies fainted?

She rubbed palms, suddenly sweaty, against her skirt.

Levi's voice responded to the call. "Unit twenty-seven to four-seven-eight Burnt Hollow. Lights and sirens."

She relaxed.

Some.

Thank you, Jesus. Levi and Adam worked together this week. Torie wrapped her arms around herself. Adam knew his stuff as well as she knew hers.

"PD's on the scene," the dispatcher said. "Hysterical woman will need assistance."

A hysterical woman?

Her breath came fast. Selene's partying and sexuality were the flip side to tears and terror.

"What'd you want me fer?"

She spun around. Harold? She shook her head, remembering she had called him.

Harold stood grinning before her. "I kin smell my Grace."

She smiled wanly.

His grin evaporated. "What's wrong?"

The unconscious patient? Trey's MRIs and CAT scans? Trey dying? Terror crept up her spine. "I've got to get to Mid-State. Will you be okay alone for an hour?" She waved her hand toward the re-decorated room, but her eyes pled with Harold. "I brought Grace downstairs. Promise me you'll stay off the stairs."

His lips quivered and the inner edges of his eyebrows rose. He looked so sad Torie threw her arms around him and buried her head against his chest. "Don't worry, but I think my boy--" She paused, had no right to think of Trey as her lover. "I think a good friend is in trouble. If he is, my best friend is, too."

Best friend? She never thought she'd use the term for Selene again. Yet, it was true. If Trey was hurting, if the headaches were life-threatening, and given his family history, they could be, Selene would be aching with grief. How lame the lack of forgiveness felt. What a waste of energy and emotions. Selene needed her now.

"With Grace's life, her smell right here, I'll never go upstairs agin. Thank you, lil' one, fer doing all this." He nodded at the bed. "You go, and I promise, I'll be a good boy."

In the Lincoln, she mashed the accelerator to the floor, barely letting up around the curves. Her heart beat faster than the rotating tires. The wheels thumped. *Please save Trey.* They bumped over a pothole. *Lord, keep the troopers away.*

She glanced in the rearview mirror.

No.

Red and blue lights flashed. The trooper gained on her. She pulled to the shoulder.

Where did Adam keep the registration? She fumbled in the glove compartment. The rearview mirror showed the trooper sitting in his car fiddling with something. She turned back to her search, this time in the console. From there, she nabbed the registration and dug in her purse for her license.

She checked the rearview mirror just as the good-looking trooper from her accident unfolded himself from his car. He strolled toward the Lincoln, sauntered like she had all the time in the world. As though Trey wasn't dying ten miles away.

God, please. Please. Please. No other words formed as she chanted her plea.

"Do you know how fast you were going?"

"Too fast."

"Do you know why I stopped you?"

"Sir, I know I drove too fast. I'll pay the ticket." Torie handed off the documents she had gathered. "Here's my paperwork. Please hurry and give me the ticket. My boyfriend's been rushed to the hospital. His girlfriend needs me."

The trooper paused. "His girlfriend, yet he's *your* boyfriend?"

Torie shook her head. Couldn't think. *Will this guy just ticket me and get out of my way?*

He bent, his face close to the window. "Didn't you land in a ditch a few weeks back?"

Torie shrugged. Words wouldn't form. She took in this man's looks. Inhaled. Did *not* want to flirt, only wanted to get to the hospital.

"If you're not careful, the next time we fish you out of the ditch, it'll be to bury you in another one. How's this guy you're killing yourself for both your boyfriend and your friend's?"

"He's my ex..." Tears strangled her words.

The trooper handed back her documents. "Follow me. I'll get you there alive."

The trooper pulled out and passed her with lights flashing. She followed.

At Mid-State's ER, the trooper slowed, killed the lights, and continued down the road at a leisurely pace while Torie swerved into the parking area.

No spaces stood open. Torie crawled up and down the aisles of the parking lot. Just as the rescue careened into the emergency bay, she found a spot.

The ambulance made no sound. Did silence mean something awful happened? Was he dead? She squeezed her eyes shut and felt the tears behind her lids.

No time for self-pity.

She ran. In flip-flops, she stumbled. Needed to slow down. She kept her eyes on the ambulance. Levi bounded out. He sprinted to the back of the truck. Too fast. So Trey was alive, in trouble, but alive.

If it *was* Trey in the transport.

If he *was*, he'd be okay. Adam was in there with him. Levi helped.

A cop car with lights flashing pulled in behind them. Torie neared the hullabaloo. The cop got out, rounded the vehicle, and opened the passenger door. A woman with shocking red hair, lacquered into place, climbed out of the car. Too slow. Too unsteady. The cop grabbed her. Held her arm.

Torie's feet melted into the tar. The terror stalling Selene welded Torie to the ground. It was Trey. Her hand clawed at her chest as though she could calm her bounding heart.

The men raced a gurney into the hospital, and Torie ran once more. The group disappeared.

She flew through the emergency room doors before anyone could stop her.

"Selene."

Selene turned. Her face, pale and tear-streaked, turned hard. She stepped back.

"Will he be okay?" Torie didn't wait for a response. She threw her arms around her friend and held her until Selene wiggled free. "I'm so sorry, but he'll be okay, Selene. I've been praying since I heard the scanner. Besides, Adam Benedict is taking care of him. He's the best."

Torie clung to Selene who stood with arms at her side. In slow motion, Selene raised them, placed them on Torie's shoulders, and slid into the hug.

Selene didn't release Torie. "They're airlifting him to Albany. It's not good."

They separated, but Torie clung to Selene's fingertips.

Adam headed down the corridor. His face told Torie her prayers for healing failed.

Selene stepped toward Adam. "How is he?"

"The doctor will be with you in a moment." He nodded and headed into an office.

Torie read his eyes. His little boy eyes could never hide his emotions. No helicopter would be taking off. Selene stood motionless in the corridor, shoulders slumped. They quivered. She understood, too.

Then? As though Selene had never stolen Trey and he had never been so crude when she caught them in bed together, the past disappeared. All Torie wanted to do was console her friend.

They waited. Said nothing. Waited some more

A doctor approached.

"Are you Mrs. Currey?" he asked Selene.

She nodded.

Torie tightened her grip on Selene's hand. The lie about being Trey's wife didn't hurt. It made her want to comfort Selene more.

"The CT showed a bleed. A massive bleed." He paused. Torie knew what he'd say next. "I'm sorry. If you want to see him now, come say good-bye."

"When will the helicopter be here? How long do we have?" Hope colored Selene's voice.

"Selene." Torie took her hand. "He's not going to make it."

"But in Albany." Selene's knees buckled, and Torie strained against her weight. "In Albany."

The doctor shook his head. He opened his mouth, but no words formed.

"Can't you...can't he go on life-support? Wait until the bleeding heals?"

"It's your decision. He's on a respirator for now. I have to warn you, there's only brain stem function. He will be in a chronic vegetative state. If he lives."

"I don't care. Save him." She shrugged off Torie's arm. "Where is he?"

Selene dashed ahead of Torie.

Torie found her friend in an ER cubicle where Trey lay on a bed. Tubes stuck out of his mouth. His chest rose and fell with the swoosh of the respirator.

Selene crawled onto the bed. She ran her hand along his strong cheekbones and kissed his forehead. Her makeup streaked like a Harlequin's. Bits of her lipstick colored Trey's forehead. The sole color his face held.

Trey didn't want this. He told her that one night when they were drunk and soppy after his uncle's death from a brain bleed. When he admitted his father was being watched for it. "If I can't party, kill me, babe. I don't want to be a breathing turnip. After you pull the plug, burn me up. Be sure to invite Jim, Jack and Jose to my celebration."

251

Her eyes questioned, then the first smile graced her face. "Beam, Daniels and Cuervo."

"Where's my boy?"

Selene bolted upright.

Torie twisted as a flurry of activity blew in from the hallway. Trey's mother raced into the cubicle, followed by his father.

"What are you doing?" She grabbed Selene's shoulder. "Can't you let my son alone?"

"Mrs. Currey. Trey's going to--"

"Get off of him, you lying--" Venom etched her voice. "Telling doctors you're his *wife*."

Mrs. Currey made the word wife sound sinful.

Torie knew what would follow. During their drunken evening, she and Trey discussed DNRs and funerals. He told her all about his parents. They had plans for him from career to wedding to the sex of his babies.

Torie wouldn't have made the cut.

Selene didn't either.

"Get out of here. Now." Mrs. Currey turned her back on the women. They'd been dismissed.

"But--"

"Nurse!" Mrs. Currey never looked at Selene. "Get this woman away from my son."

Selene backed out of the cubicle, but couldn't leave the hospital. The two women sat back in the corridor outside the emergency room.

*****

Adam finished his PCRs and returned to the lobby. He stopped when he caught sight of Torie and his patient's girlfriend. He thought they would've been with Trey, not in the corridor.

They sat unaware of everything going on around them. Selene sobbed. Torie comforted. Torie hated Selene. He heard her bitter rants against her former roommate. He'd seen how Selene had treated Torie, changing locks on her house, flaunting her relationship with the man Torie loved, refusing to aid her former friend. How could Torie love this lady?

Images arose of the woman who had washed Jesus's feet with her tears, drying them with her hair. The Pharisees had hurled invectives toward Jesus about the sinner. He showed love. Adam's bitterness burned like bitter coffee in his mouth.

Old women in church? Vibrant worship? AA meetings?

What else didn't he see?

252

Chapter Forty-Three

"But I say unto you which hear, Love your enemies, do good to them which hate you..." Luke 6:27

Two days later, Torie jolted from the reception desk at Curly Girls when Selene drifted into the room.

Selene's hair stuck out on one side, and flattened in the back. Without make-up, her crimson hair washed her out like an antique porcelain doll with bone-white skin. "Why're you helping me after all?"

"It's been two days since..." Torie swallowed the words Selene didn't need to hear. "Clients need to know you can't meet with them. Your walk-ins need to be sent away."

"But why are you helping when I stole Trey?"

Torie shrugged. How could she explain forgiveness? It was like the first slug of scotch. It burned to start, but the freeing buzz told her the booze worked its magic. Selene wouldn't understand God.

She bit the inside of her cheek. *Does God like being compared to scotch?*

Selene flopped down on the chair opposite Torie and studied her fingers. Her eyes never met Torie's. "The Curreys made all the funeral decisions. Wouldn't give me a say."

"Cremation? Albany funeral?"

Selene nodded. "How'd you know?"

Torie shrugged and hurt niggled. Trey's folks always had plans for him -- where he lived, who he married, how he'd be buried. "Once, when we were blotto, we had a long, morbid discussion about how we'd die and be buried. His folks made me glad mine had no interest in my life."

Selene's lips lifted into a half smile. "You know -- knew -- more about Trey than I did." All hints of her smile faded. She sighed. "We had no time together. No time to learn everything about each other like you." Her eyes wouldn't meet Torie's.

Torie tapped the pen on the desk, and studied Selene's bowed head. Words didn't form. Seconds ticked by. The phone remained silent. She should get back to Harold. Torie scribbled a note. "Here's my number. Call me if there's anything else you need. I added my address, or rather where I am most of the time now. Living with an old guy." She smiled. "We talked about me moving in with him." She stood. "In case you need to just drop in, stop. Harold and I are always up for a party."

Selene's fingers grazed Torie's, chilling her as Selene took the note.

She dropped her hand and laid the paper on the desk.

"I heard you got religion." Selene looked up.

No mockery showed in her eyes. Even if it had, Torie didn't care, and she couldn't stop her grin. Religion. Forgiveness. Sobriety. None of it was easy, but all of it freed her. "Not only religion. I go to AA. My best buds are all geezers and a first-grade teacher with no sass at all."

Selene raised her brows. "Why?"

"'Cause it makes me feel good. Call me."

Selene nodded, but Torie understood Selene would never resume her friendship. Guilt would keep her bitter. It would tie her to the past. "Come on out to church with me sometime."

Selene grimaced, and Torie left the salon.

Just as she opened the door to the Lincoln, a battered red truck pulled next to it.

"They're closed, Jean."

As Torie climbed into the Lincoln, Jean clambered out of the truck. "Don't look it."

Torie started the car. "Don't believe me. Your problem."

Jean slammed her hand on the hood of the Lincoln.

"What the--" Torie caught herself.

"I want a word with you." Jean rounded the car, and Torie was torn between peeling out or having it out with her mother.

"So what'd I do now?"

"Your attitude."

"My--?"

"Probation showed up." Jean's lips compressed into two scarlet lines. "Because of your lies, Darren may be sent back."

"I didn't lie." Torie began to raise the window when Jean stuck her hand into the car. For a moment, Torie pictured pinning Jean to the window and driving off. Somehow she didn't think God would approve.

"You lied about him bashing in the car windows."

"You're high, Jean." She pressed the window control. Jean nipped her hand out of the way before it closed.

"You get out of my life, Victoria. You're no daughter of mine."

At last, you've figured it out? Torie let the tires squeal as she pulled onto Burnt Hollow Road. Gravel sprayed as she stepped on the gas. She peered into the rearview mirror. Jean tottered toward Curly Girls.

The next day proved warm and quiet. Selene headed out to Albany even though the Curreys informed her she would not be recognized at the calling hours. If they froze Selene out, Torie wasn't going to attempt to go.

Her heart ached. Love for Trey dogged her. Relief at forgiving

Selene soothed. Still, grief left her needing activity. Something to wash away the pain.

Wash?

Pollen coated the Lincoln and needed to be scrubbed off. Torie threw on a pair of cut-offs and a T-shirt left over from her brief stint at The Stadium. She wished she'd realized the truth of Collin's accusation weeks ago. She'd let herself become her mother -- man crazy and booze-addled. With a tilted head, Torie searched the ceiling as though she could see Jesus. "Thank you for not killing me when I crashed."

Downstairs, Harold snoozed on the porch. She tiptoed to him, and let her lips brush the tips of his hair in a kiss while he dozed, careful not to wake him.

She lugged the gritty hose out front and filled a bucket. Suds foamed, overflowed before the water reached the midpoint of the bucket. She turned the hose on the car and sprayed. Traffic sped past the house from time to time.

In the distance, LaValley's tractor rumbled. Sniffing the air, she figured he was planting fields with corn. Planting beat the stench of manuring.

Cool water drifted in the breeze and sprayed her in rainbows. Smiling, Torie placed her finger over the nozzle to create a finer mist and painted the air in reds and blues and greens. Pretty. Maya had rubbed off on her. Water rainbows now captivated her.

As Torie lathered the car, a vehicle slowed. Tires crunched on gravel.

A red truck. A battered red truck. She let go of the lever on the nozzle and let the spray die. She widened her stance and shifted to block any entrance to the house.

*****

Adam slammed the ambulance's rear doors. The rig was as perfect as it could be. It'd been a good morning. Busy enough to fly by. Quiet enough to have energy for an afternoon of fishing. Now, with his shift over, he'd get Torie to hang out with Pop a couple more hours so he could hook some trout from Thompsons Lake for supper.

He'd con her into making dinner. What a cook she was.

Torie. Who'd ever have thought he'd come to trust her with anything, let alone Pop? *I'd have called people nuts if they told me I'd love to go to church and that Maya would change me back to Goody-Two-Shoes.*

He grinned.

"What canary are you eating, Garfinkel?" Stephenson smacked the back of Adam's head as he walked toward the door. "You going to hang out here for a second shift?"

"Nah. I'm off."

"Better have Torie shave your head, Benedict. You're beginning to look like a girl."

Adam scrubbed his hair, his goldie-curly locks long beneath his fingers. A good dinner and a free buzz-cut? Torie provided even more benefits.

Who'd have ever thought?

He slung his jacket over his shoulder and marched into the late spring sunshine. It felt more like summer.

Summer.

Not much longer. Maya's schedule would meld with his. He'd take her swimming. Swimsuits. He settled back in his truck and dreamed.

It was a little after two. The fish wouldn't bite until later in the afternoon, but Torie wouldn't know he used fishing as an excuse to take a mini-vacation. Seeing as she half-moved into his old room, she didn't mind hanging around. She'd cook up his mess of trout for him and Pop and Maya.

She was worth keeping around for her cooking.

And her haircuts.

****

"What're you doing here?" Torie held the hose tight, not much protection, but she'd use it to shock Darren.

"You little dirt bucket." Darren strode toward her.

Torie raised the hose, ready to spray him away. His fist knocked into her cheek, sending shards of pain along her face. Her arms flew up as she tumbled back. The Lincoln kept her upright, but she dropped the hose.

"You called the cops on me. Narked me out before I had a chance to change my address. Blamed me for busting windows with a tire iron. After twelve years in the slammer for giving you nothing you didn't want anyway, you do this?"

"I didn't want? I was a child." She straightened and tried to meld into the car.

"A child playing Barbie in those little skirts and no panties?"

"Get out of here before I call the cops." She fished for her phone but encountered a flat pocket. The cell lay on the kitchen counter, so she wouldn't soak it.

"Threats again? I'll give you something to report. I'll show you what

rape is, do to you what your accusations forced on me for twelve years."
He shoved her against the car, pinned both her arms in one of his.

"You." Harold approached with the rifle pointed. "You leave her be and git off my property."

Darren glanced at Harold, then turned back to Torie.

She heard the double clack of the rifle's lever, knew the bullet had been prepped for the chamber. "No, Harold, he's not worth it. Get back into the house. Call the cops."

Darren swung around, took a step toward Harold and backhanded him. The rifle fired, hit the Lincoln to the right of Torie before it flew out of his hands. He sprawled on the ground.

"Harold!" Torie jumped, and stumbled into Darren who'd turned his attention to the old man.

Darren raised a foot to kick. Torie leapt and wrenched him backwards. They tumbled to the ground. The edge of Darren's shoe caught Harold in the face.

"You--" Darren rolled on top of her and sat, pinning her to the ground.

"Leave Harold alone. You hurt him."

Darren smacked her face. "What'd you care about a senile old coot? You don't care about nobody but yourself. Gave me the clap. Killed your baby. Then sent me to prison to be raped by scum? Now you're siccing the cops on me at every turn?"

Her hammering heart and Darren's weight made breathing impossible. Torie gasped for air while Darren grabbed her hair, wrenched her face forward. She stared into pupils so dilated the blue irises looked black. Evil stared back at her.

Her years of bitterness reflected from those eyes, and pity welled for this creature who believed lies. Drugs, alcohol, lust -- Darren's trinity of demons held him in a vise tighter than he now held her.

The few sermons she'd heard flowed in her veins.

Forgiveness. I need to give it. Even to him.

The words stuck in her throat but demanded that she say them.

"I'm sorry, Darren. What happened to you in prison shouldn't happen to anyone." As she uttered the words, a swoosh of forgiveness filled her. She bit back the giddiness welling inside her chest.

"You're right." He shifted, grabbed her wrist and yanked her up. The fire went out of Darren. He didn't turn gentle, just less violent.

"I forgive you."

"You what?" A punch hurled against her fragile ribs, and Torie collapsed. The pain from her accident that had almost vanished, resurrected. Hot pokers once more knifed her rib cage.

She fell to her knees, her arms wrapped around her chest waiting for a kick and powerless to stop it.

*****

While dreaming of Maya and Torie's fried trout, Pop's farm came into view. All pastoral visions fled as chaos rolled in front of him. Pop lay on his side struggling to rise, the rifle several yards out of reach. Torie staggering to her feet, hugging her ribs while a thug grabbed for her. Adam stepped on the accelerator and swerved into the driveway, his truck stopped two feet away from the rifle.

The brute stepped back -- her step-father, Darren.

Adam hopped out and scooped up the gun. "What are you doing here?" He pointed the Winchester.

Darren stepped back, hands raised. "Just stopped by to help. Saw this guy," he nodded toward Pop, "fallen. This one here," he nodded toward Torie, "started cursing and screaming at me like a poltergeist."

Torie steadied herself against the Lincoln. With one arm wrapped around her chest, she inched away from Darren. He stepped back and blocked her.

"Let her by," Adam ordered.

Darren moved, and Torie hurried to Pop. "Let me help you up." Her husky voice betrayed her pain. She ran fingers over his grandfather's bruised face.

Bile gorged Adam's throat. "You hurt my grandfather?" Adam balanced the rifle in one arm aimed at Darren. He fished for his cell. The gun's weight forced it off-balance. It toppled, and Adam caught it before it dropped.

Darren scurried toward his truck. Adam tossed the phone to Torie and refocused. "Hold it, Darren." He fixed his gaze on the scum. "Torie, call the troopers."

As though just mentioning the troopers transported them to the farm, sirens sounded. Adam grinned and glanced at Torie. "How'd you get them so fast?"

Torie pointed at the phone on the grass in front of her.

"Ya think I'm an idiot?" Pop said. "Called the dern troopers 'fore I stepped outta the house. I shoot coyotes, not people.

*****

Torie stood on the porch as Adam helped Pop to his bed with a bag of frozen peas for his eye. Harold would have a shiner, nothing worse. If

259

she moaned once, Adam threatened he'd check out her ribs and haul her to the hospital -- sirens blaring. His wink reassured her he wouldn't. Trooper Morgan followed the men into the house for their statements. Hers would come next.

The other trooper cuffed Darren, stuffed him into the cruiser, and drove off. Pity pinged against her ribs. Darren would be sent back to Fishkill. Maybe if she'd forgiven him, and never have egged him on he could've stayed clean. Maybe.

Guilt played her heart. *I understand, Lord.* She knew God was no longer just God -- the man upstairs. He would now, forever, be her Lord. The sermons she heard weren't a vindication of the wrongs done to her, but about God forgiving sinners. Lessons teaching her to forgive -- even terrible acts like Darren's and Jean's.

For the first time since childhood, she acknowledged the wrong of her actions -- bullying a goody-two-shoes, taking advantage of friends, and rebelling against her abuse with alcohol and sex. The irony of the last sin made her chuckle.

As she admitted these sins, a warmth flooded her. She raised her face toward the sun and let peace ooze through every pore.

No matter what happened to Darren, his actions in her life were now free to heal.

"Ready for your statement?"

She turned to Trooper Morgan, and in an afternoon of firsts, she didn't fear the cops.

And this one? His eyes were warm. Sweet. She checked out his finger for a wedding band. None there. She touched his sleeve, and lowered her lashes.

"I'm ready for you." Perhaps now wasn't the time to flirt.

Chapter Forty-Four

"The wheel is come full circle." Shakespeare

The smell of beer and fried food still flooded The Stadium. All was the same as the day Collin canned her. Torie peeked at Adam and Maya and Harold as Adam opened the front door and ushered them in. *I can't do this.*

She had nowhere to run. With a deep inhale, she opened her mouth to speak, then shut it. Torie closed her eyes and whispered. "I can do all things through You, Lord." She squared her shoulders and followed her friends inside.

Her ribs ached. Harold's eye held no trace of the awful black and blue from Darren's blow. She had six weeks of sobriety to her credit. Was it enough?

The hostess ushered them to a table for four by the alcove. Everyone settled, but Torie.

"Sit down, lil' one." Harold held out a chair. "Watcha waiting for?"

Torie grinned. "I was waiting for an old coot to have manners." She nodded at the chair. "Glad you decided to be a gentleman."

"Gotta teach my grandson."

"Try the veggie polenta, Torie." Maya grinned at Adam. "The vegetables here are super fresh."

Torie grinned at Maya's tease, and instead of looking around, eyeing the bar, she leaned back and studied her masterpiece. Maya lowered her lashes, leaned into Adam who looked smitten. He hadn't stopped grinning since he picked Maya up. *Boy Scout, do you know your grandfather's watching?*

She'd taught Maya well.

Why did they insist on The Stadium? Where had her gumption gotten to? Why did she agree to come here? Yet, her pluck was going to keep her sober. The Stadium was the best restaurant in Albany county, after all. They came to celebrate, and she could handle it.

"Torie, so glad to see you." Trish laid out four menus. "You're sitting where I get to serve you." She surveyed the table. "What can I get you guys to drink?"

"A Coke." Torie answered before anyone else could wonder about her commitment.

"With a little rum?" Trish asked.

"Nope. I do want the full-calorie soda seeing as it'll be a virgin."
Torie scooted her chair into the table.

"You're foregoing the booze? I guess miracles do happen." Trish
laughed, and Torie smiled. Little did Trish realize she was, indeed,
serving a bona fide miracle.

The others gave their orders, and Torie fussed with the menu. There
was no need to read it, but it offered a cover. From behind the menu,
Torie eyed the bar. Despite her bravado, she wished for a little rum. Or
vodka. No one would smell it on her breath. She closed her eyes and
pictured her one-month sobriety coin in her purse. Wished they gave
them out for hours -- or at least weeks. Not easy, but Maya nagged her
when her resolve faltered. Made her call Celeste. Even drove her to
Albany. Twice.

She loved a good nag.

For tonight, all she needed to do was not drink while here -- two
hours. She could do two hours. With Maya sitting across from her,
believing in her, she'd make it.

Trish placed a glass in front of her. Ice clinked. A lemon perched
atop the glass. Before she could take a sip, Adam raised his Coke. "A
toast to Torie."

Torie startled. "Me?"

"Quitting your job in Albany--"

"It was part-time in an old lady salon--"

"You like us geezers." Harold's tease sounded gentle.

"It doesn't matter. You wanted out of the sticks, and you had your
chance. You gave it up, and moved in to care for Pop full time."

Torie shook her head. "How do a free room, a free salon, and a free
grandfather merit a toast?"

"No. You've never been a mooch. From the day I picked you up
from Hooksill, you insisted on giving -- buying me food--"

"Not food. Half and half. Good coffee. I was happy I had it once I
saw the garbage you used as coffee and creamer." Torie ducked her
head.

Maya leaned forward. "At my place, you wanted to buy groceries.
You gave me a makeover."

"You needed it." Torie smirked.

Adam's jaw dropped. He pulled Maya to him. "No, she didn't."

Maya ran her hands along his cheek. "She's teasing." She turned
back to Torie. "Hear Adam out."

Pop crossed his arms and nodded. Torie wasn't sure if it was the
Parkinson's or a warning to his grandson.

"I was a jerk. Still, you gave. You forgave Darren who ruined your life, while I held onto grudges I should've laid to rest. I would've lost Maya if not for you."

"How?"

"Because he was a jerk to you, Torie." Maya released Adam's hand and leaned forward. "I couldn't see past his setbacks as he tried to forgive, to release the past. You showed me his motivation. His inner core. The man his insecurity and bitterness hid."

"So you no longer have any doubts about him?" A thrill shuddered down Torie's spine almost as though *she* were the one who found true love.

Maya smiled up at Adam. "None at all," she whispered. She focused on Torie again and lifted her glass. "With Adam, I applaud your sobriety."

"I toast your giving spirit," Adam said.

Harold raised his iced tea. "Torie, dontcha ever lose your spunk. Ya keep me young."

The conversation turned to school and the latest EMS training coming up next weekend. Torie's mind drifted until she caught sight of Collin. "Excuse me." Without waiting for a response, she pushed away from the table. *Time for step five.*

"Hey, Collin." She slid onto a bar stool.

"Torie. Good to see you. What can I get you?"

"A little old crow."

"We don't carry Old Crow. How about Wild Turkey or Jim Beam?"

She grinned and dug through her purse. She laid her sobriety coin on the bar. "One month. Although, it's been over six weeks. They don't give the next coin for two more weeks."

Collin took the token, studied it and handed it back. "I'm proud of you." His hand covered hers, its warmth calming

She studied his eyes. They misted, and Torie's heart melted. It wasn't just words Collin spoke. It gave her courage to go on. "What I'm here for..." Her throat turned dry, and Jim Beam sounded wonderful. Instead, she swallowed, but couldn't meet his eyes. *Lord, will the words ever come easy?* She didn't think so, but she looked into his eyes. "You were right the night of my accident."

Collin raised his brows.

"Not only have I been sober for more than a month, I'm already at step five."

Collin tilted his head.

"I need to admit to others the exact nature of my wrongs. I had become Jean. Not a druggie, but a drunk. Looking for what I wanted in sex, getting what I wanted by flirting."

Collin reached over and took her hand. He opened his mouth.

Torie stood and placed a finger over his lips. "Shush, or I'll quit apologizing." She laughed as she settled back on the stool. "Thanks for firing me."

Collin nodded, and Torie turned toward her table. From this vantage point, she could see Maya and Adam clasping hands, hiding the sentiment under the table. A pang of jealousy gripped her heart. She took one step when the door opened. A man who had to be a foot taller than she strode inside.

The trooper looks good in street clothes. She strode toward her table, arriving at the same time as Chad Morgan.

"Join us, Morgan," Adam said.

"If no one minds. Hate to eat alone."

Torie scooted her chair over. "I don't mind. You locked Darren up."

Harold nodded. His biting back of his grin was not part of his Parkinson's.

She shook her head. She wanted no romance. Just wanted to live her life right. She turned to Chad. "It's a little tight, but I'll make room for my arresting knight."

"I hope you mean arresting as striking, not imprisoning." He smiled. She batted her lashes.

"So why didn't you press charges against Brown? I would have," Chad said.

"He's gone." She ducked her head. Didn't want to put it in words, but she knew she needed to. "Perhaps Darren would have left me alone if I ignored him." She looked at Maya. "My former roommate loved to tell me where no fuel existed, fire wouldn't burn. I insisted on drinking the poison of bitterness hoping Darren would die. I should have let it alone."

"More people should be so honorable." Chad leaned in to her.

Torie bit her lip. His closeness warmed her blood. Maybe romance was a good thing.

She leaned on her elbow, gazed up at him.

"We all did." Adam's comment shocked her back to the present. "Her actions showed me how petty I'd been."

"And me," Maya said.

"You?" Torie laughed. "You make Mr. Boy Scout there look like a hoodlum."

"No, Torie. I'd forgiven my parents, but I always held their actions against them. I never gave myself the chance to discover I believed a lie."

Before the compliments got out of hand, Trish came with their meals and a menu for Chad. Conversation turned back to the dull, real-life themes.

Life wasn't what Torie pictured it, but was everything she wanted it to be.

About Carol McClain

Carol McClain is a versatile author whose interests vary as much as the East Tennessee scenery. She plays the bassoon, creates unique stained glass pieces, is a mentor to the drug addicted, and hikes the Smokies to clear her mind of life's craziness.

For ten years she served in virtually every office of the North Country Habitat for Humanity. For more than thirty years, she taught high school English.

She's learned through experience the powerful freedom forgiveness brings. Coupled with sharing life's burdens with trusted friends, bitterness can be healed. Scripture does not lie when it states a threefold cord is not quickly broken.

She's recently traded in northern New York for the Tennessee hillside where she lives with her husband and crazy Springer spaniel.

If *Yesterday's Poison* pleased you, why not leave a review? McClain would love to hear from you. You can find out more about her, her blog and newsletter at www.carolmcclain.com.